Sparrows

The Story of an Unprotected Girl

Horace W. C. Newte

Alpha Editions

This edition published in 2024

ISBN : 9789361477768

Design and Setting By
Alpha Editions
www.alphaedis.com
Email - info@alphaedis.com

Contents

CHAPTER ONE
THE DEVITTS

Everyone at Melkbridge knew the Devitts: they lived in the new, pretentious-looking house, standing on the right, a few minutes after one left the town by the Bathminster road. It was a blustering, stare-one-in-the-face kind of house, which defied one to question the financial stability of its occupants. The Devitts were like their home in being new, ostentatious folk; their prosperity did not extend further back than the father of Montague, the present head of the family.

Montague Devitt did little beyond attending board meetings of the varied industries which his father's energy had called into being. He was a bluff, well-set-up man, who had married twice; both of his wives had brought him money. Each time Montague chose a mate, he had made some effort to follow the leanings of his heart; but money not lying in the same direction as love, an overmastering instinct of his blood had prevailed against his sentimental inclinations; in each case it had insisted on his marrying, in one instance an interest in iron works, in another, a third share of a Portland cement business.

His first wife had borne him two sons and a daughter; his second was childless.

Montague was a member of two or three Bohemian clubs in London, to which, as time went on, he became increasingly attached. At these, he passed as a good fellow, chiefly from a propensity to stand drinks to any and everyone upon any pretence; he was also renowned amongst his boon companions for his rendering of "The Village Blacksmith" in dumb show, a performance greeted by his thirsty audience with thunders of applause.

Harold, his first born, will be considered later.

Lowther, his second son, can be dismissed in a few words. He was a good-looking specimen of the British bounder. His ideas of life were obtained from the "Winning Post," and the morality (or want of it) suggested by musical comedy productions at the Gaiety Theatre. He thought coarsely of women. While spending money freely in the society of ladies he met at the Empire promenade, or in the Cafe d' l'Europe, he practised mean economics in private.

Victoria, Montague's daughter, was a bit of a puzzle to friends and relations alike, all of whom commenced by liking her, a sentiment which, sooner or later, gave place to a feeling of dissatisfaction. She was a disappointment to her father, although he would never admit it to himself;

indeed, if he had tried to explain this displeasure, he would have been hard put to it to give a straightforward cause for a distressing effect. On first acquaintance, it would seem as if she were as desirable a daughter as heart of father could want. She was tall, good-looking, well educated; she had abundance of tact, accomplishments, and refinement; she had never given her parents a moment of anxiety. What, then, was wrong with her from her father's point of view? He was well into middle age; increasing years made him yearn for the love of which his life had been starved; this craving would have been appeased by love for his daughter, but the truth was that he was repelled by the girl's perfection. She had never been known to lose her temper; not once had she shown the least preference for any of the eligible young men of her acquaintance; although always becomingly dressed, she was never guilty of any feminine foibles, which would have endeared her to her father. To him, such correctness savoured of inhumanity; much of the same feeling affected the girl's other relatives and friends, to the ultimate detriment of their esteem.

Hilda, Montague's second wife, was the type of woman that successful industrialism turns out by the gross. Sincere, well-meaning, narrow, homely, expensively but indifferently educated, her opinion on any given subject could be predicted; her childlessness accentuated her want of mental breadth. She read the novels of Mrs Humphry Ward; she was vexed if she ever missed an Academy; if she wanted a change, she frequented fashionable watering-places. She was much exercised by the existence of the "social evil"; she belonged to and, for her, subscribed heavily to a society professing to alleviate, if not to cure, this distressing ailment of the body politic. She was the honorary secretary of a vigilance committee, whose operations extended to the neighbouring towns of Trowton and Devizeton. The good woman was ignorant that the starvation wages which her husband's companies paid were directly responsible for the existence of the local evil she deplored, and which she did her best to eradicate.

Miss Spraggs, Hilda Devitt's elder sister, lived with the family at Melkbridge House. She was a virgin with a taste for scribbling, which commonly took the form of lengthy letters written to those she thought worthy of her correspondence. She had diligently read every volume of letters, which she could lay hands on, of persons whose performance was at all renowned in this department of literature (foreign ones in translations), and was by way of being an agreeable rattle, albeit of a pinchbeck, provincial genus. Miss Spraggs was much courted by her relations, who were genuinely proud of her local literary reputation. Also, let it be said, that she had the disposal of capital bringing in five hundred a year.

Montague's eldest son, Harold, was, at once, the pride and grief of the Devitts, although custom had familiarised them with the calamity attaching to his life.

He had been a comely, athletic lad, with a nature far removed from that of the other Devitts; he had seemed to be in the nature of a reversion to the type of gentleman, who, it was said, had imprudently married an ancestress of Montague's first wife. Whether or not this were so, in manner, mind, and appearance Harold was generations removed from his parents and brother. He had been the delight of his father's eye, until an accident had put an end to the high hopes which his father had formed of his future. A canal ran through Melkbridge; some way from the town this narrowed its course to run beneath a footbridge, locally known as the "Gallows" bridge.

It was an achievement to jump this stretch of water; Harold Devitt was renowned amongst the youth of the neighbourhood for the performance of this feat. He constantly repeated the effort, but did it once too often. One July morning, he miscalculated the distance and fell, to be picked up some while after, insensible. He had injured his spine. After many weeks of suspense suffered by his parents, these learned that their dearly loved boy would live, although he would be a cripple for life. Little by little, Harold recovered strength, till he was able to get about Melkbridge on a self-propelled tricycle; any day since the year of the accident his kindly, distinguished face might be seen in the streets of the town, or the lanes of the adjacent country, where he would pull up to chat with his many friends.

His affliction had been a terrible blow to Harold; when he had first realised the permanent nature of his injuries, he had cursed his fate; his impotent rage had been pitiful to behold. This travail occurred in the first year of his affliction; later, he discovered, as so many others have done in a like extremity, that time accustoms the mind to anything: he was now resigned to his misfortune. His sufferings had endowed him with a great tolerance and a vast instinct of sympathy for all living things, qualities which are nearly always lacking in young men of his present age, which was twenty-nine. The rest of the family stood in some awe of Harold; realising his superiority of mind, they feared to be judged at the bar of his opinion; also, he had some hundreds a year left him, in his own right, by his mother: it was unthinkable that he should ever marry. Another thing that differentiated him from his family was that he possessed a sense of humour.

It may be as well to state that Harold plays a considerable part in this story, which is chiefly concerned with a young woman, of whom the assembled Devitts were speaking in the interval between tea and dinner on a warm July day. Before setting this down, however, it should be said that the chief concern of the Devitts (excepting Harold) was to escape from the social orbit of successful industrialism, in which they moved, to the exalted spheres of county society.

Their efforts, so far, had only taken them to certain halfway houses on their road. The families of consequence about Melkbridge were old-fashioned, conservative folk, who resented the intrusion in their midst of those they considered beneath them.

Whenever Montague, a borough magistrate, met the buffers of the great families upon the bench, or in the hunting field, he found them civil enough; but their young men would have little to do with Lowther, while its womenfolk ignored the assiduities of the Devitt females.

The drawing-room in which the conversation took place was a large, over-furnished room, in which a conspicuous object was a picture, most of which, the lower part, was hidden by padlocked shutters; the portion which showed was the full face of a beautiful girl.

The picture was an "Etty," taken in part payment of a debt by Montague's father, but, as it portrayed a nude woman, the old Puritan had employed a Melkbridge carpenter to conceal that portion of the figure which the artist had omitted to drape. Montague would have had the shutters removed, but had been prevailed upon by his wife to allow them to remain until Victoria was married, an event which, at present, she had no justification for anticipating.

The late afternoon post had brought a letter for Mrs Devitt, which gave rise to something of a discussion.

"Actually, here is a letter from Miss Annie Mee," said Mrs Devitt.

"Your old schoolmistress!" remarked Miss Spraggs.

"I didn't know she was alive," went on Mrs Devitt. "She writes from Brandenburg College, Aynhoe Road, West Kensington Park, London, asking me to do something for her."

"Of course!" commented the agreeable rattle.

"How did you know?" asked Mrs Devitt, looking up from the letter she was reading with the help of glasses.

"Didn't you know that there are two kinds of letters: those you want and those that want something?" asked Miss Spraggs, in a way that showed she was conscious of saying a smart thing.

"I can hardly believe human nature to be so depraved as you would make it out to be, Eva," remarked Mrs Devitt, who disliked the fact of her unmarried sister possessing sharper wits than her own.

"Oh! I say, is that your own?" guffawed Devitt from his place on the hearthrug.

"Why shouldn't it be?" asked Miss Spraggs demurely.

"Anyway," continued Mrs Devitt impatiently, "she wishes to know if I am in want of a companion, or anything of that sort, as she has a teacher she is unable to keep owing to her school having fallen on bad times."

"Then she's young!" cried Lowther, who was lolling near the window.

"'Her name is Mavis Keeves; she is the only daughter of the late Colonel Keeves, who, I believe, before he was overtaken by misfortune, occupied a position of some importance in the vicinity of Melkbridge,'" read Mrs Devitt from Miss Annie Mee's letter.

"Keeves! Keeves!" echoed her husband.

"Do you remember him?" asked his wife.

"Of course," he replied. "He was a M.F.H. and knew everyone" (everyone was here synonymous with the elect the Devitts were pining to meet on equal terms). "His was Sir Henry Ockendon's place."

The prospects of Mavis Keeves securing employment with the Devitts had, suddenly, increased.

"How was it he came 'down'?" asked the agreeable rattle, keenly interested in anything having to do with the local aristocracy, past or present.

"The old story: speculatin' solicitors," replied Montague, who made a point of dropping his "g's." "One week saw him reduced from money to nixes."

Mrs Devitt raised her eyebrows.

"I mean nothin'," corrected Devitt.

"How very distressing!" remarked Victoria in her exquisitely modulated voice. "We should try and do something for her."

"We will," said her father.

"We certainly owe a duty to those who were once our neighbours," assented Miss Spraggs.

"Do you remember her?" asked Mrs Devitt of her husband.

"Of course I do, now I come to think of it," he replied.

"What was she like?"

He paused for a moment or two before replying.

"She'd reddy sort of hair and queer eyes. She was a fine little girl, but a fearful tomboy," said Devitt.

"Pretty, then!" exclaimed Mrs Devitt, as she glanced apprehensively at her step-daughter.

"She was then. It was her hair that did it," answered her husband.

"H'm!" came from his wife.

"The pretty child of to-day is the plain girl of to-morrow" commented Miss Spraggs.

"What was her real disposition?" asked Mrs Devitt.

"I know nothin' about that; but she was always laughin' when I saw her."

"Frivolous!" commented Mrs Devitt.

"Perhaps there's more about her in the letter," suggested Lowther, who had been listening to all that had been said.

"There is," said his step-mother; "but Miss Mee's writing is very trying to the eyes."

Montague took the schoolmistress's letter from his wife's hand. He read the following in his big, blustering voice:

"'In all matters affectin' Miss Keeves's educational qualifications, I find her comme il faut, with the possible exception of freehand drawing, which is not all that a fastidious taste might desire. Her disposition is winnin' and unaffected, but I think it my duty to mention that, on what might appear to others as slight provocation, Miss Keeves is apt to give way to sudden fits of passion, which, however, are of short duration. Doubtless, this is a fault of youth which years and experience will correct.'"

"Rebellious!" commented Mrs Devitt.

"Spirit!" said Harold, who all this while had been reclining in his invalid chair, apparently reading a review.

Mrs Devitt looked up, as if surprised.

"After all, everything depends on the point of view," remarked Miss Spraggs.

"Is there any more?" asked Harold.

By way of reply, his father read from Miss Mee's letter:

"'In conclusion, I am proud to admit that Miss Keeves has derived much benefit from so many years' association with one who has endeavoured to influence her curriculum with the writin's of the late Mr Ruskin, whose acquaintance it was the writer's inestimable privilege to enjoy. With my best wishes for your welfare, I remain, dear Madam, your obedient servant, Annie Allpress Mee.' That's all," he added, as he tossed the letter on to the table at his wife's side.

"Did she know Ruskin?" asked Harold.

"When I was at her school—it was then at Fulham—she, or her sister, never let a day go by without making some reference to him," replied his step-mother.

"What are you going to do for Miss Keeves?" asked Harold.

"It's so difficult to decide off-hand," his step-mother replied.

"Can't you think of anything, father?" persisted Harold.

"It's scarcely in my line," answered Montague, glancing at his wife as he spoke.

Harold looked inquiringly at Mrs Devitt.

"It's so difficult to promise her anything till one has seen her," she remarked.

"Then why not have her down?" asked Harold.

"Yes, why not?" echoed his brother.

"She can get here and back again in a day," added Harold, as his eyes sought his review.

"Very well, then, I'll write and suggest Friday," said Mrs Devitt, not too willingly taking up a pen.

"You can always wire and put her off, if you want to do anything else," remarked her sister.

"Won't you send her her fare?" asked Harold.

"Is that necessary?" queried Mrs Devitt.

"Isn't it usual?"

"I can give it to her when she comes," said Mrs Devitt, who hated parting with money, although, when it was a question of entertaining the elect of Melkbridge, she spent her substance lavishly.

Thus it came about that a letter was written to Miss Annie Mee, Brandenburg College, Aynhoe Road, West Kensington Park, London, W., saying that Mrs Devitt would expect Miss Keeves, for an interview, by the train that left Paddington for Melkbridge at ten on Friday next; also, that she would defray her third-class travelling expenses.

CHAPTER TWO
MAVIS KEEVES

The following Friday morning, Mavis Keeves sprang from bed on waking. It was late when she had gone to sleep the previous night, for she had been kept up by the festivities pertaining to breaking-up day at Brandenburg College, and the inevitable "talk over" the incidents of the event with Miss Helen and Miss Annie Mee, which conversation had been prolonged till nearly twelve o'clock; but the excitement of travelling to the place of her birth, and the certainty of getting an engagement in some capacity or another (Mavis had no doubt on this point) were more than enough to curtail her slumbers. She had fallen asleep laughing to herself at the many things which had appealed to her sense of humour during the day, and it was the recollection of some of these which made her smile directly she was awake. She tubbed and dressed quickly, although she had some bother with her hair, which, this morning, seemed intent on defying the efforts of her fingers. Having dressed herself to her somewhat exigent satisfaction, she went downstairs, passing the doors of those venerable virgins, the Misses Helen and Annie Mee, as she descended to the ground-floor, on which was the schoolroom. This was really two rooms, but the folding doors, which had once divided the apartment, had long since been removed from their hinges; they were now rotting in the strip of garden behind the house.

The appearance of Brandenburg College belied its pretentious name. Once upon a time, its name-plate had decorated the gates of a stately old mansion in the Fulham of many years ago; here it was that Mrs Devitt, then Miss Hilda Spraggs, had been educated. Since those fat days, the name-plate of Brandenburg College had suffered many migrations, always in a materially downward direction, till now it was screwed on the railings of a stuffy little road in Shepherd's Bush, which, as Mavis was in the habit of declaring, was called West Kensington Park for "short."

The brass plate, much the worse for wear, told the neighbourhood that Brandenburg College educated the daughters of gentlemen; perhaps it was as well that this definition, like the plate, was fallen on hard times, inasmuch as it was capable of such an elastic interpretation that it enabled the Misses Mee to accept pupils whom, in their prosperous days, they would have refused. Mavis looked round the familiar, shabby schoolroom, with its atmosphere of ink and slate pencil, to which she was so soon to say "good-bye."

It looked desolate this morning, perhaps because there leapt to her fancy the animated picture it had presented the day before, when it had been filled by a crowd of pupils (dressed in their best), their admiring parents and friends.

Yesterday's programme had followed that of all other girls' school breaking-up celebrations, with the difference that the passages selected for recital had been wholly culled from the writings of Mr Ruskin. Reference to the same personage had occurred in the speech to the prize-winners (every girl in the school had won a prize of sorts) made by Mr Smiley, the curate, who performed this office; also, the Misses Mee, when opportunity served, had not been backward in making copious references to the occasion on which they had drunk tea with the deceased author. Indeed, the parents and friends had breathed such an atmosphere of Ruskin that there were eight requests for his works at the local free library during the following week.

"Good old Ruskin!" laughed Mavis, as she ran downstairs to the breakfast room, which was situated in the basement. Here, the only preparation made for the meal was a not too clean table-cloth spread upon the table. Mavis went into the kitchen, where she found Amelia, the general servant, doing battle with a smoky kitchen-fire.

"How long before breakfast is ready?" asked Mavis.

"Is that you, miss? Oi can't see you properly," said Amelia, as she turned her head. "This 'ere smoke had got into my best oye."

Amelia spoke truly; there was a great difference between the seeing capacity of her two eyes, one of these being what is known as "walled." Amelia was an orphan; she had been dragged up by the "Metropolitan Association for Befriending Young Servants," known to its familiars as the "Mabys," such designation being formed by the first letter of each word of the title. Every week, dozens of these young women issued from the doors of the many branches of this institution, who became, to their respective mistresses, a source of endless complaint; in times of domestic stress, one or two of these "generals" had been known to keep their situations for three months. Amelia was a prodigy of success, a record in the annals of the society, inasmuch as she had been at Brandenburg College for two years and a half. She kept her situation because she was cheap; also, because she did her best to give satisfaction, as she appreciated the intellectual atmosphere of the place, which made her hope that she, too, might pick up a few educational crumbs; moreover, she was able to boast to her intimates, on the occasions when she visited her parent home, how her two mistresses could speak four languages, which was certainly true.

"Wasn't it all beautiful, miss?" asked Amelia, who had listened to yesterday's entertainment halfway down the stairs leading to the basement.

"Wonderful," replied Mavis, as she tied on a kitchen apron, a preliminary to giving Amelia a helping hand with the breakfast.

"And the 'reverend'! He did make me laugh when he gave four prizes to fat Miss Robson, and said she was a good all round girl."

This joke had not been intentional on Mr Smiley's part; he had been puzzled by the roar of laughter which had greeted his remark; when he divined its purport, he was quite willing to take credit for having deliberately made the sally.

"You managed to hear that?" asked Mavis.

"Yes, miss; an' what the 'reverend' said about dear Mr Fuskin. I 'eard that too."

"Ruskin," corrected Mavis, as she set about making coffee.

Amelia, with a hurt expression on her face, turned to look at Miss Keeves, who, noticing the girl's dejection, said:

"Call him what you like, Amelia. It's only the Miss Mees who're so particular."

"Dear gentleman," continued Amelia. "Next to being always with you, miss, I should like to have been with 'im."

"I'm afraid you can't even be with me. I have to earn my own living."

"Yes, miss; but when you marry a rich gentleman, I should like to come with you as 'general.'"

"Don't talk nonsense, Amelia."

"But it ain't, miss; didn't the music master, 'im with the lovely, long, shiny 'air, promise me a shillin' to give you a note?"

"Did he?" laughed Mavis. "It's nearly eight: you'd better take in the breakfast things."

"Oh, well, if I can't be here, or with you, I'd sooner be with that dear Mr—"

"Ruskin, Amelia," interrupted Mavis. "Try and get it right, if only for once."

Amelia took no notice of the interruption, but went on, as she dusted the cups, before putting them on the tray:

"Dear Mr Fuskin! 'Ow I would have looked after 'im, and 'ow carefully I'd 'ave counted 'is washing!"

Punctually, as the clock struck eight, the two Miss Mees entered the breakfast room; they kissed Mavis on the cheek before sitting down to the meal. They asked each other and Mavis how they had slept, as was their invariable custom; but the sensitive, observant girl could not help noticing that the greetings of her employers were a trifle less cordial than was their wont. Mavis put down this comparative coldness to their pride at the success of yesterday's festival.

To the indifferent observer, the Miss Mees were exactly alike, being meagre, dilapidated, white-haired old ladies, with the same beaked noses and receding chins; both wore rusty black frocks, each of which was decorated with a white cameo brooch; both walked with the same propitiatory shuffle. They were like a couple of elderly, moulting, decorous hens who, in spite of their physical disabilities, had something of a presence. This was obtained from the authority they had wielded over the many pupils who had passed through their hands.

Nearer inspection showed that Miss Annie Mee was a trifle stouter than her sister, if this be not too robust a word to apply to such a wisp of a woman; that her eyes were kinder and less watery than Helen's; also, that her face was less insistently marked with lines of care.

The Miss Mees' dispositions were much more dissimilar than their appearance. Miss Helen, the elder, loved her home and, in her heart of hearts, preferred the kitchen to any other part of the house. It was she who attended to the ordering of the few wants of the humble household; she arranged the meals, paid the bills, and generally looked after the domestic economy of the college; she took much pride in the orderliness of her housekeeper's cupboard, into which Amelia never dared to pry. In the schoolroom, she received the parents, arranged the fees and extras, and inflicted the trifling punishment she awarded to delinquents, which latter, it must be admitted, gave her a faint pleasure.

Annie Mee, her sister, had a natural inclination for the flesh-pots of life. She liked to lie abed on Sunday and holiday mornings; she spread more butter on her breakfast toast than Helen thought justified by the slenderness of their resources; she was indulgent to the pupils, and seized any opportunity that offered of going out for the evening. She frequented (and had been known to enjoy) entertainments given in schoolrooms for church purposes she welcomed the theatre or concert tickets which were sometimes sent her by the father of one of the pupils (who was behind with his account), when, however paltry the promised fare, she would be waiting at the door, clad in her faded garments, a full hour before the public were admitted, in order not to miss any of the fun. Mavis usually accompanied her on these excursions; although she was soon bored by the tenth-rate singers and the poor plays she heard and saw, she was compensated by witnessing the pleasure Miss Annie Mee got from these sorry dissipations.

The two sisters' dispositions were alike in one thing: the good works they unostentatiously performed. The sacrifices entailed by these had much contributed to their declining fortunes. This unity of purpose did not stay them from occasionally exchanging embittered remarks when heated by difference of opinion.

When they sat down to breakfast, Helen poured out the coffee.

"What day does the West London Observer come out?" asked Annie, presently, of Mavis.

"Friday, I believe."

"There should be some account of yesterday's proceedings," said Miss Helen. "The very proper references which Mr Smiley made to our acquaintance with the late Mr Ruskin are worthy of comment."

"I have never known the applause to be so hearty as it was yesterday," remarked Annie, after she had eaten her first piece of toast.

"What is the matter, Mavis?" asked Miss Helen.

"A crumb stuck in my throat," replied Mavis, saying what was untrue, as she bent over her plate. This action was necessary to hide the smile that rose to her lips and eyes at the recollection of yesterday's applause, to which Miss Annie had referred. It had amused Mavis to notice the isolated clapping which followed the execution of an item, in the programme by a solitary performer; this came from her friends in the room. The conclusion of a duet would be greeted by two patches of appreciation; whilst a pianoforte concerto, which engaged sixteen hands, merged the eight oases of applause into a roar of approval.

"How do you get to Paddington, Mavis?" asked Miss Helen, after she had finished her meagre breakfast.

"From Addison Road," replied Mavis, who was still eating.

"Wouldn't Shepherd's Bush be better?" asked Annie, who was wondering if she could find accommodation for a further piece of toast.

"I always recommend parents to send their daughters from Paddington via Addison Road," remarked Helen severely.

"There are more trains from Shepherd's Bush," persisted Annie.

"Maybe, dear Annie" (when relations between the sisters were strained, they made use of endearing terms), "but more genteel people live on the Addison Road connection."

"But, Helen dear, the class of residence existing upon a line of railway does not enable a traveller to reach his or her destination the quicker."

"I was not aware, dear Annie, that I ever advanced such a proposition."

"Then there is no reason, dearest Helen, why Mavis shouldn't reach Paddington by going to Shepherd's Bush."

"None, beyond the fact that it is decided that she shall travel by way of Addison Road. Besides, Addison Road is nearer, dear."

"But the exercise of walking to Shepherd's Bush would do Mavis good after the fatigues of yesterday, Helen."

"That is altogether beside the point, dear Annie."

"I am never listened to," complained her sister angrily.

"You argue for the sake of talking," replied the other crossly.

They continued in that strain for some moments, and were still at it when Mavis went upstairs to put on her hat; here, she gave a last look at herself in the glass.

"I wonder if I'll do?" she thought, as she dealt with one or two strands of tawny coloured hair, which were still inclined to be rebellious.

"I wonder if I'll meet anyone who remembers me?" she thought, as she left the room.

Downstairs, the two old ladies were awaiting her in the hall. Miss Helen was full of good advice for the journey, whilst Miss Annie dangled a packet of sandwiches, "In case dear Mavis should need refreshment on the way."

"Thanks so much," said Mavis, as she took the little packet, the brown-paper covering of which was already grease-stained from the fat of the sandwiches.

"Don't fail to remember me to Mrs Devitt," urged Helen.

"I won't forget," said Mavis.

"I put salt and mustard in the sandwiches," remarked Annie.

"Thanks so much," cried Mavis, as she opened the front door.

"And don't forget to be sure and travel in a compartment reserved for ladies," quavered Helen.

"I won't forget; wish me luck," answered Mavis.

"We do; good-bye," said the two old ladies together.

Directly the door was closed, Miss Annie, followed at a distance by Miss Helen, hurried into the schoolroom, where, pulling aside the Venetian blind of the front window, they watched the girl's trim figure walk down the street. The two old ladies were really very fond of her and not a little proud of her appearance.

"She has deportment," remarked Helen, as Mavis disappeared from their ken.

"Scarcely that—distinction is more the word," corrected Annie.

"I fear for her in the great world," declared Helen with trembling lips; "they say that good looks are a girl's worst enemy."

"But Mavis has profited by the example of our lives, Helen."

"There is much in that, Annie. Also, she should have derived much benefit from being, in school hours, and often out of them, in an atmosphere influenced by the writings of the late Mr Ruskin."

With these consolations, the two old ladies toiled upstairs, and set about packing for a fortnight's stay they proposed making with an old friend at Worthing, for which place they proposed starting in two days' time.

Meanwhile, the subject of their thoughts was walking to Addison Road Station, happily ignorant of the old ladies' fears concerning the perils of her path. To look at her, she seemed the least likely girl in London who was about to take a journey on the chance of obtaining a much-needed engagement. Her glowing eyes, flushed cheeks, and light step were eloquent of a joyousness not usually associated with an all but penniless girl on the look-out for something to do. Her clothes, also, supported the impression that she was a young woman well removed from likelihood of want. She was obliged to be careful with the few pounds that she earned at Brandenburg College: being of an open-handed disposition, this necessity for economy irked her; but however much she stinted her inclinations in other directions, she was determined, as are so many other young women who are thrown on their own resources, to have one good turn-out in which to make a brave show to the world. Not that Mavis spent her money, shop-girl fashion, in buying cheap flummery which was, at best, a poor and easily recognisable imitation of the real thing; her purchases were of the kind that any young gentlewoman, who was not compelled to take thought for the morrow, might becomingly wear. As she walked, most of the men she met looked at her admiringly; some turned to glance at her figure; one or two retraced their steps and would have overtaken her, had she not walked purposefully forward. She was so used to these tributes to her attractiveness, that she did not give them heed. She could not help noticing one man; he glanced at her and seemed as if he were about to raise his hat; when she looked at him to see if she knew him, she saw that he was distinguished looking, but a stranger. She hurried on; presently, she went into a draper's shop, where she bought a pair of gloves, but, when she came out, the good-looking stranger was staring woodenly at the window. She hastened forward; turning a corner, she slipped into a tobacconist's and newsagent's, where she bought a packet of her favourite cigarettes, together with a box of matches. When she got to the door, her good-looking admirer was entering the shop. He made way for her, and, raising his hat, was about to speak: she walked quickly away and was not troubled with him any more. When she got to Paddington, she disobeyed Miss Helen's injunctions to travel in a compartment reserved for ladies, but went into an ordinary carriage, which, by the connivance of the guard, she had to herself. When the train left Paddington, she put her feet on the cushions of the opposite seat, with a fine disregard of railway bye-laws, and lit a cigarette.

It was, perhaps, inevitable that the girl's thoughts should incline to the time and the very different circumstances in which she had last journeyed to Melkbridge. This was nine years ago, when she had come home for the holidays from Eastbourne, where she had been to school. Then, she had had but one care in the world, this on account of a jaundiced pony to which she was immoderately attached. Then she suffered her mind to dwell on the unrestrained grief with which she had greeted her favourite's decease; as she did so, half-forgotten fares, scenes, memories flitted across her mind. Foremost amongst these was her father's face—dignified, loving, kind. Whenever she thought of him, as now, she best remembered him as he looked when he told her how she should try to restrain her grief at the loss of her pet, as her distress gave him pain. She had then been a person of consequence in her little world, she being her father's only child; she had been made much of by friends and acquaintances, amongst whom, so far as she could recollect, no member of the Devitt family was numbered. Perhaps, she thought, they have lately come to Melkbridge. Then aspects of the old home passed through her mind. The room in which she used to sleep; the oak-panelled dining-room; the garden, which was all her very own, passed in rapid review; then, the faces of playmates and sweethearts, for she had had admirers at that early age. There was Charlie Perigal, the boy with the steely blue eyes and the pretty curls, with whom she had quarrelled on the ground that he was in the habit of catching birds in nasty little brick traps; also, because, when taxed with this offence, he had defended his conduct and, a few moments later, had attempted to stone a frog in her highly indignant presence.

Then there was Archie Windebank, whose father had the next place to theirs; he was a fair, solemn boy, who treated her with an immense deference; he used to blush when she asked him to join her in play. The day before she had left for school, he had confessed his devotion in broken accents; she had thought of him for quite a week after she had left home. How absurd and trivial it all seemed, now that she was to face the stern realities of life!

The next thing she recalled was the news of her father's ruin. This calamity was more conveyed to her by the changed look in his face, when she next saw him, than by anything else.

She had been, at once, taken away from the expensive school at which she was being educated and had been sent to Brandenburg College, then languishing in Hammersmith Terrace, while her father went to live at Dinan, in Brittany, where he might save money in order to make some sort of a start, which might ultimately mean a provision for his daughter.

Next, she remembered—this she would never forget—the terrible day on which Miss Helen Mee had called her into the study to tell her that she would never again see her dear father in this world. Tears came to Mavis's eyes whenever she thought of it. Orphaned, friendless, with no one to give her the affection for which her lonely soul craved, Mavis had stayed on at Brandenburg College, where the little her father had left sufficed to pay for her board and schooling. This sum lasted till she was sixteen, when, having passed one or two trumpery examinations, she was taken on the staff of the college. The last few months, Mavis's eyes had been opened to the straitened circumstances in which her employers lived; she had lately realised that she owed her bread and butter more to the kindness of the Miss Mees, than to the fact of her parts as a teacher being in request at the school. She informed the kind ladies that she was going to seek her bread elsewhere; upon their offering the mildest of protests, she had made every effort to translate her intentions into performance.

This was by no means an easy matter for a comparatively friendless girl, as Mavis soon discovered. Her numerous applications had, so far, only resulted in an expenditure of stationery and postage stamps. Then, Miss Annie Mee kindly volunteered to write to the more prosperously circumstanced of the few one-time pupils with whom she had kept up something of a correspondence. Those who replied offered no suggestion of help, with the exception of Mrs Devitt. So much for the past: the future stretched, an unexplored country, before her, which, to one of her sanguine disposition, seemed to offer boundless opportunities of happiness. It appeared a strange conjunction of circumstances that she should have been sent for by a person living in her native place. It seemed fortuitous to Mavis that she should earn her bread in a neighbourhood where she would be known, if only because of the high reputation which her dear father had enjoyed. It all seemed as if it had been arranged like something out of a book. Amelia's words, referring to the certainty of her marrying, came into her mind; she tried to dismiss them, but without success. Then, her thoughts flew back to Charlie Perigal and Archie Windebank, youthful admirers, rivals for her favours. She wondered what had become of them; if she should see them again: a thousand things in which she allowed her imagination to wing itself in sentimental flight.

She was of an ardent temperament; men attracted her, although, since she had been grown up, she had never exchanged anything that could be construed into a love passage with a member of the opposite sex, opportunities for meeting those whom she considered her equals being wanting in her dull round of daily teaching. Sometimes, a face she had seen in the street, or a character she encountered in a book attracted her, when she would think of her hero, allowing her mind to place him in tender situations with herself, for the few hours her infatuation lasted, showing her to be of an impressionable and romantic disposition. Although she often felt her loneliness, and the consequent need of human companionship, her pride would never suffer her to take advantage of the innumerable facilities which the streets of London offer a comely girl to make chance friendships, facilities which, for thousands of friendless young women in big towns, are their only chance for meeting the male of their species.

Mavis's pride was not of the kind with which providence endows millions of foolish people, apparently by way of preventing them from realising their insignificance, or, at the worst, making their smallness tolerable. It arose from knowledge of the great and inexhaustible treasure of love which was hers to bestow; so convinced was she of the value of this wealth, that she guarded it jealously, not permitting it to suffer taint or deterioration from commerce with those who, if only from curiosity, might strive to examine her riches.

She feared with a grave dread the giving of the contents of this treasure house, knowing full well that, if she gave at all, she would bestow with a lavish hand, believing the priceless riches of her love to be but a humble offering upon the shrine of the loved one.

For all this consciousness that she would be as wax in the hands of the man she would some day love, she had much of a conviction that, somehow, things would come right.

Beyond thanking the Almighty for the beauties of nature, sunlight, and the happiness that danced in her veins, she did not bother herself overmuch with public religious observances. She had a fixed idea that, if she did her duty in life, and tried to help others to the best of her small ability, God would, in some measure, reward her very much as her dear father would have done, if he had been spared; also, that, if she did ill, she would offend Him and might be visited with some sign of His displeasure, just as her own father might have done if he had been still on earth to advise and protect her.

Then, all such thoughts faded from her mind; she looked out of the carriage window as the train rushed through Didcot Junction. She felt hungry after the meagre breakfast she had made; she remembered the sandwiches, and, untying the greasy little parcel, was glad to eat them. When she had finished the sandwiches, she lit another cigarette; after smoking this, she closed her eyes the better to reflect.

Then she remembered nothing till the calling of "Melkbridge!" "Melkbridge!" seemed to suffuse her senses. She awoke with a start, to find that she had reached her destination.

CHAPTER THREE
FRIENDS IN NEED

Mavis scrambled out of the train, just in time to prevent herself from being carried on to the next stopping—place. She smoothed her ruffled plumage and looked about her. She found the station much smaller than she had believed it to be; she hardly remembered any of its features, till the scent of the stocks planted in the station-master's garden assisted her memory. She gave up her ticket, and looked about her, thinking that very likely she would be met, if not by a member of the Devitt family, by some conveyance; but, beyond the station 'bus and two or three farmers' gigs, there was nothing in the nature of cart or carriage. She asked the hobbledehoy, who took her ticket, where Mrs Devitt lived, at which the youth looked at her in a manner that evidently questioned her sanity at being ignorant of such an important person's whereabouts. Mavis repeated her question more sharply than before. The ticket-collector looked at her open—mouthed, glanced up the road and then again to Mavis, before saying:

"Here her be."

"Mrs Devitt?"

"Noa. Her."

"The housekeeper?"

"Noa. The trap. Mebbe your eyes hain't so 'peart' as mine."

The grating of wheels called her attention to the fact that a smart, yellow-wheeled dogcart had been driven into the station yard by a man in livery.

"Be you Miss Keeves, miss?" asked the servant.

"Yes."

"Then you're for Melkbridge House. Please get in, miss."

Mavis clambered into the cart and was driven quickly from the station. At the top of the hill, they turned sharp to the right, and rolled along the Bathminster road. Mavis first noticed how much the town had been added to since she had last set foot in it; then she became conscious that distances, which in her childhood had seemed to be considerable, were now trivial.

The man driving her had been a gentleman's servant; seeing that Mavis belonged to a class of life which he had been accustomed to serve, he treated her with becoming respect. Mavis incorrectly argued from the man's deference that it had been decided to secure her services: her heart leapt, her colour heightened at her good fortune.

If a few moments of pleasure are worth purchasing at a cost of many hours of crowded disappointment, it was as well that Mavis was ignorant of the way in which her prospects had been prejudiced by the trend of events at Melkbridge House since Mrs Devitt had replied to Miss Mee's letter. To begin with, Mavis's visit had been within an ace of being indefinitely postponed; it was owing to Harold's expressed wish that the original appointment had been allowed to stand. The reason for this indifference to Mavis's immediate future was that, the day after the schoolmistress had written, Harold had been seriously indisposed. His symptoms were so alarming that his doctor had insisted on having a further opinion; this was obtained from a Bathminster physician, who had confirmed the local medical man's diagnosis; he had also advised Harold a month's rest on his back, this to be followed by a nine months' residence abroad. As if this were not enough to interfere with Mavis's visit, Montague Devitt had met young Sir Archibald Windebank, the bachelor owner of Haycock. Abbey, when going to discharge his duties as borough magistrate, the performance of which he believed might ease his mind of the pain occasioned by his son's illness.

After he had told Windebank his bad news, and the latter had expressed his genuine concern, Devitt had said:

"Do you remember Keeves—Colonel Keeves?"

"Of Melkbridge Court? Of course. Why?"

"I heard something of his daughter the other day."

"Little Mavis!"

"She's big Mavis now," remarked Devitt.

"Have you seen her?" asked Windebank eagerly.

"Not yet, but I may very soon."

"She promised to be an awfully pretty girl. Is she?"

"I haven't seen her. But if she comes down you might care to call."

"Thanks," replied Windebank. "When you see her, you might mention I asked after her."

"I will."

"Although I don't suppose she'll remember me after all these years."

Devitt had left Windebank and gone about his business. When he came out of the court house, and was about to get into his motor, Windebank again approached him, but in such a manner that made Devitt wonder if he had been hanging about on purpose to speak to him.

Windebank made one or two remarks about nothing in particular. Devitt was about to start, when the other said:

"By the way, when you do see Miss Keeves, you might tell her that the mater and my sister will be down here next week and that they'll be awfully pleased to see her, if she'd care to come and stay."

"I won't forget," replied Devitt dryly.

"Tell her to come for as long as she cares to, as the mater and Celia were always fond of her. None of us could ever make out what became of her."

"I won't forget," said Devitt again.

"Thanks. Good-bye."

Montague told his wife of this; she had replied:

"We will decide nothing till we see her," which meant that, if Mavis had not fulfilled the promise of her childhood, and had grown up plain, there would be some prospect of her being engaged in some capacity in the Devitt family, as her acquaintance with the big people about Melkbridge might result in introducing Victoria within the charmed circle, without prejudicing the latter's chances of making a brilliant match. Mrs Devitt's words likewise meant that, if Mavis were charming or pretty, her prospects of securing an engagement would be of the slenderest.

Mavis, ignorant of these considerations, was driven to the door of Melkbridge House. On getting out of the cart, the front door was opened by Hayter, the fat butler, who showed her into the drawing-room. Left to herself, Mavis looked about the expensively furnished room. Noticing a mirror, she walked to it in order to see if hair or hat had been disarranged by her journey and drive; as she looked at her comely reflection, she could not help seeing with a thrill of satisfaction that already the change of air, together with the excitement of the occasion, had flushed her cheeks with colour; she was looking her best. She walked to the window and looked in the direction of her old home, which was on a slight eminence about a mile from where she stood: were the time of year other than summer, its familiar outlines would not have been obscured by foliage. Mavis sighed, turned her back on the window and walked towards the fireplace; something moving in the cool, carefully shaded room caught her eye. It was the propitiatory wagging of a black, cocker spaniel's tail, while its eyes were looking pleadingly up to her. Mavis loved all animals; in a moment the spaniel was in her lap, her arms were about its neck, and she was pressing her soft, red lips to its head. The dog received these demonstrations of affection with delight; although it pawed and clawed the only decent frock which Mavis possessed, she did not mind a bit.

"I shall be here a long time and we shall always be the best of friends," murmured Mavis, as she pressed the affectionate animal to her heart.

Mavis waited half an hour in the drawing-room before anyone came.

Victoria was the first to join her; she entered the room with a frank smile, together with an apology for having kept Mavis waiting. The latter took to Miss Devitt at once, congratulating herself on her good fortune at the prospect of living with such congenial companions as Miss Devitt and the dog. Victoria explained that her brother's illness was responsible for Mavis having been treated with apparent neglect.

"I am so sorry," replied Mavis. "Is it serious?"

"Not at present, but it may be."

"How dreadful it must be for you, who love him!"

"We are all of us used to seeing my brother more or less ill; he has been a cripple for the last eight years."

"How very sad! But if your brother is worse, why didn't you wire and put me off?"

"You would have been disappointed if we had."

"I should have understood."

Then, after making further sympathetic reference to Harold's condition, Mavis said:

"What a dear dog this is! Is he yours?"

"It's Harold's. She's no business to be in here. She'll dirty your dress."

"I don't mind in the least."

"Let me turn her out," said Victoria, as she rose from her seat.

"Please don't. I love to have her with me," pleaded Mavis, adding, as Victoria acceded to her request:

"Don't you like dogs?"

"In their proper place. Jill wouldn't be allowed in at all if Harold didn't sometimes wish it."

"If I had a house, it should be full of dogs," remarked Mavis.

"I understand that you were born near here."

"Yes, at Melkbridge Court."

"I don't know what time you go back, but, after luncheon—of course you'll stay—you might take the opportunity of your being down here to have a look at the old place."

"I—I might," faltered Mavis, who suddenly felt as if all the happiness had been taken out of her life; for Miss Devitt's words hinted that her family was not going to keep Mavis at Melkbridge House.

She looked regretfully at the dog, then inquiringly at Victoria, when Mrs Devitt came into the drawing-room.

Her eyes at once fell on Mavis's comeliness; looking at her step-daughter, she found herself comparing the appearance of the two girls. Before she had offered her hand to Mavis, she had decided that, beside her, Victoria appeared at a disadvantage.

Although Mavis's hair and colouring might only appeal to a certain order of taste, the girl's distinction, to which one of the Miss Mees had alluded earlier in the day, was glaringly patent to Mrs Devitt's sharp eyes; beside this indefinable personal quality, Mrs Devitt observed with a shudder, Victoria seemed middle-class. Mavis's fate, as far as the Devitts were concerned, was decided in the twinkling of an eye. For all this decision, so suddenly arrived at, Mrs Devitt greeted Mavis kindly; indeed, the friendliness that she displayed caused the girl's hopes to rise.

"Luncheon will be ready directly. We are only waiting for my husband," said Mrs Devitt.

"You must be hungry after your journey," added Victoria.

"I've always a healthy appetite, whatever I do," remarked Mavis, who was fondly regarding the black spaniel.

Then Montague Devitt, Lowther, and Miss Spraggs entered the drawing-room, to all of whom Mavis was introduced.

The men were quite cordial, too cordial to a girl who, after all, was seeking a dependant's place, thought Mrs Devitt.

Already she envied Mavis for her family, the while she despised her for her poverty.

The attentions that her husband and stepson were already paying her were a hint of what Mrs Devitt might expect where the eligible men of her acquaintance were concerned. She felt the necessity of striking a jarring note in the harmony of the proceedings. Jill, the spaniel, who, at that moment, sprang upon Mavis's lap, supplied the means.

"What is Jill doing here?"

"I really don't mind," exclaimed Mavis.

"She shouldn't be in the house. There's no reason for her being here at all, now Harold is ill."

"If you wish her to go," said Mavis ruefully.

Jill was ordered from the room, but refused to quit her new friend's side. Lowther approached the dog; to emphasise his wishes, he kicked her in the side.

Mavis looked up quickly.

"Come along, you brute!" cried Lowther, who seized the spaniel by the ear, and, despite its yell of agony, was carrying it by this means from the room.

Mavis felt the blood rush to her head.

"Stop!" she cried.

Lowther turned to look at her.

"Stop—, please don't," she pleaded, as she went quickly to Jill and caught her in her arms.

Lowther looked down, surprised, into Mavis's pleading, yet defiant face.

"It was all my fault: you're hurting her and she's such a dear," continued Mavis.

"Better let her stay," said Devitt, while Mrs Devitt, seeing the girl's flushed face, recalled the passage in Miss Mee's letter which referred to Mavis's sudden anger.

Mrs Devitt hated a display of emotion; she put down Mavis's interference with Lowther's design to bad form. She was surprised that Lowther and her husband were so assiduous in their attentions to Mavis; indeed, as Mrs Devitt afterwards remarked to Miss Spraggs:

"They hardly ever took their eyes off her face."

"Never trust a man further than you can see him," had remarked the agreeable rattle, who had never had reason to complain of want of respect on the part of any man with whom she may have been temporarily isolated.

"And did you notice how her eyes flashed when she seized Jill from Lowther? They're usually a sort of yellow. Then, as perhaps you saw, they seemed to burst into a fierce glare."

"My dear Hilda, is there anything I don't notice?" Miss Spraggs had replied, a remark which was untrue in its present application, as, at the moment when Mavis had taken Jill's part, Eva Spraggs had been looking out of the window, as she wondered if the peas, that were to accompany a roast duckling at luncheon, would be as hard and as unappetising as they had been when served two days previously.

This was later in the day. Just now, Mavis was about to be taken down to luncheon by Montague Devitt; she wondered if her defence of dear Jill had prejudiced her chance of an engagement.

"What's that picture covered with a shutter for?" asked Mavis, as her eye fell on the padlocked "Etty."

"Oh, well-it's an 'Etty': some people might think it's scarcely the thing for some young people, you know," replied Devitt, as they descended the stairs.

"Really! Is that why it's kept like that?" asked Mavis, who could scarcely conceal her amusement.

Mrs Devitt, who was immediately behind, had detected the note of merriment in Mavis's voice. "Scarcely a pure-minded girl," she said to herself, unconscious of the fact that there is nothing so improper as the thoughts implied by propriety.

It was not a very pleasant time for Mavis. Although the luncheon was a good meal, and served in a manner to which she had been unaccustomed for many years, she did not feel at home with the Devitts. Montague, the head of the house, she disliked least; no one could be long insensible to his goodness of heart. Already, she could not "stand" Lowther, for the reason that he hardly took his eyes from her face. As for the women, she was soon conscious of the social gulf that, in reality, lay between her and them; she was, also, aware that they were inclined to patronise her, particularly Mrs Devitt and Miss Spraggs: the high hopes with which she had commenced the day had already suffered diminution.

"And what are your aims in life?" Miss Spraggs asked presently; she had found the peas to be as succulent as she had wished.

"To earn my own living," replied Mavis, who had seen that it was she to whom the agreeable rattle had spoken.

"But, surely, that doesn't satisfy the young women of today!" continued Miss Spraggs.

"I fear it does me; but then I don't know any young women to be influenced by," answered Mavis.

"I thought every young woman, nowadays, was thirsting with ambition," said Miss Spraggs.

"I suppose everyone, who isn't an idiot, has her preferences," remarked Mavis.

"I don't mean that. I thought every girl was determined on living her own life to the exclusion of everything else," continued Miss Spraggs.

"Really!" asked Mavis in some surprise, as she believed that it was only the plain and unattractive women who were of that complexion of thought.

"Despise marriage and all that," put in Lowther, his eyes on Mavis as he tossed off a glass of wine.

"But I don't despise marriage," protested Mavis.

"Really!" said Mrs Devitt, whose sensibilities were a trifle shocked by this remark.

"If two people are in love with each other, and can afford to marry, it seems a particularly natural proceeding," said Mavis simply.

"One that you would welcome?" asked Miss Spraggs, as she raised her thin eyebrows.

"One that someone else would welcome," put in Devitt gallantly.

But Mavis took no notice of this interruption, as she said:

"Of course. Nothing I should wish for more."

Miss Spraggs made two or three further efforts to take a rise out of Mavis; in each case, such was the younger woman's naturalness and self-possession, that it was the would—be persecutor who appeared at a disadvantage.

After luncheon the womenfolk moved to the drawing room; when Victoria presently went to sit with her invalid brother, Mrs Devitt assumed a business-like manner as she requested Mavis to sit by her. The latter knew that her fate was about to be decided. They sat by the window where, but for the intervening foliage, Mavis would have been able to see her old home.

"This is our best chance of a quiet talk, so I'll come to the point at once," began Mrs Devitt.

"By all means," said Mavis, as Miss Spraggs took up a book and pretended to be interested in its contents.

"How soon do you require a situation?"

"At once."

"Has Miss Mee applied to anyone else in the neighbourhood on your account?"

"Not that I'm aware of."

"And you yourself, have you written to anyone here?"

"There's no one I could write to. There's not one of my father's old friends I've kept up. They've all forgotten my very existence, years ago."

"Sure?"

"Who am I to remember?" asked Mavis simply.

It was on Mrs Devitt's lips to give the girl Sir Archibald's message, but the thought of her unmarried step—daughter restrained her. She addressed Mavis rather hurriedly (she tried hard to act conscientiously):

"I may as well say at once that the opportunity that presented itself, when I wrote to Miss Mee, has passed."

The room seemed to move round Mavis. Mrs Devitt continued, as she noticed the look of dismay on the girl's face:

"But I need hardly tell you that I will do all I can to do something for you."

"Thank you," said Mavis.

"Can't you get anything to do in London?"

"I might."

"Have you tried?"

"A little."

Mavis felt tears welling into her eyes; she would never have forgiven herself if she had displayed the extremity of weeping before these people, who, after all, were not of her social world. She resolved to change the subject and keep any expression of her disappointment till she was safe from unsympathetic eyes.

"Did you know my father?" she asked.

"I didn't live here, then. I married Mr—my husband six years ago."

"I suppose he knew him?"

"I gather so."

Very soon after, the two men came into the drawing-room, having considerably curtailed the time they usually devoted to their cigars.

"We were discussing getting something to do for Miss Keeves," said Mrs Devitt.

"You haven't thought of anything?" asked her husband.

"Not yet," replied his wife.

"I suppose you wouldn't care to go into an office?" he continued.

"A lot of girls do that kind of thing nowadays," said Mavis.

"Or a shop?" put in Miss Spraggs.

Mavis glanced up.

"I mean a—flower shop," corrected Miss Spraggs, misliking the look in Mavis's yellow eyes.

Mavis looked towards where she could have seen her old home but for the intervening trees.

"I think I'd better see about my train," she said as she rose.

"Must you, dear?" asked Mrs Devitt.

The men pressed her to stay, particularly Lowther.

"I think I'll go. I want to get back in good time," said Mavis.

"I'll drive you to the station, if I may," volunteered Lowther.

"Thank you; if it's giving you no trouble," she replied.

Lowther left the room. Mavis said good-bye to the others, including Victoria, who joined her for this purpose, from whom the girl learned that Harold was asleep.

As Devitt conducted Mavis to the door, which the fat butler held open, she heard the snorting of a motor; the next minute, a superb car, driven by Lowther, pulled up before the front door. Mavis had never before been in a petrol-propelled carriage (automobiles were then coming into use); she looked forward to her new experience.

She got in beside Lowther, waved her hand to Devitt and was gone. She was surprised at the swift, easy motion, but had an idea that, soon after they left the house, Lowther Devitt was not travelling so fast as when they set out.

"How delightful!" she cried.

"Eh!"

"I've never been in a motor before."

"What?"

"I really haven't. Don't talk: I want to enjoy it."

Seeing that the girl was disinclined for speech, he increased the pace. Mavis was quite disappointed at the short time it took to reach the station. They got out, when Mavis learned that she had twenty minutes to wait. She was sorry, as she disliked the ardent way in which Lowther looked at her. She answered his remarks in monosyllables.

"I'm afraid you're no end angry with me," he said presently.

"Why?" she said coldly.

"Because I punished Jill for disobedience."

"It was cruel of you."

"I made sure she was worrying you."

"Indeed!"

"But it was almost worth while to upset you, you looked so fine when you were angry."

"Did it frighten you?" she asked half scornfully.

"Almost. You looked just like a young tigress."

"I've been told that before."

"Then you often get angry?"

"If I'm annoyed. But it's soon over."

"I go up to town sometimes," he said presently.

"How clever of you!"

"I go up to my club—the Junior Constitutional. May I look you up when I run up next?"

"Here's the train coming in."

"Bother! It's so nice talking to you. I'm no end of sorry the mater isn't taking you on."

"I am too," replied Mavis, who, at once, saw the meaning that Lowther might misread into her words.

"Can I look you up when next I'm in town?" he asked eagerly.

"Oh yes, you can look me up," she replied diffidently.

"We ought to go out to supper one evening."

"I should be delighted."

"You would! Really you would?"

"If you brought your sister. I must find a seat."

"No hurry. It always waits some time here; milk-cans and all that. By Jove! I wish I were going up alone with you. And that's what I meant. I thought we'd go out to supper at the Savoy or Kettner's by ourselves, eh?"

She looked at him coldly, critically.

"Or say the Carlton," he added, thinking that such munificence might dazzle her.

"I'll get in here," she said.

Seeing Mavis select a third-class carriage, his appreciation of her immediately lessened.

"Tell you what," he said to her through the window, "we won't bother about going out to grub; we'll have a day in the country; we can enjoy ourselves just as much there. Eh, dear? Oh, I beg your pardon, but you're so pretty, you know, and all that."

Mavis noticed the way in which he leered at her while he said these words. She bit her lip in order to restrain the words that were on her tongue; it was of no avail.

"I'll tell you something," she cried.

"Yes—yes; quickly, the train is just off."

"If my father had been alive, and we'd been living here, you'd not have dared to speak to me like that; in fact, you wouldn't have had the chance."

It was a crestfallen, tired, and heartsick Mavis who opened the door of Brandenburg College with her latch-key in the evening. The only thing that sustained her was the memory of the white look of anger which appeared in Lowther Devitt's face when she had unmistakably resented his insult.

CHAPTER FOUR
MAVIS LEAVES HER NEST

Mavis did not tell the whole truth to the two old ladies; they gathered from her subdued manner that she had not been successful in her quest.

The girl was too weary to give explanations, to talk, even to think; the contemplation of the wreck of the castles that she had been building in the air had tired her: she went to bed, resolving to put off further thought for the future until the morrow.

Several times in the night, she awoke with a start, when she was oppressed with a great fear of the days to come; but each time she put this concern from her, as if conscious that she required all the rest she could get, in order to make up her mind to the course of action which she should pursue on the morrow.

When she definitely awoke, she determined on one thing, that, unless pressed by circumstances, she would not ask the Devitts for help.

The old ladies were already down when she went in to breakfast. Miss Annie, directly she saw Mavis, took up a letter that she had laid beside her plate.

"I've heard from Mrs Devitt, dear," she said, after she had asked Mavis, according to custom, how she had slept.

"What does she say?" asked Mavis indifferently.

"That she regrets she is unable to offer you anything at present, but if, at any time, you would take a clerkship in one of the companies in which her husband is interested, they might be able to provide you with a berth," replied Annie.

"Oh!" said Mavis shortly.

"She has also sent me a postal order for your fare," continued Annie.

Mavis made no reply.

The two old maids glanced significantly at one another; presently, Annie Mee was emboldened to ask:

"Do you think you would like to earn your living in the manner indicated?"

"I have decided not to," replied Mavis shortly.

"Of course, if you would prefer to stay with us," began Miss Helen.

"If you have no objection, I will leave for good tomorrow morning," said Mavis.

"Leave for good!" cried the two old ladies together, who, now that they believed Mavis to be going, were dismayed at the prospect of living without her.

"It will be better for all of us," remarked Mavis.

"But have you anything in view, dear?" asked Miss Annie.

"Nothing very definite. But I've every hope of being settled in a day or two."

The two old ladies heaved a sigh of relief; for all their affection for the girl, they found that her healthy appetite made serious inroads into the meager profits of the college. After breakfast, Mavis went upstairs for her hat. She opened the drawers at the base of her old-fashioned looking-glass and counted up her possessions. These amounted to seven pounds, thirteen shillings and sevenpence halfpenny; in addition to which, there was a quarter's salary of four pounds ten shillings due to her; also, there was her fare which Mrs. Devitt had sent, a sum which she was undecided whether or not to accept. At any other time, Mavis would have thought that this money would have been ample provision with which to start life; but her one time ignorance on this matter had been rudely dissipated by her fruitless search after employment, when she had first decided to leave Brandenburg College. Beyond her little store of ready money, she owned a few trinkets which, at the worst, she could sell for a little; but this was a contingency on which she would not allow her mind to dwell just now. One or two things she was determined not to part with; these were her mother's wedding ring, a locket containing a piece of her father's hair, and a bracelet which he had given her. The two old ladies would be leaving for Worthing on the morrow; Amelia was going to Southend-on-Sea for a fortnight. As Mavis had resolved to sever her long connection with the college, it was necessary for her to seek lodging elsewhere.

A few minutes later, she set out upon this wearisome quest: she had never looked for London lodgings before. Although nearly every window in the less frequented streets displayed a card announcing that apartments were to let, she soon discovered how difficult it was to get anything remotely approaching her simple needs. She required a small bedroom in a house where there was a bathroom; also, if possible, she wanted the use of a sitting-room with a passable piano on which she sought permission to give lessons to any pupils whom she might be successful in getting.

Most of the doors she knocked at were answered by dirty children or by dirtier women; these, instinctively, told Mavis that she would get neither cleanliness nor comfort in a house frequented by such folk. When confronted with these, she would make some excuse for knocking at the door, and, after walking on a few yards, would attack the knocker of another house, when, more likely than not, the door would be opened by an even more slatternly person than before. Now and again she would light upon a likely place, but it soon appeared to Mavis that good landladies knew their value and made charges which were prohibitive to the girl's slender resources.

Tired with running up and down so many steps and stairs, Mavis turned into a milk-shop to buy a bun and a glass of milk. She asked the kindly-faced woman who served her if she happened to know of anyone who let clean rooms at moderate charges. The woman wrote down two addresses, said that she would be comfortable at either of these, and told her the quickest way of getting to them. The first name was a Mrs Ellis, who lived at 20 Kiva Gardens. This address proved to be a neat, two-storied house, by the side of which was a road leading to stables and a yard. Mrs Ellis opened the door. Mavis, with a sense of elation, saw that she was a trim, elderly, kindly-looking body.

The girl explained what she wanted. She learned that there was a small bedroom at the back to let; also, that she could have the use of the downstairs sitting-room, in which was a piano.

"Would you very much mind if I had one or two pupils?" asked Mavis.

"Not a bit, miss. I like young people myself, and look on music as company."

"I'd like to see the bedroom."

Mrs Ellis took Mavis upstairs, where the girl was delighted to find that the room was pleasant-looking and scrupulously clean.

"It's only a question of terms," said Mavis hesitatingly.

"You'd better see the sitting-room and try the piano, miss, before you decide," remarked Mrs Ellis.

They went downstairs to another room at the back of the house; this was adequate, although Mavis noticed that it was stuffy. Perhaps the landlady suspected the girl's thoughts on the matter, for she said:

"I have the window shut to keep out dust and smell from the yard, miss."

Mavis, satisfied with this explanation, looked through the window, and saw that the yard was much bigger than she had believed it to be. Three or four men in corduroys were lounging about and chaffing each other.

"You try the piano, miss; I shan't keep you a moment," said Mrs Ellis, who, also, had looked out of the window.

Mavis, left to herself, did as she was bid. She found the piano, although well past its prime, to be better than the generality of those that she had already tried. She got up and again looked out of the window, when she saw that the men, whom she had previously seen idling in the yard, were now hard at work.

The next moment, Mrs Ellis, looking rather hot, re-entered the room.

"I've had to talk to my men," she said.

"You employ them?" asked Mavis.

"Yes, the lazy rascals. It was my husband's business, but since he died I've kept it on."

"You must be very clever."

"It wants managing. You didn't open the window, miss?" This question was asked anxiously.

"No."

"How much did you wish to pay, miss?"

Mavis explained that she didn't wish to pay more than five shillings a week for a bedroom, but after some discussion it was agreed that she should pay six shillings a week, which would include the use of the sitting-room, together with a morning bath, bathrooms not having been supplied to Mrs Ellis's house.

"I'm letting it go reasonable to you, miss, because you're a real young lady and not like most who thinks they are."

"Here's my first week's rent in advance. I can't say how long I shall stay, because I may get a place where they may want me to live in the house," said Mavis.

"It isn't the money I want so much as the company. And if you'd like me to supply the meals, we shan't quarrel over L. s. d."

"I'm sure we shan't. I shall come in without fail tomorrow morning."

Mavis then took a bus to Kensington Church; here she got out and walked the few yards necessary to take her to the Kensington Free Library, where she put down the addresses of those advertising situations likely to suit her. This task completed, she walked to Brandenburg College. When dinner was over—the Misses Mee dined midday—Mavis wrote replies to the advertisements. After parting with the precious pennies, which bought the necessary stamps at the post-office, she came home to pack her things. This took her some time, there being so many odds and ends which had accumulated during her many years' association with the college. As it was getting dark, she slipped out to tell the nearest local agent for Carter Paterson to have her boxes removed the first thing in the morning.

Hurrying back, she ran into Bella Goss, a pupil at the college, and her father. Mr. Goss was the person who was behindhand with his account; he supplied Miss Annie Mee with the theatre and concert tickets which were the joy of her life.

"There's Miss Keeves!" cried Bella, at which her father raised his hat.

Bella, looking as if she wished to speak to Mavis, the latter stopped; she shook hands with the child and bowed to Mr. Goss.

"You're leaving the college, aren't you, Miss Keeves?" asked Bella.

"Yes, dear," replied Mavis.

"Going to be married?" asked Mr. Goss, who secretly admired Mavis.

"I'm going to earn my living; at least, I hope so," said Mavis.

"Haven't you anything to do, then?" he asked.

"Nothing settled," Mavis answered evasively.

"I suppose you wouldn't care for anything in the theatrical line?"

Mavis did not think that she would.

"Or, if you want anything very badly, I might get you into a house of business."

"Do you mean a shop?" asked Mavis.

"A big one where they employ hundreds," said Goss apologetically.

"It's awfully kind of you. I'll come to you if I really want anything badly."

"Thank you, Miss Keeves. Good night."

"Good night. Good night, Bella."

Mavis hurried home and to bed, to be kept awake for quite two hours by fears of the unknown perils which might menace the independent course which she was about to travel.

Breakfast the next morning was a dismal meal. Mavis was genuinely sorry to leave the old ladies, who had, in a large measure, taken the place of the parents she had lost.

They, on their part, were conscious of the break that Mavis's departure would make in their lives. All three women strove to conceal their distress by an affectation of cheerfulness and appetite. But little was eaten or drunk. Miss Annie Mee was so absent-minded that she forgot to spread any butter upon her toast. The old ladies were leaving for Worthing soon after eleven. Mavis purposed taking leave of them and Brandenburg College as soon after breakfast as she could get away. When she rose from the table, Miss Helen Mee said:

"I should like to see you in my study in five minutes from now."

The study was a small-sized room, which was reached by descending two steps at the end of the hall further from the front door. Mavis presented herself here at the expiration of the allotted time, where she found Miss Helen and Miss Annie solemnly seated behind the book-littered table, which stood in the middle of the room.

"Pray close the door," said Helen.

"Please take a seat," added Annie, when Mavis had obeyed the elder Miss Mee's behest.

The girl sat down and wondered what was coming. It was some moments before Helen spoke; she believed that delay would enhance the impressiveness of the occasion.

"Dear Mavis," she presently began, "before I say a few parting words, in which my sister most heartily joins, words which are not without a few hints of kindly admonishment, that may help you along the path you have—er—elected—yes, elected to pursue, I should like to press on you parting gifts from my sister and myself."

Here she handed Mavis her treasured copy of The Stones of Venice, which contained the great Mr Ruskin's autograph, together with a handsomely bound Bible; this latter was open at the fly-leaf.

"Read," said Helen, as she looked at Mavis over her spectacles.

Mavis read as follows:

"TO DEAR MAVIS, FROM HER FRIEND, HELEN ALLPRESS MEE.

"ARE NOT TWO SPARROWS SOLD FOR A FARTHING? AND ONE OF THEM SHALL NOT FALL ON THE GROUND WITHOUT YOUR FATHER.

"FEAR YE NOT THEREFORE, YE ARE OF MORE VALUE THAN MANY SPARROWS.—St Matthew x. 29, 31."

Mavis thanked Miss Mee and was about to press on her the trinket that she had previously purchased as a parting gift for her old friend; but Helen checked the girl with a gesture signifying that her sister was about to speak.

Mis Annie was less prosy than her sister.

"Take this, dear, and God bless you."

Here she handed Mavis her much-prized copy of Sesame and Lilies, likewise containing the autograph of the great Mr. Ruskin; at the same time, she presented Mavis with a box of gloves.

Mavis thanked the generous old ladies and gave them the little presents she had bought for this purpose. To Miss Helen she handed a quaint old workbox she had picked up in the shop of a dealer in antiquities; to Miss Annie she gave her A three-quarter-length photograph in a silver frame.

The two old ladies' hands shook a little when they took these offerings; they both thanked her, after which Miss Helen rose to take formal farewell of Mavis.

She spoke the words that she always made use of when taking final leave of a pupil; usually, they came trippingly to her tongue, without the least effort of memory; but this morning they halted; she found herself wondering if her dignity were being compromised in Mavis's eyes.

"Dear Mavis," she said, "in—in issuing from the doors—er—portals of Brandenburg College to the new er—er—world that awaits you beyond, you—you may rest assured that you carry—"

The old lady stopped; she did not say any more; she sat down and seemed to be carefully wiping her spectacles. Mavis rose to go, girl-like; she hated anything in the nature of a scene, especially when made over such an insignificant person as herself. At the same time, her farewell of the two old ladies, with whom she had lived for so long, affected her far more than she would ever have thought possible. Halfway to the door, she hesitated; the noise made by Miss Annie blowing her nose decided her. In a moment, she had placed her arms about Miss Helen and Miss Annie, and all three women were weeping to their hearts' content.

Some seventy minutes later, it was two very forlorn-looking old ladies who stumbled into the train that was to take them to Worthing. Meanwhile, Mavis had packed her few remaining things and had gone down to the kitchen to say good-bye to Amelia.

Directly Amelia caught sight of her and she burst into tears. Mavis, somewhat disconcerted by this evidence of esteem, gave Amelia five shillings, at which the servant wept the more.

"Oh, miss! what shall I do without you?"

"You'll get on all right. Besides, you're going for a holiday to Southend."

"Moind you let me come to you when you're married," sobbed Amelia.

"I shouldn't count on that if I were you."

"Do 'ave me, miss. I'll always troi and 'and things so no one sees my bad oye."

"It isn't that I don't want you; but it's so unlikely that I shall ever have a home."

Mavis offered her hand. Amelia wiped her wet hand (she had been washing up) upon her apron before taking it.

"Oh, miss, you are good to me, and you a reel lydy."

"Be a good girl and look after your mistresses."

"That I will, miss. Whatever should I sy to that there Mr. Fuskin, when I meet 'im in 'eaven, if I didn't?"

"Good-bye, Amelia."

"There! I forgot," cried Amelia. She went to the drawer of the dresser and brought out something wrapped in tissue paper.

Mavis undid this, to find Amelia's offering to consist of a silver brooch forming the word "May."

"It's the nearest I could get to your nime, miss," she explained.

"Thank you so much."

"It ain't good enough for you: nothin' ain't good enough for you. Wasn't you loved by the music master, 'im who was so lovely and dark?" wept Amelia.

It was with a heavy heart that Mavis left Brandenburg College, the walls of which had sheltered her for so long: she did her best to be self-possessed as she kissed the Misses Mee and walked to her new address, to which her two boxes had been taken the first thing by the carriers.

The rest of the morning, and after the simple meal which Mrs Ellis provided, Mavis unpacked her things and made her room as homelike as possible. While she was doing this, she would now and again stop to wonder if she had heard the postman's knock; although she could hear him banging at doors up and down the street, he neglected to call at No. 20, a fact which told Mavis that so far no one had troubled to seriously consider her applications for employment. A cup of tea with Mrs Ellis put a cheerful complexion upon matters; she spent the next few hours in finishing her little arrangements. These completed to her satisfaction, she leaned against the window and looked hungrily towards the heavens. It was a blue, summer evening; there was not a cloud in the sky.

Although the raucous voices of children playing in the streets assailed her ears, she was scarcely conscious of these, her thoughts being far away. She was always a lover of nature; wildflowers, especially cowslips, affected her more than she would care to own; the scent of hay brought a longing to her heart; the sight of a roadside stream fascinated her. Now, she was longing with a passionate desire for the peace of the country. Upon this July evening, the corn must now be all but ripe for the sickle, making the fields a glory of gold. She pictured herself wandering alone in a vast expanse of these; gold, gold, everywhere; a lark singing overhead. Then, in imagination, she found her way to a nook by the Avon at Melkbridge, a spot endeared to her heart by memories that she would never forget. As a child, she loved to steal there with her picture book; later, as a little girl, she would go there all alone, and, lying on her back, would dream, while her eyes followed the sun. Her fondness for this place was the only thing which she had kept from her father's knowledge. She wondered if this hiding place, where she had loved to take her thoughts, were the same. She could shut her eyes and recall it: the pollard willows, the brown river banks, the swift, running river in which the forget-me-nots (so it appeared to her) never seemed to tire in the effort to see their reflection.

Darkness came out of the east. Mavis's heart went out to the summer night. Then, she was aware of a feeling of physical discomfort. The effort of imagination had exhausted her. She became wearily conscious of the immediate present. The last post, this time, knocked at the door of Mrs

Ellis', but it brought no letter for Mavis. It seemed that the world had no need of her; that no one cared what became of her. She was disinclined to go out, consequently, the limitations of her surroundings made her quickly surrender to the feeling of desolation which attacked her. She wondered how many girls in London were, at the present moment, isolated from all congenial human companionship as she was. She declined the landlady's kindly offer to partake of cold boiled beef and spring onions in the status of guest; the girl seemed to get satisfaction from her morbid indulgence in self-pity.

As she was about to undress, her eye fell on the Bible which Helen Mee had given her earlier in the day. Mavis remembered something had been written on the fly-leaf: more from idle curiosity than from any other motive, she opened the cover of the book, to read in the old lady's meager, pointed hand:

"Are not two sparrows sold for a farthing? and one of them shall not fall on the ground without your Father.

"Fear ye not therefore, ye are of more value than many sparrows."— St Matthew x. 29, 31.

Mavis's heart was filled with contrition. She was not forgotten; there was Someone who cared what became of her. Although she was now as one of the sparrows, which are never certain of their daily food, she could not fall without the knowledge of One who cared, and He——

Mavis knelt: she implored forgiveness for having believed herself to be utterly forgotten: she thanked Him for caring that a poor, friendless girl, such as she, should not fall.

CHAPTER FIVE
BARREN WAYS

There followed for Mavis many, many anxious days, spent from the first thing in the morning till late at night in a fruitless search for work. Her experiences were much the same as those of any attractive, friendless girl seeking to earn her livelihood in London. To begin with, she found that the summer was a time of year in which the openings she sought were all obstinately closed, the heads of firms, or those responsible for engaging additional assistance, being either away on holidays, or back from these in no mood to consider Mavis' application.

Another thing that struck her was that, whenever she went to interview men, she was always treated civilly, cordially, or familiarly; but the womenfolk she saw were invariably rude, directly they set eyes upon her comeliness. Once or twice, she was offered employment by men; it was only their free and easy behaviour which prevented her accepting it. Mavis, as yet, was ignorant of the conditions on which some employers of female labour engage girls seeking work; but she had a sensible head screwed on her pretty shoulders; she argued that if a man were inclined to be familiar after three minutes' acquaintance, what would he be when she was dependent upon him for a weekly wage? It was not compatible with her vast self-respect to lay herself open to risk of insult, suggested by a scarcely veiled admiration for her person after a few moments' acquaintance. It was not as if she had any qualification of marketable value; she knew neither shorthand nor typewriting; she could merely write a decent hand, was on very fair terms with French, on nodding acquaintance with German, and had a sound knowledge of arithmetic.

On the face of it, her best course was to get a situation as governess; but Mavis, after a week's trial, gave up the endeavour. The mothers of possible pupils, with whom the girl's credentials from the college secured an interview, were scarcely civil to the handsome, distinguished-looking girl; they were sure that such looks, seeking for employment, boded ill for anyone indulgent enough to engage her. Mavis could not understand such behaviour; she had read in books how people were invariably kind and sympathetic, women particularly so, to girls in want of work; surely she furnished opportunity for her own sex to show consideration to one of the less fortunate of their kind.

Mavis next advertised in local papers for pupils to whom she would teach music. Receiving no replies, she attempted to get employment in a house of business; this effort resulted in her obtaining work as a canvasser, remuneration being made by results. This meant tramping the pavement in all weathers, going up and coming down countless flights of stairs, swallowing all kinds of humiliating rebuffs in the effort to sell some encyclopedia or somebody's set of novels, which no one wanted. She always met with disappointment and, in time, became used to it; but there were occasions when a purchaser seemed likely, when hope would beat high, only to give place to sickening despair when her offer was finally rejected. On the whole, she met with civility and consideration from the young men (mostly clerks in offices) whom she interviewed; but there was a type of person whose loud-voiced brutality cut her to the quick. This was the West-end tradesman. She would walk into a shop in Bond Street or thereabouts, when the proprietor, taking her for a customer, would advance with cringing mien, wringing his hands the while. No sooner did he learn that the girl wanted him to buy something, than his manner immediately changed. Usually, in coarse and brutal voice, he would order her from the shop; sometimes, if he were in a facetious mood, and if he had the time to spare, he would make fun of her and mock her before a crowd of grinning underlings. To this day, the sight of a West-end tradesman fills Mavis with unspeakable loathing; nothing would ever mitigate the horror which their treatment of her inspired at this period of her life.

Then Mavis, in reply to one of her many answers to advertisements, received a letter asking her to call at an office in Eastcheap, at a certain time. Arrived there, she learned how she could earn a pound a week by canvassing, together with commission, if her sales were successful. She had eagerly accepted the offer, when she learned that she was to make house-to-house calls in certain London suburbs (she was to commence at Peckham), armed with a bottle of pickles and a bottle of sauce. She was furnished with a Peckham local directory and was instructed to make calls at every house in her district, when she was to ask for the mistress by name, in order to disarm suspicion on the part of whoever might open the door. When she was asked inside, she was to do her utmost to get orders for the pickles and the sauce, supplies of which were sent beforehand to a grocer in the neighbourhood. Mavis did not relish the job, but was driven by the goad of necessity. On her way home to tell Mrs. Ellis that she would be leaving immediately to live in Peckham, she slipped on a piece of banana skin and twisted her ankle, an accident which kept her indoors for the best part of a week. When she had written to Eastcheap to say that she was well enough to commence work, she had received a letter which informed her that her place had been filled.

Now, she was sitting in her little bedroom in Kiva Street, a prey to despair; she had no one to comfort her, not even Mrs. Ellis, this person having gone out on a rare visit to an aunt.

Her little stock of money had sadly dwindled; eighteen shillings and her trinkets stood between her and want. She had fought and had been vanquished; there was nothing left for her to do but to write to Mrs Devitt and ask if the offer, that had been mentioned in her last letter to Miss Mee, still held good. During all these weeks of weary effort, Mavis had been largely kept up by the thought that she was a sparrow, who could not fall to the ground without the knowledge of the Most High. Now, it seemed to her that she could sustain her flight but a little while longer; yet, so far as she could see, there was no one to whom her extremity seemed to matter in the least.

Apart from her desire to earn a living, the girl had struggled resolutely in order that she should not seek work of the Devitts. She disliked the family; she had resolved to apply to them only as a last resource.

She had gone one day to Brandenburg College to call on her old employers, but she found that the name-plate had been removed, and that the house was to let. She had made inquiries, to learn that her old friend Miss Annie Mee had died suddenly at Worthing, and also that Miss Helen had sold the school for what it would fetch, and no one knew what had become of her. Mavis grieved at the loss of her friend, but not so deeply, or for so long, as she would if she had not been consumed with anxiety on her own account. She had not forgotten Mr Goss's offer of help: she had called at his house twice, to learn on each occasion that he was out of town. Presently, Mrs Ellis came in; finding Mavis moping, she asked her to the downstairs sitting-room for a cup of tea. The girl gladly went: she sat by the window watching the men working in the yard behind, while Mrs Ellis made tea in the kitchen. Mavis, wanting air, opened the window, although she remembered her landlady's liking for having this particular one shut. No sooner had she done so, than she heard a woman's voice raised in raucous anger, the while it made use of much bad language. It abused certain people for not having done their work. The bad language getting more forceful than before, Mavis moved from the window. Presently, the voice stopped. Soon after, Mrs Ellis, looking red and flustered, came into the room. When she saw that Mavis had opened the window, she became redder in the face, as she said:

"I'm sorry, miss; I couldn't help it."

"Help what?" asked Mavis.

"Talking to the men as I did. I always wanted the window down, so you shouldn't hear."

"It was you, then?"

"Didn't you know, miss?"

"Not altogether. It was something like your voice."

"If I were to talk to them ordinary, they wouldn't listen; so I've to talk to them in my 'usband's language, which is all they understand," said Mrs Ellis apologetically.

The contrast between Mrs Ellis's neat, unassuming respectability and her language to the men made Mavis smile.

"I'm glad you've taken it sensible," remarked her landlady. "Many's the good lodger I've lost through that there window being open."

Tea put fresh heart into Mavis. It was ten days since she had last called on Mr Goss: she resolved to make a further attempt. He was in, she learned from the maid-of-all-work, who opened the door of Mr Goss's house.

On asking to see him, she was shown into a double drawing-room, the front part of which was tolerably furnished; but Mavis could not help noticing that the back was quite shabby; unframed coloured prints, taken from Christmas numbers of periodicals, were fastened to the walls with tin tacks.

Mr Goss came into the room wiping his mouth with his handkerchief. Mavis feared that she had interrupted a meal. Whether she had or not, he was glad to see her and asked if he could help her. Mavis told him how she was situated. In reply, he said that he had a friend who was a man of some importance in a West-end emporium. He asked her if she would like a letter of introduction to this person. Mavis jumped at the offer. When he had written the letter, Mavis asked after his daughter, to learn that she was staying at Margate with her mother. When Mavis thanked and said good-bye to Mr Goss, he warmly pressed the hand that she offered.

The next day, she presented herself at the great house of business where Mr Goss's friend was to be found. His name was Evans. It was only after delay that she was able to see him. He was a grave, kindly-looking man, who scanned Mavis with interest before he read Mr Goss's letter. Mavis could almost hear the beating of her heart while she waited to see if he could offer her anything.

"I'm sorry," he said, as he folded up the letter.

Mavis could not trust herself to speak.

"Very sorry I can't oblige you or Mr Goss," continued the man. "All our vacancies were filled last week. I've nothing at present."

Mavis turned to go.

"You want something to do at once?" said Mr Evans, as he noticed the girl's dismay.

Mavis nodded. The man went on:

"They'd probably take you at Dawes'."

"Dawes'!" echoed Mavis hopefully.

"Do you know anything of Dawes'?"

"Everyone knows Dawes'," smiled Mavis.

"But do you know anything of the place, as it affects girls who live there?"

"No," answered Mavis, who scarcely heeded what Mr Evans was saying; all her thoughts were filled by a great joy at a prospect of getting work.

She was conscious of the man saying something about her consulting Mrs Goss before thinking of going there; but she did not give this aspect of the matter another moment's thought.

"What name shall I ask for?" asked Mavis.

"Mr Orgles, if you go."

"Thank you so much. May I mention your name?"

"If you decide to go there, certainly."

Mavis thanked him and was gone. She, at once, made for Dawes'. The girl knew exactly where it was, its name and situation being a household word to women living in London. Arrived there, she glanced appealingly at the splendid plate-glass windows, as if beseeching them to mitigate some of their aloofness. She approached one of the glass doors, which was opened by a gorgeously attired official. When inside, she looked about her curiously, fearfully. She was in a long room, down either side of which ran a counter, behind which were stationed young women, who bore themselves with a self-conscious, would-be queenly mien. The space between the counters, to which the public was admitted, was promenaded by frock-coated men, who piloted inexperienced customers to where they might satisfy their respective wants. One of these shop-walkers approached Mavis.

"Where can I direct you, madam?"

"I want to see Mr Orgles."

The man looked at her attentively.

"I've come from Mr Evans at Poole and Palfrey's," murmured Mavis.

The man left her and spoke to one of the regal young women, who stood behind the counter as if trying to make believe that they were there, not from necessity, but from choice.

The man returned to Mavis and told her to wait. As she stood in the shop, she saw the young woman whom the man had spoken to mouth something in a speaking tube; this person then whispered to two or three other girls who stood behind the counter, causing them to stare continuously at Mavis. Presently, the speaking tube whistled, when a message came to say that if Miss Keeves would walk upstairs, Mr Orgles would see her. The shop-walker walked before Mavis to show her the way. She could not help noticing that the man's demeanour had changed: he had approached her, when he first saw her, with the servility peculiar to his occupation; now, having fathomed her errand, he marched before her with elbows stuck out and head erect, as if to convey what an important personage he was.

She was shown into a plainly furnished office, where she was told to wait. She wondered if, at last, she would have any luck. She sat there for about ten minutes, when a man came into the room, shutting the door after him. He was about sixty-five, and walked with a stoop. His face reminded Mavis of a camel. He had large bulging eyes, which seemed to gaze at objects sideways. He looked like the deacon at a house of dissenting worship, which, indeed, he was. Mavis rightly concluded this person to be Mr Orgles.

"You wished to see me?" he asked.

"Mr Orgles?"

"That's my name."

Mavis explained why she had called: it was as much as she could do to hide her anxiety. Mr Orgles not making any reply, she went on speaking, saying how she would do her utmost to give satisfaction in the event of her being engaged.

While she was pleading, she was conscious that the man was looking in his sideways fashion at her figure. He approached her. Mavis suddenly felt an instinct of repugnance for the man. She said all she could think of, but Mr Orgles remained silent; she anxiously scanned his face in the hope of getting some encouragement from its expression, but she might as well have stared at a brick wall for all the enlightenment she got. Then followed a few moments' pause, during which her eyes were riveted on Mr Orgles's nostrils: these were prominent, large, dilating; they fascinated her. As he still remained silent, she presently found courage to ask:

"Will you take me?"

He turned his face so that one of his eyes could look into hers, fiercely as she thought. He shook his head. Mavis uttered a little cry; she rose to go.

"Don't go," said a voice beside her.

Mr Orgles was standing quite near.

"Do you badly want a place?"

"Very badly."

"H'm!"

His big nostrils were dilating more than ever; he turned his head so that one of his eyes again looked into hers.

"Something might be got you," continued the man.

"It all depends on influence."

Mavis looked up quickly.

"I was wondering if you'd like me to do my best for you?"

"Oh, of course I would."

"Excuse me," said Mr Orgles, as he took what seemed to be a tiny piece of fluff from the skirt of her coat. "You must have got it coming upstairs."

"Do you think you would speak for me?" Mavis found words to ask.

Mr Orgles's eyes again rested on Mavis, as he said:

"It depends on you."

"On me?"

"You say you have never been out in the world before?"

"Not really in the world."

"I am sorry."

"Sorry!" echoed Mavis.

"Because you haven't lived; you don't know what life can be—is," cried Mr Orgles, who now waved his arms and moved jerkily about the girl.

She looked at him in astonishment.

"Excuse me; a further bit of fluff," said Mr Orgles.

This time he placed his hand upon the breast of her coat and seemed in no hurry to remove it.

Mavis flushed and moved away; at any other time she would have hotly resented his conduct, but today she was desperately anxious to get employment, Mr Orgles took courage from her half-heartedness.

"Let me show you," he cried.

"Show me what?" she asked, perplexed.

"How to live: how to enjoy life: how to be happy. The rest is easy: you will be employed here; you will rise to great things; and it will all be owing to me."

Mavis looked at the excited, gesticulating old man in surprise; she wondered if he were right in his senses. Suddenly, his gyrations ceased; he glanced at the door and then moved his head in order to dart a horrid glance at the girl. He then approached her with arms outstretched.

Mavis intuitively knew what he meant. Her body quivered with rage; the fingers of her right hand clenched. Perhaps the man saw the anger in her eyes, because he stopped; but he was near enough for Mavis to feel his hot breath upon her cheek.

Thus they stood for a moment, he undecided, she on the defensive, when the door opened and a man came into the room. Mr Orgles, with an unpleasant look on his face, turned to see who the intruder might be.

"I've been looking for you, Orgles," said the man.

"Indeed, sir! Very sorry, sir," remarked Mr Orgles, who wore such an attitude of servility to the newcomer that Mavis could hardly believe him to be the same man.

"I see you're busy," continued the intruder. "Engaging someone in Miss Jackson's place?"

"I was thinking about doing so, sir."

"Why hesitate?"

Here the man—he was tall, dark, and fresh-coloured—looked kindly at Mavis; although not a gentleman, he had an unmistakable air of authority.

"There's no reason why I shouldn't, sir, only—"

"Only what?"

"She's had no experience, sir."

The man turned to Mavis and said:

"If your references are satisfactory, you can consider yourself as engaged from next week."

"Oh, thank you," said Mavis, trying to voice her gratitude.

"Call to-morrow with your references at eleven and ask for Mr Skeffington Dawes," said the stranger.

A great gladness and a great reproach came to the girl's heart: a great gladness at having secured work; a great reproach at having believed that there was no one who cared if a human sparrow, such as she, should fall.

She bowed her thanks to Mr Skeffington Dawes and left the room, all unconscious of the malignant glance that Mr Orgles shot at her, after turning his head to bring the girl within his range of vision.

CHAPTER SIX
"DAWES"

After securing a place in "Dawes'," which Mavis did at her interview with Mr Skeffington Dawes (one of the directors of the firm), her first sensation was one of disappointment, perhaps consequent upon reaction from the tension in her mind until she was sure of employment.

Now, she was resentful at having to earn her bread as a shop-girl, not only on account of its being a means of livelihood which she had always looked down upon, but also, because it exposed her to the insults of such creatures as Orgles. She sat in Mrs Ellis' back sitting-room three days before she was to commence her duties at "Dawes'"; she was moody and depressed; on the least provocation, or none at all, she would weep bitter tears for ten minutes at a time.

This physical lowness brought home to her the fear of possibly losing her hitherto perfect health. The prospect of being overtaken by such a calamity opened up a vista of terrifying possibilities which would not bear thinking about.

Now, she was to earn fifteen pounds a year and "live in," a term meaning that "Dawes'" would provide her with board and lodging; she might, also, add to her salary by commissions on sales. The effort of packing her belongings took her mind from brooding over troubles, real or imaginary, and served to heighten her spirits. Mrs Ellis' words, also, put heart into her.

"People will take to a nice-mannered, well-spoken, fine-looking young lady like you, miss," she said to Mavis.

"Nonsense!" replied Mavis.

"It ain't, miss. I've kep my eyes open, and I see how young ladies, such as you, either go 'up' or go 'down.' You're one of the 'go uppers,' and now you've a chance, why, you might, one day, have a business of your own."

"Mind you come and deal with me if I do. You shall always have 'tick' for as much as you like."

"Thank you very much, miss; but I couldn't enjoy wearing a thing if I didn't know it was paid for. I should think everyone was looking at it."

"Time to talk about that when I get my own business."

"And if things go wrong, which God forbid, you've always a home here!"

"Mrs Ellis!"

"I'm not so young as I was, and that yard gets me in the throat crool in the cold weather. You'd be useful there too, miss, if you wouldn't mind learning a few swear words."

"Oh, Mrs Ellis!" laughed Mavis.

"It's difficult at first, miss; but it's wonderful how soon you drop into it if you give your mind to it," declared the landlady solemnly.

Four evenings later, Mavis arrived at "Dawes'," having sent her boxes earlier in the day. She was to commence work on the morrow, and had been advised by the firm that it would be as well to take up her abode in her future quarters the night before.

Nine o'clock found her on the pavement before the firm's great windows, now securely shuttered; she wondered how she should find her way inside, there being no door in the spread of shutters by which she could gain admittance. Noticing that one or two men were dogging her footsteps, she asked a policeman how she could get into "Dawes'."

"A new hand, miss?" asked the policeman.

"Yes."

"I thought so. First to the right and first to the right again, where you'll see two or three open doors belonging to the firm," the policeman informed her. He had directed many fresh, comely young women, who had arrived from the country, to the "young ladies'" entrance; later, he had seen the same girls, when it was often with an effort that he could believe them to have been what they once were.

Mavis followed his directions and nearly missed the first on the right, this being a narrow turning. Many-storied buildings, looking like warehouses, were on either side of this; their height was such that the merest strip of sky could be seen when Mavis looked up. She then came to an open door. Above this was a fanlight, which fitfully lighted a passage terminating in a flight of uncarpeted stone steps. It was all very uninviting. The girl looked about for someone of whom to make further inquiries. No one came in or went out; all that Mavis could see was one or two over-dressed men, who were prowling about on the further side of the way. A little distance up the turning was another open door lit in the same way as the first. This also admitted to a similar passage, which, also, terminated in a flight of bare stone steps. Just as she got there, two young women flaunted out; they were in evening dress, but Mavis thought the petticoats that they aggressively displayed were cheap, torn, and soiled. They pushed past Mavis, to be joined by two of the prowlers in the street. Mavis walked inside, where she waited for some time without seeing anyone; then, an odd-looking, malformed creature came up, seemingly from a hole at the end of the passage. She had scarcely any nose; she wore spectacles and the uniform of a servant. Before she disappeared up the stairs, Mavis saw that she carried blankets in one hand, a housemaid's pail in the other. She breathed noisily through her nostrils. When she was well out of sight, Mavis thought that she might have got the information she wanted from this person. Presently, the clattering of a pail was heard, a sound which gradually came nearer. In due course, the malformed creature appeared at the foot of the stairs.

"I've come," said Mavis to this person.

"'Ave yer?"

The person vanished, seemingly through the floor.

Mavis was taken aback by the woman's rudeness; even to this creature, shop-girls were, apparently, of small account. By and by, Mavis heard her clumping up from below. When she appeared, Mavis put authority into her voice as she said:

"Can I see anyone here?"

"If you've any eyes in your 'ead," snorted the servant, as she disappeared from view.

Still no one came. Mavis was making up her mind to explore the downstair regions when the footfalls of the rude person were heard coming down.

"I've been waiting quite ten minutes," Mavis began angrily, as the person came in view.

"'Ave yer?"

"Look here, I'm not used to be answered like that," Mavis began; but she was wasting her breath; the servant went on her way in complete disregard of Mavis's wrath.

Mavis thought of trying another entrance, when a young woman came downstairs. She had a pasty face, with a turned-up nose and large, romantic eyes. She carried a book under her arm. When she saw Mavis, she stopped to look curiously at her.

"I've come here to start work tomorrow. Can you tell me where I'm to go?" asked Mavis.

"I'm in a great hurry. I've a Browning—"

"If you'll only tell me where to go," interrupted Mavis.

"It's this way," cried the girl, as she led the way up the stairs. "I've a Browning to return to—"

"If you'll only tell me where I'm to go—"

"You'd never find it. I'd have shown you round, but I've to return a Browning to a gentleman."

"It's very kind of you," remarked Mavis, who was wondering how much further she had to climb.

"Do you love Browning?" asked the girl with the big eyes.

"I can't say I do."

"You—don't—love—Browning?" asked the other in astonishment.

"I'm sorry, but I don't."

"I couldn't live without Browning. Here's your room: you'll probably find someone inside. My name's Miss Meakin."

"Mine is Mavis Keeves. Thanks so much."

Mavis opened the door of a not over-large room, which was lit by a single gas burner. Mavis looked at the four small beds, the four chests of drawers, the four washing stands, the four cane chairs, and the four framed bits of looking glass, which made up the furniture of the room. Upon three of the beds were tumbled articles of feminine attire; others had slipped on the not over-clean floor. Then Mavis noticed the back of a girl who was craning her neck out of the one window at the further end of the room. The atmosphere of the apartment next compelled attention; it was a combination of gas (the burner leaked), stale body linen, cheap scents and soapsuds; it stuck in her throat and made her cough.

"Is that Pongo?" asked the girl, who was still staring out of the window.

"It's me," said Mavis.

"Eh!"

The girl brought her body into the room. Mavis saw a girl who would have had a fine figure if she had been two or three inches taller. She was swarthy, with red lips and fine eyes; she was dressed in showy but cheap evening finery.

"Common and vulgar-minded," was Mavis's mental comment as she looked at this person.

"Are you the new girl?" the stranger asked.

"Yes."

"I took you for Bella, the slavey. Sorry! Pleased to meet you."

"Thank you."

"Have you just come in from outside?"

"Yes."

"You didn't see anything of a gentleman in a big motor car?"

"No."

"I'm expecting my boy in one. He promised to call for me in his motor car to-night and take me out to dinner and supper," continued the girl.

"I'm rather hungry too," remarked Mavis.

"Are you going out to dinner and supper?"

"Don't they give supper here?"

"They do," answered the girl, emphasising the last word, as if to disparage the meal supplied to their young ladies by "Dawes'."

"It will have to be good enough for me," said Mavis, who resented the patronising manner of the other.

"Excuse me," remarked the dark girl suddenly, as she again craned out of the window.

"Certainly," said Mavis dryly, as she wondered what had happened to the boxes she had had sent on earlier in the day.

"No sign of him yet. I'm afraid he's had a breakdown," exclaimed the girl, after looking down the street for some time, a remark to which Mavis paid no attention. The girl went on:

"You were speaking of the supper 'Dawes'' supply. I couldn't eat it myself. I simply lode their food."

"What?" asked Mavis, whose ears had caught the mispronunciation.

"Yes, I simply lode the food they give for supper, the same as Miss Potter and Miss Allen, the other young ladies who sleep in this room. Indeed, we can only eat restaurant food in the evenings."

"What's wrong with the supper here?" asked Mavis, nervously thinking of her hearty appetite and the few shillings that remained after settling up with Mrs Ellis.

"Taste and try: you've only to go right to the bottom of the 'ouse. Excuse me."

Here the swarthy young woman leaned so far out of the window that Mavis feared she would lose her balance and fall into the street. Then Mavis heard footsteps and the clatter of a pail in the passage. The door opened, and the misshapen person who had been rude to her when she was waiting downstairs appeared.

"Here she is," called this person, at which two men entered with Mavis's trunks; these they dumped on the floor.

"Thank you," said Mavis.

"Heavy work, miss," remarked one of the men.

"Be off with you," cried the servant.

"Now then, beauty," laughed the other of the men.

"Be off with you; none of your cadging here."

"But they're heavy, and if—" began Mavis.

"It's what they're paid for. Be off with you," snorted the servant.

"There he is!" cried the girl who had been leaning out of the window.

"Motor and all?" asked Mavis.

"Eh! Oh, he hasn't brought the motor; we'll 'ave to take a 'an'som. Good-bye for the present. My name's Impett—Rose Impett."

"Mine's Keeves," said Mavis, thinking she may as well be agreeable to those she had to live with. She then went to her boxes and saw that the odd-looking servant had uncorded them.

"Thank you," said Mavis.

"I dessay it's more than you deserve," remarked the servant.

"I daresay," assented Mavis.

"Let's have a look at you."

"What?"

"You needn't be jealous of me; let's have a look."

The servant urged Mavis to stand by the flaring gas, where she looked her up and down, Mavis thought maliciously.

"H'm! Wonder how long it'll be before I have to pray for you?"

"Eh!"

"Same as I has to for the others."

"I don't understand."

"Look on the bed; see 'ow they leave their clothes, and such clothes. That's what their souls is like."

"Indeed!" said Mavis, scarcely knowing what to say.

"All the same, I prays for them, though what God A'mighty thinks o' me for all the sinners I pray for, I can't think. Supper's downstairs, if you can eat it; and my name's Bella."

Bella left the room. Mavis thought that she rather liked her than otherwise, despite her rudeness earlier in the evening. Mavis unpacked her more immediate requirements before seeking supper in the basement. She descended to the floor on which was the passage communicating with the street, but the staircase leading to the supper-room was unlit, therefore she was compelled to grope her way down; as she did so, she became aware of a disgusting smell which reminded Mavis of a time at Brandenburg College when the drains went wrong and had to be put right. She then found herself in a carpetless passage lit by gas flaming in a wire cage; here, the smell of drains was even more offensive than before. There was a half-open door on the right, from which came the clatter of knives and plates. Mavis, believing that this was the supper-room, went in.

She found herself in a large, low room, the walls of which were built with glazed brick. Upon the left, the further wall receded as it approached the ceiling, to admit, in daytime, the light that straggled from the thick glass let into the pavement, on which the footsteps of the passers-by were ceaselessly heard. The room was filled by a long table covered by a scanty cloth, at which several pasty-faced, unwholesome-looking young women were eating bread and cheese, the while they talked in whispers or read from journals, books, or novelettes. At the head of the table sat a dark, elderly little woman, who seemed to be all nose and fuzzy hair: this person was not eating. Several of the girls looked with weary curiosity at Mavis, while they mentally totted up the price she had paid for her clothes; when they reached their respective totals, they resumed their meal.

"Miss Keeth?" said the dark little woman at the head of the table, who spoke with a lisp.

"Yes," replied Mavis.

"If you want thupper, you'll find a theat."

"Thank you."

Mavis sank wearily in the first empty chair. "Dawes'" had already got on her nerves. She was sick at heart with all she had gone through; from the depths of her being she resented being considered on an equality with the two young women she had met and those she saw about her. She closed her eyes as she tried to take herself, for a brief moment, from her surroundings. She was recalled to the present by a plate, on which was a hunk of bread and a piece of cheese, being thrust beneath her nose. She was hungry when she came downstairs; now, appetite had left her. Her gorge rose at the pasty-faced girls, the brick-walled cellar, the unwholesome air, and the beady-eyed little woman seated at the head of the table. She thought it better, if only for her health's sake, to try and swallow something. She put a piece of cheese in her mouth. Mavis, by now, was an authority on cheap cheese; she knew all the varieties of flavour to be found in the lesser-priced cheeses. Ordinarily, she had been enabled to make them palatable with the help of vinegar, mustard, or even with an onion; but tonight none of these resources were at hand with which to make appetising the soapy compound on her plate. Miss Striem, the dark little woman at the head of the table, noted her disinclination to tackle the cheese.

"You can have anything exthra if you care to pay for it," she remarked.

"What have you?" asked Mavis.

"Ham, bloater, or chicken pathte, and an exthellent brand of thardines."

"I'll try the ham paste," said Mavis.

An opened tin of ham paste was put before her. Mavis noticed that the other girls were looking at her out of the corners of their eyes.

She put some of the paste on to her plate; it looked unusual, even for potted meat; but ascribing its appearance to the effect of the light, Mavis spread some on a bit of bread and put this in her mouth. Only for a moment; the next, she had removed it with her handkerchief. One of the girls tittered. Miss Striem looked sharply in this person's direction.

"I can't eat this: it's bad!" cried Mavis.

"Perhaps you would prefer a thardine."

"Anything, so long as it's fit to eat."

Some of the girls raised their eyebrows at this remark. All of them were more or less frightened of Miss Striem, the housekeeper.

An opened tin of sardines was set before Mavis. She had only to glance inside to see that its contents were mildewed.

"Thanks," she said, pushing the tin away.

"I beg your pardon," remarked Miss Striem severely.

"They're bad too. I'm not going to eat them."

"You'll have to pay for them juth the thame."

"What?" cried Mavis.

"If you order, you pay. Ith a rule in the houth," said Miss Striem, as if the matter were forthwith dismissed from her mind.

"To sell girls bad food?" asked Mavis.

"I cannot discuth the matter; the thum due will be deducted from your wageth."

Mavis's blood was up. Her wage was small enough without having anything deducted for food she could not eat.

"I shall go to the management," she remarked.

"You'll what?"

"Go to the management. I'm not going to be cheated like that."

"You call me a cheat?" screamed the little woman, as she rose to her feet.

Mavis was, for the moment, taken aback by Miss Striem's vehemence. The girl next to her whispered, "Go it," under her breath.

"You call me a cheat?" repeated Miss Striem.

"I shall say what I have to say to the management," replied Mavis coolly.

"And I'll thay what I have to thay; and you'll find out who is believed in a way you won't like."

"I shall prove my case," retorted Mavis, as she grabbed the ham paste and the tin of sardines.

Miss Striem sat down. A giggle ran round the table.

"Can you tell me where the sitting-room is, please?" Mavis asked of the girl next to her.

"What?" replied the girl whom she had spoked to.

Mavis repeated her question.

"There's no such thing; there's only this place open at meal times and your bedroom."

"Thanks; I'll go there. Good night."

Mavis, carrying her ham paste and sardines, walked the evil-smelling passage and up the stairs to her room. Once outside the supper-room, she repented of having had words with Miss Striem, who was, doubtless, a person of authority; but it was done now, and Mavis reflected how she had justice and evidence on her side. The bedroom was empty. Mavis placed the ham paste and sardines on her washing-stand; she then took advantage of the absence of the other girls to undress and get into bed. She fell into a heavy slumber, which gave place to a state of dreamy wakefulness, during which she became conscious of others being in the room; of hearing herself discussed; of a sudden commotion in the apartment. A sequence of curious noises thoroughly awoke her. The unaccustomed sight of three other girls in the room in which she slept caused her to sit bolt upright. The girl, Miss Impett, to whom she had already spoken, was sitting on her bed, yawning as she pulled off her stockings. Another, a fine, queenly-looking girl, in evening dress, was sitting on a chair with her hands pressed to her stomach; her eyes were rolling as if she were in pain. The third girl, also in evening dress, but not so handsome as the sufferer, was whispering consoling words.

"Is she ill?" asked Mavis.

"It's the indigestion," replied the last girl Mavis had noticed.

"Can I do anything?" asked Mavis.

"She always has it dreadful when she goes out to supper; now she's paying for it and—" She got no further; her friend was seized with another attack; all her attention was devoted to rubbing the patient's stomach, the while the latter groaned loudly. It was a similar noise which had awakened Mavis.

"I suppose we shan't get to sleep for an hour," yawned Miss Impett, as she struggled into a not too clean nightdress.

"Oh, you cat, you!" gasped the sufferer.

"It's your own fault," retorted Miss Impett. "You always over-eat yourself and drink such a lot of that filthy creme de menthe."

"Don't you wish you had the chance?" snapped the girl who was attending her friend.

"I always drink Kummel; it's much more ladylike," remarked Miss Impett.

"You'd drink anything you can bally well get," the sufferer cried at a moment when she was free of pain.

"I am a lady. I know how to be'ave when a gentleman offers me a drink," retorted Miss Impett.

"You a lady—you—!" began the sufferer's ministering angel. She got no further, being checked by her friend casting a significant glance in Mavis's direction.

Half an hour later, Mavis fell asleep. It was a strange experience when, the next morning, she had to wash and dress with three other girls doing the same thing in the little space at their disposal.

She had asked if there were any chance of getting a bath, to be surprised at the astonished looks on the faces of the others. At a quarter to eight, they scurried down to breakfast, at which meal Miss Striem presided, as at supper.

Breakfast consisted of thick bread, salt butter, and the cheapest of cheap tea. It was as much as Mavis could do to get any of it down, although she was hungry. She could not help noticing that she was the object of much remark to the other girls present, her words with Miss Striem on the previous evening having attracted much attention. After breakfast, Mavis was taken upstairs to the department in which she was to work. It was on the roomy ground floor, for which she was thankful; she was also pleased that the girl selected to instruct her in her duties was her Browning friend of last night. Her work was not arduous, and Mavis enjoyed the handling of dainty things; but she soon became tired of standing, at which she sat on one of the seats provided by Act of Parliament to rest the limbs of weary shop assistants.

"You mustn't do that!" urged Miss Meakin.

"Why not?"

"You'll get yourself disliked if you do."

"What are they here for, if not to sit on?"

"They have to be there; but you won't be here long if you're seen using them, 'cept when the Government inspector is about."

"It's cruel, unfair," began Mavis, but her friend merely shrugged her shoulders as she moved away to wait on a customer.

Mavis was disposed to rebel against the unwritten rule that seats are not to be made use of, but a moment's reflection convinced her of the unwisdom of such a proceeding.

Later on in the morning, Miss Meakin said to Mavis:

"I hear you had a dust up with old Striem last night."

Mavis told her the circumstances.

"She's an awful beast and makes no end of money out of the catering. But no one dare say anything, as she's a relation of one of the directors. All the young ladies are talking of your standing up to her."

"I suppose she'll report me," remarked Mavis.

"She daren't; she's too keen on a good thing; but I'll bet she has her knife into you if she gets a chance."

Presently, Miss Meakin got confidential; she told Mavis how she was engaged to be married; also, that she met her "boy" by chance at a public library, where they both asked the librarian for Browning at the same time, and that this had brought them together.

The girls went down to dinner in two batches. When it was time for Mavis to go (she was in the second lot), she was weary with exhaustion; the continued standing, the absence of fresh air, her poor breakfast, all conspired to cause her mental and physical distress.

The contaminated air of the passage leading to the eating-room brought on a feeling of nausea. Miss Meakin, noticing Mavis change colour, remarked:

"We're all like that at first: you'll soon get used to it."

If the atmosphere of the downstair regions discouraged appetite, the air in the glazed bricked dining-room was enough to take it away; it was heavy with the reek arising from cooked joints and vegetables. Mavis took her place, when a plate heaped up with meat and vegetables was passed to her. One look was enough: the meat was cag mag, and scarcely warm at that; the potatoes looked uninvitingly soapy; the cabbage was coarse and stringy; all this mess was seemingly frozen in the white fat of what had once been gravy. Mavis sickened and turned away her head; she noticed that the food affected many of the girls in a like manner.

"No wonder," she thought, "that so many of them are pasty-faced and unwholesome-looking."

She realised the necessity of providing the human machine with fuel; she made an effort to disguise the scant flavour of the best-looking bits she could pick out by eating plenty of bread. She had swallowed one or two mouthfuls and already felt better for the nourishment, when her eye fell on a girl seated nearly opposite to her, whom she had not noticed before. This creature was of an abnormal stoutness; her face was covered with pimples and the rims of her eyes were red; but it was not these physical defects which compelled Mavis's attention. The girl kept her lips open as she ate, displaying bloodless gums in which were stuck irregular decayed teeth; she exhibited the varying processes of mastication, the while her boiled eyes stared vacantly before her. She compelled Mavis's attention, with the result that the latter had no further use for the food on her plate. She even refused rice pudding, which, although burned, might otherwise have attracted her.

The air of the shop upstairs was agreeably refreshing after the vitiated atmosphere of the dining-room; it saved her from faintness. Happily, she was sent down to tea at a quarter to four, to find that this, by a lucky accident, was stronger and warmer than the tepid stuff with which she had been served at breakfast. As the hours wore on, Mavis noticed that most of the girls seemed to put some heart into their work; she supposed that this elation was caused by the rapidly approaching hour of liberty. When this at last arrived, there was a rush to the bedrooms. Mavis, who was now suffering tortures from a racking headache, went listlessly upstairs; she wondered if she would be allowed to go straight to bed. When she got into the room, she found everything in confusion. Miss Potter, Miss Allen, and Miss Impett were frantically exchanging their working clothes for evening attire. Mavis was surprised to see the three girls painting their cheeks and eyebrows in complete indifference to her presence. They took small notice of her; they were too busy discussing the expensive eating-houses at which they were to dine and sup. Miss Potter, in struggling into her evening bodice, tore it behind. Mavis, seeing that Miss Allen was all behind with her dressing, offered to sew it.

"Thank you," remarked Miss Potter, in the manner of one bestowing a favour. Mavis mended the rent quickly and skilfully. Perhaps her ready needle softened the haughty Miss Potter's heart towards her, for the beauty said:

"Where are you off to to-night?"

"Nowhere," answered Mavis.

"Nowhere!" echoed Miss Potter disdainfully, while the other occupants of the room ejaculated "My!"

"Haven't you a 'boy'?" asked Miss Potter.

"A what?"

"A young man then," said Miss Potter, as she made a deft line beneath her left eye with an eye pencil.

"I don't know any young men," remarked Mavis.

"Hadn't you better be quick and pick up one?" asked Miss Impett.

"I don't care to make chance acquaintances," answered Mavis.

To her surprise, her remark aroused the other girls' ire; they looked at Mavis and then at one another in astonishment.

"I defy anyone to prove that I'm not a lady," cried Miss Impett, as she bounced out of the room.

"I'm as good as you any day," declared Miss Potter, as she went to the door.

"Yes, that we are," cried Miss Allen defiantly, as she joined her friend.

Mavis sat wearily on her bed. Her head ached; her body seemed incapable of further effort; worst of all, her soul was steeped in despair.

"What have I done, oh, what have I done to deserve this misery?" she cried out.

This outburst strengthened her: needs cried for satisfaction in her body, the chief of these being movement and air. She walked to the window and looked out on the cloudless September night; there was a chill in the air, imparting to its sweetness a touch of austerity. Mavis wondered from what peaceful scenes it came, to what untroubled places it was going. The thought that she was remote from the stillness for which her heart hungered exasperated her; she closed the window in order to spare herself being tortured by the longing which the night air awoke in her being. The atmosphere of the room was foul when compared with the air she had just breathed; it seemed to get her by the throat, to be on the point of stifling her. The next moment she had pinned on her hat, caught up her gloves, and scurried into the street. Two minutes later she was in Oxford Street, where she was at once merged into a stream of girls, a stream almost as wide as the pavement, which was sluggishly moving in the direction of the Park. This flow was composed of every variety of girl: tall, stumpy, medium, dark, fair, auburn, with dispositions as varied as their appearances. Many were aglow with hope and youthful ardour; others were well over their first fine frenzy of young blood. There were wise virgins, foolish virgins, vain girls, clever girls, elderly girls, dull girls, laughing girls, amorous girls, spiteful girls, girls with the toothache, girls radiantly happy in the possession of some new, cheap finery: all wending their way towards the Marble Arch. Most walked in twos and threes, a few singly; some of these latter were hurrying and darting amongst the listless walk of the others in their eagerness to keep appointments with men. Whatever their age, disposition, or condition, they were all moved by a common desire—to enjoy a crowded hour of liberty after the toil and fret of the day. As Mavis moved with the flow of this current, she noticed how it was constantly swollen by the addition of tributaries, which trickled from nearly every door in Oxford Street, till at last the stream overflowed the broad pavement and became so swollen that it seemed to carry everything before it. Here were gathered girls from nearly every district in the United Kingdom. The broken home, stepmothers, too many in family, the fascination which London exercises for the country-grown girl—all and each of these reasons were responsible for all this womanhood of a certain type pouring down Oxford Street at eight o'clock in the evening. Each of them was the centre of her little universe, and, on the whole, they were mostly happy, their gladness being largely ignorance of more fortunate conditions of life. Ill-fed, under-paid, they were insignificant parts of the great industrial machine which had got them in its grip, so that their function was to make rich men richer, or to pay 10 per cent, dividends to shareholders who were careless how these were earned. Nightly, this river of girls flows down Oxford Street, to return in an hour or two, when the human tide can be seen flowing in the contrary direction. Meantime, men of all ages and conditions were skilfully tacking upon this river, itching to quench the thirst from which they suffered. It needed all the efforts of the guardian angels, in whose existence Mavis had been taught to believe, to guide the component parts of this stream from the oozy marshland, murky ways, and bottomless quicksands which beset its course.

CHAPTER SEVEN
WIDER HORIZONS

Seven weeks passed quickly for Mavis, during which her horizon sensibly widened. She learned many things, the existence of which she would never have thought possible till the knowledge stared her in the face. To begin with, she believed that the shabby treatment, in the way of food and accommodation, that the girls suffered at "Dawes'" would bind them in bonds of sympathy: the contrary was the case. The young women in other departments looked down on and would have nothing to do with girls, such as she, who worked in the shop. These other departments had their rivalries and emulation for social precedence, leading to feuds, of which the course of action consisted of the two opposing parties sulking and refusing to speak to each other, unless compelled in the course of business. The young women in the showroom were selected for their figures and general appearance; these, by common consent, were the aristocracy of the establishment. After a time, Mavis found that there was another broad divergence between her fellow-workers, which was quite irrespective of the department in which they were. There was a type of girl, nearly always the best-looking, which seemed to have an understanding and freemasonry of its own, together with secrets, confidences, and conversations, which were never for the ears of those who were outsiders—in the sense of their not being members of this sisterhood. Miss Potter, Miss Allen, and Miss Impett all belonged to this set, which nearly always went out after shop hours in evening dress, which never seemed to want for ready money or pretty clothes, and which often went away for the weekend ("Dawes'" closed at two on Saturdays). When Mavis had first been introduced to the three girls with whom she shared her bedroom, she had intuitively felt that there was a broad, invisible gulf which lay between her and them; as time went on, this division widened, so far as Miss Impett and Miss Potter were concerned, to whom Mavis rarely spoke. Miss Allen, who, in all other respects, toadied to and imitated Miss Potter, was disposed to be friendly to Mavis. Miss Impett, who on occasion swore like any street loafer, Mavis despised as a common, ignorant girl. Miss Potter she knew to be fast; but Miss Allen, when alone with Mavis, went out of her way to be civil to her; the fact of the matter being that she was a weak, easily led girl, whose character was dominated by any stronger nature with which she came in contact.

Another thing which much surprised Mavis was the heartless cruelty the girls displayed to any of their number who suffered from any physical defect. Many times in the day would the afflicted one be reminded of her infirmity; the consequent tears incited the tormentors to a further display of malignity.

Bella, the servant, was an object of their attentions; her gait and manner of breathing would be imitated when she was by. She was always known by the name of "Pongo," till one of the "young ladies" had witnessed The Tempest from the upper boxes of His Majesty's Theatre; from this time, it was thought to be a mark of culture on the part of many of the girls at "Dawes'" to call her "Caliban." Mavis sympathised with the afflicted woman's loneliness; she made one or two efforts to be friendly with her, but each time was repulsed.

One day, however, Mavis succeeded in penetrating the atmosphere of ill-natured reserve with which "Pongo" surrounded herself. The servant was staggering upstairs with two big canfuls of water; the task was beyond her strength.

"Let me help you," said Mavis, who was coming up behind her.

"Shan't," snorted Bella.

"I shall do as I please," remarked Mavis, as she caught hold of one of the cans.

"Leave 'old!" cried Bella; but Mavis only grasped the can tighter.

"Go on now; don't you try and get round me and then turn an' laugh at me."

"I never laugh at you, and I only want to help you up with the water."

"Straight?"

"What else should I want?"

"Don't be kind to me," cried Bella, suddenly breaking down.

"Bella!" gasped Mavis in astonishment.

"Don't you start being kind to me. I ain't used to it," wept Bella.

"Don't be a fool, Bella!"

"I ain't a fool. I'm onny ugly and lopsided, and everyone laughs at me 'ceptin' you, and I've no one or—or nothin' to care for."

Mavis thought it advisable to take Bella into her room, which happened to be empty; here, she thought, Bella would be free from eyes that would only find food for mirth in her tears.

"I've never had a young man," sobbed Bella. "An' that's why I turned to Gawd and looked down on the young ladies here, as 'as as many young men as they want; too many sometimes. An' speaking of Gawd, it's nice to 'ave Someone yer know as cares for you, though you can't never see 'Im or walk out with 'Im."

From this time, she tried to do Bella many little kindnesses, but, saving this one instance, the servant was always on her guard and never again opened her heart to Mavis.

Miss Striem did not carry out her threat of charging Mavis for the extras she refused to eat. In time, Mavis got used to the food supplied by "Dawes'"; she did not swallow everything that was put upon her plate, indeed, she did not eat with good appetite at three consecutive meals; but she could sit at the table in the feeding-room without overwhelming feelings of repulsion, and, by shutting her eyes to the unconcealed mastication of the girl opposite, could often pick enough to satisfy her immediate needs. The evening was the time when she was most hungry; after the walk which she made a point of taking in all weathers, she would get quite famished, when the morsel of Canadian cheese and sour bread supplied for supper was wholly insufficient. At first, she was tempted to enter the cheaper restaurants with which the streets about Oxford Street abound; but these extravagances made serious inroads on her scanty capital and had to be given up, especially as she was saving up to buy new boots, of which she was in need.

She confided in Miss Meakin, who was now looking better and plumper, since nearly every evening she had taken to supping with her "boy's" mother, who owned a stationery business in the Holloway Road.

"I know, it's dreadful. I used to be like that before I met Sylvester," Miss Meakin answered to Mavis's complaint.

"But what am I to do?" asked Mavis.

"Have you ever tried brisket?"

"What's that?"

"Beef!"

"Beef?"

"You get it at the ham and beef shop. You get quite a lot for five pence, and when they get to know you they give you good weight."

"But you must have something with it," remarked Mavis.

"Then you go to a baker's and buy a penn'orth of bread."

"But where am I to eat it?" asked Mavis.

"In some quiet street," replied Miss Meakin. "Why not?"

"With one's fingers?"

"There's no one to see you."

Mavis looked dubious.

"It's either that or picking up 'boys,'" remarked Miss Meakin.

"Picking up boys!" echoed Mavis, with a note of indignation in her voice.

"It's what the girls do here if they don't want to go hungry."

"But I don't quite understand."

"Didn't you come here through old Orgles's influence?" asked Miss Meakin guardedly.

"Nothing of the kind; one of the partners got me in."

"Sorry! I heard it was that beast Orgles. But most of the 'boys' who try and speak to you in the street are only too glad to stand a girl a feed."

"But why should they?"

"Don't you know?"

"It would put me under an obligation to the man," remarked Mavis.

"Of course; that's what the gentlemen want."

"But it might lead silly girls into all sorts of trouble."

"I think most of us know how to behave like ladies and drop the gentleman when he wants to go too far."

"Good heavens!" cried Mavis, who was taken aback by the vulgarity of Miss Meakin's point of view.

Perhaps the latter resented the moral superiority contained in her friend's exclamation, for she said with aggrieved voice:

"There's Miss Searle and Miss Bone, who're taken everywhere by a REEL swell; they even went to Paris with him at Easter; and no matter what he wants, I'm sure no one can say they're not ladies."

Mavis thought for a moment before saying:

"Is that quite fair to the man?"

"That's his look-out," came the swift retort.

"I don't fancy the brisket and I don't fancy picking up men. Can't one get on and get in the showroom and earn more money?" asked Mavis.

"One can," replied Miss Meakin, much emphasising the "can."

"How is it done?"

"You ask your friend Miss Allen; she'll tell you all about it."

"She's no friend of mine. Can't you tell me?"

"I could, but don't want to; you look at things so funny. But, then, you don't like Browning," replied Miss Meakin.

Mavis was filled with blind rage at the indifference of "Dawes'" to the necessities of those they engaged; as long as the firm's big dividend was made, they were careless to what questionable shifts and expedients their staff was reduced in order to have sufficient strength to bring to the daily task of profit-earning. She pondered on the cruelty and injustice of it all in odd moments; she could not give much thought to the matter, as Christmas was approaching, which meant that "Dawes'" would be hard at work to cope with the rush of custom every minute of the working day, and for some time after the doors were closed to the public. The class of customer had, also, changed. When Mavis first went to "Dawes'," the people whom she served were mostly visitors to London who were easily and quickly satisfied; then had followed the rough and tumble of a remnant sale. But now, London was filling with those women to whom shopping is at once an art, a fetish, and a burden. Mavis found it a trying matter to satisfy the exigent demands of the experienced shopper. She was now well accustomed to the rudeness of women to those of their own sex who were less happily placed; but she was not a little surprised at a type of customer whom she was now frequently called upon to serve. This was of the male sex; sometimes young; usually, about forty; often, quite old; it was a smart, well-dressed type, with insinuating manners and a quiet, deferential air that did not seem to know what it came to buy or cared what it purchased so long as it could engage Mavis in a few moments' conversation. She soon got to know this type at a glance, and gave it short shrift. Others at "Dawes'" were not so coy. Many of the customers she got to know by sight, owing to their repeated visits. One of these she disliked from the first; later experience of her only intensified this impression. She was a tall, fine woman, well, if a trifle over-dressed; her complexion was a little more aggressive than most of the females who shopped at "Dawes'." Her name was Mrs Stanley; she appeared well known to the girls for whom Bella the servant declared she was in the habit of praying. From the first, Mrs Stanley was attracted by Mavis, into whose past life she made sympathetic and tactful inquiries. Directly she learned that Mavis was an orphan, Mrs Stanley redoubled her efforts to win the girl's confidence. But it was all of no use; Mavis turned a deaf ear to all Mrs Stanley's insinuations that a girl of her striking appearance was thrown away in a shop: it was as much as Mavis could do to be coldly civil to her. Even when Mrs Stanley gave up the girl as a bad job, the latter was always possessed by an uneasy sensation whenever she was near, although Mavis might not have set eyes on her.

Another customer who attracted much attention was the Marquis de Raffini; he was old, distinguished-looking, and the last survivor of an illustrious French family.

Mavis saw him come into "Dawes'" soon after she had commenced work, when he was accompanied by a showy, over-dressed girl, whom he referred to as Madame the Marquise, and for whom he ordered a costly and elaborate trousseau. He seemed well known to the girls, who told Mavis that he appeared every few months with a different young woman; also, that when, in the ordinary course of nature, the condition of the temporary Madame the Marquise could no longer be concealed, the Marquis was in the habit of providing a lump sum of some hundreds of pounds as dowry in order to induce someone (usually a working man) to marry his mistress. Mavis was shocked at what she heard; it seemed strange to her that such things should exist and be discussed as if they were the most everyday occurrences.

Often, while busily engaged in serving customers or in hearing and seeing things which, before she came to "Dawes'," she would never have believed to be possible, she had a strong suspicion that old Orgles was watching her from the top of a flight of stairs or the tiny window in his room; it seemed that he was a wary old spider, she a fly, and that he was biding his time. This impression saddened her; it also made her attend carefully to her duties, it being his place to deal with those of the staff who were remiss in their work. It was only of an evening, when she was free of the shop, that she could be said to be anything like her old, light-hearted self. She would wash, change her clothes, and scurry off to a ham and beef warehouse she had discovered in a turning off Oxford Street, where she would get her supper. The shop was kept by a man named Siggers. He was an affected little man, who wore his hair long; he minced about his shop and sliced his ham and beef with elaborate wavings of his carving knife and fork. Mavis proving a regular customer, he let her eat her supper in the shop, providing her with knife, fork, tablecloth, and mustard. Although married and henpecked, he affected to admire Mavis; while she ate her humble meal, he would forlornly look in her direction, sigh, and wearily support his shaggy head with his forefinger; but she could not help noticing that, when afflicted with this mood, he would often glance at himself in a large looking glass which faced him as he sat. His demonstrations of regard never became more pronounced. It was as much as Mavis could do to stop herself from laughing outright when she paid him, it being a signal mark of his confidence that he did not exact payment from her "on delivery of goods in order to prevent regrettable mistakes," as printed cards, conspicuously placed in the shop, informed customers—or clients, as Mr Siggers preferred to call them.

One night, Mavis, by the merest chance, made a discovery that gladdened her heart: she lighted upon Soho. She had read and loved her Fielding and Smollett when at Brandenburg College; the sight of the stately old houses at once awoke memories of Tom Jones, Parson Adams, Roderick Random, and Lady Bellaston, She did not immediately remember that those walls had sheltered the originals of these creations; when she realised this fact she got from the nearest lending library her old favourites and carefully re-read them. She, also, remembered her dear father telling her that an ancestor of his, who had lived in Soho, had been killed in the thirties of the eighteenth century when fighting a famous duel; this, and the sorry dignity of the Soho houses, was enough to stir her imagination. Night after night, she would elude the men who mostly followed her and walk along the less frequented of the sombre streets. These she would people with the reckless beaux, the headstrong ladies of that bygone time; she would imagine the fierce loves, the daring play, the burning jealousies of which the dark old rooms, of which she sometimes caught a glimpse, could tell if they had a mind. Sometimes she would close her eyes, when the street would be again filled with a jostling crowd of sedan chairmen, footmen, and linkboys; she could almost smell the torches and hear the cries of their bearers. It gave her much of a shock to realise how beauties, lovers, linkboys, and all had disappeared from the face of the earth, as if they had never been. She wondered why Londoners were so indifferent to the stones Soho had to tell. Then she fell to speculating upon which the house might be where her blood-thirsty ancestor had lived; also, if it had ever occurred to him that one of his descendants, a girl, would be wandering about Soho with scarce enough for her daily needs. In time, she grew to love the old houses, which seemed ever to mourn their long-lost grandeur, which still seemed full of echoes of long-dead voices, which were ill-reconciled to the base uses to which they were now put. Perhaps she, also, loved them because she grew to compare their fallen state with that of her own family; it seemed that she and they had much in common; and shared misfortunes beget sympathy.

Thus Mavis worked and dreamed.

CHAPTER EIGHT
SPIDER AND FLY

One night, Mavis went back to "Dawes'" earlier than usual. She was wearing the boots bought with her carefully saved pence; these pinched her feet, making her weary and irritable. She wondered if she would have the bedroom to herself while she undressed. Of late, the queenly Miss Potter had given up going out for the evening and returning at all hours in the morning. Her usual robust health had deserted her; she was constantly swallowing drugs; she would go out for long walks after shop hours, to return about eleven, completely exhausted, when she would hold long, whispered conversations with her friend Miss Allen.

Mavis was delighted to find the room vacant. The odour of drugs mingled with the other smells of the chamber, which she mitigated, in some measure, by opening the window as far as she was able. She pulled off her tight boots, enjoying for some moments a pleasurable sense of relief; then she tumbled into bed, soon to fall asleep. She was awakened by the noise of voices raised in altercation. Miss Potter and Miss Impett were having words. The girls were in bed, although no one had troubled to turn off the flaring jet. As they became more and more possessed with the passion for effective retort, Mavis saw vile looks appearing on their faces: these obliterated all traces of youth and comeliness, substituting in their stead a livid commonness.

"We know all about you!" cried loud-voiced Miss Impett.

"Happily, that's not a privilege desired in your case," retorted Miss Potter.

"And why not?" Miss Impett demanded to know.

"We might learn too much."

"What does anyone know of me that I'm ashamed of?" roared Miss Impett.

"That's just it."

"Just what?"

"Some people have no shame."

"Do try and remember you're ladies," put in Miss Allen, in an effort to still the storm.

"Well, she shouldn't say I ought to wash my hands before getting into bed," remarked Miss Impett.

"I didn't say you should," said Miss Potter.

"What did you say?"

"What I said was that anyone with any pretension to the name of lady would wash her hands before getting into bed," corrected Miss Potter.

"I know you don't think me a lady," broke out Miss Impett. "But ma was quite a lady till she started to let her lodgings in single rooms."

"Don't say any more and let's all go to sleep," urged pacific Miss Allen, who was all the time keeping an anxious eye on her friend Miss Potter.

Miss Impett, perhaps fired by her family reminiscence, was not so easily mollified.

"Of course, if certain people, who're nobodies, try to be'ave as somebodies, one naturally wants to know where they've learned their classy manners," she remarked.

"Was you referring to me?" asked Miss Potter.

"I wasn't speaking to you," replied Miss Impett.

"But I was speaking to you. Was you referring to me?"

"Never mind who I was referring to."

"Whatever I've done," said Miss Potter pointedly, "whatever I've done, I've never made myself cheap with a something in the City."

"No. 'E wouldn't be rich enough for you."

"You say that I take money from gentlemen," cried Miss Potter.

"If they're fools enough to give it to you."

"Ladies! ladies!" pleaded Miss Allen, but all in vain.

"I've never done the things you've done," screamed Miss Potter.

"I've done? I've done? I 'ave my faults same as others, but I can say, I can that—that I've never let a gentleman make love to me unless I've been properly introduced to him," remarked her opponent virtuously.

"For shame! For shame!" cried Miss Potter and Miss Allen together, as if the proprieties that they held most sacred had been ruthlessly and unnecessarily violated.

"No, that I h'ain't," continued irate Miss Impett. "I've watched you when you didn't know I was by and seen the way you've made eyes at gentlemen in evening dress."

Much as Mavis was shocked at all she had heard, she was little prepared for what followed. The next moment Miss Potter had sprung out of bed; with clenched fists, and features distorted by rage, she sprang to Miss Impett's bedside.

"Say that again!" she screamed.

"I shan't."

"You daren't!"

"I daren't?"

"No, you daren't."

"What would you do if I did?"

"Say it and see."

"You dare me to?"

"Yes, you damn beast, to say I'm no better than a street-walker!"

"Don't you call me names."

"I shall call you what I please, you dirty upstart, to put yourself on a level with ladies like us! We always said you was common."

"What—what's it you dared me to say?" asked Miss Impett breathlessly, as her face went livid.

"Don't—don't say it," pleaded Miss Allen; but her interference was ineffectual.

"That I picked up gentlemen in evening dress," bawled Miss Potter. "Say it: say it: say it! I dare you!"

"I do say it. I'll tell everyone. I've watched you pick up gentlemen in—"

She got no further. Miss Potter struck her in the mouth.

"You beast!" cried Miss Impett.

Miss Potter struck her again.

"You beast: you coward!" yelled Miss Impett.

"It's you who's the coward, 'cause you don't hit me. Take that and that," screamed Miss Potter, as she hit the other again and again. "And if you say any more, I'll pull your hair out."

"I'm not a coward; I'm not a coward!" wept Miss Impett. "And you know it."

"I know it!"

"If anything, it's you who's the coward."

"Say it again," threatened Miss Potter, as she raised her fist, while hate gleamed in her eyes.

"Yes, I do say it again. You are a coward; you hit me, and you know I can't hit you back because you're going to have a baby."

There was a pause. Miss Potter's face went white; she raised her hand as if to strike Miss Impett, but as the latter stared her in the eyes, the other girl flinched. Then, tears came into Miss Potter's eyes as she faltered:

"Oh! Oh, you story!"

"Story! story!" began Miss Impett, but was at once interrupted by pacific Miss Allen.

"Ssh! ssh!" she cried fearfully.

"I shan't," answered Miss Impett.

"You must," commanded Miss Allen under her breath. "Keeves might hear."

"What if she does! As likely as not she herself's in the way," said Miss Potter.

Mavis, who had been trying not to listen to the previous conversation, felt both hot and cold at the same time. The blood rushed to her head. The next moment she sprang out of bed.

"How dare you, how dare you say that?" she cried, her eyes all ablaze.

"Say what?" asked Miss Potter innocently.

"That. I won't foul my lips by repeating it. How dare you say it? How dare you say that you didn't say it?"

"Well, you shouldn't listen," remarked Miss Potter sullenly.

Mavis advanced menacingly to the side of the girl's bed.

"If you think you can insult me like that, you're mistaken," said Mavis, with icy calmness, the while she trembled in every limb.

"Haven't you been through Orgles's hands?" asked Miss Potter.

"No, I have not. I say again, how dare you accuse me of that?"

"She didn't mean it, dear," said Miss Allen appeasingly; "she's always said you're the only pretty girl who's straight in 'Dawes'.'"

"Will you answer my question?" asked Mavis, with quiet persistence. Then, as the girl made no reply, "Please yourself. I shall raise the whole question to-morrow, and I'll ask to be moved from this room. Then perhaps you'll learn not to class me with common, low girls like yourself."

It might be thought that Mavis's aspersions might have provoked a storm: it produced an altogether contrary effect.

"Don't be down on me. I don't know what's to become of me," whimpered Miss Potter.

The next moment, the three girls, other than Mavis, were clinging together, the while they wept tears of contrition and sympathy.

Mavis, although her pride had been cruelly wounded by Miss Potter's careless but base accusation, was touched at the girl's distress; the abasement of the once proud young beauty, the nature of its cause, together with the realisation of the poor girl's desperate case, moved her deeply: she stood irresolute in the middle of the room. The three weeping girls were wondering when Mavis was going to recommence her attack; they little knew that her keen imagination was already dwelling with infinite compassion on the dismal conditions in which the promised new life would come into the world. Her heart went out to the extremity of mother and unborn little one; had not her pride forbade her, she would have comforted Miss Potter with brave words. Presently, when Miss Potter whimpered something about "some people being so straitlaced," Mavis found words to say:

"I'm not a bit straitlaced. I'm really very sorry for you, and I can't see you're much to blame, as the life we lead here is enough to drive girls to anything. If I'm any different, it's because I'm not built that way."

Mavis was the only girl in the room who got next to no sleep. Long after the other girls had found repose, she lay awake, wide-eyed; her sudden gust of rage had exhausted her; all the same, her body quivered with passion whenever she remembered Miss Potter's insult. But it was the shock of the discovery of the girl's condition which mostly kept her awake; hitherto, she had been dimly conscious that such things were; now that they had been forced upon her attention, she was dazed at their presence in the person of one with whom she was daily associated. Then she fell to wondering what mysterious ends of Providence Miss Potter's visitation would serve. The problem made her head ache. She took refuge in the thought that Miss Potter was a sparrow, such as she—a sparrow with gaudier and, at the same time, more bedraggled plumage, but one who, for all this detriment, could not utterly fall without the knowledge of One who cared. This thought comforted Mavis and brought her what little sleep she got.

The next morning, Mavis was sent to a City warehouse in order to match some material that "Dawes'" had not in stock. When she took her seat on the 'bus, a familiar voice cried:

"There's 'B. C.'"

"Miss Allen."

"That's what we all call you, 'cos you're so innocent. If you're off to the warehouse, it's where I'm bound."

"We can go together," remarked Mavis.

"I say, you were a brick last night," said Miss Allen, after the two girls had each paid for their tickets.

"I'm only sorry for her."

"She'll be all right."

"Will he marry her, then?" asked Mavis.

"Good old 'B. C.'! Don't be a juggins; her boy's married already."

"Married!" gasped Mavis.

"Yes!" laughed Miss Allen. "And with a family."

When Mavis got over her astonishment at this last bit of information, she remarked:

"But you said she would be all right."

"So she will be, with luck," declared Miss Allen.

"What—what on earth do you mean?"

"What I say. Why, if every girl who got into trouble didn't get out of it, I don't know what would happen."

Mavis wondered what the other meant. Miss Allen continued:

"It's all a question of money and knowing where to go."

"Where to go?" echoed Mavis, who was more amazed than before.

"Of course, there's always a risk. That's how a young lady at 'Dawes'' died last year. But the nursing home she was in managed to hush it up."

Mavis showed her perplexity in her face.

Miss Allen, unaccustomed to such a fallow ear, could not resist giving further information of a like nature.

"You are green, 'B. C.' I suppose you'll be saying next you don't know what Mrs Stanley is."

"I don't."

"Go on!"

"What is she?"

"She's awfully well known; she gets hold of pretty young girls new to London for rich men: that's why she was so keen on you."

As Mavis still did not understand, Miss Allen explained the nature of the lucrative and time immemorial profession to which Mrs Stanley belonged.

For the rest of the way, Mavis was so astonished at all she had heard, that she did not say any more; she scarcely listened to Miss Allen, who jabbered away at her side.

On the way back, she spoke to Miss Allen upon a more personal matter.

"What did your friend mean last night by saying I'd been through Orgles's hands?"

"She thought he introduced you here?"

"What's that to do with it?"

"He sees all the young ladies who want rises and most of the young ladies who want work at 'Dawes'.' If he doesn't fancy them, and they want 'rises,' he tells them they have their latch-keys; if he fancies them, he asks what they're prepared to pay for his influence."

"Money?" asked Mavis.

"Money, no," replied Miss Allen scornfully.

"You mean—?" asked Mavis, flushing.

"Of course. He's sent dozens of girls 'on the game.'"

"On the game?"

"On the streets, then."

Mavis's body glowed with the hot blood of righteous anger.

"It can't be," she urged.

"Can't be?"

"It isn't right."

"What's that to do with it?"

"It wouldn't be allowed."

"Who's to stop it?"

"But if it's wrong, it simply can't go on."

"Whose to stop it, I say?"

It was on the tip of Mavis's tongue to urge how He might interfere to prevent His sparrows being devoured by hawks; but this was not a subject which she cared to discuss with Miss Allen. This young person, taking Mavis's silence for the acquiescence of defeat, went on:

"Of course, on the stage or in books something always happens just in the nick of time to put things right; but that ain't life, or nothing like it."

"What is life, then?" asked Mavis, curious to hear what the other would say.

"Money: earning enough to live on and for a bit of a fling now and then."

"What about love?"

"That's a luxury. If the stage and books was what life really is, we shop-girls wouldn't like 'em so much."

Mavis relapsed into silence, at which Miss Allen said:

"Of course, in my heart, dear, I think just as you do and would like to have no 'truck' with Ada Potter or Rose Impett; but one has to know which side one's bread is buttered. See?"

Later, when talking over Mavis with the girls she had disparaged, Miss Allen was equally emphatic in her condemnation of "that stuck-up 'B. C.,'" as she called the one-time teacher of Brandenburg College.

Mavis's anger, once urged to boiling point by what she had learned of old Orgles's practices, did not easily cool; it remained at a high temperature, and called into being all the feeling of revolt, of which she was capable, against the hideous injustice and the infamous wrongs to which girls were exposed who sought employment at "Dawes'," or who, having got this, wished for promotion. Luckily, or unluckily for her, the course of this story will tell which, the Marquis de Raffini, accompanied by a new "Madame the Marquise," came into the shop directly she came up from dinner on the same day, and made for where she was standing. Two or three of the "young ladies" pressed forward, but the Marquis was attracted by Mavis; he showed in an unmistakable manner that he preferred her services.

He wanted a trousseau for "Madame the Marquise." He—ahem!— she was very particular, very, very particular about her lingerie; would Mavis show "Madame" "Dawes'" most dainty and elaborate specimens?

Mavis was no prude; but this request, coming on top of all she had learned from Miss Allen, fanned the embers of resentment against the conditions under which girls, helpless as she, worked. The Marquis's demand, the circumstances in which it was made, seemed part and parcel of a system of oppression, of which old Orgles's sending dozens of girls "on the game," who might otherwise have kept straight, was another portion. The realisation of this fact awoke in Mavis a burning sense of injustice; it only needed a spark to cause an explosion. This was not long in coming. The Marquis examined the things that she set before him with critical eye; his eagerness to handle them did not prevent his often looking admiringly at Mavis, a proceeding that did not please "Madame the Marquise," who felt resentful against Mavis for marring her transient triumph. "Madame the Marquise" pouted and fretted, but without effect; when her "husband" presently put his mouth distressingly near Mavis's ear, "Madame's" feelings got the better of her; she put her foot, with some violence, upon the Marquis's most sensitive corn, at which it was as much as Mavis could do to stop herself from laughing. All might then have been well, had not the Marquis presently asked Mavis to put her bare arm into one of the open worked garments in order that he might critically examine the effect. In a moment, Mavis was ablaze with indignation; her lips tightened. The man repeated his request, but he may as well have talked to the moon so far as Mavis was concerned. The girl felt that, if only she resisted this unreasonable demand, it would be an act of rebellion against the conditions of the girls' lives at "Dawes'"; she was sure that only good would come of her action, and that He, who would not see a sparrow fall to the ground without caring, would aid her in her single-handed struggle against infamous oppression.

"I am sorry, sir; but I cannot."

"Cannot?"

"No, sir."

"Anything wrong with your plump, pretty arm?"

"No, sir."

"Then why not do as I wish?"

"Because—because it isn't right, sir."

"Eh!"

The man stared at Mavis, who looked him steadfastly in the eyes. In his heart of hearts, he respected her scruples; he also admired her spirit. But for "Madame the Marquise," nothing more would have been said, but this young person was destined to be an instrument of the fates that ruled Mavis's life. This chit was already resentful against the strangely beautiful, self-possessed shop-girl; Mavis's objection to the Marquis's request was in the nature of a reflection on "Madame the Marquise's" mode of life. She took her lover aside and urged him to report to the management Mavis's obstinacy; he resisted, wavered, surrendered. Mavis saw the Marquis speak to a shopman, of whom he seemed to be asking her name; he was then conducted upstairs to Mr Orgles's office, from which he issued, a few minutes later, to be bowed obsequiously downstairs by the man he had been to see. The Marquis joined "Madame the Marquise" (who, while waiting, had looked consciously self-possessed), completed his purchases, and left the shop.

Mavis waited in suspense, expecting every minute to be summoned to Orgles's presence. She did not regret what she had done, but, as the hours passed and she was not sent for, she more and more feared the consequences of her behaviour.

When she came upstairs from tea, she received a message saying that Mr Orgles wished to see her. Nerving herself for the interview, she walked up the circular stairs leading to his office, conscious that the eyes of the "young ladies" in the downstair shop were fixed upon her. As she went into the manager's room, she purposely left the door open. She found Orgles writing at a table; at his side were teacups, a teapot, some thinly cut bread and butter and a plate of iced cake. Mavis watched him as he worked. As her eyes fell on his stooping shoulders, camel-like face and protruding eyes, her heart was filled with loathing of this bestial old man, who made the satisfaction of his lusts the condition of needy girls' securing work, all the while careless that he was conducting them along the first stage of a downward journey, which might lead to unsuspected depths of degradation. She itched to pluck him by the beard, to tell him what she thought of him.

"Miss Keeves!" said Mr Orgles presently.

"Yes, sir."

"Don't say 'sir.'"

Mavis started in surprise. Mr Orgles put down his pen.

"We're going to have a friendly little chat," said the man. "Let me offer you some tea."

"No, thank you."

"Pooh! pooh! Nonsense!"

Mr Orgles poured out the tea; as he did so, he turned his head so that his glance could fall on Mavis.

"Bread and butter, or cake?"

"Neither, thank you."

"Then drink this tea."

Mr Orgles brought a cup of tea to where Mavis was standing. On his way, he closed the door that she had left open. He placed the tea on a table beside her and took up a piece of bread and butter.

"No, thank you," said Mavis again.

"What?"

He had taken a large bite out of his piece of bread and butter. He stared at the girl in open-mouthed surprise.

Mavis was fascinated by the bite of food in his mouth and the tooth-marks in the piece of bread and butter from which it had been torn.

"Now we'll have a cosy little chat about this most unfortunate business."

Here Mr Orgles noisily sucked up a mouthful of tea. Mavis shivered with disgust as she watched him churn the mixture of food and drink in his mouth.

"Won't you sit down?" he asked presently.

"I prefer to stand."

"Now then!" Here he joyously rubbed his hands. "Two months ago, when we had a little talk, you were a foolish, ignorant little girl. Perhaps we've learned sense since then, eh?"

Mavis did not reply. The man went on:

"Although a proud little girl, I don't mind telling you I've had my eye on you, that I've watched you often and that I've great hopes of advancing you in life. Eh!"

Here he turned his head so that his eyes leered at her. Mavis repressed an inclination to throw the teapot at his head. He went on:

"To-day, we made a mistake; we offended a rich and important customer. That would be a serious matter for you if I reported it, but, as I gather, you're now a sensible little girl, you may make it worth my while to save you."

Mavis bit her lip.

"What if you're still a little fool? You will get the sack; and girls from 'Dawes" always find it hard to get another job. You will wear yourself out trapesing about after a 'shop,' and by and by you will starve and rot and die."

Mavis trembled with anger. The man went on talking. His words were no longer coherent, but the phrases "make you manageress"—"four pounds a week"—"share the expenses of a little flat together," fell on her ear.

"Say no more," Mavis was able to cry at last.

The next moment, Mavis felt the man's arms about her, his hot, gasping breath on her cheek, his beard brushing against her mouth, in his efforts to kiss her. The attack took her by surprise. Directly she was able to recover herself, she clawed the fingers of her left hand into his face and forced his head away from her till she held it at arm's length. Orgles's head was now upon one side, so that one of his eyes was able to glare hungrily at her; his big nostrils were dilating with the violence of his passion. Mavis trembled with a fierce, resentful rage.

"Your answer: your answer: your answer?" gasped the man huskily.

"This: this: this!" cried Mavis, punctuating each word with a blow from her right hand upon Orgles's face. "This: this: this! It's men like you who drag poor girls down. It's men like you who bring them to horrible things, which they'd never have dreamed of, if it hadn't been for you. It's men like you who make wickedness. You're the worst man I ever met, and I'd rather die in the gutter than be fouled by the touch of a horrible old beast like you."

Her anger blazed up into a final flame. This gave her strength to throw the old man from her; he crashed into the grate; she heard his head strike against the coal-box. Mavis cast one look upon the shapeless and bleeding heap of humanity and left the room.

CHAPTER NINE
AWING

Mavis was again workless, this time with a capital of fifteen shillings and sixpence halfpenny.

Immediately after her interview with Orgles, she had gone to her room to change into her out-of-door clothes.

She disregarded the many questions that several of the girls came upstairs to ask her. She packed up her things as a preliminary to leaving "Dawes'" for good. For many hours she paced the streets, heedless of where her steps led her, her heart seemingly breaking with rage and shame at the insults to which she had been subjected.

About eight, she felt utterly exhausted, and turned into the first shop where she could get refreshment.

This was a confectioner's. The tea and dry biscuits she ordered enabled her to marshal her distracted thoughts into something approaching coherence; she realised that, as she was not going back to "Dawes'," she must find a roof for the night.

She had several times called on her old friend Mrs Ellis; she decided to make for her house. She asked her way to the nearest station, which was Notting Hill; here she took a ticket to Hammersmith and then walked to Kiva Street, where she knocked at the familiar door. A powerful-looking man in corduroy trousers and shirt sleeves opened it.

"Mrs Ellis?" asked Mavis.

"'Orspital."

"I'm very sorry. What's the matter with her?"

"Werry bad."

"I wanted rooms. I used to lodge here."

At this piece of information the man made as if he would close the door.

"Can you tell me where I can get a room for the night?" asked Mavis.

The man by way of reply muttered something about the lady at the end of the row wanting a lodger.

"Which hospital is Mrs Ellis at?" asked Mavis.

By way of reply, the door was slammed in her face. Mavis dragged her weary limbs to the end house in the row, where, in reply to her knock, a tall, pasty-faced, crossed-eyed woman, who carried an empty jug, answered the door.

"I thought you was Mrs Bonus," remarked the woman.

"I want a room for the night. I used to lodge with Mrs Ellis at number 20."

"Did yer? There! I do know yer face. Come inside."

Mavis followed the landlady into a faded and formal little sitting-room, where the latter sat wearily in a chair, still clasping her jug.

"Can I have a room?" asked Mavis.

"I think so. My name's Bilkins."

"Mine is Keeves."

"That's a funny name. I 'ope you ain't married."

"No."

"It's only fools who get married. You jest hear what Mrs Bonus says."

"I'm very tired," said Mavis. "Can you give me anything to eat?"

"I've nothing in the 'ouse, but I'll get you something when I go out. And, if Mrs Bonus comes, ask her to wait, an' say I've jes gone out to get a little Jacky."

Mavis waited in the dark room of the deserted house. Had she not been tired and heartsick, she would have been amused at this strange experience. A quarter of an hour passed without anyone calling, when she heard the sound of a key in the latch, and Mrs Bilkins returned.

"No Mrs Bonus?"

"No one's been."

"It isn't her washing day neither, though it would be late for a lady like 'er to be out all alone. Drink this."

"But it's stout," said Mavis, as Mrs Bilkins lit the gas.

"I call it jacky. A glass will do you good."

Mavis drank some of the liquor and certainly felt the better for it.

"I bought you a quarter of German," declared Mrs Bilkins, as she enrolled a paper parcel.

- 87 -

"You mean German sausage," said Mavis, as she caught sight of the mottled meat, a commodity which her old friend Mr Siggers sold.

"I always call it German," remarked Mrs Bilkins, a trifle huffily.

"But what am I to eat it on?"

"That is funny. I'm always forgetting," said Mrs Bilkins, as she faded from the room.

After some time, she came back with a coarse cloth, a thick plate, a wooden-handled knife, together with a fork made of some pliant material; these she put before Mavis.

The coarse food and more of the stout put fresh heart into the girl. She got a room from Mrs Bilkins for six shillings a week, on the understanding that she did not give much trouble.

"There's only one thing. I suppose you have a bath of some sort?" said Mavis.

"That is funny," said Mrs Bilkins. "I've never been asked such a thing in my life."

"Don't you wash?"

"In penny pieces; a bit at a time."

"But never all over, properly?"

"You are funny. Why, three years ago, I had the rheumatics; then I was covered all over with flannel. Now I don't know which is flannel and which is skin."

It was arranged, however, that, if Mrs Bilkins could not borrow a bath from a neighbour in the morning, she would bring Mavis her washing-tin, which would answer the same purpose. Mavis slept soundly in a fairly clean room, her wanderings after leaving "Dawes'" having tired her out.

The next morning she came down to a breakfast of which the tea was smoked and her solitary egg was scarcely warm; when she opened this latter, the yolk successfully eluded the efforts of her spoon to get it out. It may be said at once that this meal was a piece with the entire conduct of Mrs Bilkins's house, she being a unit in the vast army of incapable, stupid women who, sooner or later, drift into the letting of lodgings as a means of livelihood. After breakfast, Mavis wrote to "Dawes'," requesting that her boxes might be sent to her present address. Now that the sun of cold reason, which reaches its zenith in the early morning, illumined the crowded events of yesterday, Mavis was concerned for the consequences of the violence she had offered Orgles. Her faith in human justice had been much disturbed; she feared that Orgles, moved with a desire for vengeance, would represent her as the aggressor, himself as the victim of an unprovoked assault: any moment she feared to find herself in the clutches of the law. She was too dispirited to look for work; to ease the tension in her mind, she tried to discover what had become of Mrs Ellis, but without success.

About five, two letters came for her, one of these being, as the envelope told her, from "Dawes'." She fearfully opened it. To her great surprise, the letter regretted the firm's inability to continue her temporary engagement; it enclosed a month's salary in place of the usual notice, together with the money due to her for her present month's services; it concluded by stating that her conduct had given great satisfaction to the firm, and that it would gladly give her further testimonials should she be in want of these to secure another place.

Mavis could hardly believe her good fortune; she read and re-read the letter; she gratefully scanned the writing on the cheque. The other letter attracted her attention, which proved to be from Miss Meakin. This told her that, if Mavis could play the piano and wanted temporary work, she could get this by at once applying at "Poulter's" Dancing Academy in Devonport Road, Shepherd's Bush, which Miss Meakin attended; it also said that the writer would be at the academy soon after nine, when she would tell Mavis how she had found her address. Mavis put on her hat and cloak with a light heart. The fact of escaping from the debasing drudgery of "Dawes'," of being the possessor of a cheque for L2. 12S., the prospect of securing work, if only of a temporary nature, made her forget her loneliness and her previous struggles to wrest a pittance from a world indifferent to her needs. After all, there was One who cared: the contents of the two letters which she had just received proved that; the cheque and promise of employment were in the nature of compensation for the hurt to her pride which she had suffered yesterday at Orgles's hands. She thought her sudden good fortune justified a trifling extravagance; she had no fancy for Mrs Bilkins's smoked tea, so she turned into the first teashop she came to, where she revelled in scrambled eggs, strong tea, bread, butter, and jam. She ate these unaccustomed delicacies slowly, deliberately, hugely enjoying the savour of each mouthful. She then walked in the direction of Shepherd's Bush.

The garish vulgarity of the Goldhawk Road, along which a procession of electric trams rushed and whizzed, took away her breath. Devonport Road, in which she was to find the academy, was such a quiet, retiring little turning that Mavis could hardly believe it joined a noisy thoroughfare like the Goldhawk Road. "Poulter's" Dancing Academy took some finding; she had no number to guide her, so she asked the two or three people she met if they could direct her to this institution, but not one of them appeared to know anything about it. She walked along the road, keeping a sharp look-out on either side for door plate or lamp, which she believed was commonly the out-ward and visible sign of the establishment she sought. A semicircle of brightly illuminated coloured glass, placed above an entrance gate, attracted her, but nearer inspection proved this to be an advertisement of "painless dentistry."

Further down the road, a gaily coloured lamp caught her eye, the lettering on which read "Gellybrand's Select Dancing Academy. Terms to suit all pockets. Inquire within." Mavis was certain that the name of which she was in search was none other than Poulter: she looked about her and wondered if it were possible for such a down-at-heel neighbourhood to support more than one dancing academy. The glow of a light in an open doorway on the other side of the way next attracted her. She crossed, to find this light came from a lamp which was held aloft by a draped female statue standing just inside the door: beyond the statue was another door, the upper part of which was of glass, the lower of wood. Written upon the glass in staring gilt letters was the name "Poulter's."

Mavis walked up the steps to the front door. Her heart sank as she noticed that the plaster had worn away and was broken from various parts of the house, which had a shabby and dilapidated appearance. Mavis set going a bell, which could be heard faint-heartedly tinkling in the distance; she employed the time that she was kept waiting in examining the statue. This was as depressing as the house: its smile was cracked in the middle; a rude boy had reddened the lady's nose; its dress cried aloud for some kindly disposed person to give it a fresh coat of paint. Presently, a drab of a little servant opened the inner door.

"'Pectus?" said the girl, directly she caught sight of Mavis.

"I want to see Mr Poulter."

"Not a 'pectus?"

Mavis repeated her request.

"Come insoide. 'E's 'avin' 'is tea."

Mavis followed the drab along a passage: at the end of this was a door, above which was inscribed "Ladies' Cloak Room."

Opening this, the drab said mechanically:

"Walk insoide. What nime?"

"Miss Keeves. I've come from Miss Meakin."

Mavis walked inside, to find herself in a smallish room, the walls of which were decorated with rows of hooks, beneath each of which was a number printed in large type. There were a cracked toilette glass, a few rickety chairs, a heavy smell of stale toilet powder, and little else. A few moments later, a little, shrivelled-up, elderly woman walked into the room with a slight hobble. Mavis noticed her narrow, stooping shoulders, which, although the weather was warm, were covered by a shawl; her long upper lip; her snub nose; also that she wore her right arm in a sling.

"Was you waiting to see Mr Poulter particular?" she asked.

"I was rather."

"'E's 'avin' 'is tea, and—and you know what these artists are at meal-time," said the little woman confidentially.

"I'm in no hurry. I can easily wait," said Mavis.

"Was you come about 'privates'?" asked the little woman wistfully.

"Privates?"

"I mean private lessons. 'Poulter's' always calls 'em 'privates.'"

"I heard you were in want of an accompanist. I came to offer my services."

"It won't be for long; my fingers is nearly healed of the chilblains."

"Anything is better than nothing," remarked Mavis.

"Would you mind if I heard you play?"

"Not at all."

"My word might go some way with Mr Poulter. See?" said the little woman confidentially.

"It's very good of you," remarked Mavis, who was beginning to like the little, shrivelled-up old thing.

The woman with the chilblains led the way to a door in a corner of the cloak-room, which Mavis had not noticed before. Mavis followed her down an inclined, boarded-in gangway, decorated with coloured presentation plates from long forgotten Christmas numbers of popular weeklies, to the ballroom, which was a portable iron building erected in the back garden of the academy. At the further end was a platform, which supported a forlorn-looking piano.

"Be careful not to slip," said Mavis's conductor.

"Thank you, I won't," replied Mavis, who was not in the least danger of losing her foothold.

"'E invented it."

"Invented what?"

"This floor wax. It's Poulter's patent," the little woman reverently informed Mavis.

"He must be rather clever!"

"Rather clever! It's plain you've never met 'im."

Mavis sat down to the piano, but did not do herself justice over the first waltz she played, owing to the faultiness of the instrument. As with many other old pianos, the keys were small; also, the treble was weak and three notes were broken in the bass.

"Try again!" said the little woman dubiously.

By this time, Mavis had mastered the piano's peculiarities; she played her second waltz resonantly, rhythmically.

"I think you're up to 'Poulter's,'" said the little woman critically, when Mavis had finished. "And what about terms?"

"What about them?" asked Mavis pleasantly.

"It's a great honour being connected with 'Poulter's,'" the little woman hazarded.

"No doubt."

"And what with the undercutting and all, on the part of those who ought to know better, it makes it 'ard to make both ends meet."

"I'm sure it does."

"But there! We'll leave it to Mr Poulter."

"That's the best thing to do."

"I'll see if Mr Poulter's finished 'is tea."

Mavis followed the woman across the ballroom, and back to the cloak-room, where she was left alone for quite five minutes. Then the little woman put her head into the room to say:

"Mr Poulter won't be many minutes now. 'E's come to the cake," at which Mavis smiled as she said:

"I can wait any time."

Mavis already quite liked the odd little woman. She waited some minutes longer, till at last her friend excitedly re-entered to say, in the manner of one conveying information of much moment:

"Mr Poulter is reelly coming on purpose to see you."

Mavis nerved herself for the ordeal of meeting the dancing-master.

CHAPTER TEN
"POULTER'S"

When, a few moments later, Mr Poulter came into the room, his appearance surprised Mavis. She expected and braced herself to interview a person with greasy, flowing locks and theatrical manners; instead, she saw a well-preserved old man with one of the finest faces she had ever seen. He had a ruddy complexion, soft, kindly blue eyes, and a noble head covered with snow-white hair. His presence seemed to infect the coarsely scented air of the room with an atmosphere of refinement and unaffected kindliness. He was shabbily dressed. Directly Mavis saw him, she longed to throw her arms about his neck, to kiss him on the forehead.

He bowed to Mavis before saying:

"Have you 'ad your tea?"

"Yes, thank you," she replied.

"Miss Nippett has told me of your errand."

"She has also heard me play."

"It is now only a question of terms," said Mr Poulter gently.

"Quite so."

"The last wish of 'Poulter's' is to appear ungenerous, but, with remorseless competition in the Bush," here Mr Poulter's kindly face hardened, "everyone suffers."

"The Bush?" queried Mavis.

"Shepherd's Bush," explained Poulter. "Many of 'Poulter's' clients, who are behindhand with their cheques for family tuition, have made payment with the commodities which they happen to retail," remarked Poulter. "Assuming that you were willing, you might care to take whole or part payment in some of these."

Mavis was sorry, but money was a necessity to her.

"I quite understand," said Poulter sympathetically. "On 'Ordinary Days,' 'Poulter's' would require you from eleven in the morning till—" Here he turned inquiringly to Miss Nippett.

"Carriages at ten thirty," put in Miss Nippett promptly.

"Yes, carriages at ten thirty," repeated Mr Poulter, who took a simple enjoyment in the reference to the association of vehicles, however imaginary, with the academy.

"And on 'Third Saturdays'?" said Poulter, as he again turned to Miss Nippett, as if seeking information.

"Special and Select Assembly at the Athenaeum, including the Godolphin String Band and light refreshments," declared Miss Nippett.

"Ah! carriages at twelve," said Mr Poulter with relish. "That means your getting home very late."

"I don't mind. I don't live far from here. I can walk."

It was ultimately arranged that Mavis should be supplied with dinner, tea, and supper, and receive a shilling a day for five days of the week; on Saturdays, in consideration of her staying late, she was to get an extra shilling.

Mention was made with some pride of infrequent "Long Nights," which were also held at the Athenaeum, when dancing was kept up till three in the morning; but, as Miss Nippett's chilblains would probably be cured long before the date fixed for the next Terpsichorean Festival, as these special dances were called, no arrangement was made in respect of these.

"It is usual for 'Poulter's' to ask for references," declared Mr Poulter. "But needless to say that one who has pioneered 'Poulter's' into the forefront of such institutions can read character at a glance."

Mavis thanked him for his confidence, but said that she could supply him with testimonials from her last two employers. Mr Poulter would not dream of troubling her, and asked Mavis if she could commence her duties on that evening. Upon Mavis saying that she could, Mr Poulter looked at his watch and said:

"It still wants an hour till 'Poulter's' evening classes commence. As you've joined 'Poulter's' staff, it might be as well if you shared one of the privileges of your position."

This particular privilege consisted of Mavis's being taken downstairs to Mr Poulter's private sitting-room. This was a homely apartment furnished with much-worn horsehair furniture, together with many framed and unframed flashlight photographs of various "Terpsichorean Festivals," in all of which, conspicuous in the foreground, was Mr Poulter, wearing a big white rosette on the lapel of his evening coat.

"Smoke if you want to, won't you?" said Mavis.

"Thank you," replied Mr Poulter, "but I only smoke after 'Poulter's' is closed. It might give 'Poulter's' a bad reputation if the young lady pupils went 'ome smelling of smoke."

"'E thinks of everything," declared Miss Nippett admiringly.

"'Poulter's' is not deficient in worldly wisdom," remarked the dancing-master with subdued pride.

"I'm sure of that," said Mavis hypocritically, as she looked at the simple face of the kindly old man.

"Suppose we have a game of cards," suggested Mr Poulter presently.

"Promise you won't cheat," said Mavis.

Mr Poulter laughed uneasily before saying:

"'Poulter's' would not occupy its present position if it were not for its straightforward dealing. What shall we play?"

Mavis, feeling light-hearted, was on the point of saying "Snap," but feared that the fact of her suggesting such a frivolous game might set her down as an improper person in the eyes of "Poulter's."

"Do you know 'Casino'?" asked Mr Poulter.

"I'm afraid I don't," replied Mavis.

"A grand old game; we must teach you another time. What do you say to 'Old Maid'?"

They played "Old Maid" deliberately, solemnly. After a time, Mavis had a strong suspicion that Miss Nippett was cheating in order that Mr Poulter might win; also, that Mr Poulter was manoeuvring the cards so that Mavis might not be declared "old maid."

This belief was strengthened when Mavis heard Miss Nippett say to Mr Poulter, at the close of the game:

"She ought to 'ave been 'old maid.'"

"I know, I know," replied Mr Poulter. "But I want her first evening at 'Poulter's' to be quite 'appy and 'omelike."

"Did you easily find 'Poulter's'?" asked Mr Poulter presently of Mavis.

"I had no number, so I had to ask," she replied.

"Then, of course, you were directed at once," suggested Mr Poulter eagerly.

Mavis's consideration for the old man's feelings was such that she thought a fib was justified.

"Yes," she said.

Mr Poulter's eyes lit with happiness.

"That's the advantage of being connected with 'Poulter's,'" he said. "You'll find it a great help to you as you make your way in the world."

"I'm sure of it," remarked Mavis, with all the conviction she could muster. After a few moments' silence, she said:

"There's another dancing academy on the other side of the road."

Mavis was surprised to see Mr Poulter's gentle expression at once change to a look of intense anger.

"Gellybrand's! Gellybrand's! The scoundrel!" cried Mr Poulter, as he thumped his fist upon the table.

"I'm sorry. I didn't know," said Mavis.

"What? You haven't heard of the rivalry between mushroom Gellybrand's and old-established 'Poulter's'?" exclaimed Mr Poulter.

Mavis did not know what to say.

"Some people is ignorant!" commented Miss Nippett at her silence.

"Gellybrand is the greatest scoundrel and blackleg in the history of dancing," continued Poulter. Then, as if to clinch the matter, he added, "Poulter's 'Special and Select' is two shillings, with carriages at eleven. Gellybrand's is one and six, with carriages at eleven thirty."

"Disgraceful!" commented Mavis, who was anxious to soothe Poulter's ruffled sensibilities.

"That is not all. Poulter's oranges, when light refreshments are supplied, are cut in eights; Gellybrand's"—here the old man's voice quivered with indignation—"oranges are cut in sixes."

"An unfair advantage," remarked Mavis.

"That's not all. Gellybrand once declared that I had actually stooped so low as to kiss a married pupil."

"Disgraceful!" said Mavis gravely.

"Of course, the statement carried its own refutation, as no gentleman could ever demean himself so much as to kiss another gentleman's wife."

"That's what I say," cried Miss Nippett.

"But Gellybrand foully libelled me," cried Mr Poulter, with another outburst of anger, "when he stated that I only paid one and fourpence a pound for my tea."

This last recollection so troubled Mr Poulter that Miss Nippett suggested that it was time for him to go and dress. As he left the room, he said to Mavis:

"Pray never mention Gellybrand's name in my presence. If I weren't an artiste, I wouldn't mind; as it is, I'm all of a tremble."

Mavis promised that she would not, at which the old man's face wore its usual kindly expression. When he was gone, Miss Nippett exclaimed:

"Oh, why ever did you?"

"How was I to know?" Mavis asked.

"I thought everyone knew. Don't, whatever you do, don't again. It makes him angrier than he was when once the band eat up all the light refreshments."

"He's a very charming man," remarked Mavis.

"But his brains! It's his brains that fetches me."

"Really!"

"In addition to 'Poulter's Patent Floor Wax,' he's invented the 'Clacton Schottische,' the 'Ramsgate Galop,' and the 'Coronation Quadrilles.'"

"He must be clever."

"Of course; he's on the grand council of the 'B.A.T.D.'"

"What is that?"

"What? You don't know what 'B.A.T.D.' is?" cried Miss Nippett in astonishment.

"I'm afraid I don't," replied Mavis.

"You'll be saying you don't know the Old Bailey next."

"I don't. But I know a lot of people who should."

"Don't send 'em to 'Poulter's,'" said Miss Nippett. "There's enough already who're be'ind with their accounts."

A few minutes later, Mr Poulter entered the room, wearing evening dress, dancing pumps, and a tawdry-looking insignia in his coat.

"That's the 'B.A.T.D.,' Grand Council Badge," Miss Nippett informed Mavis.

"Wonderful!" exclaimed Mavis, who felt that her hypocrisy was justified by the pleasure it gave kindly Mr Poulter.

"Say we enjoy a whiff of fresh air before commencing our labours," suggested Mr Poulter.

Upon Mavis and Miss Nippett rising as if to fall in with his suggestion, Mr Poulter went before them, up the stairs, past the "Ladies' Cloak Room," along the passage to the front door.

As Miss Nippett and Mavis followed the dancing-master, the former said, referring to Mr Poulter:

"'E once took the 'Olborn Town 'all for an 'All Night,' didn't you, Mr Poulter?"

"The night the 'Clacton Schottische' was danced for the first time," replied Poulter.

"And what do you think the refreshments was contracted at a 'ead?" asked Miss Nippett.

"Give it up," replied Mavis.

"Why, no less than three shillin's, wasn't it, Mr Poulter?"

"True enough," replied Mr Poulter. "But I must admit the attendants did look 'old-fashioned' at you, if you 'ad two glasses of claret-cup running."

By this time, they were outside of the front door, where Mr Poulter paused, as if designing not to go any further into the night air, which, for the time of year, was close and warm.

"I don't want to give the 'Bush' the chance of saying Poulter never shows himself outside the walls of the academy," remarked the dancing-master complacently.

"There's so much jealousy of fame in the 'Bush,'" added Miss Nippett.

As they stood on the steps, Mavis could not help noticing that whereas Miss Nippett had only eyes for Mr Poulter, the latter's attention was fixed on the plaster figure of "Turpsichor" to the exclusion of everything else.

"A classic figure"—(he pronounced it "clarsic")—"gives a distinction to an academy, which is denied to mongrel and mushroom imitations," he presently remarked.

"Quite so," assented Mavis.

"She has been with 'Poulter's' fifteen years."

"Almost as long as I have," put in Miss Nippett.

"The figure?" asked Mavis.

"The statue 'Turpsichor,'" corrected Mr Poulter.

"Turpsichor," in common with other down-at-heel people, had something of a history. She was originally the plaster cast model of a marble statue ordered by a sorrowing widow to grace the last resting-place of the dear departed, a widow, whose first transports of grief were as extravagant as the order she gave to the monumental mason. But when the time came for the statue to be carved, and a further deposit to be paid, the widow had been fascinated by a man whom she had met in a 'bus, when on her way to visit the cemetery where her husband was interred. She was now loth to bear the cost of the statue and, as she had changed her address, she took no notice of the mason's repeated applications. "Turpsichor" had then been sold cheap to a man who had started a tea-garden, in the vain hope of reviving the glories of those forgotten institutions; when he had drifted into bankruptcy, she had been knocked down for a song to a second-hand shop, where she had been bought for next to nothing by Mr Poulter as "the very thing." Now she stood in the entrance hall of the academy, where, it can truthfully be said, that no heathen goddess received so much adoration and admiration as was bestowed on "Turpsichor" by Mr Poulter and Miss Nippett. To these simple souls, it was the finest work of art to be found anywhere in the world, while the younger amongst the pupils regarded the forlorn statue with considerable awe.

When a move was made to the ballroom, Miss Nippett whispered to Mavis:

"If Mr Poulter wins the great cotillion prize competition 'e's goin' in for, I 'ope to stand 'Turpsichor' a clean, and a new coat of paint."

When all three had waited in the ballroom some minutes, the pupils for the night classes straggled in, the "gentlemen" bringing their dancing shoes in their overcoat pockets, the "ladies" theirs, either in net-bags or wrapped in odd pieces of brown paper. These "ladies" were much of a type, being either shop-girls or lady clerks, with a sprinkling of maid-servants and board school teachers. They were pale-faced, hard-working, over-dressed young women who read Marie Corelli, and considered her "deep"; who had one adjective with which to express appreciation of things, this "artistic"; anything they condemned was spoken of as "awful"; one and all liked to be considered what they called "up-to-date." Marriage they desired more than anything else in the world, not so much that they wished to live in an atmosphere of affection, but because they believed that state promised something of a respite from their never-ending, poorly recompensed toil. The "gentlemen" were mostly shopmen or weekly paid clerks with social aspirations; they carried silver cigarette cases, which they exhibited on the least provocation.

Mavis played, whilst Mr Poulter put the pupils through their steps. She had no eyes for the dancers, these not interesting her; her attention, of which she had plenty to spare, was fixed upon the kindly, beaming face and the agile limbs of Mr Poulter. It was a pleasure to watch him, he so thoroughly enjoyed his work; he could not take enough pains to instruct his pupils in the steps that they should take. Miss Nippett sat beside Mavis. Presently, in a few minutes' interval between the dances, the former said:

"Don't you ever be a fool an' teach dancing."

"Why 'a fool'?" asked Mavis.

"Look at me an' the way I 'obble; it's all the fault of teaching the 'gentlemen.'"

"Indeed!"

"The 'gentlemen' is such clumsy fellers; they always tread on my right foot. I tried wearing flannel, but they come down on it jess the same, 'arder if anything."

Soon after nine, Miss Meakin came in, having travelled from "Dawes'" with all dispatch by the "Tube." She warmly greeted Mavis, congratulated her on getting employment at "Poulter's," and told her that, after she (Mavis) had left "Dawes'," the partners had made every inquiry into her habit of life. Miss Meakin had been summoned to one of the partner's rooms to say what she knew of the subject, and had sat near a table on which was lying Mavis's letter; she had made a note of the address, to write to her directly she was able to do so.

"We must have a long talk, dear; but not to-night."

"Why not to-night?"

"Mr Napper, my 'boy,' will be waiting for me outside."

"Bring him in and introduce me."

"He'd never forgive me if I did. He's all brains, dear, and would never overlook it, if I insisted on his entering a dancing academy."

"What is he?"

"He's a lawyer. But his cleverness is altogether outside of that."

"A barrister?"

"Scarcely."

"A solicitor?"

"Not yet. He works for one."

After the pupils had gone, Mavis, pressed by Mr Poulter, stayed to a supper that consisted of bread, cheese, and cocoa.

When this was over, Mr Poulter said:

"I don't know of what religious persuasion you may be, but would you be offended if I asked you to stay for family prayers?"

"I like you for asking me," declared Mavis.

"I am overjoyed at a real young lady like you caring to stay," replied Poulter.

Mr Poulter read a chapter from the Bible. He then offered up a brief extempore prayer. He prayed for Miss Nippett, for Mavis, for past and present pupils, the world at large. The Lord's Prayer, in which the two women joined, ended the devotions.

When Miss Nippett had put on her goloshes, bonnet, and cloak, and Mavis her things, Mr Poulter accompanied them to the door.

"I live in the 'Bush': where do you?" asked Miss Nippett of Mavis.

"Kiva Road, Hammersmith."

"Then we go different ways. Good night, Mr Poulter; good night, Miss Keeves."

Mavis wished her and Mr Poulter good night. The two women walked together to the gate, when Miss Nippett hobbled off to the left.

As Mavis turned to the right, she glanced at Mr Poulter, who was still standing on the steps; he was gazing raptly at "Turpsichor." A few minutes later, when she encountered the insolent glances of the painted foreign women who flock in the Goldhawk Road, Mavis found it hard to believe that they and Mr Poulter inhabited the same world.

CHAPTER ELEVEN
MAVIS'S PRAYER

The next morning, Mavis was awakened by Mrs Bilkins bringing her a cup of tea.

"Bless my soul!" cried Mrs Bilkins, almost spilling the tea in her agitation.

"What's the matter?"

"You've got your window open. It's a wonder you're alive."

"I always sleep with it open."

"Well, you are funny. What will you do next?"

Mrs Bilkins sat on the bed, seemingly inclined to gossip. Mavis did not discourage her; for some reason, the landlady was looking different from when she had seen her the day before. Curious to discover the cause, she let the woman ramble on unchecked about the way in which "her son, a Bilkins," had "demeaned himself" by marrying a servant.

Then it occurred to Mavis that the way in which Mrs Bilkins had done her hair was the reason for her changed appearance: she had arranged it in imitation of the manner in which Mavis wore hers.

Presently, Mavis told the woman how she had got temporary employment, and added:

"But it's work I'm quite unaccustomed to."

To her surprise, Mrs Bilkins bridled up.

"Just like me. I ain't used to letting lodgin's; far from it."

"Indeed!" remarked Mavis.

"Oh, well, if you don't believe me, ask Mrs Bonus."

When Mavis came downstairs, she found Mrs Bilkins busy trimming a hat. The next day, the landlady wore it about the house, when Mavis was surprised and amused to see that it was a shabby imitation of her own. At first, she could scarcely believe such emulation to be possible, but when, after buying a necessary pair of gloves, she found that her landlady had got a new pair for herself, she saw that Mrs Bilkins was possessed by jealousy of her lodger. This belief was strengthened by the fact of Mrs Bilkins making copious reference to past prosperity directly Mavis made innocent mention of former events in her life which pointed to her having been better off than she was at present. It was fourteen days before Miss Nippett's chilblains were sufficiently healed to allow her to take her place at "Poulter's" piano. During this time, Mavis became on friendly terms with the dancing-master; the more she saw of him, the more he became endeared to the lonely girl. Apart from his vanity where the academy was concerned (a harmless enough foible, which saddened quite as much as it amused Mavis), he was the simplest, the kindliest of men. He was very poor; although his poverty largely arose from the advantage which pupils and parents took of his boundless good nature, Mavis did not hear him utter a complaining word of a living soul, always excepting Gellybrand.

She learned how Mr Poulter had been happily married, although childless; also, that his wife had died of a chill caught by walking home, insufficiently clad, from an "All Night" in bleak weather. For all the pain that her absence caused in his life, he looked bravely, confidently forward (sometimes with tears in his eyes) to when they should meet again, this time never to part. When the evenings were fine, Mr Poulter would take Miss Nippett and Mavis for a ride on a tram car, returning in time for the night classes. Upon one of these excursions, someone in the tram car pointed out Mr Poulter to a friend in the hearing of the dancing-master; this was enough to make Mr Poulter radiantly happy for the best part of two days, much to Mavis's delight.

Another human trait in the proprietor of "Poulter's" was that he was insensible to Miss Nippett's loyalty to the academy, he taking her devotion as a matter of course.

Miss Nippett and Mavis, also, became friends; the latter was moved by the touching faith which the shrivelled-up little accompanist had in the academy, its future, and, above all, its proprietor. If the rivalry between "Poulter's" and "Gellybrand's" could have been decided by an appeal to force, Miss Nippett would have been found in the van of "Poulter's" adherents, firmly imbued with the righteousness of her cause. She lived in Blomfield Road, Shepherd's Bush, a depressing, blind little street, at the end of which was a hoarding; this latter shut off a view of a seemingly boundless brickfield. Miss Nippett rented a top back room at number 19, where, on one Sunday afternoon, Mavis, being previously invited, went to tea. The little room was neat and clean; tea, a substantial meal, was served on the big black box which stood at the foot of Miss Nippett's bed. After tea, Miss Nippett showed, with much pride, her little treasures, which were chiefly pitiful odds and ends picked up upon infrequent excursions to Isle of Thanet watering-places. Her devotion to these brought a lump to Mavis's throat. After the girl had inspected and admired these household gods, she was taken to the window, in order to see the view, now lit by a brilliant full moon. Mavis looked over a desert of waste land and brickfield to a hideous, forbidding-looking structure in the distance.

"Ain't it beautiful?" asked Miss Nippett.

"Y—yes," assented Mavis.

"Almost as good as reel country."

"Almost."

"Why, I declare, you can see the 'Scrubbs': you are in luck to-day."

"What's the 'Scrubbs'?"

"The 'Scrubbs' prison. Oh, I say, you are ignorant!"

"I'm afraid I am," sighed Mavis.

"It ain't often you can see the 'Scrubbs' at this time of year 'cause of the fog," remarked Miss Nippett, whose eyes were still glued to the window.

Presently, when she drew the curtains, she looked contentedly round the little room before saying:

"I often think that, after all, there's no place like a good 'ome."

"If you're lucky enough to have one," assented Mavis heartfully.

"Sometimes I like it even better than 'Poulter's'; you know, when you've got a waltz in your 'ead, and 'ate it, and 'ave to play it over and over again. But every bit of this here furniture is mine and paid for."

"Really?" asked Mavis, feigning surprise to please her friend.

"I can show you the receipts if you don't b'lieve me."

"But I do."

"Being at the academy makes me business-like. But there! if I haven't forgotten something; reelly I 'ave."

"What?"

"One moment: let me bring the light."

Miss Nippett led the way to the landing immediately outside her door, where she unlocked a roomy cupboard, crammed to its utmost capacity with odds and ends of cheap feminine adornment. Mangy evening boas, flimsy wraps, down-at-heel dancing shoes, handkerchiefs, gloves, powder puffs, and odd bits of ribbon were jumbled together in heaped disorder.

"D'ye know what they is?" asked Miss Nippett.

"Give it up," replied Mavis.

"They're the 'overs.'"

"What on earth's that?"

"Oh, I say, you are ignorant; reelly you are. 'Overs' is what's left and unclaimed at 'Poulter's.'"

"Really?"

"They're my 'perk,'" which last word Mavis took to be an abbreviation of perquisite.

Mavis looked curiously at the heap of forgotten finery: had she lately lived among more prosperous surroundings, she might have glanced contemptuously at this collection of tawdry flummery; but, if her sordid struggles to make both ends meet had taught her nothing else, they had given her a keen sympathy for all forms of endeavour, however humble, to escape, if only for a crowded hour, from the debasing round of uncongenial toil. Consequently, she looked with soft eyes at the pile of unclaimed "overs." None knew better than she of the sacrifices that the purchase of the cheapest of these entailed; her observation had told her with what pride they were worn, the infinite pleasure which their possession bestowed on their owner. The cupboard's contents seemed to Mavis to be eloquent of pinched meals, walks in bad weather to save 'bus fares, mean economies bravely borne; to cry aloud of pitiful efforts made by young hearts to secure a brief taste of their rightful heritage of joy, of which they had been dispossessed.

Mavis turned away with a sigh.

Presently, in the cosiness of the bed-sitting room, Miss Nippett became confidential.

"Are you ambitious?" she asked.

"I don't know," replied Mavis.

"I mean REELLY ambitious."

"What do you mean by that?"

"Well, like I am. I'm reelly ambitious."

"Indeed!"

"I want to be a partner in 'Poulter's.' Not for the money, you understand, but for the honour. If I was made a partner, I'd die 'appy. See?"

"I don't see why you shouldn't be some day. Mr Poulter might reward you that way for your years of faithful service."

As Mavis walked back to Kiva Street, she asked herself the question that Miss Nippett had asked her, "Was she ambitious?"

Now, her chief concern was to earn her daily bread. It was not so very long ago that her ambition was in some way bound up with the romantic fancies which she was then so fond of weaving. Now, the prospect of again having to fight for the privilege of bread-winning drove all thought from her mind beyond this one desire—to keep afloat without exhibiting signals of distress to the Devitts.

Three days before Mavis left "Poulter's," she assisted at a Third Saturday Night which was held, as usual, on that Saturday of the month at the Athenaeum, Shepherd's Bush.

Mavis, dressed in her one evening frock and wearing her few trinkets, went to the Athenaeum an hour before the public was expected, in order to rehearse with the "Godolphin Band," which was always engaged for these occasions. She was in some trepidation at having to accompany professional musicians on the piano; she hoped that they would not find fault with her playing. When she got to the hall, she found Mr Poulter already there in evening dress, vainly striving to conceal his excitement.

"Aren't you nervous?" he asked.

"I am rather," she replied, as she took off her coat.

"Oh, my dear, may an old man say how beautiful you look?"

"Why not?" asked Mavis, whose eyes were shining at the unexpectedness of the compliment.

Mr Poulter looked at her intently for a few moments before saying:

"Haven't you a father or mother?"

Mavis shook her head.

"Neither kith nor kin?"

"I'm all alone in the world," she replied sadly.

A sorrowful expression came over the old man's face as he said with much fervour:

"God bless you, my dear. May He keep you from pain and all harm."

Mavis was seized with a sudden impulse. She took the white head in her warm arms and kissed him fondly on the forehead.

Mr Poulter turned away and pretended to have trouble with one of his dancing pumps.

A minute or two later, three grimy, uncouth-looking men came into the hall, whom Mavis took to be gasmen.

"Here's the 'Godolphin Band,'" said Mr Poulter, as he caught sight of them.

"All except Baffy: 'e's always late," remarked one of the men.

Mavis was introduced to the three members of the band, all of whom seemed to be somewhat abashed by her striking appearance.

"What about evening dress?" asked Mr Poulter of the trio.

Two of the men coughed and hesitated before saying:

"Very sorry, Mr Poulter, but Christmas coming and all that, sir—"

"I understand," sighed the dancing-master sympathetically; he then turned to the tallest of the three to ask:

"And you, Mr Cheadle?"

"What a question to ask a cornet-player!" replied Mr Cheadle, as he undid his overcoat to reveal a much worn evening suit, together with a frayed, soiled shirt.

"Excellent! excellent!" cried Mr Poulter on seeing the cornet-player's garb.

"One 'ud think I played outside pubs," grumbled Mr Cheadle.

"Now, if only Mr Baffy would come, you artistes could get to work," remarked Mr Poulter pleasantly.

"Let's start without him," suggested Cheadle, who seemed pleased at being referred to as an artiste.

A move was made to the platform at the further end of the hall; when this was reached, a little old man staggered into the hall, bearing on his shoulders a bass viol.

"Here's Baffy!" cried the three musicians together.

When the man disentangled himself from his burden, Mavis saw that the bass viol player was short, unkempt, greyhaired and bearded; he stared straight before him with vacant, watery eyes; his mouth was always agape; he neither greeted nor spoke to anyone present.

In obedience to Mr Poulter's instructions, two of the band brought a big screen from a side-room; this was set up by the piano, at which instrument Mavis took her seat. The screen was arranged so that she and Cheadle, the cornet-player, would be in full sight of the dancers; the three musicians not in evening dress were hidden behind the screen. They commenced a waltz. Mr Baffy did not start with the others; he was set going by a kick from Mr Cheadle. He played without music, seemingly at random, vilely, unconcernedly. Mr Baffy seemed to be ignorant of when a figure was ended, as he went on scraping after the others had ceased, and only stopped after receiving a further kick from Cheadle; he then stared feebly before him, till again set going by a forcible hint from the cornet-player.

Mavis acquitted herself to the grudging satisfaction of Cheadle. A few minutes before the doors were open, Miss Nippett approached her, wearing, besides her usual shawl, a coquettish cap and apron.

"Have you come to the dance?" asked Mavis.

"I'm 'ladies cloak-room' to-night? What do you think of Baffy?"

"I don't know what to think."

"No class, is 'e?"

"Do you know anything about him?"

"I don't 'old with the feller. 'Is presence is a disgrace to the academy," replied the "ladies' cloak-room."

A few minutes later, the first of Mr Poulter's patrons self-consciously entered the room; soon after, dancing commenced.

As if to give Mavis heart for her unaccustomed task, Mr Poulter kept an eye upon her; he encouraged her with smiles whenever she looked in his direction. Mavis's playing was much jeopardised by the conduct of the other musicians; they did not give the least attention to what they were at, but performed as if their efforts were second nature. Soon after the dancing started, Mr Cheadle brought from a pocket a greasy pack of cards, at which he and the two musicians who had arrived with him began to play at farthing "Nap," a game which the most difficult passages of their performance did not interrupt, each card-player somehow contriving to play almost directly it came to his turn. Mr Cheadle, playing the cornet, had one hand always free; he shuffled the cards, dealt them, and put down the winnings. When Mavis became more used to the vagaries of their instrumental playing, she was amused at the way in which they combined business with diversion. Mr Baffy, also, interested her; he still continued to stare before him, as he played with watery, purposeless eyes, and with mouth agape.

Halfway through the programme, there was an interval for refreshments. Mavis was conducted by Mr Poulter to a table set apart for the artistes in the room in which the lightest of light refreshments were served to his patrons.

Mavis sat down to a plateful of what looked uncommonly like her old friend, brisket of beef; she was now so hungry that she was glad to get anything so substantial.

"'Ow are you gettin' on?" asked a familiar voice over her shoulder.

Mavis looked up, to see Miss Nippett, who had discarded her cap and apron; she was now in her usual rusty frock, with her shawl upon her narrow, stooping shoulders.

"All right, thank you. Why don't you have some?"

"No, thank you. I can't spare the time. I'm 'light refreshments.'"

"But they're all eaten!" remarked Mavis, as her eye ranged along a length of table-cloth innocent of food or decoration.

"'Poulter's' ain't such a fool as to stick nothink out; it would all be 'wolfed' in a second. Let 'em ask."

"Some people mightn't like to."

"That's their look-out," snapped Miss Nippett, who had a heart of stone where the interests of anything antagonistic to "Poulter's" were concerned.

At the conclusion of the evening, the band was paid.

Mr Baffy got a shilling for his services, which he held in his hand and looked stupidly before him, till he got a cut with a bow from the second violinist, at which he put the money in his pocket. He then shouldered his bass viol and plunged out into the darkness.

Mavis's heart went out to Mr Baffy. She wondered where and how he lived; how he passed his time; what had reduced him to his present condition.

She spoke of him to Mr Poulter, who looked perplexed before replying:

"Ah, my dear young lady, it's as well for such as you not to inquire too closely into the lives of we who are artistes."

When Mavis had put on her hat and cloak, and was leaving the Athenaeum, Miss Nippett called out:

"It's all right; you can sleep sound; 'e's pleased with you."

"Who?" asked Mavis.

"Mr Poulter. Who else d'ye think I meant?"

Three days later, Mavis severed her connection with "Poulter's." Upon her going, Mr Poulter presented her with a signed photograph of himself in full war-paint, an eulogistically worded testimonial, also, an honorarium (this was his word) of five shillings. Mavis was loth to take it; but seeing the dancing-master's distress at her hesitation, she reluctantly pocketed the money.

Miss Nippett also gave her a specially taken photograph of herself.

"Where's your shawl?" asked Mavis, who missed this familiar adjunct from the photograph.

"I took it off to show off me figure. See?" replied Miss Nippett confidentially.

Mr Poulter asked Mavis if she had further employment in view. She knew how poor he was; also, that if she told him she was workless, he would probably insist on retaining her services, although he could not afford to do so. Mavis fibbed to Mr Poulter; she hoped that her consideration for his poverty would atone for the lie.

For five weeks Mavis vainly tried to get work. She soon discovered how, when possible employers considered her application, the mere mention of her being at "Dawes'" was enough to spoil her chances of securing an engagement.

She had spent all her money; she was now living on the sum she had received from a pawnbroker in exchange for two of her least prized trinkets. Going out in all weathers to look for employment had not improved her clothes; her best pair of boots let in water; she was jaded, heartsick, dispirited. As with others in a like plight, she dared not look into the immediate future, this holding only terrifying probabilities of disaster; the present moment was all sufficient; little else mattered, and, although to-morrow promised actual want, there was yet hope that a sudden turn of fortune's wheel would remove the dread menace of impending ruin. One evening, Mavis, dazed with disappointment at failing to secure an all but promised berth, wandered aimlessly from the city in a westerly direction. She scarcely knew where she was going or what quarter of London she had reached. She was only aware that she was surrounded by every evidence of well-being and riches. The pallid, worried faces of the frequenters of the city were now succeeded by the well-fed, contented looks of those who appeared as if they did not know the meaning of the word care. Splendid carriages, costly motor cars passed in never-ending procession. As Mavis glanced at the expensive dresses of the women, the wind-tanned faces of the men, she thought how, but for a wholly unlooked-for reverse of fortune, these would be the people with whom she would be associating on equal terms. The thought embittered her; she quickened her steps in order to leave behind her the opulent surroundings so different from her own, A little crowd, consisting of those entering and waiting about the door of a tea-shop, obstructed her. An idea suddenly possessed her. Confronted with want, she wondered if she had enough money to snatch a brief half-hour's respite from her troubles. She looked in her purse, to find it contained three shillings. The next moment, she was moving in the direction of the tea-room, her habitual husbandry making a poor fight against the over-mastering desire possessing her.

She walked up a steep, narrow flight of carpeted stairs; this terminated in a long, low room, the walls of which were of black oak, and which was nearly filled with a gaily dressed crowd of men and women. The sensuous music of a string band fell on her ear; the smell of tea and the indefinable odour of women were borne to her nostrils. A card was put in her hand, telling her that a palmist could be consulted on the next floor. In and out among the tables, attendants, clad in the garb of sixteenth century Flemish peasant women, moved noiselessly.

Mavis got a table to herself in a corner by a window which overlooked the street. She ordered tea and toast. When it was brought, she did her best to put her extremity out of sight; she tried hard to believe that she, too, led a happy, butterfly existence, without anxious thought for the morrow, without a care in the world. The effort was scarcely a success, but was, perhaps, worth the making. As she sat, she noticed a kindly-looking old gentlewoman who was pointing her out to a companion; for all the old woman's somewhat dowdy garb, she had rich woman stamped all over her. The old lady kept on looking at Mavis; once or twice, when the latter caught her eye, the elder woman smiled. When she rose to go, she came over to Mavis and said:

"Forgive me, my dear, but your hair looks wonderful against that imitation oak."

"Does it? But it isn't imitation too," replied Mavis.

"Forgive me, won't you?"

"Of course."

"May I ask your name?"

"Keeves. Mavis Keeves."

"A good name," muttered the old lady. "Good-bye."

"Good-bye."

Mavis saw her move towards the door; when she reached it, she turned to smile again to Mavis before going out.

"What a fool I am!" thought Mavis. "If I'd only told her I wanted work, she'd have helped me to something. What a fool I am!"

Mavis rose as if to follow the kindly old soul; but she was too late. As she got up, she saw her step into a fine carriage, which, after the footman had closed the door and mounted the box, had driven away. Mavis sat helplessly. It seemed as if she were as a drowning person who had been offered the chance of clutching a straw, but had refused to take it. There was little likelihood of her getting a second chance. She must resign herself to the worst. She had forgotten; one hope was still left, one she had, hitherto, lost sight of: this to pray to her Heavenly Father, to remind Him that she, as a human sparrow, was in danger of falling; to implore succour. Although she had knelt morning and evening at her bedside, it had lately been more from force of habit than anything else; her heart had not inspired her lips. There had been some reason for this: every morning she had been devoured by eagerness to get work; at night, she had been too weary and dispirited to pray earnestly. Mavis covered her eyes with her hands; she prayed heartfully and long for help. Words welled from her being; their burden was:

"I am young; I love life; help me to live, if only for a little while, in this glorious, wonderful world of Thy making. I only ask for bread, for which I am eager to work. Help me! Help me! Help me!"

Mavis uncovered her eyes. The tea-shop, the music, the indefinable odour of women all seemed bizarre after her communion with the Most High. She made ready to go.

"Are you in trouble?" said a voice at her elbow.

"Yes," she replied.

"I must help you," said the voice.

Mavis saw a richly dressed, bejewelled, comfortable-looking woman at her side.

She was not in the least surprised; a friend had been sent in answer to her prayer.

- 113 -

"Is it over money?" asked the instrument.

Mavis nodded.

"I thought as much. I saw you outside the tea-shop and followed you in. Is your time your own?"

"Absolutely."

"No parents or anyone?"

"I haven't a friend or relation in the world."

"Ah! I must really help you. Come with me. Let me pay for your tea."

Mavis, before she went, found time to offer up brief, heartfelt thanks for having speedily received an answer to her prayer.

CHAPTER TWELVE
MRS HAMILTON'S

Mavis followed her new friend past the pay box, down the carpeted stairs, into the street. She could not help seeing how bedraggled a sparrow she appeared when contrasted with the brilliant plumage of the woman at her side. A superb motor drew up to the pavement, from which a man got down to open the door.

"Get inside, dear," said the woman.

Mavis did as she was bid, hardly realising the good fortune which had so unexpectedly overtaken her.

"Telegraph office, then home," said the woman, who had, also, got into the car.

The man touched his hat and they were off. The woman did not speak at first, being seemingly absorbed in anxious thought. Mavis became conscious of a vague feeling of discomfort like to when—when—she tried to remember when this uneasy feeling had before possessed her. She glanced at her companion; she noticed that the woman's eyes were hard and cold; it was difficult to reconcile their expression with the sentiments she had professed. Then the woman turned to her.

"What is your name?"

"Mavis Weston Keeves."

"My name's Hamilton; it's really West-Hamilton, but I'm known as Mrs Hamilton. How old are you?"

"Eighteen. I'm nineteen in three months."

"Tell me more of yourself."

Mavis briefly told her story; as she finished, the car drew up at a post-office. Mrs Hamilton scanned Mavis's face closely before getting out.

"I shan't be a moment; it's only to someone who's coming to dinner."

Mavis, left alone in the motor, wondered at the strangeness of the adventure. She knew that Mrs Hamilton was scarcely a gentlewoman—even in the broad interpretation nowadays given to the word. But it was not this so much as the fact of her having such hard eyes which perplexed the girl. She had little time to dwell on this matter, as, in a very few moments, Mrs

Hamilton was again beside Mavis, and they were speeding up Oxford Street.

"The fact is I live alone," said Mrs Hamilton. "I am in need of a companion, young and nice-looking, like yourself. I wonder if you'd care for the job."

"I wonder if you'd care to have me."

"I entertain a good deal, mostly gentlemen; two gentlemen are coming to dinner to-night."

"But you don't expect me—?"

"Why not?"

"But my clothes."

"Is that all? I've some things that will suit you down to the ground."

"You're very kind," said Mavis, as the motor, having turned into Regent Street, whizzed past the Langham Hotel.

"You play and sing?" asked Mrs Hamilton.

"A little."

"That always helps. And as to terms, if we get along well together, you'll be grateful to me till the day of your death."

Although the words were spoken without a suspicion of feeling, Mavis replied:

"I'm sure I shall."

"Here we are!" said Mrs Hamilton.

Mavis was much surprised that no word had been said about references.

A man-servant opened the door. Mavis passed in with Mrs Hamilton, for whom a telegram was waiting.

"Dinner at eight to-night, Jarvis; an hour earlier than usual. Lay for four," said Jarvis's mistress, after opening the telegram.

"Yes, ma'am," replied Jarvis, as Mrs Hamilton walked upstairs to the drawing-room, followed by Mavis.

Accustomed as Mavis had been of late to bed-sitting rooms or shabby lodging-house parlours, her first glimpse of Mrs Hamilton's richly-furnished drawing-room almost took away her breath. It was not so much the richness of the furniture which astonished her, as the daring scheme of decoration and the profusion of expensive nicknacks scattered about the room; these last were eloquent of Mrs Hamilton's ability to satisfy any whim, however costly it might be. The walls were panelled in white; white curtains were drawn across the windows; black bearskins covered the floor; the furniture was dark, formal, much of it carved; here and there on the white panelling of the walls were black Wedgwood plaques; black Wedgwood china stood audaciously upon and inside cabinets. A large grand piano and the cheerful blaze of a wood fire mitigated the severity of the room.

"How beautiful!" exclaimed Mavis.

"You like it?"

"It's the loveliest room I've ever been in."

"It's your home if we hit it off."

"Do you think we shall?"

"Up to now I don't see any reason why we shouldn't."

Mavis again breathed thanks to Heaven for having so generously answered her prayer. She felt how she would like to tell of her experience to any who denied the efficacy of personal supplication to God.

"Shall I play to you?" asked Mavis, after they had talked for some minutes.

"I don't like music," replied Mrs Hamilton.

"Not?"

"I don't understand it. Let's go upstairs to my room."

If she did not care for music, Mavis wondered why she had made a point of asking if she (Mavis) could play.

Mrs Hamilton's bedroom was a further revelation to the girl; she looked wide-eyed at the Louis Seize gilt furniture, the tapestry, the gilt-edged screens, the plated bath in a corner of the room, the superb dressing-table bestrewed with gold toilet nicknacks.

"Do you like my bed?" asked Mrs Hamilton, who was watching the girl's undisguised wonder.

"I haven't had time to take in the other things."

Mavis looked at the bed; it stood in an alcove on the side of the room furthest from where she was. It was long, low, and gilded; plum-coloured curtains rose in voluptuous folds till they were joined near the ceiling by a pair of big silver doves.

"Do you like it?" asked Mrs Hamilton.

"Like is scarcely the word. I've never imagined anything like it in my life."

"It belonged to Madame du Barri, the mistress of a French king."

"I've read something about her."

"He always wished to give her a toilette set of pure gold, but could never quite afford it. I hope to get one next year if things go well."

Mavis stared at Mrs Hamilton in wide-eyed amazement. The rich woman appeared to take no notice of the girl's surprise, and said:

"Sit by the fire with me a moment. It will soon be time for you to dress."

"Dress! I've only what I've got on with me. My one poor evening dress would look absurd in this house."

"I told you I'd see to that," replied Mrs Hamilton. "I've had a young friend staying with me who was just about your build. She left one or two of her evening dresses behind her. If they don't quite fit, my maid will take them in."

"You are good to me," said Mavis.

"If you like it, I'll give you one."

"How can I ever thank you?"

"You can to-night."

"To-night?"

"Listen. I've two old friends coming to dinner. One is a Mr—Mr Ellis, but he won't interest you a bit."

"Why not?"

"He's old and is already infatuated."

"Isn't the other, then?" asked Mavis lightly.

"Mr—Mr Williams! No. I wonder if you'd interest him."

"I don't suppose so for one moment," remarked Mavis.

"You're too modest. Mr Williams is young, good-looking, rich."

"Money doesn't interest me."

"Nonsense!"

"Really, it doesn't."

"Not after your wanting work for so long?"

"Not a bit."

"Not when you see it can buy things like mine?"

"Of course money is wonderful, but it isn't everything."

"You say that because you don't know. Money is power, happiness, contentment, life. And you know it in your heart of hearts. Every woman, who is anything at all, knows it. Surely, after all you've gone through, it appeals to you?"

Mrs Hamilton anxiously watched Mavis's face.

"Not a bit like it seems to—to some people," replied Mavis.

Mrs Hamilton's face fell. She was lost in anxious thought for some moments.

"Do you mind?" asked Mavis.

"Of course not. But we'll talk it over after you've seen Mr Williams."

"But is it so necessary for his happiness that he should be infatuated with anyone?"

"It might keep him from worse things. He's very impulsive and romantic. I've quite a motherly interest in the boy. You might assist me to reclaim him."

[Footnote:]Although Mrs Hamilton spoke such maternal sentiments, Mavis looked in vain for the motherly expression upon her face, which she felt should inevitably accompany such words. Mrs Hamilton's face was hard, expressionless, cold. Presently she said:

"If you would care to go to your room, it's on the next floor, and the second door you come to on the right. If it isn't good enough, let me know."

"It's sure to be," remarked Mavis.

"Parkins, my maid, will come to you in ten minutes. Rest till then, as to-night I want you to look your best."

Mavis thanked and left Mrs Hamilton. She then found her way to her chamber. She was as surprised and delighted with this as she had been with the other two rooms, perhaps more so, because she reflected, with an immense satisfaction, that it might be her very own. The room was furnished throughout with satinwood; blue china bowls decorated the tops of cabinets; a painted satinwood spinet stood in a corner; the hearth was open and tiled throughout with blue Dutch tiles; the fire burned in a brass brazier which was suspended from the chimney.

Thought Mavis, as she looked rapturously about her:

"Just the room I should love to have had for always, if—if things had been different."

A door on the right of the fireplace attracted her. She turned the handle of this, to find it opened on to a luxuriously fitted bathroom, in a corner of which a fire was burning. Mavis returned to the bedroom, still wondering at the sudden change in her fortunes; even now, with all these tangible evidences of the alteration in her condition, she could scarcely believe it to be true: it all seemed like something out of a book or on the stage, two forms of distraction which, according to Miss Allen, did anything but represent life as it really was. She was still mentally agape at her novel surroundings when Parkins, Mrs Hamilton's maid, entered the room to dress Mavis.

Parkins's appearance surprised her; she was wholly unlike her conception of what a lady's-maid should be. Instead of being unassumingly dressed, quiet, self-effacing, Parkins was a bold, buxom wench, with large blue eyes and a profusion of fair hair. She wore white lace underskirts, openwork silk stockings, and showy shoes. Her manner was that of scarcely veiled familiarity. She carried upon her arm a gorgeous evening gown.

Mavis made an elaborate toilette. She bathed, presently to clothe herself in the many delicate garments which Mrs Hamilton had provided. Her hair was dressed by Parkins; later, when she put on the evening frock, she hardly knew herself. The gown was of grey chiffon, embroidered upon the bodice and skirt with silver roses; grey silk stockings, grey silver embroidered shoes completed the toilette.

"Madam sent you these," said Parkins, returning to the room after a short absence.

"Those!" cried Mavis, as her eyes were attracted by the pearl necklaces and other costly jewels which the maid had brought.

"Madam entertains very rich gentlemen; she likes everyone about her to look their best."

Mavis, with faint reluctance, let Parkins do as she would with her. The pearl necklaces were roped about her neck; gold bracelets were put upon her arms; a thin platinum circlet, which supported a large emerald, was clasped about her head.

Mavis stood to look at herself in the glass. She could scarcely believe that the tall, queenly, ardent-looking girl was the same tired, dispirited creature who had listlessly pinned on her hat of a morning before tramping out, in all weathers, to search for work. She gazed at herself for quite two minutes; whatever happened, the memory of how she looked in all this rich finery was something to remember.

"Will I do?" she asked of Mrs Hamilton, when that person, very richly garbed, came into the room.

Mrs Hamilton looked her all over before replying:

"Yes, you'll do."

"I'm glad."

"I never make a mistake. You can go, Parkins."

When the maid had left the room, Mrs Hamilton said:

"I'm going to introduce you to my friends as Miss Devereux."

"But—"

"I wish it."

"But—"

Mavis did not at all like this resolve.

"It was the name of my last companion, and I've got used to it. Besides, I wish it."

Mavis resented Mrs Hamilton's sudden assumption of authority; it quickened the vague feelings of dislike which she had felt in her presence, the vague feelings of dislike which reminded her of—of—ah! She remembered now. It was the same uncomfortable sensation which she had always experienced when Mrs Stanley stood by her in "Dawes'."

This discovery of the identity of the two emotions set Mavis wondering if either had anything to do with the character of the two women who had inspired them, and, if so, whether Mrs Hamilton followed the same loathsome calling as Mrs Stanley. Mavis comforted her mind's disquiet by reflecting how Miss Allen had, most likely, not told the truth about Mrs Stanley's occupation; also, by remembering how her present situation was the result of a direct, personal appeal to the Almighty, which precluded the remotest possibility of her being exposed to risk of insult or harm. She had little time for thinking on the matter, for Mrs Hamilton said:

"Mr Ellis has already come. Mr Williams will be here any moment. We'd better go down."

Mavis followed Mrs Hamilton to the drawing-room, where a man rose at their entrance, to whom Mavis was introduced as Miss Devereux.

He scarcely glanced at Mavis, gave her the most formal of bows, and, as the few remarks he made were directed to Mrs Hamilton, the girl had plenty of time in which to observe him. He was elderly, tall, distinguished-looking. He had the indefinable air of being, not only a man of wealth, but a "somebody." She was chiefly attracted by his grey eyes, which seemed dead and lifeless. The underlids of these were pencilled with countless small lines, which, with the weary, dull eyes, seemed quite out of keeping with the otherwise keenly intellectual face.

Mavis secretly resented the man's indifference to her comeliness. A few minutes later, the servant opened the door to announce Mr Williams, whereupon a tall, sun-bronzed, smart-looking man sauntered into the room. Something in his carriage and face suggested soldier to Mavis's mind. He was by no means handsome, but what might have been a somewhat plain face was made pleasant-looking by the deep sunburn and the kindliness of his expression.

Williams shook hands with Mrs Hamilton, nodded to Ellis, and then turned to Mavis. Directly he saw her, a look of surprise came into his face; the girl could not help seeing how greatly he was struck by her appearance. Mrs Hamilton introduced them, when he at once came to her side.

"Just think of it," he said, "I was in no hurry to get here. If I had only known!"

"Known what?" asked Mavis.

"That's asking something. In return I'm going to ask you a question."

"Well?"

"What is it like to be so charming?"

The same question asked by another man might have offended her. There was such a note of sincere, boyish admiration in the man's voice, that she had said, almost before she was aware of it:

"Rather nice."

He said more in the same strain. Mavis found herself greatly enjoying the thinly veiled compliments which he paid her. It was the first time since she had grown up that she had spoken to a smart man, who was obviously a gentleman. If this were not enough to thaw her habitual reserve, there was something strangely familiar in the young man's face and manner; it almost seemed to Mavis as if she were talking with a very old friend or acquaintance, which was enough to justify the unusual levity of her behaviour.

Once or twice, she caught Mrs Hamilton's eye, when she could not help seeing how her friend was much pleased at the way in which she attracted Mr Williams.

When he was taking the girl down to dinner, he murmured:

"May I call here often?"

"There's no charge for admission," replied Mavis.

"It wouldn't make any difference to me if there were."

"How nice to be so reckless!"

"I'm a lot in town for the next three months. I want to get as much out of life as I can."

"From school?"

"Aldershot."

"Are you in the service?"

"Eh!"

"If you are, haven't you any rank at your age?" asked Mavis.

"How do you know I'm not a Tommy?" he asked.

"That's what I thought you were," she retorted.

Mavis and Mrs Hamilton faced each other at table; Williams sat on her right, Ellis on her left. The conversation at the dinner-table was, almost exclusively, between the soldier and Mavis. Ellis scarcely spoke to his hostess, and then only when compelled.

"What will you drink?" asked Mrs Hamilton of Mavis.

"Water, please."

"Water?" echoed Mrs Hamilton.

Mr Ellis looked keenly at Mavis.

"Have some champagne," continued Mrs Hamilton.

"I'd fall under the table if I did. I'll have water. I never drink anything else," said Mavis.

"I never drink anything else except champagne," retorted Mrs Hamilton. "Look here, if Miss Devereux drinks water I shall," declared Williams.

"Do. The change will do you good," replied Mavis.

"See what I've let myself in for," said Williams, as he kept his word.

As the servant was about to pour out champagne for Mr Ellis, Mrs Hamilton said:

"Stop! I've something special for you."

She then whispered to the servant, who left the room to bring back a curious, old bottle. When this was opened, a golden wine poured into Mr Ellis's glass, where it bubbled joyously, as if rejoicing at being set free from its long imprisonment.

As the wine was poured out, Mavis noticed how Mr Ellis's eye caught Mrs Hamilton's.

The meal was long, elaborate, sumptuous. Mavis wondered when the procession of toothsome delicacies would stop. She enjoyed herself immensely; her unaccustomed personal adornment, the cosy room, the shaded lights, the lace table-cloth, the manner in which the food was served, above all, the manly, admiring personality of Mr Williams, all irresistibly appealed to her, largely because the many joyous instincts of her being had been starved for so long.

She surrendered herself body and soul to the exhilaration of the moment, as if conscious that it was all too good to be true; that her surroundings might any moment fade; that her gay clothes would disappear, and that she would again find herself, heartsick and weary, in her comfortless little combined room at Mrs Bilkins's. At the same time, her natural alertness took in everything going on about her.

As the dinner progressed, she could not help seeing how Mr Ellis's eyes seemed to awaken from their torpor; but the life that came into them was such that Mavis much preferred them as they originally were. They sparkled hungrily; it seemed to the girl as if they had a fearful, hunted, and, at the same time, eager, unholy look, as if they sought refuge in some deadly sin in order to escape a far worse fate. Mavis's and Williams's gaiety was infectious. Ellis frequently joined in the raillery proceeding between the pair; it was as if Mavis's youth, comeliness, and charm compelled homage from the pleasure-worn man of the world. Mrs Hamilton, all this while, said little; she left the entertaining to Mavis, who was more than equal to the effort; it seemed to the joy-intoxicated girl as if she were the bountiful hostess, Mrs Hamilton a chance guest at her table. The appearance of strawberries at dessert (it was January) made a lull in Mavis's enjoyment: the out-of-season fruit reminded her of the misery which could be alleviated with the expenditure of its cost. She was silent for a few moments, which caused Ellis to ask:

"I say, Windebank, what have you said to our friend?"

Mavis looked up quickly, to see a look of annoyance on Mrs Hamilton's face.

"Williams, I should have said," corrected Ellis. "I muddled the two names. What have you said to our friend that she should be so quiet all at once?"

"Give it up," replied Williams. "Perhaps she's offended at our childishness."

The men talked. Mrs Hamilton, with something of an effort, joined in the conversation. Mavis was silent; she wondered how Mr Ellis came to address Mr Williams as "Windebank," which was also the name of the friend of the far-away days when her father was alive. She reflected how Archie Windebank would be now twenty-eight, an age that might well apply to Mr Williams. Associated with these thoughts was an uneasy feeling, which had been once or twice in her mind, that the two men at table were far too distinguished-looking to bear such commonplace names as Ellis and Williams. The others rallied her on her depression. Striving to believe that she must be mistaken in her suspicions, she made an effort to end the perplexities that were beginning to confront her.

"Are you at Aldershot for long?" asked Mavis of Mr Williams.

"I scarcely know: one never does know these things."

"Do you come up often?"

"I shall now."

"To see your people?"

"They live in the west of England."

"Wiltshire?"

"How did you know?"

"I didn't; I guessed."

"Wherever they are, I don't see so much of them as I should."

"How considerate of you!"

"Isn't it? But they're a bit too formidable even for one of my sober tastes."

"I see. They're interesting and clever."

"If Low Church and frumpy clothes are cleverness, they're geniuses," he remarked.

"Of course, you prefer High Church and low bodices," retorted Mavis.

Soon after, Mrs Hamilton and Mavis left the men and went upstairs to the drawing-room. The girl was uneasy in her mind as to how Mrs Hamilton would take the fact of her having considerably eclipsed her employer at table; now that they were alone together, she feared some token of Mrs Hamilton's displeasure.

To her surprise and delight, this person said:

"You're an absolute treasure."

"You think so?"

"I don't think; I know. But then, I never make a mistake."

"I'm glad you're pleased."

"I'm not pleased; delighted is more the word. You're worth your weight in gold."

"I wish I were."

"But you will be, if you follow my advice. At first, I thought you a bit of a mug. I don't mind telling you, now I see how smart you are."

Mavis looked puzzled; the extravagant eulogy of her conduct seemed scarcely to be justified.

"You can see Williams is head over ears in love with you. So far, he's been beastly stand-offish to anyone I put him on to," continued Mrs Hamilton.

"Indeed!" said Mavis coldly. She disliked Mrs Hamilton's coarse manner of expressing herself.

Mrs Hamilton did not notice the frown on the girl's forehead, but went on:

"As for that idea of drinking water, it was a stroke of genius."

"What?"

"My heart went out to you when you insisted on having it, although I pretended to mind."

Mavis was about to protest her absolute sincerity in the matter, when Parkins, the maid who had dressed her, came into the room. She whispered to her mistress, at which Mrs Hamilton rose hurriedly and said:

"I must leave you for a little time on important business."

"What would you like me to do?" asked Mavis.

"Particularly one thing: don't leave this room."

"Why should I?"

"Quite so. But I want someone here when Mr Williams comes upstairs."

"I'll stick at my post," laughed Mavis, at which Mrs Hamilton and the comely-looking maid left the room.

Left alone, Mavis surrendered herself to the feeling of uneasiness which had been called into being, not only by her employer's strange words, but, also, by the fact of Mr Williams having been addressed by the other man as Windebank. The more she thought of it, the more convinced was she that Mr Ellis had not made a mistake in calling the other man by a different name to the one by which she had been introduced to him. The fact of his having admitted that his home was in Wiltshire, together with the sense of familiarity in his company, seemingly begotten of old acquaintance, tended to strengthen this conviction. On the other hand, if he were indeed the old friend of her childhood, there seemed a purposed coincidence in the fact of their having met again. She did not forget how her presence in Mrs Hamilton's house was the result of an appeal to her Heavenly Father, who, she firmly believed, would not let a human sparrow such as she fall to the ground. She was curious to discover the result of this seemingly preordained meeting. The sentimental speculation engendered a dreamy languor which was suddenly interrupted by a sense of acute disquiet. She was always a girl of abnormal susceptibility to what was going on about her; to such an extent was this sensibility developed, that she had learned to put implicit faith in the intuitions that possessed her. Now, she was certain that something was going on in the house, something that was hideous, unnatural, unholy, the conviction of which seemed to freeze her soul. She had not the slightest doubt on the matter: she felt it in the marrow of her bones.

She placed her hand on her eyes, as if to shut out the horrid certainty; the temporary deprivation of sight but increased the acuteness of her impression, consequently, her uneasiness. She felt the need of space, of good, clean air. The fine drawing-room seemed to confine her being; she hurried to the door in order to escape. Directly she opened it, she found Parkins, the over-dressed maid, outside, who, directly she saw Mavis, barred her further progress.

"What is it, miss?" she asked.

"Mrs Hamilton! I must see her."

"You can't, miss."

"I must. I must. There's something going on. I must see her."

A fearsome expression came over the maid's face as she said:

"I was coming to remind you from madam of your promise to her not to leave the drawing-room."

"I must. I must."

"If I may say so, miss, it will be as much as your place is worth to disobey madam."

These words brought a cold shock of reason to Mavis's fevered excitement.

She looked blankly at the servant for a moment or two, before saying:

"Thank you, Parkins; I will wait inside."

If her many weeks of looking for employment had taught her nothing else, they now told her how worse than foolish it would be to shatter at one blow Mrs Hamilton's good opinion of her. In compliance with her employer's request, she returned to the drawing-room, her nerves all on edge.

Although more convinced than before of the presence of some abomination, she made a supreme effort to divert her thoughts into channels promising relief from her present tension of mind.

She caught up and eagerly examined the first thing that came to hand. It was a large, morocco-bound, gold-edged photograph album; almost before she was aware of it, she was engrossed in its contents. It was full from cover to cover of coloured photographs of women. There were dark girls, fair girls, auburn girls, every type of womanhood to be met with under Northern skies; they ranged from slim girls in their teens to over-ripe beauties, whose principal attraction was the redundance of their figures. For all the immense profusion of varied beauty which the women displayed, they had certainly two qualities in common—they all wore elaborate evening dress; they were all photographed to display to the utmost advantage their physical attractions. Otherwise, thought Mavis, there was surely nothing to differentiate them from the usual run of comely womanhood. Always a lover of beauty, Mavis eagerly scanned the photographs in the book. To her tense imagination, it was like wandering in a highly cultivated garden, where there were flowers of every hue, from the timid shrinking violet and the rosebud, to the over-blown peony, to greet the senses. It was as if she wandered from one to the next, admiring and drinking in the distinctive beauty of each. There were supple, fair-petalled daffodils, white-robed daisies, scarlet-lipped poppies, and black pansies, instinct with passion, all waiting to be culled. It seemed as if a paradise of glad loveliness had been gathered for her delight. They were all dew-bespangled, sun-worshipping, wind-free, as if their only purpose was to languish for some thirsty bee to come and sip greedily of their sweetness. As Mavis looked, another quality, which had previously eluded her, seemed to attach itself to each and all of the flowers, a quality that their calculated shyness now made only the more apparent. It was as if at some time in their lives their petals had been one and all ravaged by some relentless wind; as if, in consequence, they had all dedicated themselves to decorate the altars raised to the honour and glory of love.

Mavis, also, noticed that beneath each photograph was written a number in big figures. Then the book repelled her. She put it down, not before she noticed that, scattered about the room, were other albums filled presumably in the same way as was the other. She had no mind to look at these, being already surfeited with beauty; also, she was more than ever aware of the sense of disquiet which had troubled her before. To escape once more from this, she walked to the piano, opened it, and let her fingers stray over the keys. She had not touched a piano for many weeks, consequently her fingers were stiff and awkward; but in a few minutes they got back something of their old proficiency: almost unconsciously, she strayed into an Andante of Chopin's.

The strange, appealing, almost unearthly beauty of the movement soothed her jangled nerves; before she was aware of it, she was enrapt with the morbid majesty of the music. Although she was dimly conscious that someone had come into the room, she went on playing.

The next definite thing that she knew was that two strong arms were placed about her body, that she was being kissed hotly and passionately upon eyes and lips.

"You darling; you darling; you perfect darling!" cried a voice.

Mavis was too overcome by the suddenness of the assault to know what to be at; her first instinct was to deliver herself from the defiling touch of her assailant. She freed herself with an effort, to see that it was Mr

Williams who had so grossly insulted her. Blind rage, shame, outraged pride all struggled for expression; blind rage predominated.

"Oh, you beast!" she cried.

"Eh!"

"You beast! You beast! To do a thing like that!" Then, as she became on better terms with the nature of the vulgar insult to which she had been subjected, her anger blazed out.

"How dare you insult a defenceless girl?"

"But—" the man stammered.

"What have I ever done but try and work to keep away from such things, and now you come and—Oh, you beast—you cruel beast! You'll never know what you have done."

A sense of shame possessed her. She turned away to drop scalding tears. Anger quickly succeeded this brief fit of dejection. It caused her inexpressible pain to think that she, a daughter of a proud family, the girl with the aloof soul, should have been treated in the same way as any fast London shop-girl. She was consumed with passion; she feared what form her rage might take. At least she was determined to have the man turned out of the house. She moved towards the bell.

"If I've made a mistake," began the man, who all this time had been fearfully watching her.

"If you've made a mistake!" she echoed scornfully.

"The best of us do sometimes, you know," he continued.

"Why to me—to me? What have I said or done to encourage you? Why to me?" she cried.

"If I've made a mistake, I'm more sorry than I can say, more sorry than you can guess."

"What's the use of that to me? You touched my lips. Oh, I could tear them!" she cried desperately.

"Will you hear my excuse?"

"There's no excuse. Nothing—nothing will ever make me forget it. Oh, the shame of it!"

Here bitter tears again welled to her eyes.

The man was moved by her extremity.

"I am so very sorry. I wouldn't have had it happen for anything. I didn't know you were in the least like this."

"Why not? If you had met me as I was before I came here there might have been the shadow of an excuse. Do you usually behave to girls you meet at friends' houses like you did to me?"

"In friends' houses?" he asked, emphasising the word "friends."

"You heard what I said?"

"This is scarcely a friend's house."

"Why not?"

"Eh?"

"Why not? Why not? Can't you tell me?"

"But—"

"Why not? Why not? Answer!"

"Is it possible?"

"Is what possible?"

"You don't know the house you're in?"

"What house?" she asked wildly.

The look of terror, of fear, which accompanied this question was enough to dissipate any doubts of the girl's honesty which may have lingered in the man's mind.

"How long have you been here?"

"Three hours."

"And you don't know what Mrs Hamilton is?"

"No."

"What?" he cried excitedly.

"Tell me! Tell me!"

"Just tell me how you met her."

She told him in short words; she was reluctant to make a confidant of the man who had ravished her lips; she was dimly conscious that he may have had a remote excuse for his behaviour. When she had done, he said:

"Mrs Hamilton is one of the worst women in London. She'd have been 'run in' long ago if she weren't so rich and if her clients weren't so influential."

Mavis looked at him wide-eyed.

"That chap at dinner, didn't, you know he was Lord Kegworth? If you don't, you must have heard of the rotten life he's led."

"But—" stammered Mavis.

"Have you seen any photographs since you've been here?"

"Just now—these."

"She's their agent, go between. Here! What am I telling you? You can thank your stars you've met me."

Mavis's frightened eyes looked into his.

"I'm going to get you out of it."

"You?"

"There's not a moment to lose. Get on your things and clear out."

"But Mrs Hamilton—"

"She's busy for a moment. Slip on something over your dress and join me outside the drawing-room. If anyone interferes with you, shout."

"But—"

"Do as I tell you. Hang it! I must do something to try and make up for my blackguard behaviour."

Mavis went from the room, her heart beating with fear of discovery. For the time being, she had forgotten the insult offered her by the man she had left: her one thought was to put as great a space as possible between this accursed house and herself in the least imaginable time. She scarcely knew what she did. She tore off the pearls, the head circlet with its shining emerald, bracelets and other costly gee-gaws, and threw them on the table; she was glad to be rid of them; their touch meant defilement. She kicked off the grey slippers, tore off the silk stockings, and substituted for these her worn, down-at-heel shoes and stockings. There was no time to change her frock, so she pulled the cloak over her evening clothes; she meant to return these latter to their owner the first thing in the morning. She turned her back on the room, that such a short while back she had looked upon as her own, ran down the stairs and joined the man, who was impatiently waiting for her on the landing. Without exchanging a word, they descended to the ground floor. The front door was in sight and Mavis's heart was beating high with hope, when Mrs Hamilton, who looked tired and heated, stood in the passage.

"Where are you going?" she asked.

"Out for the evening," replied Williams.

"What time shall I expect you back?" she asked of Mavis.

"I'm not coming back," replied Mavis. "I wish I'd never come."

"Then—?"

"Yes," interrupted Williams, anticipating Mrs Hamilton's question.

"You believe and trust a notorious seducer like this man?" asked Mrs Hamilton of Mavis.

"Whatever I am, I ain't that," cried Williams.

"To a man who has ruined more girls than anyone else in London?" continued Mrs Hamilton. "I solemnly warn you that if you go with that man it means your ruin—ruin body and soul."

Mrs Hamilton spoke in such a low, earnest voice, that Mavis, who now recollected Mr Williams's previous behaviour to her, was inclined to waver.

Mrs Hamilton saw her advantage and said:

"Since you disbelieve in me, the least you can do is to go upstairs and take off my clothes."

"She'll do nothing of the kind," cried out the man.

"He doesn't want to lose his prey," Mrs Hamilton remarked to Mavis, who was inclined to falter a little more.

Perhaps Williams saw the weakening of the girl's resolution, for he made a last desperate effort on her behalf.

"Look here," he said, "I'm not a sneak, but, if you don't own up and let Miss Devereux go, I'll fetch in the police."

"You'll what?" cried Mrs Hamilton.

"Fetch in the police. Not to Mrs Hamilton, but to Mrs Bridgeman, Mrs Knight, or Mrs Davis."

Mrs Hamilton's face went white; she looked intently at the man to see if he were in earnest. His resolute eyes convinced her that he was.

The next moment, a torrent of foul words fell from her lips. She abused Mavis; she reviled the man; she accused the two of sin, the while she made use of obscene, filthy phrases, which caused Mavis to put her hands to her ears.

Mavis no longer wavered. She put her hand on the man's arm; the next minute they were out in the street.

CHAPTER THIRTEEN
MAVIS GOES OUT TO SUPPER

"Where now?" asked the man, as the two stood outside in the street.

"Good night," replied Mavis.

"Good night?"

"Good-bye, then."

"Oh no."

"I'm grateful to you for getting me out of that place, but I can never see you or speak to you again."

"But—"

"We needn't go into it. I want to try to forget it, although I never shall. Good-bye."

"I can't let you go like this. Let me drive you home."

"Home!" laughed Mavis scornfully. "I've no home."

"Really no home?"

"I haven't a soul in the world who cares what becomes of me: not a friend in the world. And all I valued you've soiled. It made me hate you, and nothing will ever alter it. Good-bye."

She turned away. The man followed.

"Look here, I'll tell you all about myself, which shows my intentions are straight."

"It wouldn't interest me."

"Why not? You liked me before—before that happened, and, when you've forgiven me, there's no reason why you shouldn't like me again."

"There's every reason."

"My name's Windebank—Archibald Windebank. I'm in the service, and my home is Haycock Abbey, near Melkbridge—"

"You gave me your wrong name!" cried Mavis, who, now that she knew that the man was the friend of her early days, seized on any excuse to get away from him.

"But—"

"Don't follow me. Good-bye."

She crossed the road. He came after her and seized her arm.

"Don't be a fool!" he cried.

"You've hurt me. You're capable of anything," she cried.

"Rot!"

"Oh, you brute, to hurt a girl!"

"I've done nothing of the kind. It would almost have served you right if I had, for being such a little fool. Listen to me—you shall listen," he added, as Mavis strove to leave him.

His voice compelled submission. She looked at him, to see that his face was tense with anger. She found that she did not hate him so much, although she said, as if to satisfy her conscience for listening to him:

"Do you want to insult me again?"

"I want to tell you what a fool you are, in chucking away a chance of lifelong happiness, because you're upset at what I did, when, finding you in that house, I'd every excuse for doing."

"Lifelong happiness?" cried Mavis scornfully.

"You're a woman I could devote my life to. I want to know all about you. Oh, don't be a damn little fool!"

"You're somebody: I'm a nobody. Much better let me go."

"Of course if you want to—"

"Of course I do."

"Then let me see you into a cab."

"A cab! I always go by 'bus, when I can afford it."

"Good heavens! Here, let me drive you home."

"I shouldn't have said that. I'm overwrought to-night. When I'm in work, I'm ever so rich. I know you mean kindly. Let me go."

"I'll do nothing of the kind. It's all very important to me. I'm going to drive you home."

He caught hold of her arm, the while he hailed a passing hansom. When this drew up to the pavement, he said:

"Get in, please."

"But—"

"Get in," he commanded.

The girl obeyed him: something in the man's voice compelled obedience.

He sat beside her.

"Now, tell me your address."

Mavis shook her head.

"Tell me your address."

"Nothing on earth will make me."

"The man's waiting."

"Let him."

"Drive anywhere. I'll tell you where to go later," Windebank called to the cabman.

The cab started. The man and the girl sat silent. Mavis was not reproaching herself for having got into the cab with Windebank; her mind was full of the strange trick which fate had played her in throwing herself and her old-time playmate together. There seemed design in the action. Perhaps, after all, their meeting was the reply to her prayer in the tea-shop.

The cab drove along the almost deserted thoroughfare. It was now between ten and eleven, a time when the flame of the day seems to die down before bursting out into a last brilliance, when the houses of entertainment are emptied into the streets.

Mavis stole a glance at the man beside her. Her eye fell on his opera hat, the rich fur lining of his overcoat; lastly, on his face. His whole atmosphere suggested ample means, self-confidence, easy content with life. Then she looked at her cloak, the condition of which was now little removed from shabbiness. The pressure of her feet on the floor of the cab reminded her how sadly her shoes were down at heel. The contrast between their two states irked Mavis: she was resentful at the fact of his possessing all the advantages in life of which she had been deprived. If he had been visited with the misfortune that had assailed her, and if she had been left scathless, it would not have been so bad: he was a man, who could have fought for his own hand, without being hindered by the obstacles which weigh so heavily on those of her own sex, who seek to win for themselves a foothold on the slippery inclines of life. She found herself hating him more for his prosperity than for the way in which he had insulted her.

"Have you changed your mind?" asked Windebank presently.

"No."

"Likely to?"

"No."

"We can't talk here, and a fog's coming up. Wouldn't you like something to eat?"

"I'm not hungry—now."

"Where do you usually feed?"

"At an Express Dairy."

"Eh!"

"You get a large cup of tea for tuppence there."

"A tea-shop! But it wouldn't be open so late."

"Lockhart's is."

"Lockhart's?"

"The Cocoa Rooms. In the 'First Class' you find quite a collection of shabby gentility. And you'd never believe what a lot you can get there for tuppence."

"Eh!"

"I'll tell you, you might find it useful some day; one never knows. You can get a huge cup of tea or coffee—a bit stewed—but, at least, it's warm; also, four huge pieces of bread and butter, and a good, long, lovely rest."

"Good God!"

"For tuppence more you can get sausages; sixpence provides a meal; a shilling a banquet. Can't we find a 'Lockhart'?"

The man said nothing. The cab drove onward. Mavis, now that her resentment against Windebank's prosperity had found relief in words, was sorry that she had spoken as she had. After all, the man's well-being was entirely his own affair; it was not remotely associated with the decline in the fortunes of her family. She would like to say or do something to atone for her bitter words.

"Poor little girl! Poor little girl!"

This was said by Windebank feelingly, pityingly; he seemed unconscious that they had been overheard by Mavis. She was firmly, yes, quite firmly, resolved to hate him, whatever he might do to efface her animosity.

Meanwhile, the cab had fetched something of a compass, and had now turned into Regent Street.

"Here we are: this'll do," suddenly cried Windebank.

"What for?"

"Grub. Hi, stop!"

Obedient to his summons, the cabman stopped. Mavis got out on the pavement, where she stood irresolute.

"You'll come in?"

Mavis did not reply.

"We must have a talk. Please, please don't refuse me this."

"I shan't eat anything."

"If you don't, I shan't."

"I won't—I swear I won't accept the least favour from you."

She looked at him resentfully: she would go any lengths to conceal her lessening dislike for him.

"You'd better wait," he called to the cabman, as he led the way to a restaurant.

Two attendants, in gold-laced coats, opened double folding doors at the approach of the man and the girl.

Mavis found herself in a large hall, elaborately decorated with red and gold, upon the floor of which were many tables, that just now were sparsely occupied.

Windebank looked from table to table, as if in search of something. His eye, presently, rested on one, at which an elderly matron was supping with a parson, presumably her husband.

"Good luck!" Windebank murmured, adding to the girl, "This way."

Mavis followed him up the hall to the table next the one where the elderly couple were sitting.

"This is about our mark," he said.

"Why specially here?" she asked.

"Those elderly geesers are a sort of chaperone for unprotected innocence; a parson and all that," he remarked.

She could hardly forbear smiling at his conception of protection.

A waiter assisted her with her cloak. When she took a seat opposite to Windebank, he said:

"I like this place; there's no confounded music to interfere with what one's got to say."

"I like music," Mavis remarked.

"Then let's go where they have it," he suggested, half rising.

"I want to go straight home, if you'll let me."

"Then we'll stay here. What are you going to eat?"

"Nothing."

"Rot! Here's the waiter chaps. Tell 'em what you want."

Two waiters approached the table, one with a list of food, the other with like information concerning wines, which, at a nod from Windebank, they put before Mavis.

She glanced over these; beyond noticing the high prices charged, she gave no attention to the lists' contents.

"Well?" said Windebank.

"I'm not hungry and I'm not thirsty," remarked Mavis.

"You heard what I said, and I'm awfully hungry!"

"That's your affair."

"If you won't decide, I'll decide for you."

The waiters handed him the menus, from which, after much thought, he ordered an elaborate meal. When the waiters hastened to execute his orders, he found Mavis staring at him wide-eyed.

"Are you entertaining your regiment?" she asked.

"You," he replied.

"But—"

"It isn't much, but it's the best they've got. Whatever it is, it's in honour of our first meeting."

"I shan't eat a thing," urged Mavis.

"You won't sit there and see me starve?"

"There won't be time. I have to get back."

"But, however much you hate me, you surely haven't the heart to send me supperless to bed?"

"You shouldn't make silly resolutions."

As Windebank did not speak for some moments, Mavis looked at her surroundings. Men and women in evening dress were beginning to trickle in from theatres, concerts, and music hall. She noticed how they all wore a bored expression, as if it were with much of an effort that they had gone out to supper.

"Don't move! Keep looking like that," cried Windebank suddenly.

"Why?" she asked, quickly turning to him.

"Now you've spoiled it," he complained.

"Spoiled what?"

"Your expression. Good heavens!"

The exclamation was a signal for retrospection on Windebank's part. When he next spoke, he said:

"Is your name, by any wonderful chance, Mavis Keeves?"

"What?"

"Answer my question. Is your name Mavis Keeves: Mavis Weston Keeves in full?"

"You know it isn't. That woman told you what it was."

"She didn't tell you my name, and I thought she might have done the same by you. And when I saw that expression in your face—"

"Who is Mavis Keeves?"

"A little girl I knew when I was a kid. She'd hair and eyes like yours, and when I saw you then—but you haven't answered my question. Is your name Mavis Weston Keeves?"

Mavis had decided what to reply if further directly questioned.

"No, it isn't," she answered.

"Confound! I might have known. It's much too good to be true."

While Mavis was tortured with self-reproach at having told a lie, soup, in gilt cups, was set before Windebank and Mavis, the latter of whom was more than ever resolved to accept no hospitality from the man who appeared sincerely anxious to befriend her. The fact of her having told him a lie seemed, in the eyes of her morbidly active conscience, to put her under an obligation to him, an indebtedness that she was in no mind to increase. She folded her hands on the napkin, and again looked about her.

"Don't you want that stuff?" Windebank asked.

"No, thank you."

"Neither do I. Take it away!"

The waiters removed the soup, to substitute, almost immediately, an appetising preparation of fish. At the same time an elderly, important-mannered man poured out wine with every conceivable elaboration of his office.

"Don't refuse this. The place is famous for it," urged Windebank.

"You know what I said. I mean it more than ever."

"Don't you know that obstinacy is one of the seven deadly sins?"

"Is it?"

"If it isn't, it ought to be. Do change your mind."

"Nothing will make me," she replied icily.

He signalled to the waiters to remove the food.

"What a jolly night we're having!" he genially remarked, when the men were well out of hearing.

"I'm afraid I've spoiled your evening."

"Not at all. I like a good feed. It does one good."

Mavis would have been hard put to it to repress a smile at this remark, had she not suddenly remembered how she had left her purse in the pocket of the frock that she had left behind her at Mrs Hamilton's; she realised that she would have to walk to Mrs Bilkins's. The fact of having no money to pay a 'bus fare reminded her how the cab was waiting outside.

"You've forgotten your cab," she remarked.

"What cab?"

"The one you told to wait outside."

"What of it?"

"Won't he charge?"

"Of course. What of it?"

"What an extravagance!" she commented.

She could say no more; a procession of dishes commenced: meats, ices, sweetmeats, fruit, wines, coffee, liqueurs; all of which were refused, first by Mavis, then by Windebank.

Mavis, who had been accustomed to consider carefully the spending of a penny, was appalled at the waste. She had hoped that Windebank, after seeing how she was resolved to keep her word, would have countermanded the expensive supper he had ordered; failing this, that the management of the restaurant would not charge for the unconsumed meats and wine. Windebank would have been flattered could he have known of Mavis's consideration for his pocket.

He and the girl talked when the attendants were out of the way, to stop conversing when they were immediately about them; the two would resume where they had left off, directly they were sure of not being overheard.

"Just imagine, if you were little Mavis Keeves grown up," began Windebank.

"Never mind about her," replied Mavis uneasily.

"But I do. I loved her, the cheeky little wretch."

"Was she?"

"A little flirt, too."

"Oh no."

"Fact. I think it made me love her all the more."

"Are you trying to make me jealous?" she asked, making a sad little effort to be light-hearted.

"I wish I could. There was a chap named Perigal, whom the little flirt preferred to me."

"Perigal?"

"Charlie Perigal. We were laughing about it only the week before last."

"He loved her too?"

"Rather. I remember we both subscribed to buy her a birthday present. Anyway, the week before last, we both asked each other what had become of her, and promised to let each other know if we heard anything of her."

"If I were Mavis Keeves, would you let him know?"

"No fear."

Mavis smiled at the reply.

"Then we come to to-day," continued Windebank.

"The least said of to-day the better."

"I'm not so sure; it may have the happiest results."

"Don't talk nonsense."

"Do let me go on. Assuming you were little Mavis, where do I find her—eh?"

Here Windebank's face hardened.

"That woman ought to be shot," he cried. "As it is, I've a jolly good mind to show her up. And to think she got you there!"

"Ssh!"

"You've no idea what a house it is. It's quite the worst thing of its kind in London."

"Then what were you doing there?"

"Eh!"

"What were you doing there?"

"I'm not a plaster saint," he replied.

"Who said you were?"

"And I'm interested in life: curious to see all sides of it. She's often asked me, but to-night, when she wired to say she'd a paragon coming to dinner, I went."

"She wired?"

"To-night. It all but missed me. I'm no end of glad it didn't."

"I suppose I ought to be glad too," remarked Mavis.

"I know you think me a bad egg, but I'm not; I'm not really," he went on, to add, after a moment's pause, "I believe at heart I'm a sentimentalist."

"What's that?"

"A bit of a bally fool where the heart is concerned. What?"

"I think all nice people are that," she murmured.

"Thanks."

"I wasn't including you," she remarked.

"Eat that ice."

"Wild horses wouldn't make me."

"You'd eat it if you knew what pleasure it would give me."

"You want me to break my word?" she said, with a note of defiance in her voice.

"Have your own way."

"I mean to,"

The ices were taken away. Windebank went on talking.

"You've no idea how careful a chap with domestic instincts, who isn't altogether a pauper, has to be. Women make a dead set at him."

"Poor dear!" commented Mavis.

"Fact. You mayn't believe it, but every woman—nearly every woman he meets—goes out of her way to have a go at him."

"Nonsense!"

Windebank did not heed the interruption; he went on:

"Old Perigal, Charlie Perigal's father, is a rum old chap; lives alone and never sees anyone and all that. One day he asked me to call, and what d'ye think he said?"

"Give it up."

"Boy! you're commencing life, and you should know this: always bear in mind the value of money and the worthlessness of most women. Good-bye."

"What a horrid old man!"

"Yes, that's what he said."

"And do you bear it in mind?"

"Money I don't worry about. I've more than I know what to do with. As to women, I'm jolly well on my guard."

"You're as bad as old Perigal, every bit."

"But one has to be. Have some of these strawberries?"

"No, thank you."

"You ate 'em fast enough at Mrs What's-her-name's."

"It was different then."

"Yes, wasn't it? Take 'em away."

These last words were spoken to the waiters, who were now accustomed to removing the untasted dishes almost as soon as they were put upon the table.

"Have the coffee when it comes. It'll warm you for the fog outside."

"Thanks, I'm not used to coddling."

"Then you ought to be. But about what we were saying: then, I quite thought old Perigal a pig for saying that about women; now, I know he's absolutely right."

"Absolutely wrong."

"Eh!"

"Absolutely wrong. It's the other way about. It's men who're worthless, not poor women; and they don't care what they drag us down to so long as they get their own ends," cried Mavis.

"Nonsense!" he commented.

"I've been out in the world and have seen what goes on," retorted Mavis.

"It isn't my experience."

"Men are always in the right. No coffee, thank you."

"Sure?"

"Quite."

"No; it is not my experience," he went on. "Take the case of all the chaps I know who've married women who played up to them. Without exception they curse in their hearts the day they met them."

"If anything's wrong, it's owing to the husband's selfishness."

"Little Mavis—I'm going to call you that—you don't know what rot you're talking."

"Rot is often the inconvenient common sense of other people," commented Mavis.

"It isn't as if marriage were for a day," he went on, "or for a week, or two years. Then, it wouldn't matter very much whom one married. But it's for a lifetime, whether it turns out all right or whether it don't. What?"

"I see; you'd have men choose wives as you would a house or an umbrella," she suggested.

"People would be a jolly sight happier if they did," he replied, to add, after looking intently at Mavis: "Though, after all, I believe I'm talking rot. When one's love time comes, nothing else in the world matters; every other consideration goes phut, as it should."

"Goes what?"

"Goes to blazes, then, as it should."

"As it should," echoed Mavis.

"Dear little Mavis!" smiled Windebank, "But it's big Mavis now."

He called the waiter, to give him a note with which to pay the bill.

"What wicked waste!" remarked Mavis in an undertone.

"When it's been time spent with you?"

When the bill and the change were brought, Windebank would not look at either.

"How can you be so extravagant?" she murmured.

"When one's with you, it's a crime to think of anything else."

"What a good thing I'm leaving you!" she laughed.

He insisted on getting and helping her into her coat. As she put her arms into the sleeves, he murmured:

"Where did you get your hair?"

"Do try and talk sense," she pleaded, not insensible to the man's ardent admiration.

Then, with something like a sigh, she left the warmth and comfort of the restaurant for the bleakness of the street, on which a thick fog had descended.

This enveloped the man and the woman. As they stood on the pavement, it seemed to cut them off from the rest of the world.

CHAPTER FOURTEEN
THE SEQUEL

"Will you let me drive you home?"

"No, thank you."

"Then you must let me walk with you."

"There's no necessity."

"I insist. London, at this time of night, isn't the place for a plain little girl like Mavis."

"Now you're talking sense."

"I wish I thought it," he remarked bitterly.

He paid the cabman and piloted Mavis through the fog to the other side of Regent Street; they then made for Piccadilly.

"Am I going right?" he asked.

"At present," she replied, to ask, after a moment or two, "Why are you so extravagant?"

"I'm not."

"That supper and keeping that cab waiting! It must have run into pounds."

"Eh! What if it did?"

"It's wicked. Just think of the good you could have done with it."

"Good? Who to?" he asked blankly.

"You've only to look about you. Don't you know of all the misery there is in the world?"

"To tell you the truth, I've never thought very much about it."

"Then you ought to."

"You think so?"

"Most certainly."

"Then I'll have to."

They were now in Piccadilly. The pavement on which they walked was crowded with women of all ages; some walked in pairs, others, singly.

Whatever their age and appearance, all these women had two qualities in common—artificial complexions and bold, inviting eyes. It was the nightly market of the women of the town. This mart has much in common with any other market existing for the buying or selling of staple commodities. Amongst this assembly of women of all ages and conditions (many of whom were married), there were regular frequenters, who had been there almost from time immemorial; occasional dabblers; chance hucksterers: most were there compelled by the supreme necessity of earning a living; others displayed their wares in order to provide luxuries; whilst a few were present merely for the fun of an infrequent bargain. As at other marts, there were those who represented the interests of sellers, and extracted a commission for their pains on all sales effected by their principals. Also, most of the chaffering was negotiated over drink, to obtain which adjournment was made to the handiest bar.

This exchange was as subject to economic laws as ruthlessly as are all other markets. There were fat times, when money was plentiful; lean nights, when buyers were scarce or sellers suffered from over-supply. To complete the resemblance, this mart was sensibly affected by world events, political happenings, the robustness or weakness of other markets of industry.

Men of all ages swarmed on the pavement; some were buyers, others were attracted by the fun of the fair. The family parties which were occasionally to be met with, as they scurried home to remote suburbs, seemed sadly out of place in this seething collection of vicious men and women.

An over-dressed black woman was there, as if to prove, if proof were needed, the universality of sin.

As the procession of painted faces loomed out of the fog, it seemed to Mavis as if they were lost souls in the spume of the pit.

She drew closer to the man at her side. London, life itself, seemed to the girl's jangled nerves to be a concentrated horror, from which, so it now appeared, the man beside her was her only safeguard. He had certainly insulted her, she reflected; but his conduct was, perhaps, excusable under the circumstances in which he had found her. Directly he had learned his mistake, he had rescued her from further contact with infamy, and had been gentle with her. In return, she had been scarcely civil to him, and had told him a lie when he had asked her if she were his old playmate.

As she walked with him, she bitterly reproached herself for her falsehood; she also tried to hide from herself that her rudeness had been largely assumed in order to conceal her growing regard for him. It would seem another world when he was not at her side to protect her from possible harm.

As they passed Burlington House, a beggar whined his tale of woe in their ears. Mavis saw Windebank give the man something, the handsomeness of which made the recipient open his eyes. A flower-seller, who had witnessed the generous act, immediately pestered Windebank to buy of her wares, an example at once followed by others of her calling. He gave them all money, at which some of them forced their wired flowers upon him, whilst others overwhelmed him with thanks.

"Don't thank me," he protested, as he glanced towards Mavis, who was the recipient of countless blessings, mechanically uttered.

Beggars and loafers, with their keen scent for prey, were about him in less time than it takes to tell. He gave largely, generously; he was soon the centre of a struggling, unsavoury crowd, which was growing larger every minute.

"Whatever are you doing?" protested Mavis.

"Wasn't it your wish?" he asked.

"Not this. Please, please get me out and away."

The next moment, Windebank, dragging Mavis after him, was vigorously making a passage through those who surrounded them. Once he saw his way clear, he ran forward, still keeping hold of her, and dragged her up Bond Street. They were still followed by the more persistent of the loafers, but a friendly policeman came to their aid, enabling them to pursue their unmolested way down Piccadilly.

"It is good of you to let me stay with you all this time," he said presently.

"What time is it?" she asked.

"I'll see. Why, I've lost my watch!"

"Not really?"

"I suppose it was stolen just now."

"Stolen?"

"Yes, you can see where the chain is snapped."

"Can't we do something?"

"What's the use?"

"But it must be got back. If it isn't, I shall feel it's all my doing."

"How can that be? Don't talk rot."

"I talked you into giving money away, and—"

"If you say any more, I'll be very angry," he interrupted. "What's a watch!"

Although she made no further reference to the matter, she thought the more of the loss he had sustained, which was owing to the representations she had made upon his duty to the needy. His indifference to the theft of his property the more inclined her in his favour.

As they walked, he was full of kindly anxiety for her present and future welfare. His ardent sincerity filled her with self-reproaches, the while he continued to express concern for her well-being. Presently, when they were passing St George's Hospital, she said:

"I wish you wouldn't talk so much about myself."

"It's so interesting," he pleaded.

"Why not talk more about yourself?"

"Never mind me."

"But I do. What on earth time will you get to bed?"

"Any time. It doesn't matter."

"Won't you be tired in the morning?"

"I shouldn't notice. I should be thinking of you."

"Nonsense; you'll be thinking about breakfast. Where do you sleep?"

"When I'm up like this, at a hotel in Jermyn Street."

"Are you comfortable there?"

"I only sleep there. I breakfast at the club."

"Where's that?"

"We passed it on the way down."

"How you must have wanted to get away! Your coat's undone."

"What of it?"

"Do it up."

"But—"

"You'll take cold. Do it up or I'll leave you at once."

"Don't be so considerate," he said, as he obeyed her behest. "It isn't kind."

"Why not?"

"It makes me fonder—I mean like you ever so much."

When they reached Sloane Street, he remarked:

"Do let me drive you. It's a shame to make you walk. You must be quite tired out."

"I'll leave you and get a 'bus," she replied.

"And you won't give me your address?"

"No."

Although heavily laden 'buses were constantly passing, she made no pretence of stopping one; not because she had no money: she had forgotten for the time being that she was penniless. Her mind was a welter of emotion. She regretted her sudden tenderness in the matter of his unbuttoned overcoat; she reproached herself for not leaving him directly she had got away from Mrs Hamilton's; she knew she would never forgive him for having insulted her; the fact of his having kissed her lips seemed in some mysterious way to bind them together; she hated herself for having denied that she was Mavis Keeves. The many leanings of her mind struggled for precedence; very soon, concern for the lie that she had told the man, who it was now evident wished her well, possessed her to the exclusion of all else. She suffered tortures of self-reproach, which became all but unendurable.

Windebank, who had been walking between her and the curb, suddenly moved so that she was on the outside.

"Why did you do that?" she asked.

"The wind. Little Mavis might take cold."

She could bear it no longer.

"Stop!" she cried.

He looked at her in surprise.

"I've something to tell you. I can't go on like this."

"What is it?" he asked, all concern.

"When you know, you'll never forgive me. I lied to you."

"Lied?"

"Yes, lied, lied, lied. But I can't let it go on. I hate myself for doing it. Why was I so wicked?"

"Give it up."

"My name. I told you a lie about it."

"Is that all?"

"Isn't that enough? I am Mavis Keeves. I am—"

"What?" he interrupted.

"I didn't like to confess it before. Don't, please don't think very badly of me."

"YOU—little Mavis after all?"

"Yes," she answered softly.

"What wonderful, wonderful luck! I can't believe it even now. You little Mavis! How did it all come about?"

"It's simple enough."

"Simple!" He laughed excitedly. "You call it simple?"

"Let me tell you. I was very miserable to-day and I prayed and—and—"

She could say no more; her overcharged feelings were such that they got the better of her self-control. Careless of what he might think, she leaned against him, as if for protection—leaned against him to weep bitter-sweet, unrestrained tears upon his shoulder.

"Poor little girl! Poor little Mavis!" he murmured.

The remark reinforced her tears.

The fog again enveloped them and seemed to cut them off from the observation of passers-by. It was as if their tenderness for each other had found an oasis in the wilderness of London's heartlessness.

Mavis wept unrestrainedly, contentedly, as if secure or sympathetic understanding. Although he spoke, she gave small heed to his words. She revelled in the unaccustomed luxury of friendship expressed by a man for whom she, already, had something in the nature of an affectionate regard.

Presently, when she became calmer, she gave more attention to what he was saying.

"You must give me your address and I'll write to my people at once," he said. "The mater will be no end of glad to see you again, and you must come down. I'll be down often and—and—Oh, little Mavis, won't it be wonderful, if all our lives we were to bless the day we met again?"

Although her sobs had ceased, she did not reply.

Two obsessions occupied her thoughts: one was an instinct of abasement before the man who had such a tender concern for her future; the other, a fierce pride, which revolted at the thought of her being under a possibly lifelong obligation to the man with whom, in the far-off days of her childhood, she had been on terms of economic equality. He produced his handkerchief and gently wiped her eyes. She did not know whether to be grateful for, or enraged at, this attention. The two conflicting emotions surged within her; their impulsion was a cause which threatened to exert a common effect, inasmuch as they urged her to leave Windebank.

This sentiment was strengthened by the reflection that she was unworthy of his regard. She had, of set purpose, lied to him, denied that she was the friend of his early youth. True, he had previously insulted her, but, considering the circumstances, he had every excuse for his behaviour. He certainly led a fast life, but, if anything, Mavis the more admired him for this symptom of virility; she also dimly believed that such conduct qualified him to win a wife who, in every respect, was above reproach. She was poor and friendless, she again reflected. Above all, she had lied to him. She was hopelessly unworthy of one who, in obedience to the sentimental whim she had inspired, seemed contemptuous of his future. She would be worse than she already was, if she countenanced a course of action full of such baleful possibilities for himself. Almost before she knew what she was doing, she kissed him lightly on the cheek, and snatched the violets he was wearing in his coat, before slipping away, to lose herself in the fog.

CHAPTER FIFTEEN
A GOOD SAMARITAN

Mavis heard him calling her name, first one way, then another; once, he approached and came quite near her, but he changed his direction, to pass immediately out of her ken.

She then hurried in the direction of what she believed to be Hammersmith; she could not know for certain, as the fog increased in intensity every minute. Her mind was too confused to ask anyone if she were going the right way, even if she had cared to know, which, at present, she did not. She was seized with a passion for movement, anything to distract her mind from the emotions possessing it. One moment, she blamed herself for having left Windebank as she had done; the next, she told herself and tried hard to believe that she had done the best conceivable thing under the circumstances.

She walked quickly, careless to where her footsteps led her, as if hurrying from, or to Windebank's side; she was not certain which she desired. She had walked for quite twenty minutes when she was brought up short by a blow on the forehead. Light flashed in her eyes; she put out her arms to save herself from a fall. She had walked into a tree, contact with which had bruised her face and torn skin from her forehead. Pain and dizziness brought her to the realisation of the fact that it was late, and that she was penniless; also, that she was unaware of her whereabouts. She resolved to get back to her lodging with as little delay as possible. She groped about, hoping to find someone who would tell her where she was and direct her to Kiva Street. After some minutes, she all but walked into a policeman, who told her how she was near the King's Road, Chelsea, also how to get to her destination. She hastened on, doing her utmost to follow his directions. This was not easy, the fog and the pain in her head both confusing her steps. Once or twice, she was almost overcome by faintness; then, she was compelled to cling to railings for support until she had strength to continue her way.

There came a time when her legs refused to carry her further; her head throbbed violently; a dark veil seemed to gradually blot out things as she knew them. She remembered no more.

When next she became dimly conscious, she seemed to be in a recumbent position in a strange room, where she was watching the doings of a woman who was unknown to her.

When Mavis first set eyes on this person, she appeared to be a decent, comely, fair-haired, youngish woman, who was dressed in the becoming black of one who had recently emerged from the mourning of widowhood. But as Mavis watched the woman, a startling transformation took place before her eyes. The woman began by removing her gloves and bonnet before a dressing glass, which was kept in position by a mangy hair brush thrust between the frame and its supports. Then, to the girl's wondering astonishment, the woman unpinned and took off her fair curls, revealing a mop of tangled, frowsy, colourless hair, which the wig had concealed. Next, she removed her sober, well-cut costume, also, her silk underskirt, to put on a much worn, greasy dressing-gown. Then, she pulled off her pretty shoes and silk stockings, to thrust her feet into worn slippers, through which her naked toes showed in more than one place.

Mavis rubbed her eyes; she expected every moment to find herself again in the street, clinging to the railings for support, at which moment of returning sense she would know that what she was now witnessing would prove to be an effect of her disordered imagination.

If what she saw were the result of a sick brain, it was a convincing, consistent picture which fascinated her attention.

The woman had taken up a not over-clean towel, to dip a corner of it in a jug upon the washstand before applying it to one side of her face. Mavis suffered her eyes to leave the woman in order to wander round the room. She was lying on a sofa at the foot of an iron bed. That part of the wall nearest to her was filled by the fireplace, in which a cheerful fire was burning; it looked as if it had recently been made up. Upon the mantelshelf were faded photographs of common, self-conscious people, the tops of which all but touched a framed print of the late Mr Gladstone. In the complementary recess to the one in which the washstand stood, was a table littered with odds and ends of food, some of which were still wrapped in the paper in which they had come from the shop. A smoking oil lamp, of which the glass shade had disappeared, and which was now shaded with the lid of a cardboard shoe box, cast elongated shadows of the occupier of the room on walls and ceiling as she moved. The atmosphere of the room was heavy with the mingled smell of paraffin oil and fugginess.

"Where—where am I?" asked Mavis.

"You've come round, then?" said the woman, who had just cleansed one side of her face of artificial complexion.

"How did I get here?"

"I found you outside as I came 'ome. I couldn't very well leave you like that."

"You're very kind."

"'Elp that you may be 'elped is my motto. An' then you didn't smell of drink. I wouldn't 'ave took you in if you had. Girls who're 'on the game' who drink ought to know better, and don't deserve sympathy."

Mavis stared at her wide-eyed, striving to recalled where she had heard that expression before, also what it meant.

"You sit quiet, dear; you'll be better directly," said the woman. "I've got to wash this stuff off. Beastly nuisance, but, if you don't, it stains the sheets and pillers, as I daresay you know."

Had Mavis possessed sufficient strength she would have combated this suggestion; it was as much as she could do to concentrate her wandering attention on the doings of the woman who had played good Samaritan in her extremity.

Mavis saw her cleanse the other side of her face and remove two false teeth from her mouth, actions which completed the transformation from that of a comely, interesting-looking, youngish woman to that of an elderly, extremely commonplace person with foxy, shifty eyes.

"Now I'm 'done.' I never feel reely at home till I get into my shirt sleeves, as you might say," remarked the woman.

Mavis sat up.

"'Ave a drink?" asked her benefactor.

"No, thank you."

"I don't mind a drop out of business hours, when I feel I've earned it, as you might say. I've got a quartern in a bottle. If I'd expected visitors, I'd have got more, but I'll go 'alves."

"No, thank you," repeated Mavis.

"Ah! Don't mind if I do?" said the woman, in the manner of one relieved of the possibility of parting with something that she would prefer to keep.

"Not at all."

The woman heated some water in a tin kettle, before mixing herself hot gin and water in a tooth glass, the edge of which was smudged with tooth powder.

"Smoke?"

"I do, sometimes," replied Mavis.

"Have a fag? A gentleman brought me these to-night."

Mavis somewhat reluctantly took and lit a cigarette. The woman did likewise, sipped her grog, and then brought a chair in order that she might sit by Mavis.

"What might your name be?"

"Keeves," answered Mavis shortly.

"Mine's Ewer—'Tilda Ewer. Miss, thank Gawd."

"You wear a wedding ring."

"Eh! That's business. And 'ow did you come to be overtook outside this 'ouse?"

"I walked far and was very tired."

"Rats!"

"I beg your pardon."

"Don't tell me. 'Ad a row with your boy, an' 'e biffed you on the 'ead. That's nearer the truth. And that's the worst of gentlemen in drink; but then, at other times, they're generous enough when they're in liquor, and don't mind if you help yourself to any spare cash they may 'appen to 'ave about them. It's as long as it's broad."

"You're quite wrong in thinking—" began Mavis.

"Don't come the toff with me," interrupted the woman. "If you was a reel young lady, you wouldn't be out on such a night, and alone. So don't tell me. I ain't lived forty—twenty-six years for nothink."

Mavis did not think it worth while to argue the point.

"What time is it?" she asked.

"'Alf-past two. I suppose I shall 'ave to keep you till the morning."

"I'll go directly. I can knock my landlady up."

"She's one of the right sort, eh? Ask no questions, but stick it on the rent!"

"If my head wasn't so bad, I'd go at once," remarked Mavis, who liked Miss Ewer less and less.

The woman took no notice of Mavis' ungracious speech: she was staring hard at Mavis' shoes.

"Fancy wearin' that lovely dress with them tuppenny shoes!" cried Miss Ewer suddenly.

"They are rather worn."

"Oh, you young fool! Beginner, I s'pose."

"I beg your pardon."

"Must be. No one else could be such a fool. Don't you know the gentlemen is most particular about underclothes, stockings and shoes?"

"It's a matter of utter indifference to me what the 'gentlemen' think," said Mavis with conviction.

"Go on!"

"Very well, if you don't believe me, you needn't."

"Here, I say, what are you?" asked Miss Ewer. "Tell me, and then we'll know where we stand."

"Tell you what?"

"Are you a naughty girl or a straight girl?"

"What do you mean?"

"Straight girls is them as only takes presents like silk stockings an' gloves from the gentlemen, like them girls in 'Dawes'."

"Girls in 'Dawes'!" echoed Mavis.

"They do a lot of 'arm; but yet you can't blame 'em: gentlemen will pay for anything rather than plank money down to them naughty girls as live by it."

"While I'm here, do you mind talking about something else?" asked Mavis angrily.

"I 'ave it. I 'ave it," cried Miss Ewer triumphantly. "You're one of the lucky ones. You're kep'."

"I beg your pardon."

"And good luck to you. Don't drink, keep him loving and generous, and put by for a rainy day, my dear: an' good luck to you."

"I'm well enough to go now," said Mavis, as she rose with something of an effort.

"Eh!"

"Thank you very much. Would you kindly show me the way out?"

"You've forgotten something, ain't yer?"

"What?"

"A little present for me."

"I've no money on me: really I haven't."

"Go on!"

"See!" cried Mavis, as she turned out the pockets of her cloak.

To her great surprise, many gold coins rolled on to the floor.

"Gawd in 'Eaven!" cried Miss Ewer, as she stooped to pick them up.

Mavis wondered how they had got there, till it occurred to her how Windebank, pitying her poverty, must have taken the opportunity of putting the money in her pocket when he insisted upon getting and helping her into her coat at the restaurant.

She at once told herself that she could not touch a penny piece of it, indeed the touch of it would seem as if it burnt her fingers. Her present concern was to get away as far from the money as possible.

"'Ow much can I 'ave?" cried Miss Ewer, who was on her knees greedily picking up the coins.

"All."

"All? Gawd's trewth!"

"Every bit. Only let me go; at once."

"'Ere, if you're so generous, ain't you got no more?" said Miss Ewer, the while her eyes shone greedily.

"I'll see," said Mavis, as she thoroughly turned out her pockets.

Another gold piece fell out; also, a bunch of violets.

"Vilets!" laughed Miss Ewer.

"Don't touch those. No one else shall have them," cried Mavis, as she wildly snatched them.

"You're welcome to that rubbage, and as you've given me all this, in return I'll give you a tip as is worth a king's money box."

"You needn't bother."

"You shall 'ave it. I've never told a soul. It's 'ow you can earn a living on the streets like me, and keep, like me, as good a maid as any lady married at St George's, 'Anover Square."

"Thank you, but—".

"Listen; listen; listen! It's dress quiet, pick up soft-looking gents, refuse drink, and pitch 'em a Sunday school yarn," said Miss Ewer impressively.

"But—".

"It's four pound a week I'm giving away. Tell 'em it's the first time you're going wrong; talk about your dead 'usband in 'is grave, an' the innocent little lovely baby girl in 'er cot (the gentlemen like baby girls better'n boys), as prayed for 'er mummy before she went to sleep. Then, squeeze a tear an' see if that don't touch their 'earts an' their pockets."

"Let me go! Let me go!" cried Mavis, horrified at the woman's communication.

"I thought I'd astonish you," said Miss Ewer complacently.

"Let me go. This way?"

"Too grateful to thenk me! Never mind; leave it till nex' time we meet. You can thenk me then. I thought I'd take your breath away."

"Let me out! Let me out!" cried Mavis, as she fumbled at the chain of the front door.

"Lemme. Good night, and Gawd bless yer," said Miss Ewer, furtively counting the gold pieces in her pocket.

Mavis did not reply.

"Thought I'd astonish yer. Fer Gawd's sake, don't whisper what I told you to a livin' soul. An' work 'ard and keep virtuous like me. Before Gawd, I'm as good a maid—"

These were the last words Mavis heard as she hurried away from Miss Ewer.

CHAPTER SIXTEEN
SURRENDER

Four weeks later, Mavis got out of the train at Melkbridge. She breathed a sigh of relief when her feet touched the platform; her one regret was that she was not leaving London further away than the hundred miles which separated Melkbridge from the metropolis. It seemed to her as if the great city were exclusively peopled with Mr. Orgles', Mrs Hamiltons, Miss Ewers, and their like. Ignorant of London's kindness, she had only thought for its wickedness. With the exception of one incident, she had resolved to forget as much as possible of her existence since she had left Brandenburg College; also, to see what happiness she could wrest from life in the capacity of clerk in the Melkbridge boot manufactory, a position she owed to her long delayed appeal to Mr Devitt for employment. The one incident that she cared to dwell upon was her meeting with Windebank and the kindly concern he had exhibited in her welfare. The morning following upon her encounter with him, she had long debated, without arriving at any conclusion, whether she had done well, or otherwise, in leaving him as she had done. As the days passed, if things seemed inclined to go happily with her, she was glad that she had put an end to their budding friendship, to regret her behaviour when vexed by the slings and arrows of outrageous fortune.

Her few hours' acquaintance with Windebank had ruffled the surface of the deep, unexplored waters of the girl's passion, which, rightly or wrongly, caused her to surrender her personal preferences and to regard the matter entirely from the man's point of view. This self-abasement was, largely, the result of the girl's natural instincts where her affections were concerned; these had been reinforced by the sentimental pabulum which enters so much into the fiction that is devoured by girls of Mavis' age and habit of thought. She argued how it would be criminally selfish of her to presume on his boyish attachment of the old days, which might lead him to believe that it was a duty for him to extend to his old-time playmate the lifelong protection of marriage.

Her lack of personal vanity was such that it never once occurred to her that she was eminently desirable in his eyes; that he wished for nothing better than for her to bestow herself, together with her affections, upon him for lifelong appreciation. She resolved to stifle her inclinations in order that the man's career should not suffer from legal companionship with a portionless, friendless girl.

Her unselfish resolutions faltered somewhat when, in resuming the weary search for chances of employment in the advertising columns of the newspapers, she came across the following, which was every day repeated for the remainder of the week:—

"To M...s, who foolishly lost herself in the fog on the night of last Thursday. She is earnestly urged to write to me, care of Taylor & Wintle, 43 Lincoln's Inn Fields. Do not let foolish scruples delay you from letting me hear from you."

She had got as far as writing a reply, but could never quite bring herself to post it.

A miserable Sunday had urged her to send it to its destination; the chance purchase of a Sunday paper decided the letter's, and, incidentally, her own fate. In it she read how, owing to threatened disturbance on the Indian frontier, Sir Archibald Windebank, D.S.O., would shortly leave Aldershot by S.S. Arabia with a reinforcing draft of the Rifle Brigade.

Mavis tore up her letter, to write another, which she addressed to the steamer which was to carry him the greater part of his long journey. She did not give her address; she told him how she believed it would be for his advantage not to encumber his noble career with concern for her. She had added that, if it were destined for them to meet, nothing would give her greater pleasure than to see him again. She ended by wishing him God-speed, a safe return, a successful and happy life. As the days passed, with all the indignities and anxieties attending the quest for employment, the girl's thoughts more and more inclined to Melkbridge. She longed to breathe its air, tread its familiar ways, steep herself in the scarcely awakened spirit of the place. She constantly debated in her mind whether or not she should write to Mr. Devitt to ask for employment. She told herself how, in doing what she had resolved upon doing only in the last extremity, she was giving no more hurt to her pride than it received, several times daily, in her hopeless search for work. A startling occurrence had put the fear of London into her heart and decided her to write to Melkbridge. She had been walking down Victoria Street, raging with anger at the insult that a rich photographer had offered her, to whom, in reply to an advertisement, she had applied for work, when her attention was attracted by a knot of people gathered about a hospital nurse, a girl, and a policeman.

The nurse, a harsh, forbidding-looking woman, was endeavouring to coax the girl into a waiting cab. The girl was excitedly appealing for release to the policeman, to the knot of spectators, to passers-by. When anyone displayed a sign of active interest in the matter, the nurse had put her finger to her forehead to signify that her charge was insane.

Mavis was about to avoid the gathering by crossing the road, when she caught a glimpse of the girl's face, to recognise it as belonging to Miss Meakin. Wondering what it could mean, she hastened to her old acquaintance, who, despite her protests, was being urged towards the cab.

"It's all a mistake. Let me go! Oh! won't anyone help?" Miss Meakin had cried as Mavis reached her side.

"What is it? What has happened?" asked Mavis.

"It's you: it's you! Thank Heaven!" cried Miss Meakin.

"What has happened? I insist on knowing," Mavis had asked, as she glanced defiantly at the forbidding-looking nurse.

"It's not a nurse. It's a man. I know he is. He's followed me, and now he's trying to get me away," sobbed the girl.

Mavis turned to the nurse, who put her finger to her forehead, as if to insist that Miss Meakin's mind was unhinged.

Mavis had appealed to the policeman, to declare there must be some mistake, as she knew Miss Meakin to be of sound mind; but this man had replied that it was not his place to interfere. Mavis, feeling anxious for her friend, was debating in her mind whether she should get into the cab with the girl and the nurse, when a keen-faced-looking man, who had listened to all that had been said, came forward to tell the policeman that if he did not interfere, his remissness, together with his number, would be reported to Scotland Yard.

The policeman, stirred to action, stepped forward, at which the nurse had sprung into the cab, to be driven away, when Miss Meakin had gone into hysterics upon Mavis' shoulder.

Later, after she had come to herself in a chemist's shop, she had told Mavis that she had left "Dawes'," and was now keeping house for an aunt who was reduced to taking in paying guests somewhere in North Kensington. She had been to Vincent Square to look up a late paying guest of her aunt's, who had taken with her some of the household linen by mistake. Upon her setting out for home, she had met with the uncanny adventure from which Mavis' timely arrival had released her.

Directly Mavis reached home, she had written to Mr Devitt. Four days passed, during which she heard nothing in reply. The suspense filled her soul with a sickening dread. Work at Melkbridge now promised alluring possibilities, qualities that had never presented themselves to her mind in the days when she believed that a letter from her would secure from Mr Devitt what she desired. To her surprised delight, the fifth morning's post had brought her a letter from Mr Devitt, which told her that, if she would start at once for Melkbridge, she could earn a pound a week in the office of a boot manufactory, of which he was managing director; the letter had also contained postal orders for three pounds to pay the expenses of her moving from London to Wiltshire. Mavis could hardly believe her eyes. She had already pawned most of her trinkets, till now there alone remained her father's gifts, from which she was exceedingly loath to part. The three pounds, in relieving her of this necessity, was in the nature of a godsend.

Now she stood on the platform at Melkbridge. Her luggage had been put out of the train, which had steamed away. Mavis thought that she would ask the station-master if he knew of a suitable lodging. The man whom she judged to be this person was, at present, engaged with the porters. While she waited till he should be at liberty, her mind went back to the time when she had last stood on the same platform. It had been on the day when she had come down to Melkbridge fully confident of securing work with the Devitt family. This had only been a few months ago, but to Mavis it seemed long years: she had experienced so much in the time. Then it occurred to her how often Archie Windebank had walked on the same platform—Archie Windebank, who was now on the sea so many hundreds of miles from where she stood. She wondered if he ever found time to think of her. She sighed.

Seeing that the station-master was disengaged, she approached the spectacled, dapper little man and told him of her wants.

"Would it be for long?" he asked.

"Possibly for years. I'm coming to work here."

"Work!"

"In the office of one of Mr Devitt's companies."

The man assumed an air of some deference.

"Mr Devitt! Our leading inhabitant—sings baritone," remarked the station-master.

"Indeed!"

"A fair voice, but a little undisciplined in the lower register. This is quite between ourselves."

"Of course. Do you think you can help me to find rooms?"

"I wish I could. Let me think."

Mr Medlicott, as he was called, put the tips of his fingers together, while he reflected. Mavis watched his face for something in the nature of encouragement.

"Dear! dear! dear! dear!" he complained.

"Don't bother. It's good of you to think of it at all," said Mavis.

"Stay! I have it. Why didn't I think of it before? Mrs Farthing: the very thing."

"Where does she live?"

"The Pennington side of Melkbridge—over a mile from here; but I know you'd find there everything that you desire."

"Thanks. I'll leave my boxes here and walk there."

"I can save you the trouble. Her husband is guard on the 4.52. If you can fill up the time till then, it will save you walking all that way, perhaps, for no purpose."

Mavis thanked the station-master, left her luggage in his care and walked to the town, where the unmistakable London cut of her well-worn clothes attracted the attention of the female portion of the population. She had a cup of tea in a confectioner's, and felt better for it. She then set out to walk to her old favourite nook on the banks of the river, a spot rich with associations of her childhood. Her nearest way was to walk across the churchyard to the meadows, the third of which bordered the Avon. It only needed a quarter of an hour's walk along its banks to find the place she wanted. Unconsciously, her steps led her in a contrary direction from that in which she had purposed going. Almost before she knew what she had done, she had taken the road to Haycock Abbey, which was Windebank's Wiltshire home. It required something of an effort to enable her to retrace her steps. She reached and crossed the churchyard, where long forgotten memories crowded upon her; it was with heavy heart that she struck across the meadows.

When she reached the Avon, she found the river to be swollen with the winter's rain. The water, seamed with dark streaks, flowed turbulently, menacingly, past her feet. She walked along the river's deserted bank to the place that she had learned to look upon as her own. Its discovery gave her much of a shock. She had always pictured it in her mind as when she had last seen it. Then, it had been in early July. The river had lazily flowed past banks gaily decorated with timid forget-me-nots and purple veitch; the ragged robin had looked roguishly from the hedge. Such was the heat, that the trees of her nook had looked longingly towards the cool of the water, while the scent of lately mown hay seemed to pervade the world. That was then.

Now, a desolation had invaded the spot. In place of summer gaiety there was only dreariness. The flowers had gone; a raw wind soughed along the river's banks; instead of the scent of the hay there was only the smell of damp earth, as if to proclaim to the girl that such desolation was the certain heritage of all living things.

Mavis could not get rid of the impression that the contrast between the place as she remembered it and as it was now resembled her own life. She made her way, with all dispatch, to the station. Here she learned that Mrs Farthing could not take her in until the following day, as her present "visitors" were not leaving till then. Mavis pricked up her ears at the mention of visitors; she did not think such polite euphemisms had penetrated so far afield.

She had little thought to give the matter, as she was concerned to know where she was going to spend the night. Mr Medlicott solved her perplexity; he insisted upon Mavis seeing Mrs Medlicott, who proved to be a simple, kindly countrywoman, who dropped an old-fashioned curtsey directly she set eyes on the girl. The station-master's wife showed Mavis a little room and told her that she was welcome to the use of it for the night, if she were not afraid of being kept awake by the passing and shunting of trains. Mavis jumped at the offer, whereat Mrs Medlicott insisted on her sitting down to a solid, homely tea, a meal which was often interrupted by Mr Medlicott getting up to attend to his duties upon the platform. When tea was over, there was yet another hour's daylight. Mrs Medlicott suggested to Mavis that it might be as well for her to call on Mrs Farthing, to see if she liked her; she mentioned that Mr Farthing was a very nice man, but that his wife was not a person everyone could get on with.

Mavis set out for the Pennington end of Melkbridge, where, after some inquiry, she found that Mrs Farthing lived in an old-world cottage, which was situated next door to a farm.

The girl's knock brought Mrs. Farthing, first to the window, then to the door, whereupon Mavis explained her errand, not forgetting to mention who had recommended her to come.

"Please to come inside," said Mrs. Farthing.

Mavis followed the woman, who was little and sharp-eyed, into a clean, orderly living room, where she was asked to take a seat. She was surprised to see her prospective landlady also sit, for all the world as if she were entertaining a guest.

"Did you say you were taking up church work?" asked Mrs Farthing.

"No, I did not."

"I thought you did," said Mrs Farthing, as her face fell.

"You see, my father was a sea captain, so I have to be so careful to whom I let my rooms."

"If I thought they weren't respectable, I shouldn't have come here," retorted Mavis.

Mrs Farthing winced, but recovered herself.

"Since I have been resident at Pennington Cottage, one colonel, three doctors, two lawyers, seven reverends, and one banker have visited here."

"I'm glad to see others appreciate you," remarked Mavis.

"Professional gentlemen and their ladies take to me at once. Did you tell me your uncle was a reverend?"

"No, I did not," replied Mavis, who was beginning to lose patience.

"You see, my father being a sea captain—"

"I can't see how that's anything to do with letting lodgings," said Mavis.

"Pardon me, it raises the question of references."

"Of course, I must have yours. I have only your word for the sort of people you've had here."

Mrs Farthing looked at Mavis in astonishment; she was unaccustomed to being tackled in this fashion.

"Perhaps, perhaps you'd like to see the sitting-room?" she faltered.

"I should," said Mavis.

Mrs Farthing led the way to a quaint little room, the window of which overlooked the neighbouring farmyard.

Mavis, although she took a fancy to it at once, was sufficiently diplomatic to say:

"It might, perhaps, suit me."

Mrs. Farthing pointed out the beauty of the view, a recommendation to which Mavis subscribed.

The girl's acquiescence emboldened Mrs Farthing to say:

"Did you say that your mother would sometimes visit you?"

Mavis trembled with indignation.

"I did nothing of the kind, and you know it," she cried. "If you wish to know, I'm employed by Mr Devitt, and should probably have stayed here for years. If you can't see at a glance what I am, all I can say is that you've been used to a tenth-rate lot of lodgers."

Mrs. Farthing capitulated.

"Wouldn't you like to see the bedroom?"

"If you don't ask any more silly questions."

"It's hard to forget my father was a sea captain," explained Mrs Farthing.

A door in the passage opened on to winding stairs, up which vanquished and victor walked.

From the first floor, a sort of gangway led to the door of a room that was raised some three feet from the level of where the two women stood.

"Now we ascend the Kyber Pass," cried Mrs Farthing gaily, as she set foot on the gangway.

As Mavis followed, it occurred to her how this remark might be invariably retailed to prospective lodgers by Mrs Farthing.

The bedroom's neat appointments made it even more attractive in Mavis' eyes than the sitting-room.

Mrs. Farthing wanted eight shillings a week for a permanency, but Mavis stuck out for seven. The issue was presently compromised by the landlady's agreeing to accept seven and sixpence.

"There's only one thing," said Mrs Farthing, as she sat on the bed; "and that's my husband."

"What about him?" asked Mavis, who had believed that everything was settled.

"He simply can't abide my letting rooms; he's on to me about it morning, noon, and night."

"I'm sorry."

"To think," as he says, "the daughter of a sea captain—" Here Mrs Farthing caught Mavis' eye, to substitute for what she was about to say: "But there," he says, "work your fingers to the bone; go and commit suicide by overdoing it; kill yourself outright with making other people comfortable, so long as you get your own way."

"Really!"

"That's what he says every minute of the time that he's at home."

When Mavis left Mrs Farthing to walk to the station, she could not help noticing how the rough and tumble of her experiences had had a hardening effect upon her once soft heart. It was not so long ago that, although presumption on a landlady's part would have goaded Mavis into making an apposite retort, she would have bitterly regretted the pain that her words may have inflicted. Now, she was indifferent to any annoyance that she may have caused Mrs Farthing. If anything, she was rather pleased with herself for having shown the woman her place.

It was something of an experience for Mavis to spend the evening in the sitting-room of a country railway station. Stillness violently alternated with the roar and rush of the trains. Mr Medlicott spent his spare time in the sitting-room, where his eyes never deserted the faded, uncanny-looking cabinet piano, which spread its expanse of faded green silk at one end of the room.

Mavis noticed his preoccupation.

"I wonder if you would do me a favour?" she asked.

"And what might that be?"

"If you would sing?"

"Delighted!" he cried, as he excitedly sprang to his feet.

"How nice of you!"

"Stay! What about the accompaniment?"

"I can manage that."

"At sight?"

"I think so."

"You're an acquisition to Melkbridge. There's one other thing."

"I knew you'd disappoint me. What is it?"

"The 7.53," replied the station-master, looking at his watch. "It's almost due."

"We can make a start," suggested Mavis.

Mr Medlicott quickly produced a collection of old-fashioned ballads, the covers of many of which were decorated with strange, pictorial devices.

"Stay! What say to 'Primrose Farm'?"

"Anything, so long as you sing," replied Mavis.

Mr Medlicott delightedly cleared his throat. It did not take Mavis long to discover that the station-master had little ear for music; he sang flat, although Mavis did her best to assist him by including in her accompaniment the notes of the vocal score. The song was no sooner concluded than the station-master caught up his braided cap and ran downstairs to meet the 7.53. Upon his return, he sang many songs. No sooner was one ended than he commenced another; they were only interrupted by the arrival of trains.

The room became insupportably hot. During one of Mr Medlicott's absences, Mavis asked his wife if she might open the window that overlooked the platform. Where Mavis sat by it, she could see Mr Medlicott performing his duties below. Once or twice, she fancied her ear caught strange sounds, which could be heard above the shouts of the porters and the noises of escaping steam; they proceeded from where Mr Medlicott stood. The noises became more insistent, when it occurred to Mavis that the station-master was taking advantage of the din to practise the more uncertain of his notes.

The next morning, when Mavis wanted to pay Mrs Medlicott, the station-master's wife would not hear of it. She declared that she was amply repaid by Mavis' accompanying her husband's songs, which was enough to make him happy for many weeks to come. Mrs Medlicott also observed that her husband would like to take singing lessons from Mavis, if the latter cared to teach him.

Mavis walked the good mile necessary to take her to the Melkbridge boot manufactory with a light heart. She reached it at nine, to find a square, unlovely building, enclosed by a high stone wall of the usual Wiltshire type, broken slabs of oolitic formation loosely thrown together. She explained her errand to the first person she met inside the gate, and was told to await the arrival of Mr Gaby, the manager, who was due in half an hour, the time, she afterwards learned, at which the lady clerks were expected. When Mr Gaby came, she found him to be a nervous, sandy-haired man, who blushed like any school-girl when he addressed Mavis. A few minutes later, two colleagues arrived, to whom she was formally introduced. The elder of these was Miss Toombs, a snub-nosed, short, flat-chested, unhealthy-looking woman, who was well into the thirties. She took Mavis' proffered hand limply, to drop it quickly and set about commencing her work. Her conduct was in some contrast to the other girl's, who was introduced to Mavis as Miss Hunter. She was tallish, dark, good-looking, with a self-possessed manner. The first two things Mavis noticed about her were that she was neatly and becomingly dressed, also that her eyebrows met above her nose. She looked at Mavis critically for a few moments, and gave the latter the impression that she had taken a dislike to her. Then Miss Hunter advanced to Mavis with outstretched hand to say:

"I hope we shall all be great friends and work together comfortably."

"Thank you," replied Mavis, at which Miss Hunter proceeded to instruct her in her duties. These were of the kind usually allotted to clerical beginners, and consisted of the registering, indexing, and sorting of all letters received in the course of the day.

Mavis worked with a will; her bold, unaffected handwriting emphasised the niggling scrawliness of Miss Hunter's previous entries in the book.

"Don't work so fast," said Miss Hunter presently, at which Mavis looked up in surprise.

"If you do, you won't have anything to go on with," continued Miss Hunter.

About eleven, Mavis learned from Mr Gaby that Mr. Devitt would like to see her. The manager conducted Mavis to the board room, where she found Mr Devitt standing before the fire. Directly he saw her, he came forward with outstretched hand.

"Good morning, Miss Keeves. Why—" He paused, to look at her with some concern.

"What's the matter?" she asked.

"You're different. If I may say so, you look so much more grown up."

"I've had rather a rough time since I last saw you."

"I can well believe it to look at you. Why didn't you write?"

"I didn't like to. It's good of you to do what you've done."

Mr Devitt appeared to think for a few moments before saying:

"I'm sorry I can't do more; but one isn't always in a position to do exactly what one would like."

"Quite so," assented the girl.

More was said to the same effect, although Mavis could not rid herself of the impression that he was patronising her. A further thing that prejudiced her against Devitt was his absence of self-possession. While speaking, he gesticulated, moved his limbs, and seemed incapable of keeping still.

"I'll pay you back the three pounds you so kindly sent me, gradually," said Mavis presently.

"Wouldn't hear of it; nothin' to me; only too happy to oblige you," declared Devitt, showing by his manner that he considered the interview at an end.

As she walked towards the door, he said:

"By the way, where are you stayin'?"

"At Mrs Farthing's; it's quite near here."

"Quite two miles from us," remarked Devitt, as if more pleased than otherwise at the information.

"Quite," answered Mavis.

"Well, good-bye! Let me know if I can ever do any-thin' for you," he cried from the fireplace.

Mavis went back to her work. She had an hour's liberty at one, which she spent at Mrs Farthing's, who provided an appetising meal of stewed steak and jam roly-poly pudding.

About three, Miss Toombs made tea on the office fire; she asked Mavis if she would like to join the tea club.

"What's that?" asked Mavis.

"You pay fourpence a week for tea and biscuits. We take it in turn to make the tea and wash up: profits equally divided at Christmas."

"I shall be delighted," said Mavis, as she produced her purse.

"Not till tomorrow. Today you're a guest," remarked Miss Toombs listlessly.

About four, there was so little to do that Miss Toombs produced a book, whilst Miss Hunter rather ostentatiously opened the Church Times. Mavis scribbled on her blotting paper till Miss Toombs brought out a brown-paper-covered book from her desk, which she handed to Mavis.

"It's 'Richard Feverel'; if you haven't read it, you can take it home."

"Thanks. I'll take great care of it. I haven't read it."

"Not read Richard Feverel?" asked Miss Toombs, as she raised her eyebrows, but did not look at Mavis.

"Is it always easy like this?" Mavis asked of Miss Hunter, as they were putting on their things at half-past four.

"You call it easy?"

"Very. Is it always like this?"

"Always, except just before Christmas, when there's a bit of a rush, worse luck," replied Miss Hunter, to add after a moment: "It interferes with one's social engagements."

Mavis walked to her rooms with a light heart. It was good to tread the hard, firm roads, with their foundation of rock, to meet and be greeted by the ruddy-faced, solidly built Wiltshire men and women, many of whom stopped to stare after the comely, graceful girl with the lithe stride.

When Mavis had had tea and had settled herself comfortably by the fire with her book, she felt wholly contented and happy. Now and again, she put down Richard Feverel to look about her, and, with an immense satisfaction, to contrast the homely cleanliness of her surroundings with the dingy squalor of Mrs Bilkins's second floor back. It was one of the happiest evenings she ever spent. She often looked back to it with longing in her later stressful days.

About seven, she heard a knock at her door. She called out "Come in," at which, after much fumbling at the door handle, a big fair man, with wide-open blue eyes, stood in the doorway. He looked like a huge, even-tempered child; he carried two paper-covered books in his hand.

"I'm Farthing, miss," the man informed her.

"Good evening," said Mavis, who would scarcely have been surprised if Farthing had brought out a handful of marbles and started playing with them.

"The driver's out, miss, so—"

"The driver?" interrupted Mavis.

"Mrs Farthing, miss. I be only fireman when her be about," he humbly informed her.

"Won't you sit down?"

"I? No, thankee, miss. I thought you might want summat to read, so I brought you these."

Here Mr Farthing handed Mavis a Great Western Railway time table, together with "Places of Interest on the Great Western Railway."

"How kind of you! I shall be delighted to read them," declared Mavis untruthfully.

Then, as Mr Farthing was about to leave the room, she said:

"I'm afraid I'm in your bad books."

"Bad what, Miss?" he asked, perplexed.

"Books—that you're offended with me."

"I, miss?"

"For coming here as your lodger?"

Mr Farthing stared at her in round-eyed amazement.

"I understood from Mrs Farthing that you object to her taking lodgers," explained Mavis.

Mr Farthing's jaw dropped; he seemed dumbfounded.

"That you're complaining about Mrs Farthing overworking herself every minute you're at home," continued Mavis.

Mr Farthing backed to the door.

"And you tell her she's only killing herself by doing it."

Hopelessly bewildered, Mr Farthing clumped downstairs.

Mavis laughed long and softly at this refutation of Mrs Farthing's pretensions. Before she again settled down to the enjoyment of her book, she looked once more about the cleanly, comfortable room, which had an indefinable atmosphere of home.

"Yes, yes," thought Mavis, "it is—it is good to be alive."

CHAPTER SEVENTEEN
SPRINGTIME

Days passed swiftly for Mavis; weeks glided into months, months into seasons. When the anniversary of the day on which she had commenced work at the boot factory came round, she could not believe that she had been at Melkbridge a year. When she had padded the streets of London in quest of work, she had many times told herself that she had only to secure a weekly wage in order to be happy. Now this desire was attained, she found (as who has not?) that satisfaction in one direction breeds hunger in another. Although her twenty shillings a week had been increased to twenty-five, and she considerably augmented this sum by teaching music to pupils to whom Mr Medlicott recommended her, Mavis was by no means content. Her regular hours, the nature of her employment, the absence of friendship in the warm-hearted girl's life, all irked her; she fearfully wondered if she were doomed to spend her remaining days in commencing work at nine-thirty and leaving off at half-past four upon five days of the week, and one on Saturdays. If the fifty-two weeks spent in Melkbridge had not brought contentment to her mind, the good air of the place, together with Mrs Farthing's wholesome food, had wrought a wondrous change in her appearance. The tired girl with the hunted look in her eyes had developed into an amazingly attractive young woman. Her fair skin had taken on a dazzling whiteness; her hair was richer and more luxuriant than of yore; but it was her eyes in which the chief alteration had occurred. These now held an unfathomable depth of tenderness, together with a roguish fear that the former alluring quality might be discovered. If her figure were not as unduly stout as the skinny virgins of Melkbridge declared it to be, there was no denying the rude health apparent in the girl's face and carriage.

So far as her colleagues at the boot factory were concerned, Miss Toombs hardly took any notice of her, whilst Miss Hunter gave her the impression of being extremely insincere, all her words and actions being the result of pose rather than of conviction.

The only people Mavis was at all friendly with were Mr and Mrs Medlicott, whom she often visited on Sunday evenings, when they would all sing Moody and Sankey's hymns to the accompaniment of the cabinet piano.

When she had been some months at Melkbridge, a new interest had come into her life. One day, Mr Devitt, who, with his family, had showed no disposition to cultivate Mavis's acquaintance, sent for her and asked her if she would like to have a dog.

"Nothing I should like better," she replied.

"There's only one objection."

"One can't look gift dogs in the mouth."

"It's a she, a lady dog: there's risk of an occasional family."

"I'll gladly take that."

"She's rather a dear, but she's lately had pups, and some people might object to her appearance."

"I know I should love her."

"She's a cocker spaniel—her name's Jill. She belongs to my boy, Harold. But as he's away—"

"Then we've already met. I saw her the day I came down to see you from London. You're right—she is a dear."

"My boy, who is still away for his health—"

"I am sorry," Mavis interrupted.

"Thanks. He wrote to say that, as we—some of us—appeared to find her a nuisance, we'd better try and find her a happy home."

"I'm sure she'd be happy with me."

"What about your landlady?"

"I'd forgotten her. I must ask."

"If she doesn't mind, Jill's licence is paid till the end of the year."

"I do hope Mrs Farthing won't mind," declared Mavis hopefully.

Rather to her surprise, Mrs Farthing made little objection to Jill's coming to live with Mavis, her surrender being partly due to the fact of the girl's winsome presence having softened the elder woman's heart, but largely because it had got about Melkbridge that Mavis came of a local county family.

Mr Devitt, being told of this decision, sent Jill up in charge of a maid, who asked that its collar and chain might be returned to Melkbridge House.

Mavis took Jill in her arms, when it would seem by the dog's demonstrations of delight as if it had long been a stranger to affectionate regard.

"Be you agoing to keep un?" asked the maid.

"Why not?"

"I shouldn't. Hev a good look at un."

Mavis looked, to see that Jill's comparatively recent litter had been responsible for the temporary abnormal development of the parts of her body by which she had nourished her young.

"It's why Mrs Devitt wouldn't have un in the house. I don't blame her. I call it disgusting," continued this chip of Puritanical stock.

"I see nothing to object to. It's nature," retorted Mavis, who inwardly smiled to see how the Puritanical-minded young woman, who had looked askance at Jill's appearance, did not hesitate to grab the girl's proffered shilling.

Jill and Mavis were at once fast friends. The dog accompanied her mistress in all her rambles, where its presence routed the forces of loneliness which were beginning to lay siege to the girl's peace of mind. Jill slept on Mavis's bed, pined when she left her in the morning, madly rejoiced at her mistress' return from work, when the vigorous wagging of Jill's tail, together with the barks of delight which greeted Mavis, gave her a suggestion of home which she had never experienced since the days of Brandenburg College.

This year, spring came early, like a beautiful mistress who joins an enraptured lover before he dares to hope for her coming. With the lengthening days Mavis knew an increasing distress of mind. She became unsettled: outbreaks of violent energy alternated with spells of laziness, which, more often than not, were accompanied by headaches. Books of historical memoirs, hitherto an unfailing solace, failed to interest her. Love stories she would avoid for weeks on end, as if they were the plague, suddenly to fall to and devour them with avidity, when the inclination seized her.

It was not yet warm enough for her to sit in her nook; it was doubtful if she would have done so if the weather had been sufficiently propitious. The reason for her present indifference to the spot, which she had always loved, was that it bordered the Avon, and just now the river was swollen and turbulent with spring rains. Her soul ached for companionship with something stable, soothing, still. Perhaps this was why she preferred to walk by the canal that touched Melkbridge in its quiet and lonely course. The canal had a beauty of its own in Mavis' eyes: its red-brick, ivy-grown bridges, its wooden drawbridges, deep locks, and deserted grass-grown tow-paths were all eloquent of the waterways having arrived at a certain philosophic repose, which was in striking contrast to the girl's unquiet thoughts. Soon, as if in celebration of spring, both banks were gay with borders of great yellow butter-cups. It seemed to Mavis as if they decorated the tables of a feast to which she had not been asked. The great awakening in the heart of life proceeded exquisitely, inevitably. Mavis believed that, as the sun's rays had no real meaning for her, it was only by some cruel mischance that she was enabled to bear witness to their daily increasing warmth. She would tell the troubles of her disturbed mind to Jill, who tried to show her sympathy by licking her face. At night, she would often waken out of a deep sleep with a start, when her eagerly outstretched arms would grasp a vast emptiness. The sight of lovers walking together would bring hot blood to her head; the proximity of a young man would make her heart beat strangely.

She frequently found herself wondering why intercourse between man and woman was hedged about by innumerable restrictions. It seemed to her that what people called the conventionalities were a device of the far-seeing eye of the Most High to regulate the relations of His children. If any of these appeared to escape the ends for which they were made, she put down the failure to the imperfect construction of the human organism, the constant aberrations of which necessitated the restraints imposed by religion and morality.

Mavis soon descended from the general to the particular. Her mind continually dwelt on every incident of her brief acquaintance with Windebank: she found that it was as much as she could do to justify the exigent scruples which had made her repel the man's approaches. One day, the scales fell from her eyes. She had deserted the canal and was sitting in a field, some two miles from the town, where the few trees it contained were disposed as if they were continually setting to partners, in some arboreous quadrille. The surrounding fields were tipped at all angles, as if in petulant discontent of one-time flatness. With an effort she could discern, Jill's tail wagging delightedly from a hole in a ditch, where she was hunting a rabbit. The voice, the sights, the sounds of nature, all served to obliterate the effect of life, as she had, hitherto, regarded it, upon her processes of thought. Archie Windebank's wealth, social position and career were as nought to her; he appealed to her only as a man, and her conceivable relationship to him was but as female to male.

All other considerations, which she had before believed of importance, now seemed trivial and inept. She wondered how she could have been blinded for so long. She bitterly reproached herself for her high-flown scruples, which now savoured of unwholesome affectation; but for these, she might not only have been a happy wife, but she might, also, have proved the means of conferring happiness upon another, and he a dearly loved one.

She called to Jill and sorrowfully went home. Three weeks later was Whit Monday, a day which, being a holiday, she was able to devote to her own uses. She had planned to walk to the village of Preen, an ancient hamlet set upon a hill that overlooked Salisbury Plain, which was distant some five miles from Melkbridge; but, at the last moment, her distress of mind was such that she abandoned the excursion. Lethargy had succeeded to her disturbed thoughts—lethargy that made her look on life through grey spectacles. Instead of setting out for Preen, she walked aimlessly about the town, accompanied by Jill. Presently she went up Church Walk, at the top of which she saw that the church door was open. She had a fancy for walking by the grave-stones, so Mavis tied Jill up to the gate of the churchyard with the lead which she usually carried.

As Mavis wandered among the moss-grown stones, which bore almost undecipherable inscriptions, she wondered if those they covered had led happy, contented lives, or if they were afflicted with unquiet thoughts, unsatisfied longings, and dull despair, as she was. The church was empty and cool; she walked inside, to sit in the first pew she chanced upon. It was the first time that she had sat all alone in the church; its venerable appearance now cried aloud for recognition and appreciation. As if to accentuate its antiquity, some of the aisles and walls bore the disfiguring evidences of an unfinished electric light and electric organ-blowing installation, which was in the process of being made, despite the protests of the more conservative among the worshippers. She did not know whether to stay or to go; she seemed incapable of making up her mind. Then, almost before she was aware of it, the organ commenced to play softly, appealingly; very soon, the fane was filled with majestic notes. Mavis was always acutely sensitive to music. In a moment, her troubles were forgotten; she listened enrapt to the soaring melody. The player was not the humdrum organist of the church, neither did his music savour of the ecclesiastical inspiration which makes its conventional appeal on Sundays and holy days. Instead, it spoke to Mavis of the travail, the joy of being, the night, sunlight, sea, air, the gay and grey pageant of life: the player appeared to be moved by all these influences. Not only was he eloquent of life, but he seemed to read and understand Mavis' soul and the perplexities with which it was confronted. Her heart went out to this sympathetic and intimate understanding of her needs; body and soul, she surrendered herself to the musician's mood. Very soon, he was playing upon her being as if she were but another instrument, of which he had acquired the mastery. Her imagination, stirred to its depths, took instant wing. It seemed as if the hand of time were put back for many hundreds of years to a day in a remote century. The building, bare of memorial inscriptions, was crowded with ecclesiastics, monks, nobles and simple; she could see the gorgeous ceremonial incidental to the occasion; the chanting of monks filled her ears; the rich scent of incense lay heavy on the air; lights flickered on the altar. Night came, when silence seemed to have forever enshrouded the world; many nights, till one on which the moonlight shone upon the figure of a young man keeping his vigil beside his armour and arms. Then, in a moment, the church was filled with sunlight, and gay with garlands and bright frocks. The knight and his bride stood before the altar, while the world seemed to laugh for very joy. As the newly-made man and wife left the church, old-world wedding music sounded strangely in Mavis' ears. The best part of a year passed. A little group stood about the font, where the life, that love had called into being, was purged of taint of sin by holy church.

Next, martial music rent the air; a venerable ecclesiastic blessed the arms and aims of a goodly company of stout-hearted men. When the echoes of the martial music had died away, the fane was deserted, save for one lone woman, who offered up continual supplication for her absent lord.

Cries and lamentations fell on Mavis' ears: to the music of a military march, the brave young knight was borne to burial. Soon, the moonlight fell upon the church's first monument, beside which the tearless and kneeling figure of a woman often prayed. It was not so very long before the widow was carried to rest beside her husband; it seemed but little longer when the offspring of her love stood before the altar with the bride of his choice.

The foregoing scenes were many times repeated, as, thus, life moved down the centuries, differing not at all but for changes in personality and dress. The church looked on, unmoved, unaltered, save for signs of age and an increasing number of memorials raised to the dead. The procession of life began by fascinating and ended by paining Mavis.

It was as if she were the spectator of a crowd in which her heart ached to mix, despite the distressing penalties of pain to which those she envied were, at all times, subject. It was as if she were forever cut off from the pleasures of her kind, to gain which the risk of mental and physical torments was well worth the running. It seemed as if her youth, sweetness, and immense capacity for loving, were doomed to wither unsought, unappreciated in the desert of her destiny. As if to save herself from such an unkind fate, she involuntarily fell on her knees; but she did not pray, indeed, she made no attempt to formulate prayer in her heart. Perhaps she thought that her dumb, bruised loneliness was more eloquent than words.

She remained on her knees for quite a long time. When she got up, the music stopped. The contrast between the sound and the succeeding silence was such that the latter seemed to be more emphatic than the melody.

When she, presently, rose to go, she saw a man standing just behind her in the aisle; he was elderly and homely-looking, with soft, far-away eyes.

"Good morning, miss," said the man.

"Good morning," replied Mavis, wondering who he could be.

"I hoped—you zeemed to like my playing."

"Was it you who played so beautifully?"

"I was up there practising just now."

"Do you often practise like that?"

"It isn't often I get the chance; I'm mostly busy varming."

"Farming?"

"That's it. And what with bad times, one doesn't get much time for the organ. And when one does, one's vingers run away with one."

"You a farmer?"

"At Pennington Varm. My name's Trivett, miss. If ever you would come in to tea, Mrs Trivett would be proud to welcome 'ee."

"I should be delighted. Perhaps, if you would like to teach me, I'd have organ lessons."

"I get so little time, miss. What day will 'ee come to the varm?"

"Next Saturday, if I may,"

"That's zettled. I'm glad you be coming zoon; the colour of the young grass be wonderful."

"Indeed!" remarked Mavis, as she looked at him, surprised.

"That's the advantage of varming," continued Trivett: "you zee natur in zo many colours and zo many moods."

Thus talking, they reached the churchyard gates, where Mavis released Jill, who was delighted at being set at liberty.

Mavis said goodbye to Trivett and recrossed the churchyard on her way to the river. As she walked, she wondered at Trivett's strange conjunction of pursuits; also, if he were as good a farmer as he was a musician.

She found the part of the river nearest to the church crowded with holiday bathers, so turned aside in the direction of her nook, where she was tolerably certain of getting quiet. Arrived there, she found her expectation was not belied. She felt dazed and tired with the emotions she had experienced; she reclined on the ground to look lazily at the beauty spread so bountifully about her.

Nature was now at her best. She was like a fair young mother radiant with the joys attaching to the birth of her firstborn. The striking of the quarter on the church clock was borne to her on the light wind; she heard a rumble and caught a glimpse through the young foliage of the white panelled carriages of a train speeding to Weymouth.

She settled herself for a repose of suspended thought, thankful that there was no prospect of her peace being interfered with. She had not lain long when she was disturbed by a plashing of water, at which Jill was vigorously barking.

She raised her head to see a man swimming; her eyes were fascinated by the whiteness of the man's flesh. After a while, he returned, to pass and repass her two or three times. Then, to her consternation, he approached the bank near to where she lay. She sat up; a few moments later, the man's head and shoulders appeared among the grasses upon the river bank.

"Good morning," said the man.

Mavis took no notice, but called to Jill.

"Good morning," repeated the man, who was young and pleasant-looking.

Mavis did not reply.

"Would little Mavis mind moving a little further up the bank?" continued the man.

Mavis looked at him in astonished anger.

"Because I can't get to my clothes until you do."

Mavis got up, called to Jill, and turned her back on the nook, wondering how on earth the man could have known her name; also, why he had the impertinence to address her so familiarly.

She did not get very far, because, call as she might to Jill, the spoiled dog took no notice of her summons, but remained about the place that her mistress had left.

Mavis called vainly for some minutes, till, at last, Jill appeared, carrying the man's collar in her mouth. Mavis tried to induce the dog to come to her, but, instead, Jill raced madly round and round, delighted with her find.

Very soon the man appeared, now dressed in a flannel suit, but collarless; a bath towel was thrown over his shoulder. He advanced to Mavis in leisurely fashion.

"Bother the man!" she thought.

"May I introduce myself?" he asked, as he lifted his hat.

"No, thank you," she replied coldly.

"There's no occasion. We've already met," he continued.

"I'm sure we haven't, and I haven't the least wish to know you."

"Rot! I'm Charlie Perigal."

"Charlie Perigal!"

"Yes. And how is little Mavis after all these years? But there's little need to ask."

Here he stared at her with an immense admiration in his eyes.

CHAPTER EIGHTEEN
CHARLIE PERIGAL

Mavis looked at the friend of her youth. As she saw him now, he was, in appearance, but a grown-up replica of the boy she remembered. There were the same steely blue eyes, curly hair, and thin, almost bloodless lips. With years and inches, the man had acquired a certain defiant self-possession which was not without a touch of recklessness; this last rather appealed to Mavis; she soon forgot the resentment which his earlier familiarity had excited.

"You haven't altered a bit!" she declared.

"But you have."

"I know. I'm quite an old woman."

"That's what I was going to say."

"Thanks."

"I knew you'd be pleased. May I have my collar?"

"It's that naughty Jill. I am so sorry."

Mavis rescued the collar from the dog's unwilling mouth.

"How did you know it was me?"

"I guessed."

"Nonsense!"

"Why nonsense?"

"You aren't clever enough."

"Quite right. The pater told me you were to be found in Melkbridge."

"Your father! How did he know?"

"He knows everything that goes on here, although he never goes anywhere. And then, when I asked one or two people about you, they said you were always about with a black cocker."

"Is this the first time you've seen me?"

"Why shouldn't it be?"

"I've been here fifteen months."

"Working for old Devitt. I've only been back a week."

"From where?"

"Riga."

"In Russia! How interesting!"

"Don't you believe it. Beastly hole."

"It's abroad."

"Any place is beastly when one has to be there. And you've been here a whole fifteen months. Think what I've missed!"

Mavis had, by now, got over her first excitement at meeting her old friend: her habitual prudence essayed to work—essayed, because its customary vigour was just now somewhat impaired.

"I'm glad to have met you again. Good-bye," she said.

"Eh!"

"It's time I got back."

The man stared at her in some astonishment.

"Perhaps you're right," he remarked presently.

"Right!" she echoed, faintly surprised.

"I'm only a waster. Nobody wants anything to do with me."

Something in the tone of the man's voice stirred her heart to pity.

"I'm not a bit like that," she said.

"Rot! All women are alike. When a chap's down, they jump on him. After all, you can't blame 'em."

Mavis stood irresolute.

"Good-bye," said Perigal.

"One moment!"

"I can't wait. I must be off too."

"I want to ask you something."

"What is it? Remember, I didn't ask you to wait."

"Who has given you a bad name, and why?"

"Most people who know me."

"I read the other day that majorities are always wrong," she remarked.

"Majorities are always right, just the same as minorities and everybody else."

"Everybody right!"

"According to their lights. We are as we are made, and, whatever some people say, we can never be anything else. And that's the devil of it. It's all so unfair."

"Why unfair?"

"It's just one's confounded luck what temperament one's inflicted with. I should think you were to be congratulated. You look as if you could be infernally happy."

"Aren't you?"

"Who is?"

"Loads of people," she declared emphatically.

"The very vain and the very stupid. Who else?"

Mavis was beginning to be interested. It amused and, at the same time, touched her to notice the difference between the dreary nature of the sentiments and the youthful, comely face of the speaker.

"I'm going now," she said.

"Frightened of being seen with me?" he asked.

"When I've Jill for a chaperone?"

"Why don't you come as far as Broughton with me?"

"Across the river?"

"I've a punt moored not far from here."

"But I've got to get back to a meal."

"We can get something to eat there."

"I don't think I will."

"Is it too far?"

"I can walk any distance."

"Someone was asking about you the other day."

"Who?"

"Archie Windebank. He wrote from India."

"What did he say?" asked Mavis, striving to conceal the interest she felt.

"I forget, for the moment, what it was. If I remember, I'll tell you."

"Don't forget."

"He's rather keen on you, isn't he?"

"How should I know?"

"He's a fool if he isn't."

"What makes you think he is?"

"I'd only an idea. Are you coming to Broughton?"

"I'll compromise. I'll come as far as your punt."

"Spoken like a good little Mavis."

They followed the course of the river. The stream's windings were so vigorous that, when they had walked for some way, they had made small progress in the direction in which Perigal was going.

Mavis was strangely happy. With the exception of her brief acquaintance with Windebank, she had never before enjoyed the society of a man, who was a gentleman, on equal terms. And Windebank was coming home unharmed from the operations in which he had won distinction; she had read of his brave doings from time to time in the papers: she rejoiced to learn that he had not forgotten her.

"Thinking of Windebank?" asked Perigal, noticing her silence.

"Yes."

"Lucky chap! But he's an awfully good sort, straight-forward and all that."

Mavis again assented.

"A bit obvious, though."

"What do you mean by that?"

"Eh! Oh, well, you always know what his opinions are going to be on any given subject."

"I think he's delightful."

"So do I," assented Perigal, to add, as a qualifying afterthought, "A bit tiring to live with."

"I'm sorry, but I can't speak from experience," retorted Mavis, who disliked Perigal to criticise her friend.

They had now reached the spot where the punt was moored. It was a frail craft; the bows seemed disposed to let in water.

"Is it goodbye?" asked Perigal.

"Of course," replied Mavis irresolutely.

"Then it isn't good-bye," smiled Perigal.

"Why?"

"Because you're going to do what I wish."

Mavis was sure that she was going to do nothing of the kind, but as Perigal looked at her and smiled she became conscious of a weakening in her resolution: it was as if he had fascinated her; as if, for his present purpose, she were helpless in his hands. Consequently, she said:

"To disappoint you, I'll come as far as the other side of the river."

"What did I tell you? But it's only fair to let you know the river runs a bit just here, and it's too deep to pole, so you have to hit the opposite bank when you can."

"Is there any danger?"

"Nothing to speak of."

"I'd love to cross."

"Jump in, then."

"You don't mind if I leave you on the other side?"

"Yes, I do. You hang on to Jill."

Mavis enticed Jill into the punt, where the dog sat in the stern in her usual self-possessed manner. Perigal struggled with the rope by which the punt was moored to the stump of a tree. Very soon, they were all adrift on the stream. They made little progress at first, merely scraping along the overhanging branches of pollard willows; now and again, the punt would disturb long-forgotten night lines, which, more often than not, had hooked eels that had been dead for many days. Mavis began to wonder if they would ever get across.

"Stand by!" cried Perigal suddenly, at which Mavis gripped both sides of the punt.

It was well she did so, for the next moment the punt swerved violently, to blunder quickly down stream as it felt the strength of the current.

"Are you frightened?" asked Perigal.

"Not a bit."

"Hold tight to the bank if your end strikes first."

"Right you are."

Perigal did his best to steer the punt, but without much success. Presently, the bows hit the side, at which Perigal clutched at the growth on the bank.

"Step ashore quickly," he cried. "It's beginning to let in water."

"How exciting!" remarked Mavis, as she stepped on to the bank.

"Just wait till I tie her up."

"Where's Jill?" asked Mavis suddenly.

"Isn't she with you?"

"See if she's in the river."

"If she is, the punt striking the bank must have knocked her overboard."

They looked, but no sign could be seen of the dog. Mavis called her name loudly, frantically, but no Jill appeared.

"What shall I do? Oh, what shall I do?" she cried helplessly.

"Look!" cried Perigal suddenly. "Look, those weeds!"

Mavis looked in the direction indicated. About six feet from the bank was a growth of menacing-looking weeds under the water, which just now were violently agitated.

"I'll bet anything it's Jill. She's caught in the weeds," said Perigal.

"Let me come. Let me come," cried Mavis.

"It's ten feet deep. You're surely not going in?"

"I can't let her drown."

"Let me—"

"But—"

"I'm going in. I can swim."

Perigal had thrown off his coat, kicked off his boots.

The next moment, he had dived in the direction in which he believed Jill to be.

Mavis was all concern for her pet. Although she knew that, more likely than not, she would never see her alive again, she scarcely suffered pain at all. Although incapable of feeling, her mind noted trivial things with photographic accuracy—a bit of straw on a bush, a white cloud near the sun, the lonely appearance of an isolated pollard willow. Meantime, Perigal had unsuccessfully dived once; the second time, he was under the water for such a long time that Mavis was tempted to cover her eyes with her hands. Then, to her unspeakable relief, he reappeared, much exhausted, but holding out of the water a bedraggled and all but drowned Jill.

"Bravo! bravo!" cried Mavis.

"Give me a hand, or have Jill!" gasped Perigal.

Mavis put one foot in the punt in order to take Jill. She held her beloved friend for a moment against her heart, to put her on the floor of the punt and extend a helping hand to Perigal.

"How can I ever thank you?" she asked, as he stood upon the bank with the water dripping from his clothes.

"Easily."

"How?"

"By coming with me to Broughton."

"But Jill!"

"She'll be all right. See, she's better already."

He spoke truly. Jill was alternately licking her paws and feebly shaking herself.

"But what about you? You ought to go home at once and run all the way."

"I shall be all right. Are you going to Broughton?"

"On one condition."

"And what might that be—that I don't go with you?"

"That you run all the way and, when you get there, you borrow a change of clothes."

"Then you'll really come?"

"Since you wish it. I couldn't do less."

"What did I tell you? But there's an inn on the left, the first one you come to. Wait for me there; if they can't lend me a change I'll have to get one somewhere else and come back there."

"Only if you go at once. You've waited too long already."

Perigal started, carrying his dry boots and coat.

"Faster! faster!" cried Mavis, seeing that he was inclined to linger.

She followed behind; she did not move with her customary swinging stride, Jill's extremity having sapped her strength. Directly Perigal was out of sight, she caught Jill in her arms, to smother her wet head and body with kisses.

"Oh, my darling! my darling!" she murmured. "To think how nearly we were parted forever!"

It was with something of an effort that she pursued her way to Broughton. Her steps dragged; her mind was filled with a picture of her dearly loved Jill, cold, lifeless, unresponsive to her caress.

When she reached the inn, she learned that Perigal was upstairs changing into the landlord's clothes. When he came down, clad in corduroys, with a silk handkerchief about his throat, she was surprised to see how handsome he looked.

"So you've got here!" he remarked, as he saw Mavis.

"Didn't I say I was coming?" she asked, as she sank on a seat in the tiny sitting-room.

"You look bad. You must have something."

"I'd like a little milk, please."

"Rot! You must have brandy."

"I'd prefer milk."

"You do as you're told," replied Perigal.

Fortunately, the inn had a spirit licence, so Mavis sipped the stuff that Perigal brought her, to feel better at once. She then soaked a piece of biscuit in the remainder of the brandy, to force it down Jill's throat. Next, she turned to Perigal.

"Have you had any?" she asked.

"What do you think?"

"I don't know how to thank you for saving Jill's life."

"Rot!"

"If you won't let me thank you, perhaps you'll let Jill."

Mavis held Jill in Perigal's face, when, to the girl's surprise, Jill growled angrily.

"What wicked ingratitude!" cried Mavis. "Oh, you naughty Jill!"

"Perhaps she's sorry I didn't let her drown," remarked Perigal.

"What!" cried Mavis.

"She may have wanted to commit suicide."

"Jill want to leave me?"

"She felt unworthy of you. I suppose she growls because she sees right through me."

"Don't be so fond of disparaging yourself. It was very brave of you to dive in as you did."

"I'm going to ask you to do something really brave."

"What's that?"

"Tackle eggs and bacon for lunch. It's all they've got."

"I'll be very brave. I'm hungry."

A red-cheeked, bright-eyed young woman laid a coarse cloth, and, upon this, black-handled knives and forks.

"What will you have to drink?" asked Perigal.

"Milk."

"Have some wine."

"I always drink milk."

"Not in honour of our meeting?"

"You seem to forget I've got to walk home."

"Perhaps you're right. Goodness knows what they'd give you here. Not like the Carlton or the Savoy."

"I've never been to such places."

"Not?" he asked, in some surprise, to remain silent till the fried eggs and bacon were brought in.

"You ought to drink something warm," said Mavis, as he piled food on her plate.

"I've ordered ginger brandy. It's the safest thing they've got."

The food enabled Mavis to recover her spirits. It appeared to have a contrary effect on Perigal; the little he ate seemed to incline him to gloomy thoughts.

"I'm afraid you're going to be ill," she remarked.

"I'm all right. Don't worry about me."

"I won't. I'll worry the eggs and bacon instead."

Presently, he raised the glass of ginger brandy in his hands.

"Here's to the unattainable!" he said.

"And that?"

"Happiness."

"Nonsense! Everyone can be happy if they like."

"Little Mavis, let me tell you something."

"Something dismal?"

"No one ever was, is, or can be really happy: it's a law of nature."

"I've come across people who're absolutely happy."

"Listen. Nature, for her own ends, the survival of the fittest, has arranged matters so that we're always, always striving. We think that a certain end will bring happiness, and struggle like blazes to get it, to find that satisfaction is a myth; to discover that, no sooner do we possess a thing than we weary of what was once so ardently desired, and immediately crave for something else which, if obtained, gives no more satisfaction than the last thing hungered for."

"I don't believe it for a moment. Besides, why should it be?"

"Because it's necessary to keep the species going. By constantly fighting with others for some goal, it sharpens our faculties and makes us more fitted to hold our own; if it weren't for this struggle, we should stagnate and very soon go under."

"Even if some of what you say is true, there's the pleasure of getting."

"At first. But if one 'spots' this clever trick of nature and one is convinced that nothing, nothing on earth is worth struggling for—what then?"

"That it's a very foolish state of mind to get into, and the sooner you get out of it the better."

"You said just now there was the pleasure of getting. I know something better."

"And that?"

"The pleasure of forgetting."

He glanced meaningly at her.

"Are you forgetting now?" she asked.

"Can you ask?"

Mavis blushed; she bent down to pat Jill in order to conceal the pleasure his words gave her.

"Tell me what Archie Windebank said about me," she presently said.

"Blow Windebank!"

"I want to know."

"Then I suppose I must tell you."

"Of course: out with it and get it over."

"You met him once in town, didn't you?"

"Only once."

"Where?"

"Quite casually. Tell me what he said."

"He wanted to know if I'd ever run across you, and, if I did, I was at once to wire to him and let him know."

"Are you going to?"

"No fear," replied Perigal emphatically.

"Aren't men very selfish?" she asked.

"They are where those women they admire are concerned."

At the conclusion of the meal, they sat in the inn garden. They spoke of old times, old associations. Mavis gave Perigal an abridged account of her doings since she had last seen him, omitting to mention her experience with Mr Orgles, Mrs Hamilton, and Miss Ewer.

"I suppose you've run across a lot of chaps in London?" he presently remarked.

"No, I haven't run against any 'chaps', as you call them."

"Rot!"

"It's a fact."

"Do you mean to say you've never yet had a love affair?"

"That's a business that requires two, isn't it?"

"Usually."

"Well, I've always made a point of standing out."

"Eh!"

"I suppose it's vanity—call it that if you like—but I think too much of myself to be a party to a mere love affair, as you would call it."

Perigal glanced at her as if to see if she were speaking seriously. Then he was lost in thought for some minutes, during which he often looked in her direction.

"What are you thinking of?" she asked.

"That, to a decent chap, little Mavis would be something of a find, as women go."

"You don't think much of women, then?"

"What's it my pater's always saying?"

"I can tell you: Always learn the value of money and the worthlessness of most women."

"Eh!"

"Don't look so astonished. It's the advice he gave to Archie Windebank."

"I see: and he told you. But the pater's right over that."

"How do you know?"

"That's telling."

Later in the afternoon, at tea, Mavis learned from Perigal much of his life since they had last met. It appeared that he had been to Oxford, to be sent down during his first term; that he had tried (and failed) for Sandhurst; also a variety of occupations, all apparently without success, until his father, angered at some scrape he had got into, had packed him off to Riga, where he had secured some sort of a billet for his son. Finally, in defiance of parental orders, he had left that "beastly hole" and was living at home until his father should turn him out.

"Isn't it all rather a pity?" Mavis asked.

"All what?"

"Your wasted life? And you've had so many good chances."

"I've had some fun out of it all. And, after all, what's the use of trying?"

"Just think of the thousands who would give their eyes for your chances," she urged.

"If their fathers had plenty of money like mine, they'd probably do as I."

"Your father wants to see you worthy of it."

"I am. I've all sorts of expensive tastes."

Later, when they walked in the direction of Melkbridge, it seemed to Mavis as if she were talking to a friend of many years; he seemed to comprehend her so intimately that she felt wholly at home with him. He had changed into his flannel suit, which had been dried before the inn kitchen fire. He walked with his careless stride, his cap thrust into his pocket. Now and again, Mavis found herself glancing at his fair young face, his steely blue eyes, the wind-disturbed curls upon his head. Their way led them past a field carpeted with cowslips.

"Oh, look!" she cried, delightedly.

"Cowslips! Are you keen on wildflowers?"

"They're the only ones I care for."

"I only care for artificial ones. Shall I get you some cowslips?"

"If you wouldn't mind. We'll both go."

They gathered between them a big bunch. Now and again they would race like children for a promising clump.

"This bores you awfully," she remarked presently.

"I don't believe I've ever been so happy in my life," he replied seriously.

"Nonsense!"

"A fact. Am I not with you?"

Mavis did not reply.

"And, again, it's all so natural, you and I being here alone with nature; it's all so wonderful; one can forget the beastly worries of life."

He spoke truly. Although it was getting late, the light persisted, as if reluctant to leave the gladness of newborn things. All about her, Mavis could see the trees were decked in fresh green foliage, virginal, unsoiled; everywhere she saw a modest pride in unaffected beauty. Human interests and emulations seemed to have no lot in this serenity: no habitation was in sight; it was hard for Mavis to believe how near she was to a thriving country town. Strange unmorality, with which immersion in nature affects ardent spirits, influenced Mavis; nothing seemed to matter beyond present happiness. She made Perigal carry the cowslips, the while she frolicked with Jill. He watched her coolly, critically, appraisingly; she had no conception how desirable she appeared in his eyes. Lengthening shadows told them that it was time to go home. They left the cowslip field regretfully to walk the remaining two miles to Melkbridge.

"I want you to promise me something," she said, after some moments of silence.

"What?"

"To promise me to do something with your life."

"Why should you wish that?"

"You saved Jill's life. If you hadn't, I should now be miserable and heart-broken, whereas—Will you promise me what I ask?"

He did not speak immediately; she put her hand on his arm.

"I was wondering if it were any use promising," he said, "I've had so many tries."

"Will you promise you'll try once more?"

"Yes."

"Thank you."

"I promise I'll try, for your sake."

They talked till they were within half a mile of the town. Then he said:

"I'm going to leave you here."

"Ashamed of being seen with me?"

"Why should I be ashamed?" he asked.

"I'm only a clerk in a boot factory."

"You needn't rub it in. No, I was thinking how people in Melkbridge would talk if they saw you with me or any other chap."

"People aren't quite so bad as that," she urged.

"No woman would ever forgive you for your looks."

"Well, goodbye; thank you for saving Jill's life, and thank you for a very happy day."

"Rot! It's I who should be thankful. You've taken me out of myself."

Neither of them made any move. Mavis caught hold of Jill and held her towards Perigal as she said:

"Thank him for saving your life, you ungrateful girl."

Jill growled at Perigal even more angrily than before.

"Oh, you naughty Jill!" cried Mavis.

"Not a bit of it; she's cleverer than you; she's a reader of character," said Perigal.

CHAPTER NINETEEN
THE MOON GODDESS

"Do you know anything of Mr. Charlie Perigal?" asked Mavis of Miss Toombs and Miss Hunter the following day, as they were sipping their afternoon tea.

"Why?" asked Miss Hunter.

"I met him yesterday," replied Mavis.

"Do you mean that you were introduced to him?" asked Miss Hunter calmly.

"There was no occasion. I knew him when I was a girl."

"I can't say I knew him when I was a girl," retorted Miss Hunter. "But I know this much: he never goes to church."

"What of that?" snapped Miss Toombs.

Miss Hunter looked at the eldest present, astonished.

"Is that you talking?" she asked.

"Why, what did I say?"

"You spoke as if it were a matter of no consequence, a man not going to church."

"I can't have been thinking what I said," remarked Miss Toombs, as she put aside her teacup to go on with her work.

"I thought not," retorted Miss Hunter.

"You haven't told me very much about him," said Mavis.

"I've never heard much good of him," declared Miss Hunter.

"Men are scarcely expected to be paragons," said Mavis.

"When he was last at home, he was often about with Sir Archibald Windebank."

"I know him too," declared Mavis.

"Nonsense!"

"Why shouldn't I? His father was my father's oldest friend."

Miss Hunter winced; she stared fixedly at Mavis, with eyes in which admiration and envy were expressed. Later, when Mavis was leaving for the day, Miss Hunter fussed about her with many assurances of regard.

To Mavis's surprise, Miss Toombs joined her outside the factory—surprise, because the elder woman rarely spoke to her, seeming to avoid rather than cultivate her acquaintance.

"I can say here what I can't say before that little cat," remarked Miss Toombs.

Mavis stared at the plainly clad, stumpy little figure in astonishment.

"I mean it," continued Miss Toombs. "She's a designing little hypocrite. I know you're too good a sort to give me away."

"I didn't know you liked me well enough to confide in me," remarked Mavis.

"I don't like you."

"Why not?" asked Mavis, surprised at the other woman's candour.

"Look at you!" cried Miss Toombs savagely, as she turned away from Mavis. "But what I was also going to say was this: don't have too much to do with young Perigal."

"I'm not likely to."

"Don't, all the same. You're much too good for him."

"Why? Is he fast?" asked Mavis.

"It wouldn't matter if he were. But he is what some people call a 'waster.'"

"He admits that himself."

"He's a pretty boy. But I don't think he's the man to make a woman happy, unless—"

"Unless what?"

"She despised him or knocked him about."

"I won't forget," laughed Mavis.

"Good day."

"Won't you come home to tea?"

"No, thanks," said Miss Toombs, as she made off, to leave Mavis gazing at the ill-dressed, squat figure hurrying along the road.

As might be expected, Miss Hunter's and Miss Toombs' disparagement of Charlie Perigal but served to incline Mavis in his favour. She thought of him all the way home, and wondered how soon she would see him again. When she opened the door of her room, an overpowering scent of violets assailed her nostrils; she found it came from a square cardboard box which lay upon the table, having come by post addressed to her. The box was full of violets, upon the top of which was a card.

She snatched this up, to see if it would tell her who had sent the flowers. It merely read, "With love to Jill."

Her heart glowed with happiness to think that a man had gone to the trouble and expense of sending her violets. Before sitting down to her meal, she picked out a few of the finest to pin them in her frock; the others she placed in water in different parts of the room. If Mavis were inclined to forget Perigal, which she was not, the scent of the violets was enough to keep him in her mind until they withered.

She did not write to acknowledge the gift; she reserved her thanks till their next meeting, which she believed would not long be delayed. The following Saturday (she had seen nothing of Perigal in the meantime) she called on Mrs. Trivett at Pennington Farm. The farmyard, with its poultry, the old-world garden in which the house was situated, the discordant shrieks which the geese raised at her coming, took the girl's fancy. While waiting for the door to be opened, she was much amused at the inquisitive way in which the geese craned their heads through the palings in order to satisfy their curiosity.

The door was opened by a homely, elderly woman, who dropped a curtsey directly when she saw Mavis, who explained who she was.

"You're kindly welcome, miss, if you'll kindly walk inside. Trivett will be in soon."

Mavis followed the woman to the parlour, where her hostess dusted the chair before she was allowed to sit.

"Do please sit down," urged Mavis, as Mrs Trivett continued to stand.

"Thank you, miss. It isn't often we have such a winsome young lady like you to visit us," said Mrs Trivett, as she sat forward on her chair with her hands clasped on the side nearest to Mavis, a manner peculiar to country women.

"I can't get over your husband being a farmer as well as a musician," remarked Mavis.

Mrs Trivett shook her head sadly.

"It's a sad pity, miss; because his love of music makes him forget his farm."

"Indeed!"

"And since you praised his playing in church, he's spent the best part of the week at the piano."

"I am sorry."

"At least, he's been happy, although the cows did get into the hay and tread it down."

Mavis expressed regret.

"You'll stay to tea and supper, miss?"

"Do you know what you're asking?" laughed Mavis.

"It's the anniversary of the day on which I first met Trivett, and I've made a moorhen and rabbit-pie to celebrate it," declared Mrs Trivett.

Mavis was a little surprised at this piece of information, but she very soon learned that Mrs Trivett's life was chiefly occupied with the recollection and celebration of anniversaries of any and every event which had occurred in her life. Custom had cultivated her memory, till now, when nearly every day was the anniversary of something or other, she lived almost wholly in the past, each year being the epitome of her long life. When Trivett shortly came in from his work, he greeted Mavis with respectful warmth; then, he conducted his guest over the farm. Under his guidance, she inspected the horses, sheep, pigs and cows, to perceive that her conductor was much more interested in their physical attributes than in their contributive value to the upkeep of the farm.

"Do 'ee look at the roof of that cow barton," said Trivett presently.

"It is a fine red," declared Mavis.

"A little Red Riding Hood red, isn't it? But it's nothing to the roof of the granary. May I ask you to direct your attention to that?"

Mavis walked towards the granary, to see that thatch had been superimposed upon the tiles; this was worn away in places, revealing a roof of every variety of colour. She looked at it for quite a long time.

"Zomething of an artist, miss?" said Trivett.

"Quite uncreative," laughed Mavis.

"Then you're very lucky. You're spared the pain artists feel when their work doesn't meet with zuccess."

They returned to the kitchen, where Mavis feasted on newly-baked bread smoking hot from the oven, soaked in butter, home-made jam, and cake.

"I've eaten so much, you'll never ask me again," remarked Mavis.

"I'm glad you've a good appetite; it shows you make yourself at home," replied Mrs Trivett.

After tea, they went into the parlour, where it needed no second request on Mavis' part to persuade Mr Trivett to play. He extemporised on the piano for the best part of two hours, during which Mavis listened and dreamed, while Mrs Trivett undisguisedly went to sleep, a proceeding that excited no surprise on the musician's part. Supper was served in the kitchen, where Mavis partook of a rabbit and moorhen pie with new potatoes and young mangels mashed. She had never eaten the latter before; she was surprised to find how palatable the dish was. Mr and Mrs Trivett drank small beer, but their guest was regaled with cowslip wine, which she drank out of deference to the wishes of her kind host and hostess.

After supper, Mr Trivett solemnly produced a well-thumbed "Book of Jokes," from which he read pages of venerable stories. Although Mrs Trivett had heard them a hundred times before, she laughed consumedly at each, as if they were all new to her. Her appreciation delighted her husband. When Mavis rose to take her leave, Trivett, despite her protest, insisted upon accompanying her part of the way to Melkbridge. She bade a warm goodbye to kindly Mrs Trivett, who pressed her to come again and as often as she could spare the time.

"It do Trivett so much good to see a new face. It help him with his music," she explained.

"We might walk back by the canal," suggested Trivett. "It look zo zolemn by moonlight."

Upon Mavis' assenting, they joined the canal where the tow-path is at one with the road by the railway bridge.

"How long have you been in Pennington?" asked Mavis presently.

"A matter o' ten years. We come from North Petherton, near Tarnton."

"Then you didn't know my father?"

"No, miss, though I've heard tark of him in Melkbridge."

"Do you know anything of Mr Perigal?" she asked presently.

"Which one: the old or the young un?"

"Th—the old one."

"A queer old stick, they zay, though I've never set eyes on un. He don't hit it off with his zon, neither."

"Whose fault is that?"

"Both. Do 'ee know young Mr Charles?"

"I've met him."

"H'm!"

"What's the matter with him?"

Mr Trivett solemnly shook his head.

"What does that mean?"

"It's hard to zay. But from what I zee an' from what I hear tell, he be a deal too clever."

"Isn't that an advantage nowadays?"

"Often. But he's quarrelled with his feyther and zoon gets tired of everything he takes up."

Trivett's remarks increased Mavis' sympathy for Perigal. The more he had against him, the more necessary it was for those who liked him to make allowance for flaws in his disposition. Kindly encouragement might do much where censure had failed.

Days passed without Mavis seeing more of Perigal. His indifference to her existence hurt the little vanity that she possessed. At the same time, she wondered if the fact of her not having written to thank him for the violets had anything to do with his making no effort to seek her out. Her perplexities on the matter made her think of him far more than she might have done had she met him again. If Perigal had wished to figure conspicuously in the girl's thoughts, he could not have chosen a better way to achieve that result.

Some three weeks after her meeting with him, she was sitting in her nook reading, when she was conscious of a feeling of helplessness stealing over her. Then a shadow darkened the page. She looked up, to see Perigal standing behind her.

"Interesting?" he asked.

"Very."

"Sorry."

He moved away. Mavis tried to go on with her book, but could not fix her attention upon what she read. Her heart was beating rapidly. She followed the man's retreating figure with her eyes; it expressed a dejection that moved her pity. Although she felt that she was behaving in a manner foreign to her usual reserve, she closed her book, got up and walked after Perigal.

He heard her approaching and turned round.

"There's no occasion to follow me," he said.

"I won't if you don't wish it."

"I said that for your sake. You surely know that I didn't for mine."

"Why for my sake?"

"I've a beastly 'pip.' It's catching."

"Where did you catch it?"

"I've always got it more or less."

"I'm sorry. I've to thank you for those violets."

"Rot!"

"I was glad to get them."

"Really, really glad?" he asked, his face lightening.

"Of course. I love flowers."

"I see," he said coldly.

She made as if she would leave him, but, as before, felt a certain inertness in his presence which she was in no mood to combat; instead of going, she turned to him to ask:

"Anything happened to you since I last saw you?"

"The usual."

"What?"

"Depression and rows with my father."

"I thought you'd forget your promise."

"On the contrary, that's what all the row was about."

"How was that?"

"First of all, I told him that I had met you and all you told me about yourself."

"That made him angry?"

"And when I told him I wanted to have another shot at something, a jolly good shot this time, he said, 'I suppose that means you want money?'"

"What did you say?"

"One can't make money without. That's what all the row's been about. He's a fearful old screw."

"As well as I remember, my father always liked him."

"That was before I grew up to sour his life."

"Did you tell him how you saved Jill's life?" asked Mavis.

"I'd forgotten that, and I'm also forgetting my fishing."

"May I come too?"

"I've a spare rod if you care about having a go."

"I should love to. I've often thought I'd go in for it. It would be something to do in the evenings."

She walked with him a hundred yards further, where he had left two rods on the bank with the lines in the water; these had been carried by the current as far as the lengths of gut would permit.

"Haul up that one. I'll try this," said Perigal.

Mavis did as she was told, to find there was something sufficiently heavy at the end of her line to bend the top joint of her rod.

"I've got a fish!" she cried.

"Pull up carefully."

She pulled the line from the water, to find that she had hooked an old boot.

Perigal laughed at her discomfiture.

"It is funny, but you needn't laugh at me," she said, slightly emphasising the "you."

"Never mind. I'll bait your hook, and you must have another shot."

Her newly baited line had scarcely been thrown in the water when she caught a fine roach.

"You'd better have it stuffed," he remarked, as he took it off the hook.

"It's going to stuff me. I'll have it tomorrow for breakfast."

In the next hour, she caught six perch of various sizes, four roach, and a gudgeon. Perigal caught nothing, a fact that caused Mavis to sympathise with his bad luck.

"Next time you'll do all the catching," she said.

"You mean you'll fish with me again?"

"Why shouldn't I?"

"Really, with me?"

"I like fish for breakfast," she said, as she turned from the ardour of his glance.

Presently, when they had "jacked up," as he called it, and walked together across the meadows in the direction of the town, she said little; she replied to his questions in monosyllables. She was wondering at and a little afraid of the accentuated feeling of helplessness in his presence which had taken possession of her. It was as if she had no mind of her own, but must submit her will to the wishes of the man at her side. They paused at the entrance to the churchyard, where he asked:

"And what have you been doing all this time?"

She told him of her visit to the Trivetts.

His face clouded as he said:

"Fancy you hobnobbing with those common people!"

"But I like them—the Trivetts, I mean. Whoever I knew, I should go and see them if I liked them," she declared, her old spirit asserting itself.

He looked at her in surprise, to say:

"I like to see you angry; you look awfully fine when that light comes into your eyes."

"And I don't like you at all when you say I shouldn't know homely, kindly people like the Trivetts."

"May I conclude, apart from that, you like me?" he asked. "Answer me; answer me!"

"I don't dislike you," she replied helplessly.

"That's something to go on with. But if I'd known you were going to throw yourself away on farmers, I'd have hung after you myself. Even I am better than that."

"Thanks. I can do without your assistance," she remarked.

"You think I didn't come near you all this time because I didn't care?"

"I don't think I thought at all about it."

"If you didn't, I did. I was longing, I dare not say how much, to see you again."

"Why didn't you?" she asked.

"For once in my life, I've tried to go straight."

"What do you mean?"

"You're the sort of girl to get into a man's blood; to make him mad, reckless, head over ears—"

"Hadn't we better go on?" she asked.

"Why—why?"

She had not thought him capable of such earnestness.

"Because I wish it, and because this churchyard is enough to give one the blues."

"I love it, now I'm talking to you."

"Love it?" she echoed.

"First of all, you in your youth, and—and your attractiveness—are such a contrast to everything about us. It emphasises you and—and—it tells me to snatch all the happiness one can, before the very little while when we are as they."

Here he pointed to the crowded graves.

"I'm going home," declared Mavis.

"May I come as far as your door?"

"Aren't you ashamed of being seen with me?"

"I'm very, very proud, little Mavis, and, if only my circumstances were different, I should say much more to you."

His vehemence surprised Mavis into silence; it also awoke a strange joy in her heart; she seemed to walk on air as they went towards her lodging.

"What are you thinking of?" he asked presently.

"You."

"Really?"

"I was wondering why you went out of your way to give people a bad opinion of you."

"I wasn't aware I was especially anxious to do that."

"You don't go to church."

"Are you like that?"

"Not particularly; but other people are, and that's what they say."

"Church is too amusing nowadays."

"I'm afraid my sense of humour isn't sufficiently developed."

"It's the parsons I'm thinking of. Once upon a time, when people went in for deadly sins, it gave 'em something to preach about. Now we all lead proper, discreet lives, they have to justify their existence by inventing tiny sins for their present congregations."

"What sins?" asked Mavis.

"Sins of omission: any trifles they can think of that a more robust race of soul-savers would have laughed at. No. It's the parsons who empty the churches."

"I don't like you to talk like that."

"Why? Are you that way?"

"Sometimes more than others."

"I congratulate you."

She looked at him, surprised.

"I mean it," he went on. "People are much the happier for believing. The great art of life is to be happy, and, if one is, nothing else matters."

"Then why don't you believe?"

"Supposing one can't."

"Can't?"

"It isn't given to everyone, you know."

"Then you think we're just like poor animals—"

"Don't say 'poor' animals," he interrupted. "They're ever so much happier than we."

"Nonsense! They don't know."

"To be ignorant is to be happy. When will you understand that?"

"Never."

"I know what you're thinking of—all the so-called mental development of mankind—love, memory, imagination, sympathy—all the finer susceptibilities of our nature. Is it that what you were thinking of?"

"Vaguely. But I couldn't find the words so nicely as you do."

"Perhaps I read 'em and got 'em by heart. But don't you see that all the fine things I mentioned have to be paid for by increased liability to mental distress, to forms of pain to which coarse natures are, happily, strangers?"

"You talk like an unpleasant book," she laughed.

"And you look like a radiant picture," he retorted.

"Ssh! Here we are."

"The moon's rising: it's full tonight. Think of me if you happen to be watching it," he said.

"I shall be fast asleep."

"And looking more charming than ever, if that be possible. I shall be having a row with my father."

"I daresay you can hold your own."

"That's what makes him so angry."

Mrs. Farthing, upon opening the door, was surprised to see Mavis standing beside young Mr Perigal.

"I think you can get home safely now," he remarked, as he raised his straw hat.

"Thanks for seeing me home."

"Don't forget your fish. Good night."

Mavis thought it well not to enter into any explanation of Perigal's presence to her landlady. She asked if supper were ready, to sit down to it directly she learned that it was. But she did not eat; whether or not her two hours spent in Perigal's company were responsible for the result, it did not alter the fact that her mind was distracted by tumult. The divers perplexities and questionings that had troubled her with the oncoming of the year now assailed her with increased force. She tried to repress them, but, finding the effort unavailing, attempted to fathom their significance, with the result of increasing her distress. The only tangible fact she could seize from the welter in her mind was a sense of enforced isolation from the joys and sorrow of everyday humanity. More than this she could not understand.

She picked her food, well knowing that, if she left it untouched, Mrs Farthing would associate her loss of appetite with the fact of her being seen in the company of a man, and would lead the landlady to make ridiculously sentimental deductions, which would be embarrassing to Mavis.

When she went upstairs, she did not undress. She felt that it would be useless to seek sleep at present. Instead, she stood by the open window of her room, and, after lighting a cigarette and blowing out the candle, looked out into the night.

It was just another such an evening that she had looked into the sky from the window of Mrs Ellis' on the first day of her stay on Kiva Street. Then, beyond sighing for the peace of the country, she had believed that she had only to secure a means of winning her daily bread in order to be happy. Now, although she had obtained the two desires of her heart, she was not even content. Perigal's words awoke in her memory:

"No sooner was a desire satisfied, than one was at once eager for something else."

It would almost seem as if he had spoken the truth—"almost," because she was hard put to it to define what it was for which her being starved.

Mavis looked out of the window. The moon had not yet emerged from a bank of clouds in the east; as if in honour of her coming, the edge of these sycophants was touched with silver light. The stars were growing wan, as if sulkily retiring before the approach of an overwhelming resplendence. Mavis's cigarette went out, but she did not bother to relight it; she was wondering how she was to obtain the happiness for which her heart ached: the problem was still complicated by the fact of her being ignorant in which direction lay the promised land.

Her windows looked over the garden, beyond which fields of long grasses stretched away as far as she could see. A profound peace possessed these, which sharply contrasted with the disquiet in her mind.

Soon, hitherto invisible hedges and trees took dim, mysterious shape; the edge of the moon peeped with glorious inquisitiveness over the clouds. Calmly, royally the moon rose. So deliberately was she unveiled, that it seemed as if she were revealing her beauty to the world for the first time, like a proud, adored mistress unrobing before an impatient lover, whose eyes ached for what he now beheld.

Mystery awoke in the night. Things before unseen or barely visible were now distinct, as if eager for a smile from the aloof loveliness soaring majestically overhead.

Mavis stood in the flood of silver light. For the moment her distress of soul was forgotten. She gazed with wondering awe at the goddess of the night. The moon's coldness presently repelled her: to the girl's ardent imaginings, it seemed to speak of calm contemplation, death—things which youth, allied to warm flesh and blood, abhorred.

Then she fell to thinking of all the strange scenes in the life history of the world on which the moon had looked—stricken fields, barbaric rites, unrecorded crimes, sacked and burning cities, the blackened remains of martyrs at the stake, enslaved nations sleeping fitfully after the day's travail, wrecks on uncharted seas, forgotten superstitions, pagan saturnalias—all the thousand and one phases of life as it has been and is lived.

Although Mavis' tolerable knowledge of history told her how countless must be the sights of horror on which the moon had gazed, as indifferently as it had looked on her, she recalled, as if to leaven the memory of those atrocities (which were often of such a nature that they seemed to give the lie to the existence of a beneficent Deity), that there was ever interwoven with the web of life an eternal tale of love—love to inspire great deeds and noble aims; love to enchain the beast in woman and man; love, whose constant expression was the sacrifice of self upon the altar of the loved one.

Then her mind recalled individual lovers, famous in history and romance, who were set as beacon lights in the wastes of oppression and wrong-doing. These lovers were of all kinds. There were those who deemed the world well lost for a kiss of the loved one's lips; lovers who loved vainly; those who wearied of the loved one.

Mavis wondered, if love were laid at her feet, how it would find her.

She had always known that she was well able to care deeply if her heart were once bestowed. She had, also, kept this capacity for loving unsullied from what she believed to be the defilement of flirtation. Now were revealed the depths of love and tenderness of which she was possessed. They seemed fathomless, boundless, immeasurable.

The knowledge made her sick and giddy. She clung to the window sill for support. It pained her to think that such a treasure above price was destined to remain unsought, unbestowed. She suffered, the while the moon soared, indifferent to her pain.

Suffering awoke wisdom: in the twinkling of an eye, she learned that for which her being starved. The awakening caused tremors of joy to pass over her body, which were succeeded by despondency at realising that it is one thing to want, another to be stayed. Then she was consumed by the hunger of which she was now conscious.

She seemed to be so undesirable, unlovable in her own eyes, that she was moved in her passionate extremity to call on any power that might offer succour.

For the moment, she had forgotten the Source to which in times of stress she looked for help. Instead, she lifted her voice to the moon, the cold wisdom of which seemed to betoken strength, which seemed enthroned in the infinite in order to listen to and to satisfy yearnings, such as hers.

"It's love I want—love, love. I did not know before; now I know. Give me—give me love."

Then she cried aloud in her extremity. She was so moved by her emotions that she was not in the least surprised at the sound of her voice. After she had spoken, she waited long for a sign; but none came. Mavis looked again on the night. Everything was white, cold, silent.

It was as if the world were at one with the deathlike stillness of the moon.

CHAPTER TWENTY
THE WAY OF ALL FLESH

Mavis invested a fraction of her savings in the purchase of rod, fishing tackle, landing net, and bait can; she also bought a yearly ticket from the Avon Conservancy Board, entitling her to fish with one rod in the river at such times as were not close seasons. Most evenings, her graceful form might be seen standing on the river bank, when she was so intent on her sport that it would seem as if she had grown from the sedge at the waterside. Womanlike, she was enthusiastic over fishing when the fish were on the feed and biting freely, to tire quickly of the sport should her float remain for long untroubled by possible captures nibbling at the bait. She avoided those parts of the river where anglers mostly congregated; she preferred and sought the solitude of deserted reaches. Perigal, at the same time, developed a passion for angling. Most evenings, he would be found on the river's bank, if not in Mavis' company, at least near enough to be within call, should any assistance or advice be required. It was remarkable how often each would want help or counsel on matters piscatorial from the other. Sometimes Mavis would want a certain kind of hook, or she would be out of bait, or she would lose one of the beaded rings on her float, all being things which she had no compunction in borrowing from Perigal, inasmuch as he always came to her when he wanted anything himself. It must also be admitted that, as the days flew by, their excuses for meeting became gradually more slender, till at last they would neglect their rods to talk together for quite a long time upon any and every subject under the sun, save fishing.

Once or twice, when owing to Perigal's not making an appearance, Mavis spent the evening alone, she would feel keenly disappointed, and would go home with a strong sense of the emptiness of life.

During her day at the office, or when in her lodgings, she was either absent-minded or self-conscious; she was always longing to get away with only her thoughts for company. She would sometimes sigh for apparently no reason at all. Then Miss Toombs lent her a volume of Shelley, the love passages in which Mavis eagerly devoured. Her favourite time for reading was in bed. She marked, to read and reread, favourite passages. Often in the midst of these she would leave off, when her mind would pursue a train of thought inspired by a phrase or thought of the poet. Very soon she had learned 'Love's Philosophy' by heart. The next symptom of the ailment from which she was suffering was a dreamy languor (frequently punctuated by sighs), which disposed her to offer passionate resentment to all forms of physical and mental effort. This mood was not a little encouraged by the fact of the hay now lying on the ground, to the scent of which she was always emotionally susceptible.

Perigal renounced fishing at the same time as did Mavis. He had a fine instinct for discovering her whereabouts in the meadows bordering the river.

For some while, she had no hesitation in suffering herself to cultivate his friendship. If she had any doubts of the wisdom of the proceeding, there were always two ample justifications at hand.

The first of these was that her association with him had effected a considerable improvement in his demeanour. He was no longer the mentally down-at-heel, soured man that he had been when Mavis first met him. He had taken on a lightness of heart, which, with his slim, boyish beauty, was very attractive to Mavis, starved as she had been of all association with men of her own age and social position. She believed that the beneficent influence she exercised justified the hours she permitted him of her society.

The other reason was that she deluded herself into believing that her sighs and Shelley-inspired imaginings were all because of Windebank's imminent return. She thought of him every day, more especially since she had met Perigal. She often contrasted the two men in her thoughts, when it would seem as if Windebank's presence, so far as she remembered it, had affected her life as a bracing, health-giving wind; whereas Perigal influenced her in the same way as did appealing music, reducing her to a languorous helplessness. She had for so long associated Windebank with any sentimental leanings in which she had indulged, that she was convinced that her fidelity to his memory was sufficient safeguard against her becoming infatuated with Perigal.

Thus she travelled along a road, blinding herself the while to the direction in which she was going. But one day, happening to obtain a glimpse of its possible destination, she resolved to make something of an effort, if not to retrace her way (she scarcely thought this necessary), to stay her steps.

Perigal had told her that if he could get the sum he wanted from his father, he would shortly be going somewhere near Cardiff, where he would be engaged in the manufacture of glazed bricks with a partner. The news had frightened her. She felt as if she had been dragged to the edge of a seemingly bottomless abyss, into which it was uncertain whether or not she would be thrown. To escape the fate that threatened, she threw off her lethargy, to resume her fishing and avoid rather than seek Perigal. Perhaps he took the hint, or was moved by the same motive as Mavis, for he too gave up frequenting the meadows bordering the river. His absence hurt Mavis more than she could have believed possible. She became moody, irritable; she lost her appetite and could not sleep at night. To ease her distress of mind, she tried calling on her old friends, the Medlicotts, and her new ones, the Trivetts. The former expressed concern for her altered appearance, which only served to increase her despondency, while the music she heard at Pennington Farm told of love dreams, satisfied longings, worlds in which romantic fancy was unweighted with the bitterness and disappointment of life, as she now found it, all of which was more than enough to stimulate her present discontent.

She had not seen or heard anything of Perigal for two weeks, when one July evening she happened to catch the hook of her line in her hand. She was in great pain, her efforts to remove the hook only increasing her torment. She was wondering what was the best way of getting help, when she saw Perigal approaching. Her first impulse was to avoid him. With beating heart, she hid behind a clump of bushes. But the pain in her hand became so acute that she suddenly emerged from her concealment to call sharply for assistance. He ran towards her, asking as he came:

"What's the matter?"

"My hand," she faltered. "I've caught the hook in it."

"Poor dear! Let me look."

"Please do something. It hurts," she urged, as she put out her hand, which was torn by the cruel hook.

"What an excellent catch! But, all the same, I must get it out at once," he remarked, as he produced a pocket knife.

"With that?" she asked tremulously.

"I won't hurt you more than I can help, you may be sure. But it must come out at once, or you'll get a bad go of blood poisoning."

"Do it as quickly as possible," she urged.

She set her lips, while he cut into the soft white flesh.

However much he hurt her, she resolved not to utter a sound. For all her fortitude, the trifling operation pained her much.

"Brave little Mavis!" he said, as he freed her flesh from the hook, to ask, as she did not speak, "Didn't it hurt?"

"Of course it did. See how it's bleeding!"

"All the better. It will clear the poison out."

Mavis was hurt at the indifference he exhibited to her pain.

"Would you please tie my handkerchief round it?" she asked.

"Let it bleed. What are you thinking of?"

"I want to get back."

"Where's the hurry?"

"Only that I want to get back."

"But I haven't seen you for ages."

"Haven't you?" she asked innocently.

"Cruel Mavis! But before you go back you must wash your hand in the river."

"I'll do nothing of the kind."

"Not if it's for your good?"

"Not if I don't wish it."

"As it's for your good, I insist on your doing what I wish," he declared, as he caught her firmly by the wrist and led her, all unresisting, to the river's brink. She was surprised at her helplessness and was inclined to criticise it impersonally, the while Perigal plunged her wounded hand into the water. Her reflections were interrupted by a sharp pain caused by the contact of water with the torn flesh.

"It's better than blood poisoning," he hastened to assure her.

"I believe you do it on purpose to hurt me," she remarked, upon his freeing her hand.

"I'm justified in hurting you if it's for your good," he declared calmly. "Now let me bind it up."

While he tied up her hand, she looked at him resentfully, the colour heightening on her cheek.

"I wish you'd often look like that," he remarked.

"I shall if you treat me so unkindly."

He took no notice of the accusation, but said:

"When you look like that it's wonderful. Then certain verses in the 'Song of Solomon' might have been written to you."

"The 'Song of Solomon'?"

"Don't you read your Bible?"

"But you said some of them might have been written to me. What do you mean?"

"They're the finest love verses in the English language. They might have been written to you. They're quite the best thing in the Bible."

She was perplexed, and showed it in her face; then, she looked appealingly to him for enlightenment. He disregarded the entreaty in her eyes. He looked at her from head to foot before saying:

"Little Mavis, little Mavis, why are you so alluring?"

"Don't talk nonsense. I'm not a bit," she replied, as something seemed to tighten at her heart.

"You are, you are. You've soul and body, an irresistible combination," he declared ardently.

His words troubled her; she looked about her, large-eyed, afraid; she did not once glance in his direction.

Then she felt his grasp upon her wrist and the pressure of his lips upon her wounded hand.

"Forgive me: forgive me!" he cried. "But I know you never will."

"Don't, don't," she murmured.

"Are you very angry?"

"I—I—" she hesitated.

"Let me know the worst."

"I don't know," she faltered ruefully.

His face brightened.

"I'm going to ask you something," he said earnestly.

Mavis was filled with a great apprehension.

"If I weren't a bad egg, and could offer you a home worthy of you, I wonder if you'd care to marry me?"

An exclamation of astonishment escaped her.

"I mean it," he continued, "and why not? You're true-hearted and straight and wonderful to look at. Little Mavis is a pearl above price, and she doesn't know it."

"Ssh! ssh!" she murmured.

"You're a rare find," he said, to add after a moment or two, "and I know what I'm talking about."

She did not speak, but her bosom was violently disturbed, whilst a delicious feeling crept about her heart. She repressed an inclination to shed tears.

"Now I s'pose your upset, eh?" he remarked.

"Why should I be?" she asked with flashing eyes.

It was now his turn to be surprised. She went on:

"It's a thing any woman should be proud of, a man asking her to share her life with him."

His lips parted, but he did not speak.

She drew herself up to her full, queenly height to say:

"I am very proud."

"Ah! Then—then—"

His hands caught hers.

"Let me go," she pleaded.

"But—"

"I want to think. Let me go: let me go!"

His hands still held hers, but with an effort she freed herself, to run from him in the direction of her lodging. She did not once look back, but hurried as if pursued by danger, safety from which lay in the companionship of her thoughts.

Arrived at Mrs Farthing's, she made no pretence of sitting down to her waiting supper, but went straight upstairs to her room. She felt that a crisis had arisen in her life. To overcome it, it was necessary for her to decide whether or not she loved Charlie Perigal. She passed the best part of a sleepless night endeavouring, without success, to solve the problem confronting her. Jill, who always slept on Mavis' bed, was alive to her mistress' disquiet. The morning sun was already high in the heavens when Jill crept sympathetically to the girl's side.

Mavis clasped her friend in her arms to say:

"Oh, Jill, Jill! If you could only tell me if I truly loved him!"

Jill energetically licked Mavis' cheek before nestling in her arms to sleep.

The early morning post brought a letter from Perigal to Mavis, which she opened with trembling hands and beating heart. It ran:—

"For your sake, not for mine, I'm off to Wales by the early morning train. If you care for me ever so little (and I am proud to believe you do), in clearing out of your life, I am doing what I conceive to be the best thing possible for your future happiness. If it gives you any pleasure to know it, I should like to tell you I love you. My going away is some proof of this statement, C. P.

"P.S.—I have written by the same post to Windebank to give him your address."

Mavis looked at her watch, to discover it was exactly half-past seven. She ran downstairs, half dressed as she was, to look at the time-table which Mr Medlicott presented to her on the first of every month. After many false scents, she discovered, that for Perigal to catch the train at Bristol for South Wales, he must leave Melkbridge for Dippenham by the 8.15. Always a creature of impulse, she scrambled into her clothes, swallowed a mouthful of tea, pinned on her hat, caught up her gloves, and, almost before she knew what she was doing, was walking quickly towards the station. She had a little under twenty minutes in which to walk a good mile. Her one concern was to meet, say something (she knew not what) to Perigal before he left Melkbridge for good. She arrived breathless at the station five minutes before his train started. He was not in the booking office, and she could see nothing of him on the platform. She was beginning to regret her precipitancy, when she saw him walking down the road to the station, carrying a much worn leather brief bag. Her heart beat as she went out to meet him.

"Little Mavis!" he cried.

"Good morning."

"What are you doing here at this time?"

"I came out for a walk."

"To see me off?"

"Perhaps."

"Well, I will say this, you will bear looking at in the morning."

"Why, who won't?"

"Lots of 'em."

"How do you know?"

"Eh! But we can't talk here. It will be all over the town that we were—were—"

"Going to elope!" she interrupted.

"I wish we were. But, seriously, you got my letter?"

"It's really why I came."

"What?" he asked, astonished.

"It's really why I came."

"What have you to say to me?"

"I don't know."

"Don't you want me to go to Wales?"

"I don't know."

"I must decide soon. Here's the train."

They mechanically turned towards the platform.

"Must you go?" she impulsively asked.

"I could either chuck it or I could put it off till tomorrow."

"Why not do that?"

"But would you see me again?"

"Yes."

"And will you decide then?"

"Perhaps."

"Then I'll see you tonight," he said, as he raised his hat, as if wishing her to leave him.

Mavis bit her lip as she turned to leave Perigal.

"Goodbye till tonight, little Mavis!"

"Goodbye," she called back curtly.

"One moment," he cried.

She paused.

He went on:

"It was charming of you to come. It's like everything to do with you—beautiful."

"There's still time for you to get your train," she said, feeling somewhat mollified by his last words.

"And miss seeing you tonight!" he replied.

Mavis walked to the factory wondering how many people had seen her talking to Perigal. During her morning's work, her mind was in a turmoil of doubt as to the advisability of meeting Perigal in the evening. She could not help believing that, should she see him, as was more or less arranged, it would prove an event of much moment in her life, holding infinite possibilities of happiness or disaster. She knew herself well enough to know that if she were wholly possessed by love for him she would be to him as clay in the hands of the potter. She could come to no conclusion; even if she had, she could not be certain if she could keep to any resolve she might arrive at. During her midday meal she remembered how Perigal had said that the "Song of Solomon" might have been written to her. She opened her Bible, found the "Song" and greedily devoured it. In her present mood its sensuous beauty entranced her, but she was not a little perplexed by the headings of the chapters. As with so many others, she found it hard to reconcile the ecclesiastical claims here set forth at the beginning of each chapter with the passionate outpourings of the flesh which followed. She took the Bible with her to the office, to read the "Song" twice during the interval usually allotted to afternoon tea.

When she got back to Mrs Farthing's, she was long undecided whether she should go out to meet Perigal. The leanings of her heart inclined her to keep the appointment, whilst, on the other hand, her strong common sense urged her to decide nothing until Windebank came back. Windebank she was sure of, whereas she was not so confident of Perigal; but she was forced to admit that the elusive and more subtle personality of the latter appealed more to her imagination than the other's stability. Presently, she left her lodgings and walked slowly towards the canal, which was in a contrary direction to that in which lay the Avon. The calm of the still water inclined her to sadness. She idled along the towpath, plucking carelessly at the purple vetch which bordered the canal in luxuriant profusion. More than once, she was possessed by the idea that someone was following her. Then she became aware that Perigal was also idling along the towpath some way behind her. The sight of him made her heart beat; she all but decided to turn back to meet him. Common sense again fought for the possession of her mind. It told her that by dawdling till she reached the next bend, she could be out of sight of Perigal, without exciting his suspicions, when it would be the easiest thing in the world to hurry till she came to a track which led from the canal to the town. She was putting this design into practice, and had already reached the bend, when odd verses of the "Song of Solomon" occurred to her:

"Behold, thou art fair, my love; behold, thou art fair; thou hast doves' eyes.

"As the lily among thorns, so is my love among the daughters.

"Thou art all fair, my love; there is no spot in thee.

"Thou hast ravished my heart, my sister, my spouse; thou hast ravished my heart with one of thine eyes, with one chain of thy neck.

"Thy lips, O my spouse, drop as the honeycomb: honey and milk are under thy tongue.

"A garden enclosed is my sister, my spouse; a spring shut up, a fountain sealed.

"How fair and how pleasant art thou, O love, for delights!

"And the roof of thy mouth like the best wine for my beloved, that goeth down sweetly, causing the lips of those that are asleep to speak.

"I am my beloved's, and his desire is towards me.

"I am my beloved's, and my beloved is mine."

The influence of air, sky, evening sun, and the peace that lay over the land reinforced the unmoral suggestions of the verses that had leapt in her memory. Her blood quickened; she sighed, and then sat by the rushes that, just here, invaded the towpath.

As Perigal strolled towards her, his personality caused that old, odd feeling of helplessness to steal over her. She, almost, felt as if she were a fly gradually being bound by a greedy spider's web.

He stood by her for a few moments without speaking.

"You've broken your promise," he presently remarked.

"Haven't you, too?" she asked, without looking up.

"No."

"Sure?"

"I was so impatient to see you, I hung about in sight of your house, so that I could catch sight of you directly when you came out."

"What about Melkbridge people?"

"What do I care!"

"What about me?"

He turned away with an angry gesture.

"What about me?" she repeated more insistently.

"You know what I said to you, asked you last night."

Mavis hung her head.

"What did you tell Windebank in your letter?" she asked presently.

"Don't talk about him."

"I shall if I want to. What did you say about me?"

"Shall I tell you?" he asked suddenly, as he sat beside her. "I told him how wholesome and how sweet you were. That's what I said."

"Ssh!"

"Do you know what I should have said?"

Mavis made a last effort to preserve her being from the thraldom of love. It was in her heart to leave Perigal there and then, but although the spirit was all but willing, the flesh was weak. As before in his presence, Mavis was rendered helpless by the odd fascination Perigal exercised.

"Do you know what I should have said?" he repeated.

Mavis essayed to speak; her tongue would not give speech.

"I'll tell you. I should have said that I love you, and that nothing in heaven or earth is going to stop my getting you."

"I must go," she said, without moving.

"When I love you so? Little Mavis, I love you, I love you, I love you!"

She trembled all over. He seized her hand, covered it with kisses, and then tried to draw her lips to his.

"My hand was enough."

"Your lips! Your lips!"

"But—"

"I love you! Your lips!"

He forced his lips to hers. When he released them, she looked at him as if spellbound, with eyes veiled with wonder and dismay—with eyes which revealed the great awakening which had taken place in her being.

"I love little Mavis. I love her," he whispered.

The look in her eyes deepened, her lips trembled, her bosom was violently disturbed. Perigal touched her arm. Then she gave a little cry, the while her head fell helplessly upon his shoulder.

CHAPTER TWENTY-ONE
THE AWAKENING

Mavis was in love, consequently the world was transformed. All her previous hesitations in surrendering to her incipient love for Perigal were forgotten; the full, flowing current of her passion disregarded the trifling obstacles which had once sought to obstruct its progress. Life, nature, the aspect of things took on the abnormally adorable hues of those who love and are beloved. Such was the rapture in her heart, that days, hours, moments were all too fleeting for the enjoyment of her newborn felicity. The radiant happiness which welled within her, in seemingly inexhaustible volume, appeared to fill the universe. Often, with small success, she would attempt to realise the joy that had come into her life. At other times, when alone, she would softly shed tears—tears with which shy, happy laughter mingled. She would go about all day singing snatches of gay little songs. There was not a happier girl in the world. As if, perhaps, to give an edge to her joy, the summer sky of her gladness was troubled by occasional clouds. She would wake in the night with a great presage of fear, which nothing she could do would remove. At such times, she would clasp with both hands a ring that her lover had given her, which at night she wore suspended from her neck, so that it lay upon her heart. At other times, she would be consumed by a passion for annihilating all thoughts and considerations for self in her relations with Perigal; she was urged by every fibre in her body to merge her being with his. When thus possessed, she would sometimes, if she were at home when thus moved, go upon her knees to pray long and fervently for the loved one's welfare; as likely as not her thoughts would wander, when thus engaged, to be wholly concerned with the man she adored.

Thus, she abandoned herself whole-heartedly, unreservedly to the ecstasy of loving.

Mavis and Perigal were to be quietly married by special licence in London, in five weeks' time, which would be in the early days of September. Perigal urged Mavis not to speak to anyone of the wedding, saying, as a reason for this silence, that his father had not yet quite decided upon giving him the money he wanted, and the news of the engagement and early marriage might cause him to harden his heart. The honeymoon was to be spent in the retirement of Polperro, a Cornish village, the beauty and seclusion of which Perigal never tired of describing. As far as they could both see at present, Mavis was to keep on with her work at the office (the honeymoon was to consist of her fortnight's annual holiday), till such time as he could prepare a home for her in Wales. Although not welcoming, she did not offer the least objection to this arrangement, as she saw that it was all that could be done under their present circumstances. She wrote out and placed over her bed a list of dates, which culminated in the day on which she was to throw in her lot with the loved one; every day, as soon as she awoke, she crossed off one more of the slowly dwindling days. Nearly every Saturday she took the train to Bathminster, where she spent a considerable fraction of the forty pounds she had saved in buying a humble equivalent for a trousseau.

As boxes and parcels of clothes began to arrive at her lodgings, she would try on the most attractive of these, the while her eyes shone with happiness. Those with whom she was commonly brought in contact noticed the change in her demeanour. Mrs Farthing smiled mysteriously, as if guessing the cause. Miss Hunter made many unsuccessful efforts to worm confidences from Mavis; while plain Miss Toombs showed her displeasure of the alteration that had occurred in her by scarcely ever addressing her, and then only when compelled.

"You look like a bride," she remarked one day, when Mavis was glowing with happiness.

Mavis saw something of Perigal pretty well every day. Sometimes, they would meet quite early of a morning by the canal; if they did not see each other then, they made a point of getting a few minutes together of an evening, usually by the river. So that no hint of their intentions should reach Major Perigal, the lovers met furtively, a proceeding which enhanced the charm of their intercourse.

At all times, Mavis was moved by an abiding concern for his health. There was much of the maternal in her love, leading her frequently to ask if his linen were properly aired and if he were careful to avoid getting damp feet; she also made him solemnly promise to tell her immediately if he were not feeling in the best of health. Mavis, with a great delight, could not help noticing the change that had taken place in her lover ever since their betrothal. He, too, was conscious of the difference, and was fond of talking about it.

"I never thought I'd grow young again!" he would remark.

"What about second childhood?" laughed the irrepressible Mavis.

"Seriously, I didn't. I always felt so old. And it's little Mavis who has done it all."

"Really, sweetheart?"

"All, dear."

She rewarded him with a glance of love and tenderness.

He went on:

"The past is all over and done with. I made a fresh start from the day you promised to throw in your exquisite self with me."

Thus he would talk, expressing, at the same time, boundless confidence in the future, forgetful or ignorant of what has been well said, "That the future is only entering the past by another gate."

One evening, when he had made bitter reference to the life that he had led, before he had again met with her, she asked:

"What is this dreadful past you're always regretting so keenly?"

"You surely don't want to know?"

"Haven't I a right to?"

"No. Not that it's so very terrible. Far from it, it isn't. There's an awful sameness about it. The pleasure of to day is the boredom of tomorrow. It all spells inherent incapacity to succeed in either good or evil."

"Good or evil?" she queried.

"It's going to be good now, since I've little Mavis and her glorious hair to live for."

One evening, he brought a brick to show her, which was a sample of those he intended manufacturing, should he get the assistance he now daily expected from his father. She looked at it curiously, fondly, as if it might prove the foundation stone of the beloved one's prosperity; a little later, she begged it of him. She took it home, to wrap it carefully in one of her silk handkerchiefs and put it away in her trunk. From time to time, she would take the brick out, to have it about her when she was at her lodgings. She also took an acute interest in bricks that were either built into houses, or heaped upon the roadside. She was proudly convinced there were no bricks that could compare with the one she prized for finish or durability. Perigal was much diverted and, perhaps, touched by her interest in his possible source of success.

The clamourings of Mavis' ardent nature had been so long repressed, that the disturbing influences of her passion for Perigal were more than sufficient to loose her pent up instincts. Her lover's kisses proved such a disturbing factor, that, one evening when he had been unusually appreciative of her lips, she had not slept, having lain awake, trembling, till it was time for her to get up. For the future, she deemed it prudent to allow one kiss at meeting, and a further one at parting.

Perigal protested against this arrangement, when he would say:

"I love to kiss you, little Mavis, because then such a wistful, faraway look comes into your eyes, which is one of the most wonderful things I've seen."

Mavis, with an effort, resisted Perigal's entreaties.

One August evening, when it was late enough for her to be conscious that the nights were drawing in, she was returning from a happy hour spent with her lover. It now wanted but a week to their marriage; their hearts were delirious with happiness.

"Don't you miss all the bridesmaids and all the usual thing-uma-jigs of a wedding?" he had asked her.

"Not a bit."

"Sure, darling?"

"Quite. I only want one thing. So long as I get that, nothing else can possibly matter."

"And that?"

"You," she had replied, at which Perigal had said after a moment or two of silence:

"I will, I really will do all I know to make my treasure of a little Mavis happy."

Mavis was walking home with a light step and a lighter heart: more than one red-cheeked, stolid, Wiltshire man and woman turned to look after the trimly-built, winsome girl, who radiated distinction and happiness as she walked.

A familiar voice sounded in Mavis's ear. "At last," it said heartfully.

She turned, to see Windebank standing before her, a Windebank stalwart as ever, with his face burned to the colour of brick red, but looking older and thinner than when she had last seen him. Mavis' heart sank.

"At last," he repeated. He looked as if he would say more, but he did not speak. She wondered if he were moved at seeing her again.

Mavis, not knowing what to say, put out her hand, which he clasped.

"Aren't you glad to see me?" he asked.

"Of course."

"And you're not going to run away again?"

She looked at him inquiringly.

"I mean as you did before, into the fog!"

"There's no fog to run into," she remarked feebly.

"Little Mavis! Little Mavis! I'd no idea you could look so well and wonderful as you do."

"Hadn't we better walk? People are staring at us already."

"I can't see you so well walking," he complained.

They strolled along; as they walked, Windebank half turned, so that his eyes never left her face.

"What a beautiful girl you are!" he said.

"You mustn't say that."

"But it's true. And to think of you working for that outsider Devitt!"

"He means well. And I've been very happy there."

"You won't be there much longer! Do you know why?"

"Tell me about yourself," she said evasively, as she wondered if talking to Windebank were unfair to Perigal.

"Do you remember this?" he asked, as he brought out a crumpled letter for her inspection.

"It's my writing!" she cried.

"It's the foolish, dear letter you wrote to me."

She took it, to recall the dreary day at Mrs Bilkins's on which she had penned the lines to Windebank, in which she had refused to hamper his career by acceding to his request.

"Give it back," he demanded.

"You don't want it?"

"Don't I! A girl who can write a letter like that to a chap isn't easily forgotten, I can tell you."

Mavis did not reply. Windebank, seeing how she was embarrassed, told her of his more recent doings; how, after getting Perigal's letter, he had set out for England as soon as he could start; how he had saved three days by taking the overland route from Brindisi (such was his anxiety to see his little Mavis, who had never been wholly out of his thoughts), to arrive home before he was expected.

"I had an early feed and came out hoping to see you," he concluded.

Mavis did not speak. She was deliberating if she should tell Windebank of her approaching marriage; if he cared seriously for her, it was only fair that he should know her affections were bestowed.

"Aren't you glad to see me?" he asked.

"Of course, but—"

"There are no 'buts.' You're coming home with me."

"Home!"

"To meet my people again. They're just back from Switzerland. It isn't your home—yet."

This decided her. She told him, first enjoining him to silence. To her relief, also to her surprise, he took it very calmly. His face went a shade whiter beneath his sun-tanned skin; he stood a trifle more erect than before; and that was all.

"I congratulate you," he said. "But I congratulate him a jolly sight more. Who is he?"

Mavis hesitated.

"You can tell me. It won't go any further."

"Charlie Perigal."

"Charlie Perigal?" he asked in some surprise.

"Why not?" she asked, with a note of defiance in her voice.

"But he's upside down with his father, and has been for a long time."

"What of that?"

"What are you going to live on?"

"Charlie is going to work."

"Charlie work!" The words slipped out before he could stop them. "Of course, I'd forgotten that," he added.

"You're like a lot of other people, who can't say a good word for him, because they're jealous of him," she cried.

He did not reply for a moment; when he did, it was to say very gravely:

"Naturally I am very, very jealous; it would be strange if it were otherwise. I wish you every happiness from the bottom of my heart."

"Thank you," replied Mavis, mollified.

"And God bless you."

He took off his cap and left her. Mavis watched his tall form turn the corner with a sad little feeling at her heart. But love is a selfish passion, and when Mavis awoke three mornings later, when it wanted four days to her marriage, she would have forgotten Windebank's existence, but for the fact of his having sent her a costly, gold-mounted dressing-case. This had arrived the previous evening, at the same time as the frock that she proposed wearing at her wedding had come from Bathminster. She looked once more at the dressing-case with its sumptuous fittings, to turn to the wrappings enclosing her simple wedding gown. She took it out reverently, tenderly, to kiss it before locking the door and trying it on again. With quick, loving hands she fastened it about her; she then looked at the reflection of her adorable figure in the glass.

"Will he like me in it? Do you think he will love me in it?" she asked Jill, who, blinking her brown eyes, was scarcely awake. She then took Jill in her arms to murmur:

"Whatever happens, darling, I shall always love you."

Mavis was sick with happiness; she wondered what she had done to get so much allotted to her. All her struggles to earn a living in London, the insults to which she had been subjected, the disquiet that had troubled her mind throughout the spring, were all as forgotten as if they had never been. There was not a cloud upon the horizon of her joy.

As if to grasp her present ecstasy with both hands, she, with no inconsiderable effort, recalled all the more unhappy incidents in her life, to make believe that she was still enduring these, and that there was no prospect of escape from their defiling recurrence. She then fell to imagining how envious she would be were she acquainted with a happy Mavis Keeves who, in three days' time, was to belong, for all time, to the man of her choice.

It was with inexpressible joy that she presently permitted herself to realise that it was none other than she upon whom this great gift of happiness unspeakable had been bestowed. The rapture born of this blissful realisation impelled her to seek expression in words.

"Life is great and noble," she cried; "but love is greater."

Every nerve in her body vibrated with ecstasy. And in four days—

Two letters, thrust beneath her door by Mrs Farthing, recalled her to the trivialities of everyday life. She picked them up, to see that one was in the well-known writing of the man she loved; the other, a strange, unfamiliar scrawl, which bore the Melkbridge postmark. Eager to open her lover's letter, yet resolved to delay its perusal, so that she could look forward to the delight of reading it (Mavis was already something of an epicure in emotion), she tore open the other, to decipher its contents with difficulty. She read as follows:—

"SHAW HOUSE, MELKBRIDGE.

"MADAM,—My son has told me of his intentions with regard to yourself. This is to tell you that, if you persist in them, I shall withdraw the assistance I was on the point of furnishing in order to give him a new start in life. It rests with you whether I do my utmost to make or mar his future. For reasons I do not care to give, and which you may one day appreciate, I do what may seem to your unripe intelligence a meaningless act of cruelty.—I remain, dear Madam, Your obedient servant,

"JOHN VEZEY PERIGAL."

The sun went out of Mavis' heaven; the gorgeous hues faded from her life. She felt as if the ground were cut from under her feet, and she was falling, falling, falling she knew not where. To save herself, she seized and opened Perigal's letter.

This told her that he knew the contents of his father's note; that he was still eager to wed her as arranged; that they must meet by the river in the evening, when they could further discuss the situation which had arisen.

Mavis sank helplessly on her bed: she felt as if her heart had been struck a merciless blow. She was a little consoled by Perigal's letter, but, in her heart of hearts, something told her that, despite his brave words, the marriage was indefinitely postponed; indeed, it was more than doubtful if it would ever take place at all. She suffered, dumbly, despairingly; her torments were the more poignant because she realised that the man she loved beyond anything in the world must be acutely distressed at this unexpected confounding of his hopes. Her head throbbed with dull pains which gradually increased in intensity; these, at last, became so violent that she wondered if it were going to burst. She felt the need of action, of doing anything that might momentarily ease her mind of the torments afflicting it.

Her wedding frock attracted her attention. Mavis, with a lump in her throat, took off and folded this, and put it out of sight in a trunk; then, with red eyes and face the colour of lead, she flung on her work-a-day clothes, to walk mechanically to the office. The whole day she tried to come to terms with the calamity that had so suddenly befallen her; a heavy, persistent pressure on the top of her head mercifully dulled her perceptions; but at the back of her mind a resolution was momentarily gaining strength—a resolution that was to the effect that it was her duty to the man she loved to insist upon his falling in with his father's wishes. It gave her a certain dim pleasure to think that her suffering meant that, some day, Perigal would be grateful to her for her abnegation of self.

Perigal, looking middle-aged and careworn, was impatiently awaiting her arrival by the river. Her heart ached to see his altered appearance.

"My Mavis!" he cried, as he took her hand.

She tried to speak, but a little sob caught in her throat. They walked for some moments in silence.

"I told him all about it; I thought it better," said Perigal presently. "But I never thought he'd cut up rough."

"Is there any chance of his changing his mind?"

"Not the remotest. If he once gets a thing into his head, as he has this, nothing on earth will move him."

"I won't let it make any difference to you," she declared.

"What do you mean?" he asked quickly.

"That nothing, nothing will persuade me to marry you on Thursday."

"What?"

"I mean it. I have made up my mind."

"But I've set my mind on it, darling."

"I'm doing it for your good."

He argued, threatened, cajoled, pleaded for the best part of two hours, but nothing would shake her resolution. To all of his arguments, she would reply in a tone admitting no doubt of the unalterable nature of her determination:

"I'm doing it for your good, beloved."

Shadows grew apace; light clouds laced the west; a hush was in the air, as if trees, bushes, and flowers were listening intently for a message which had evaded them all the day.

Perigal's distress wrung Mavis' heart.

"I can bear it no longer," she presently cried.

"Bear what, sweetheart?"

"Your pain. My heart isn't made of stone. I almost wish it were. Listen. You want me?"

"What a question!"

"Then you shall have me."

He looked at her quickly. She went on:

"We will not get married. But I give you myself."

"Mavis!"

"Yes; I give you myself."

Perigal was silent for some minutes; he was, evidently, in deep thought. When he spoke, it was to say with deliberation:

"No, no, little Mavis. I may be bad; but I'm not up to that form—not yet."

"I love you all the more for saying that," she murmured.

"Since I can't move you, I'll go to Wales tomorrow," he said.

"Then that means—"

"Wait, wait, little Mavis; wait and hope."

"I shall never love anyone else."

"Not even Windebank?"

She cried out in agony of spirit.

"Forgive me, darling," he said. "I will keep faithful too."

They walked for some moments in silence.

"Do one thing for me," pleaded Mavis.

"And that?"

"We are near my nook—at least I call it that. Let us sit there for just three minutes and think Thursday was—was going to be our—" She could not trust her voice to complete the sentence.

"If you wish it."

"Only—"

"Only what?"

"Promise—promise you won't kiss me."

"But—"

"I'm not myself. Promise."

He promised. They repaired to Mavis' nook, where they sat in silence, while night enwrapped them in gloom. Instinctively, their hands clasped. Mavis had realised that she was with her lover perhaps for the last time. She wished to snatch a moment of counterfeit joy by believing that the immense happiness which had been hers was to continue indefinitely. But her imaginative effort was a dismal failure. Her mind was a blank with the promise of unending pain in the background.

Perigal felt the pressure of Mavis's hand instinctively tighten on his; it gripped as if she could never let him go: tears fell from her eyes on to his fingers. With an effort he freed himself and, without saying a word, walked quickly away. With all her soul, she listened to his retreating steps. It seemed as if her life were departing, leaving behind the cold shell of the Mavis she knew, who was now dead to everything but pain. His consideration for her helplessness illumined her suffering. The next moment, she was on her knees, her heart welling with love, gratitude, concern for the man who had left her.

"Bless him! Bless him, oh God! He's good; he's good; he's good! He's proved it to a poor, weak girl like me!"

Thus she prayed, all unconscious that Perigal's consideration in leaving her was the high-water mark of his regard for her welfare.

CHAPTER TWENTY-TWO
O LOVE, FOR DELIGHTS!

"Beloved!"

"My own!"

"Are you ready to start?"

"I'll see if they've packed the luncheon."

"One moment. Where are we going today?"

"Llansallas; three miles from here."

"What's it like?" she asked.

"The loveliest place they knew of."

"How wonderful! And we'll have the whole day there?"

"Only you and I," he said softly.

"Be quick. Don't lose a moment, sweetheart. I dislike being alone—now."

"Why?" he asked.

Mavis dropped her eyes.

"Adorable, modest little Mavis," he laughed. "I'll see about the grub."

"You've forgotten something," she pouted, as he moved towards the door.

"Your kiss!"

"Our kiss."

"I hadn't really. I wanted to see if you'd remember."

"As if I'd forget," she protested.

Their lips met; not once, but many times; they seemed reluctant to part.

Mavis was alone. She had spoken truly when she had hinted how she was averse to the company of her own thoughts. It was then that clouds seemed disposed to threaten the sun of her joy.

She went to the window of the hotel sitting-room, which overlooked the narrow road leading to Polperro village; beyond the cottages opposite was bare rock, which had been blasted to find room for stone habitations; above the naked stone was blue sky. Mavis tried to think about the sky in order to exclude a certain weighty matter from her mind. She had been five days in Cornwall, four of which had been spent with Perigal in Polperro. Mavis did her best to concentrate her thoughts upon the cerulean hue of the heavens; she wondered why it could not faithfully be matched in dress material owing to the peculiar quality of light in the colour of the sky. It was just another such a blue, so she thought, as she had seen on the morning of what was to have been her wedding day, when, heavy-eyed and life-weary, she had crept to the window of her room; then the gladness of the day appeared so indifferent to her sorrow that she had raged hopelessly, helplessly, at the ill fortune which had over-ridden her. This paroxysm of rebellion had left her physically inert, but mentally active. She had surveyed her life calmly, dispassionately, when it seemed that she had been deprived by cruel circumstance of parents, social position, friends, money, love: everything which had been her due. She had been convinced that she was treated with brutal injustice. The joyous singing of birds outside her window, the majestic climbing of the sun in the heavens maddened her. Her spirit had been aroused: she had wondered what she could do to defy fate to do its worst. The morning's post had brought a letter from Perigal, the envelope of which bore the Polperro postmark. This had told her that the despairing writer had gone to the place of their prospective honeymoon, where the contrast between his present agony of soul and the promised happiness, on which he had set so much store, was such, that if he did not immediately hear from Mavis, he was in danger of taking his life. There had been more to the same effect. Immediately, all thought of self had been forgotten; she had hurried out to send a telegram to Perigal, telling him to expect a surprise to-day.

She had confided her dear Jill to Mrs Farthing's care. After telling her wondering landlady that she would not be away for more than one night, she had hurried (with a few belongings) to the station, ultimately to get out at Liskeard, where she had to take the local railway to Looe, from which an omnibus would carry her to Polperro. Perigal had met her train at Liskeard, her telegram having led him to expect her.

He was greatly excited and made such ardent love to her that, upon her arrival at Looe, she already regretted her journey and had purposed returning by the next train. But there was nothing to take her back before morning; against her wishes, she had been constrained to spend the night at Looe.

Here Perigal insisted on staying also.

Mavis, as she looked back on the last four days, and all that had happened therein, could not blame herself. She now loved Perigal more than she had ever believed it possible for woman to love man; she belonged to him body and soul; she was all love, consequently she had no room in her being for vain regrets.

When she was alone, as now, her pride was irked at the fact of her not being a bride; she believed that the tenacious way in which she had husbanded her affections gave her every right to expect the privilege of wifehood. It was, also, then she realised that her very life depended upon the continuance of Perigal's love: she had no doubt that he would marry her with as little delay as possible. Otherwise, the past was forgotten, the future ignored: she wholly surrendered herself to her new-born ecstasy begotten of her surrender. He was the world, and nothing else mattered. So far as she was concerned, their love for each other was the beginning, be-all, and end of earthly things.

It was a matter of complete indifference to her that she was living at Polperro with her lover as Mrs and Mr Ward.

It may, perhaps, be wondered why a girl of Mavis's moral susceptibilities could be so indifferent to her habit of thought as to find such unalloyed rapture in a union unsanctified by church and unprotected by law. The truth is that women, as a sex, quickly accommodate themselves to such a situation as that in which Mavis found herself, and very rarely suffer the pangs of remorse which are placed to their credit by imaginative purists. The explanation may be that women live closer to nature than men; that they set more store on sentiment and passion than those of the opposite sex; also, perhaps, because they instinctively rebel against a male-manufactured morality to which women have to subscribe, largely for the benefit of men whose observance of moral law is more "honoured in the breach than in the observance." Indeed, it may be regarded as axiomatic that with nine hundred and ninety-nine women out of a thousand the act of bestowing themselves on the man they love is looked upon by them as the merest incident in their lives. The thousandth, the exception, to whom, like Mavis, such a surrender is a matter of supreme moment, only suffers tortures of remorse when threatened by the loss of the man's love or by other inconvenient but natural consequences of sexual temerity.

Mavis was recalled to the immediate present by an arm stealing about her neck; she thrilled at the touch of the man who had entered the room unobserved; her lips sought his.

"Ready, darling?" he asked.

"If you are."

She caught up her sunbonnet, which had been thrown on one side, to hand it to him.

"You put it on me," she said.

When he had expended several unnecessary moments in adjusting the bonnet, they made as if they would start.

"Got everything you want?" he asked, looking round the room.

"I think so. Take my sunshade."

"Right o'."

"My gloves."

"I've got 'em."

"My handkerchief."

"I've got it."

"Now kiss me."

His all too eager lips met on hers.

"Now we can start," she remarked.

She stood on the steps of the little hotel, while Perigal grasped a luncheon basket.

"Quick march!" he cried.

"Wait one moment. I so love the sunlight," she replied.

"Little pagan!"

She stood silent, while the rays of the September sun warmly caressed her face and neck.

She looked about her, to see that the sky was on all sides a faultless blue, with every prospect of its continuance.

"One of the rare days I love," she murmured.

She shut her eyes to appreciate further the sun's warmth.

"If it were only like this all the year round," she thought.

"This is going to be all my day," she said to Perigal, who was impatiently awaiting her. "I want to enjoy every moment of it for all I am worth."

They turned to the left, walking up the road to the hamlet of Crumplehorn; when they reached the mill, worked by the stream which crosses the road, they turned sharp to the left and continued to ascend. Their progress was accompanied by the music of moving water, the singing of larks. When they emerged on the Fowey road, they caught frequent glimpses of the sea, which they lost as they approached Llansallas. Arrived at this tiny, forgotten village, there was not a sign of the sea, although Perigal had been told at the inn that he would find it here. He asked the way, to be directed to a corner of the churchyard from which a track led to the shore. To their surprise, this path proved to be a partially dry watercourse which, as it wound in a downward direction, was presently quite shut in by an overgrowth of bushes. Mavis, sorry to lose the sunlight, if only for a few minutes, was yet pleased at exploring this mysterious waterway. Now and again, where the water had collected in wide pools, she had, with Perigal's assistance, to make use of stepping stones, to espy which was often difficult. They picked their way down and down for quite a long time, till Mavis began to wonder if they would ever discover an outlet. When, at last, the passage was seen to emerge into a blaze of sunlight, they ran like children to see who would be out first. In a few moments they were blinking their eyes to accustom these to the sudden sunlight. It was hard to believe that the sun had been shining while their way had been steeped in gloom. When they were shortly able to look about them, they glanced at one another, to see if the spot they reached had made anything of an impression. There was occasion for surprise. The lovers were now in an all but land-locked stretch of water, shut in by tall rocks or high ground. Before the water of the inlet could reach the sea, it would have to pass sheer, sentinel rocks which seemed to guard jealously the bay's seclusion.

From several places very high up in the ground on either side of them, water gushed out in continuous currents, making music the while, presently to merge by divers channels into a stream which straggled down to the sea. The surface of this stream was covered with watercress: this was green where the water was fresh, a bright yellow as far as the salt tide had prevailed. Between where they stood and the distressed waters of the bay was a stretch of yellow sand. A little to their right was a dismantled, tumble-down cottage, which served to emphasise the romantic remoteness of the place.

"Isn't it—isn't it exquisite?" cried Mavis.

"It might have been made for us," Perigal remarked.

"It was. Say it was."

"Of course it was. Let me make my darling comfortable. She must be tired after her walk."

"She isn't a bit—but—"

"But what, sweetheart?"

"It's a long time since she had a kiss."

Perigal insisted upon making Mavis comfortable, with her back to a conveniently situated hummock of earth. He lit a cigarette, to pass it on to her before lighting one for himself.

Mavis lay back with the cigarette between her red lips, the while her eyes lazily took in the strange loveliness about her. The joy that burned so fiercely in her heart seemed to have been communicated to the world. Sea, cliff, waterfalls were all resplendent in the bountiful sunlight.

"It's not real: it's not real," she presently murmured.

"What isn't real?" he asked.

"This: you: love."

He reassured her with kisses.

"If it would only go on for ever!" she continued. "I'm so hungry for happiness."

"Why shouldn't it?" he laughed.

"Will it be just the same when we're married?"

"Eh! Of course."

"Sure?"

"So long as you don't change," he declared.

She laughed scornfully, while he sauntered down to the sea, cigarette in mouth. Mavis settled herself luxuriously to watch the adored one through lazy, half-closed eyelids. He had previously thrown away his straw hat; she saw how the wind wantoned in his light curls. All her love seemed to well up into her throat. She would have called to him, but her tongue refused speech; she was sick with love; she wondered if she would ever recover. As he idled back, her eyes were riveted on his face.

"What's up with little Mavis?" he asked carelessly, as he reached her side.

"I love you—I love you—I love you!" she whispered faintly.

He threw himself beside her to exclaim:

"You look done. Is it the heat?"

"Love—love for you," she murmured.

He kissed her neck, first lifting the soft hair behind her ear. Her head rested helplessly on his shoulder.

"I'll see about luncheon when little Mavis will let me," he remarked.

"Don't fidget: I want to talk."

"I'll listen, provided you only talk about love."

"That's what I wanted to talk about."

"Good!"

"No one's ever loved as we do?" she asked anxiously.

"No one."

"Or ever will?"

"Never."

"Sure?"

"Quite."

"I'm sure too. And nothing's ever—ever going to change it."

"Nothing. What could?"

"I love you. Oh, how I love you!" she whispered, as she nestled closer to him.

"Don't you believe I love you?" he asked hoarsely.

"Prove it."

"How?"

"By kissing my eyes."

As they sat, her arms stole about him; she wished that they were stronger, so that she could press him closer to her heart. Presently, he unpacked the luncheon basket, spread the cloth, and insisted on making all the preparations for their midday meal. She watched him cut up the cold chicken, uncork the claret, mix the salad—this last an elaborate process.

"It's delicious," she remarked, when she tasted his concoction.

"That's all I'm good for, Tommy rotten things of no real use to anyone."

"But it is of use. It's added to the enjoyment of my lunch."

"But there's no money in it: that's what I should have said."

He filled her glass and his with claret. Before either of them drank, they touched each other's glasses.

"Suggest a toast!" said Mavis.

"Love," replied Perigal.

"Our love," corrected Mavis, as she gave him a glance rich with meaning.

"Our love, then: the most beautiful thing in the world."

"Which, unlike everything else, never dies," she declared.

They drank. Mavis presently put down her knife and fork, to take Perigal's and feed him with tid-bits from her or his plate. She would not allow him to eat of anything without her sanction; she stuffed him as the dictates of her fancy suggested. Then she mixed great black berries with the Cornish cream. When they had eaten their fill, she lit a cigarette, while her lover ate cheese. When he had finished, he sat quite close to her as he smoked. Mavis abandoned herself to the enjoyment of her cigarette; supported by her lover's arm, she looked lazily at the wild beauty spread so bountifully about her. The sun, the sea, the sky, the cliff, the day all seemed an appropriate setting to the love which warmed her body. The man at her side possessed her thoughts to the exclusion of all else; she threw away her half-smoked cigarette to look at him with soft, tremulous eyes. Suddenly, she put an arm about his neck and bent his face back, which accomplished, she leant over him to kiss his hair, eyes, neck, and mouth.

"I love you! I love you! I love you!" she murmured.

"You're wonderful, little Mavis—wonderful."

Her kisses intoxicated him. He closed his eyes and slept softly. She pulled him towards her, so that his head was pillowed on her heart; then, feeling blissfully, ecstatically happy, she closed her eyes and turned her head so that the sunlight beat full on her face. She lost all sense of surroundings and must have slept for quite two hours. When she awoke, the sun was low in the heavens. She shivered slightly with cold, and was delighted to see the kettle boiling for tea on a spirit-lamp, which Perigal had lit in the shelter of the luncheon basket.

"How thoughtful of my darling!" she remarked.

"It's just boiling. I won't keep you a moment longer than I can help."

She sipped her tea, to feel greatly refreshed with her sleep. They ate heartily at this meal. They were both so radiantly happy that they laughed whenever there was either the scantiest opportunity or none at all. The most trivial circumstance delighted them; sea and sky seemed to reflect their boundless happiness. The sea had, by now, crept quite close to them: they amused themselves by watching the myriads of sand-flies which were disturbed by every advancing wave.

"We must soon be thinking of jacking up," said Perigal.

"Surely not yet, dearest."

"But it's past six."

"Don't let us go a moment sooner than is necessary," she pleaded. "It's all been too wonderful."

As the September sun had sunk behind the cliffs, they no longer felt his warmth. When Perigal had packed the luncheon basket, they walked about hand in hand, exploring the inmost recesses of their romantic retreat. It was only when it was quite dusk that they regretfully made a start for home.

"Go on a moment. I must take a last look of where I have been so happy," said Mavis.

"Alone?"

"If you don't mind. I want to see what it's like without you. I want to carry it in my mind all my life."

It was not long before Mavis rejoined her lover. When she had looked at the spot where she had enjoyed a day of unalloyed rapture, it appeared strangely desolate in the gathering gloom of night.

"Serve you right for wishing to be without me," he laughed, when she told him how the place had presented itself to her.

"You're quite right. It does," she assented.

They had some difficulty in finding foothold on the covered way, but Perigal, by lighting matches, did much to dissipate the gloom.

"Isn't it too bad of me?" asked Mavis suddenly, "I've forgotten all about dear Jill."

"But you were talking about her a lot yesterday."

"I mean to-day. She'd never forgive me if she knew."

"You must explain how happy you've been when you see her."

When they got out by the churchyard, they found that the night was spread with innumerable stars. She nestled close to his side as they walked in the direction of Polperro. Now and again, a thick growth of hedge flowers would fill their pathway with scent, when Mavis would stop to drink her fill of the fragrance.

"Isn't it delicious?" she asked.

"It knew you were coming and has done its best to greet you."

"It's all too wonderful," she murmured.

"Like your good-night kisses," he whispered.

A love tremor possessed her body.

"Say I love you," she said at another of their frequent halts.

"I love you! I love you! I love you!"

"I love music. But there's no music like that."

He placed his arm caressingly about her soft, warm body.

"Don't!" she pleaded.

"Don't!" he queried in surprise.

"It makes me love you so."

She spoke truly: from her lips to her pretty toes her body was burning with love. Her ecstasy was such that one moment she felt as if she could wing a flight into the heavens; at another, she was faint with love-sickness, when she clung tremulously to her lover for support.

Above, the stars shone out with a yet greater brilliance and in immense profusion. Now and again, a shooting star would dart swiftly down to go out suddenly. The multitude of many coloured stars dazzled her brain. It seemed to her love-intoxicated imagination as if night embraced the earth, even as Perigal held her body to his, and that the stars were an illumination and were twinkling so happily in honour of the double union. For all the splendid egotism born of human passion, the immense intercourse of night and earth seemed to reduce her to insignificance. She crept closer to Perigal's side, as if he could give her the protection she needed. He too, perhaps, was touched with the same lowliness, and the same hunger for the support of loving sympathy. His hand sought hers; and with a great wonder, a great love and a great humility in their hearts, they walked home.

CHAPTER TWENTY-THREE
THE CURSE OF EVE

A little one was journeying to Mavis. A great fear, not unmixed with a radiant wonder, filled her being. It was now three months since her joyous stay with Perigal at Polperro. At the expiration of an all-too-brief fortnight, she had gone back, dazed, intoxicated with passion, to her humdrum work at the Melkbridge boot factory; while Perigal, provided by his father with the sinews of war, had departed for Wales, there to lay siege to elusive fortune. During this time, Mavis had seen him once or twice, when he had paid hurried visits to Melkbridge, and had heard from him often. Although his letters made copious reference to the never-to-be-forgotten joys they had experienced at Polperro, she scanned them anxiously, and in vain, for any reference to his marrying her now, or later. The omission caused her many painful hours; she realised more and more that, after the all-important part she had suffered him to play in her life, it would not be meet for her to permit any other man to be on terms other than friendship with her. It was brought home to her, and with no uncertain voice, how, in surrendering herself to her lover, she was no longer his adored Mavis, but nothing more nor less than his "thing," who was wholly, completely in his power, to make or mar as he pleased.

During these three months, she had seen or heard nothing of Windebank, so concluded that he was away.

She was much perturbed with wondering what she should do with the sumptuous dressing-case he had given her for a wedding present.

Directly there was no longer room for doubt that her union with Perigal would, in the fulness of time, bear fruit, she wrote telling him her news, and begging him to see her with as little delay as possible. In reply, she received a telegram, curtly telling her to be outside Dippenham station on Saturday afternoon at four.

This was on a Wednesday. Mavis's anxiety to hear from Perigal was such that her troubled blood set up a raging abscess in the root of a tooth that was scarcely sound. The least movement increased her torments; but what troubled her even more than the pain, was that, when the latter began to subside, one of her cheeks commenced to swell. She was anxious to look her very best before her lover: her lopsided face gave her a serio-comic expression. The swelling had diminished a little before she set out on the bleak December afternoon to meet her lover. Before she went, she looked long and anxiously in the glass. Apart from the disfigurement caused by the swelling, she saw (yet strove to conceal from herself) that her condition was already interfering with her fresh, young comeliness: her eyes were drawn; her features wore a tense, tired expression. As she looked out of the carriage window on her train journey to Dippenham, the gloom inspired by the darkening shadows of the day, the dreariness of the bleak landscape, chilled her to the heart. She comforted herself by reflecting with what eager cheerfulness Perigal would greet her; how delighted he would be at receiving from her lips further confirmation of her news; how loyally he would fulfil his many promises by making the earliest arrangements for their marriage. Arrived at her destination, she learned she would have to wait twelve minutes till the train arrived that would bring her lover from Wales. She did not stay in the comparative comfort of the waiting-room, but, despite the pain that movement still gave her, preferred to wander in the streets of the dull, quaint town till his train was due. A thousand doubts assailed her mind: perhaps he would not come, or would be angry with her, or would meet with an accident upon the way. Her mind travelled quickly, and her body felt the need of keeping pace with the rapidity of her thoughts. She walked with sharp, nervous steps down the road leading from the station, to be pulled up by the insistent pain in her head. She returned so carefully that Perigal's train was steaming into the station as she reached the booking office. She walked over the bridge to get to his platform, to be stopped for a few moments by the rush, roar, and violence of a West of England express, passing immediately under where she stood. The disturbance of the passing train stunned and then jarred her overwrought nerves, causing the pain in her face to get suddenly worse. As she met those who had got out of the train Perigal would come by, she wondered if he would so much as notice the disfigurement of her face. For her part, if he came to her one-armed and blind, it would make no difference to her; indeed, she would love him the more. Perigal stepped from the door of a first class compartment, seemingly having been aroused from sleep by a porter; he carried a bag.

Mavis noticed, with a great concern, how careworn he was looking—a great concern, because, directly she set eyes on him, she realised the immensity of her love for him. At that moment she loved him more than she had ever done before; he was not only her lover, to whom she had surrendered herself body and soul, but also the father of her unborn little one. Faintness threatened her; she clung to the handle of a weighing machine for support.

"More trouble!" he remarked, as he reached her.

She looked at him with frightened eyes, finding it hard to believe the evidence of her ears.

"W-what?" she faltered.

"Heavens!"

"What's the matter, dear?"

"What have you done to your face?"

"I—I hoped you wouldn't notice. I've had an abscess."

"Notice it! Haven't you looked in the glass?"

Mavis bit her lip.

"I shouldn't have thought you could look so—look like that," he continued.

"What trouble did you mean?" she found words to ask.

"This. Why you sent for me."

She felt as if he had stabbed her. She stopped, overwhelmed by the blow that the man she loved so whole-heartedly had struck her.

"What's up?" he asked.

"Nothing—only—"

"Only what?"

"You don't seem at all glad to see me."

She spoke as if pained at and resentful of his coldness. He looked at her, to watch the suffering in her eyes crystallise into a defiant hardness.

"I am, no end. But I'm tired and cold. Wait till we've had something to eat," he said kindly.

Mavis melted. Her love for him was such that she found it no easy matter being angry with him.

"How selfish of me! I ought to have known," she remarked. "Let someone take your bag."

"I don't know where I'm going to stop. I'll leave it at the station for the present."

"Aren't you going home?" she asked in some surprise.

"We'll talk over everything when I've got warm."

She waited while he left his bag in the cloak-room. When he joined her, they walked along the street leading from the station.

"I could have seen what's up with you without being told," he remarked ungenially.

"It won't be for so very long. I shall look all right again some day," she declared, with a sad little laugh.

"That's the worst of women," he went on. "Just when you think everything's all right, this goes and happens."

His words fired her blood.

"I should have thought you would have been very proud," she cried.

"Eh!"

"However foolish I've been, I'm not the ordinary sort of woman. Where I've been wrong is in being too kind to you."

She paused for breath. She was also a little surprised at her bold words; she was so completely at the man's mercy.

"I do appreciate it. I'd be a fool if I didn't. But it's this development that's so inconvenient."

"Inconvenient! Inconvenient you call it—!"

"This will do us," he interrupted, pausing at the doorway of the "King's Arms Hotel."

"I'm not sure I'll come in."

"Please yourself. But it's as well to have a talk, so that we can see exactly where we stand."

His words voiced the present desire of her heart. She was burning to put an end to her suspense, to find out exactly where she stood. The comparative comfort of the interior of the hotel thawed his coldness.

"Rather a difficult little Mavis," he smiled as they ascended the stairs.

"I'm all right till I'm roused. Then I feel capable of anything."

"The sort of girl I admire," he admitted.

He engaged a sitting-room and bedroom for the night. Mavis did not trouble to consider what relation to Perigal the hotel people believed her to be. Her one concern was to discover his intentions with regard to the complication which had arisen in her life. She ordered tea. While it was being got ready, she sat by the newly-lit fire, a prey to gloomy thoughts.

The pain in her face had, in a measure, abated. She was alone, Perigal having gone to the bedroom to wash after his journey. She contrasted her present misery with the joyousness that had possessed her when last she had been under the same roof as her lover. Tears welled into her eyes, but she held them back, fearing they would further contribute to the undoing of her looks.

When the tea was brought, she made the waiter wheel the table to the fire; she also took off her cloak and hat and smoothed her hair in the glass. She put the toast by the fire in order to keep it warm. She wanted everything to be comfortable and home-like for her lover. She then poked the fire into a blaze and moved a cumbrous arm chair to a corner of the tea table. When Perigal came in, he was smoking a cigarette.

"Trying to work up a domestic atmosphere," he laughed, with a faint suggestion of a sneer in his hilarity.

Mavis bit her lip.

"It was the obvious thing to do. Don't be obvious, little Mavis. It jars."

"Won't you have some tea?" she faltered.

"No, thanks. I've ordered something a jolly sight better than tea," he said, warming his hands at the fire.

Mavis was too stunned to make any comment. She found it hard to believe that the ardent lover of Polperro and the man who was so indifferent to her extremity, were one and the same. She felt as if her heart had been hammered with remorseless blows. They waited in silence till a waiter brought in a bottle of whisky, six bottles of soda water, glasses, and a box of cigarettes.

"Have some whisky?" asked Perigal of Mavis.

"I prefer tea!"

"Have some in that?"

"No, thank you."

While Mavis sipped her tea, she watched him from the corner of her eyes mix himself a stiff glass of whisky and soda. She would have given many years of her life to have loved him a little less than she did; she dimly realised that his indifference only fanned the raging fires of her passion.

"I feel better now," he said presently.

"I'm glad. I must be going."

"Eh!"

Mavis got up and went to get her hat.

"I wish you to stay for dinner."

"I'm sorry. But I must get back," she said, as she pinned on her hat.

"I wish you to stay," he declared, as he caught her insistently by the arm.

The touch of his flesh moved her to the marrow. She sat helplessly. He appeared to enjoy her abject surrender.

"Now I'll have some tea, little Mavis," he said.

She poured him out a cup, while he got the toast from the fender to press some on her. He began to recover his spirits; he talked, laughed, and rallied her on her depression. She was not insensible to his change of mood.

When the tea was taken away, he pressed a cigarette on her against her will.

"You always get your own way," she murmured, as he lit it for her.

"Now we'll have a cosy little chat," he said, as he wheeled her chair to the fire. He brought his chair quite near to hers.

Mavis did not suffer quite so much.

"Now about this trouble," he continued. "Tell me all about it."

She restated the subject of her last letter in as few words as possible. When she had finished, he asked her a number of questions which betrayed a familiar knowledge of the physiology of her extremity. She wondered where he could have gained his information, not without many jealous pangs at this suggestion of his having been equally intimate with others of her sex.

"Hang it all! It's not nearly so bad as it might be," he said presently.

"What do you mean?"

"Why that, if every woman who got into the same scrape did nothing to help herself, the world would be over-populated in five minutes."

Mavis sat bolt upright. Her hands grasped the arms of her chair; her eyes stared straight before her. There arose to her quick fancy the recollection of certain confidences of Miss Allen, which had hinted at hideous malpractices of the underworld of vice, affecting women in a similar condition to hers.

"Well?" said Perigal.

The sound of his voice recalled her to the present.

Mavis rose, placed a hand on each arm of Perigal's chair, and leant over so as to look him full in the eyes, as she said icily:

"Do you know what you are saying?"

"Eh! Dear little Mavis. You take everything so seriously," he remarked, as he kissed her lightly on the cheek.

She sat back in her chair, uneasy, troubled: vague, unwholesome, sordid shadows seemed to gather about her.

"Ever gone in for sea-fishing?" Perigal asked, after some minutes of silence.

"No."

"I'm awfully keen. I'm on it all day when the wind isn't east."

This enthusiasm for sea-fishing struck a further chill to Mavis's forlorn heart. She could not help thinking that, if he had been moved by a loving concern for her welfare, he would have devoted his days to the making of a competence on which they could live.

"Now about this trouble," said Perigal, at which Mavis listened with all her ears. He went on: "I know, of course, the proper thing, the right thing to do is to marry you at once." Here he paused.

Mavis waited in suspense for him to go on; it seemed an epoch of time till he added:

"But what are we going to live upon?"

She kept on repeating his words to herself. She felt as if she were drowning in utter darkness.

"I can tell you at once that there's precious little money in bricks. I'm fighting against big odds, and if I were worrying about you—if you had enough to live upon and all that—I couldn't give proper attention to business."

"It would be heaven for me," she remarked.

"So you say now. All I ask you to do is to trust implicitly in me and wait."

"How long?" she gasped.

"I can't say for certain. It all depends."

"On what?"

"Circumstances."

She did not speak for some moments, the while she repressed an impulse to throw herself at his feet, and implore him to reconsider his indefinite promise.

"Will you pour me out a little whisky?" she said presently.

"What about your face? It might make it throb."

"I'll chance that."

"Aren't you well, little Mavis?" he asked kindly.

"Not very. It must be the heat of the room."

She gulped down the spirit, to feel the better for it. It seemed to give her heart to face her misfortunes. She could say no more just then, as a man came into the room to lay the table.

Whilst this operation was in progress, she thought of the unlooked-for situation in which she found herself. It was not so very long since Perigal was the suppliant, she the giver; now, the parts were reversed, except that, whereas she had given without stint, he withheld that which every wholesome instinct of his being should urge him to bestow without delay.

She wondered at the reason of the change, till the words he had spoken on the day of their jaunt to Broughton occurred to her:

"No sooner was one want satisfied than another arose to take its place. It's a law of nature that ensures the survival of the fittest, by making men always struggle to win the desire of the moment."

She had been Perigal's desire, but, once won, another had taken its place, which, so far as she could see, was sea-fishing. She smiled grimly at the alteration in his taste. Then, an idea illuminated, possessed her mind.

"Why not make myself desirable so that he will be eager to win me again," she thought.

So Mavis, despite the pain in her face, which owing to the spirit she had drunk was beginning to trouble her again, set out on the most dismal of all feminine quests—that of endeavouring to make a worldly, selfish man pay the price of his liberty, and endure poverty for that which he had already enjoyed to the full. With a supreme effort of will, she subdued her inclination to unrestrained despair; with complete disregard of the acute pain in her head, she became gay, light-hearted, irresponsible, joyous. There was an undercurrent of suffering in her simulated mirth, but Perigal did not notice it; he was taken by surprise at the sudden change in her mood. He responded to her supposititious merriment; he laughed and joked as irrepressibly as did Mavis.

"Quite like the old Polperro days," he replied to one of Mavis' sallies.

His remark reduced her to momentary thoughtfulness. The staple dish of the extemporised meal was a pheasant. Perigal, despite her protests, was heaping up her plate a second time, when he said:

"Do you know what I was dreading the whole way up?"

"That you'd got into the right train!"

"Scarcely that. I was funky you'd do the obvious sentimental thing, and wear the old Polperro dress."

"As if I would!"

"Anyway, you haven't. Besides, it's much too cold."

He ordered champagne. Further to play the part of Circe to his Ulysses, she drank a little of this, careless of the pain it might inflict. Although she was worn down by her anxieties and the pain of her abscess, it gave her an immense thrill of pleasure to notice how soon she recovered her old ascendancy over him. Now, his admiring eyes never left her face. Once, when he got up to hand her something, he went out of his way to come behind her to kiss her neck.

"Little Mavis is a fascinating little devil," he remarked, as he resumed his seat.

"That's what you thought when I met you at the station."

"I was tired and worried, and worry destroys love quicker than anything. Now—"

"Now!"

"You've gone the shortest way to 'buck' me up."

Thus encouraged, Mavis made further efforts to captivate Perigal, and persuade him to fulfill the desire of her heart. Now, he was constantly about her on any and every excuse, when he would either kiss her or caress her hair. After dinner, they sat by the fire, where they drank coffee and smoked cigarettes. Presently, Perigal slipped on the ground beside her, where he leaned his head against her knee, while he fondled one of her feet. Her fingers wandered in his hair.

"Like old times, sweetheart!" he said,

"Is it?" she laughed.

"It is to me, little Mavis. I love you! I love you! I love you!"

Mavis's heart leapt. Life held promise of happiness after all.

"What have you arranged about tonight?" he asked, after a few moments' silence.

"Nothing unusual. Why?"

"Must you go back?"

"Why?" she asked, wondering what he was driving at.

"I thought you might stay here."

"Stay here!" she gasped.

"With me—as you did in Polperro." Then, as she did not speak: "There's no reason why you shouldn't!"

A great horror possessed Mavis. This, then, was all she had laboured for; all he thought of her. She had believed that he would have offered immediate marriage. His suggestion helped her to realise the hopelessness of her situation; how, in the eternal contest between the sexes, she had not only laid all her cards upon the table, but had permitted him to win every trick. She fell from the summit of her blissful anticipations into a slough of despair. She had little or no hope of his ever making her the only possible reparation. Ruin, disgrace, stared her in the face. And after all the fine hopes with which she had embarked on life! Her pride revolted at this promise of hapless degradation. Anything rather than that. There was but one way to avoid such a fate, not only for her, but for the new life within her. The roar and rush of the express, when she had crossed the footbridge at the station, sounded hopefully in her ears.

"There's no reason why you shouldn't!" he repeated.

"Indeed?" she said mechanically.

"Is there? After all that's happened, what difference can it make?" he persisted, as he reached for a cigarette.

"What difference can it make?" she repeated dully.

"Good! Dear little Mavis! Have another cigarette."

Unseen by him, she had caught up coat, gloves, and hat, and moved towards the door. Here she had paused, finding it hard to leave him whom she loved unreservedly for other women to caress and care for.

The words, "What difference can it make?" decided her. They spurred her along the short, quick road which was to end in peaceful oblivion. She opened the door noiselessly, and slipped down the stairs and out of the front door with out being seen by any of the hotel people. Once in the street, where a drizzle was falling, she turned to the right in the direction of the station. It seemed a long way. She would have liked to have stepped from the room, in which she had been with Perigal, on to the rails before the passing express. She hurried on. Although it was Saturday night, there were few people about, the bad weather keeping many indoors who would otherwise be out. She was within a few paces of the booking office when she felt a hand on her arm.

"Don't stop me! Let me go!" she cried.

"Where to?" asked Perigal's voice.

She pressed forward.

"Don't be a little fool. Are you mad? Stop!"

He forced her to a standstill.

"Now come back," he said.

"No. Let me go."

"Are you so mad as to do anything foolish?"

By way of reply, she made a vain effort to free herself. He tried to reason with her, but nothing he urged could change her resolution. Her face was expressionless; her eyes dull; her mind appeared to be obsessed by a determination to take her life. He changed his tactics.

"Very well, then," he said, "come along."

She looked at him, surprised, as she started off.

"Where you go, I go; whatever you do, I do."

She paused to say:

"If you'd let me have my own way, I should be now out of my misery."

"You only think of yourself," he cried. "You don't mind what would happen to me if you—if you—!"

"A lot you'd care!" she interrupted.

"Don't talk rot. It's coming down worse than ever. Come back to the hotel."

"Never that," she said, compressing her lip.

"You'll catch your death here."

"A good thing too. I can't go on living. If I do, I shall go mad," she cried, pressing her hands to her head.

Passers-by were beginning to notice them.

Without success, Perigal urged her to walk.

She became hysterically excited and upbraided him in no uncertain voice. She seemed to be working herself into a paroxysm of frenzy. To calm her, perhaps because he was moved by her extremity, he overwhelmed her with endearments, the while he kissed her hands, her arms, her face, when no one was by.

She was influenced by his caresses, for she, presently, permitted herself to walk with him down the street, where they turned into the railed-in walk which crossed the churchyard.

He redoubled his efforts to induce in her a more normal state of mind.

"Don't you love me, little Mavis?" he asked. "If you did, you wouldn't distress me so."

"Love you!" she laughed scornfully.

"Then why can't you listen and believe what I say?"

He said more to the same effect, urging, begging, praying her to trust him to marry her, when he could see his way clearly.

Perhaps because the mind, when confronted with danger, fights for existence as lustily as does the body, Mavis, against her convictions, strove with some success to believe the honeyed assurances which dropped so glibly from her lover's tongue. His eloquence bore down her already enfeebled resolution.

"Go on; go on; go on!" she cried. "It's all lies, no doubt; but it's sweet to listen to all the same."

He looked at her in surprise.

"Your love-words, I mean. They're all I've got to live for now. What you can't find heart to say, invent. You've no idea what good it does me."

"Mavis!" he cried reproachfully.

"It seems to give me life," she declared, to add after a few moments of silence: "Situated as I am, they're like drops of water to a man dying of thirst."

"But you're not going to die: you're going to live and be happy with me!"

She looked at him questioningly, putting her soul into her eyes.

"But you must trust me," he continued.

"Haven't I already?" she asked.

He took no notice of her remark, but gave utterance to a platitude.

"There's no love without trust," he said.

"Say that again."

"There's no love without trust," he repeated. "What are you thinking of?" he asked, as she did not speak.

A light kindled in her eyes; her face was aglow with emotion; her bosom heaved convulsively.

"You ask me to trust you?" she said.

He nodded.

"Very well, then: I love you; I will."

"Mavis!" he cried.

"More, I'll prove it. You asked me to stay here with you. I refused. I love you—I trust you. Do with me as you will."

"Mavis!"

"I distrusted you. I did wrong, I atone."

CHAPTER TWENTY-FOUR
SNARES

The Sunday week after Mavis' meeting with Perigal at Dippenham, she left the train at Paddington a few minutes after six in the evening. She got a porter to wheel her luggage to the cloak-room, reserving a small handbag for her use, which contained her savings.

She then made for the refreshment room, where she ordered and sipped a cup of tea. She would have liked more, but as she had so much to do with her money, she did not think she dare afford the threepence which she would have to pay for another cup. As she rested for some moments in the comparative seclusion of the refreshment room, she derived satisfaction from the fact that she had got away from Melkbridge before any suspicions had arisen of her condition. Upon her return to her lodging after seeing Perigal, she had, at his instigation, written to Mr Devitt, telling him that she would be leaving his employment in a week's time. She gave no reason for throwing up her work, beyond saying that the state of her health necessitated a change of occupation. She had also given notice to Mrs Farthing, and had spent her spare time in packing up and saying goodbye to her few friends. Her chief difficulty was with her dear Jill, as she knew how many London landladies objected to having dogs in lodgings. At last, she arranged for Mrs Trivett to look after her pet till such time as she could be sent for. Mavis had offered the farmer's wife a shilling or two a week for Jill's keep, but her kind friend would not hear of any such arrangement being made. Then had followed Mavis' goodbye to her dog, a parting which had greatly distressed her. Jill had seemed to divine that something was afoot, for her eyes showed a deep, pleading look when Mavis had clasped her in her arms and covered her black face with kisses. She thought of her now as she sat in the waiting room; tears welled to her eyes. With a sigh she realised that she must set about looking for a lodging. She left the waiting room in order to renew the old familiar quest. Mavis walked into the depressing ugliness of Eastbourne Terrace, at the most dismal hour of that most dismal of all days, the London Sunday in winter. The street lamps seemed to call attention to the rawness of the evening air. The roads, save for a few hurrying, recently released servants, were deserted; every house was lit up—all factors that oppressed Mavis with a sense of unspeakable loneliness. She became overwhelmed with self-consciousness; she believed that every passer-by, who glanced at her, could read her condition in her face; she feared that her secret was known to a curious, resentful world. Mavis felt heartsick, till, with something of an effort, she remembered that this, and all she had to endure in the comparatively near future, should be and were sacrifices upon the shrine of the loved one. She had walked some distance along Praed Street, and was now in the wilderness of pretentious, stucco-faced mansions, which lie between Paddington and the north side of Hyde Park. She knew it was useless to seek for lodgings here, so pressed on, hoping to arrive at a humbler neighbourhood, where she would be more likely to get what she wanted. As she walked, the front doors of the big houses would now and again open, when she was much surprised at the vulgar appearance of many of those who came out. It seemed to her as if the district in which she found herself was largely tenanted by well-to-do, but self-made people. After walking for many minutes, she reached the Bayswater Road, which just now was all but deserted. The bare trees on the further side of the road accentuated the desolation of the thoroughfare. She turned to the left and pressed on, fighting valiantly against the persistent spirit of loneliness which seemed to dog her footsteps. Men and girls hurried by to keep appointments with friends or lovers. Buses jogged past her, loaded with people who all had somewhere to go, and probably someone who looked for their coming. She was friendless and alone. Ever since her interview with Perigal she had realised how everything she valued in life, if not life itself, depended on her implicit faith in him. He had told her that there could be no love without trust; she had believed in this assertion as if it had been another revelation, and it had enabled her to go through the past week with hardly a pang of regret (always excepting her parting from Jill) at breaking with all the associations that had grown about her life during her happy stay at Melkbridge.

Now doubts assailed her mind. She knew that if she surrendered to them it meant giving way to despair; she thought of any and all of Perigal's words which she could honestly construe into a resolve on his part to marry her before her child was born. As she thus struggled against her unquiet thoughts, two men (at intervals of a few minutes) followed and attempted to speak to her. Their unwelcome attentions increased her uneasiness of mind; they seemed to tell her of the dubious ways by which men sought to entangle in their toils those of her own sex who were pleasing to the eye: just now, she lumped all men together, and would not admit that there was any difference between them. Arrived in the neighbourhood of the Marble Arch, she was sure of her ground. She was reminded of her wanderings of evenings from "Dawes'," when, if not exploring Soho, she had often walked in this direction. Memories of those long-forgotten days, which now seemed so remote, assailed her at every step. Then she had believed herself to be unhappy. Now she would have given many years of her life to be able to change her present condition (including her trust in Perigal) to be as she was before she had met him. Directly she crossed Edgware Road, the pavement became more crowded.

Shop-girls (the type of young woman she knew well) and hobbledehoyish youths, the latter clad in "reach-me-down" frockcoat suits, high collars, and small, ready-made bow ties, thronged about her. She could not help contrasting the anaemic faces, the narrow, stooping shoulders of these youths with the solidly-built, ruddy-cheeked men whom she had seen in Wiltshire. She was rapidly losing her old powers of physical endurance; she felt exhausted, and turned into the small Italian restaurant on the left, which she had sometimes gone to when at "Dawes'."

"It hasn't changed one bit," she thought, as she entered and walked to the inner room. There was the same bit of painted canvas at the further end of the place, depicting nothing in particular. There were the same shy, self-conscious, whispering couples seated at the marble-topped tables, who, after critically looking over the soiled bill of fare, would invariably order coffee, roll and butter, or, if times were good, steak and fried potatoes. The same puffy Italian waiter stood by the counter, holding, as of old, coffee-pot in one hand and milk-pot in the other. Mavis always associated this man with the pots, which he never relinquished; she remembered wondering if he slept, still holding them in his grasp.

She ordered a veal cutlet and macaroni, for which the place was famous among the epicures of "Dawes'." While it was being prepared, she brought notepaper, envelope, and pencil from her bag, to write a short note to Perigal.

The morning post had brought her a letter from him, which had enclosed notes to the value of ten pounds towards the expenses of her enforced stay in London. Her reply told him that, as she had enough for present needs, she returned his money. She suggested that if he had no use for it, he could put it towards the expenses of providing their home; that she had arrived safely in London; that she was about to look for a lodging. She ended with passionately affectionate wishes for his wellbeing. When she had put the money and letter into the envelope, and this into her bag, her meal was banged down before her. She ordered a bottle of stout, for had she not to nourish another life beside her own? After Mavis had finished, she did not feel in the least disposed to go out. She sat back on the dingy plush seat, and enjoyed the sensation of the food doing her good. It was seven o'clock when she paid the waiter and joined the crowd now sauntering along Oxford Street. She walked towards Regent Circus, hoping to find a post-office, where she could get a stamp for Perigal's letter. She wondered if she should go to church, if only for a few minutes, but decided to keep away from a place of worship, feeling that her thoughts were too occupied with her troubles to give adequate attention to the service. A new, yet at the same time familiar dread, oppressed her. She seemed to get relief from hurrying along the crowded pavement. She longed to get settled for the night, but was still uncertain where to seek a lodging. She had some thought of taking the Tube, and looking about her in the direction of Hammersmith, but her one thought now was to get indoors with as little delay as possible. She remembered that there was a maze of private houses along the Tottenham Court Road, in many of which she had often noticed that there was displayed a card, announcing that apartments were to let. She took a 'bus to the Tottenham Court Road. Arrived there, she got out and walked along it, to turn, presently, to the right. Most of the houses, for all their substantial fronts, had an indefinable atmosphere of being down at heel, perhaps because many were almost in darkness. They looked like houses that were in no sense of the word homes. She selected one of the least forbidding and knocked at the door. After waiting some time, she heard footsteps scuffling along the passage. A blowsy, elderly, red-faced woman opened the door. She was clad in a greasy flannel dressing gown; unbrushed hair fell on her shoulders; naked, unclean toes protruded through holes in her stockings and slippers.

"Good evening, dear," said the woman. Mavis turned to go.

"Was you wanting rooms, my dear?"

"I was."

"I've the very thing you want. Don't run away."

Mavis hesitated.

"Don't judge of 'em by me. I ain't been quite myself, as you, being another lady, can quite understand, an' I overslep' myself a bit; but if you'll walk inside, you'll be glad you didn't go elsewhere."

Mavis was so tired, that she persuaded herself that the landlady's appearance might not be indicative (as it invariably is) of the character of the rooms.

"One moment. Oo sent yer?" asked the woman.

"No one. I saw—"

"Didn't Foxy?"

"No one did. I saw the card in the window."

"Please to walk upstairs."

Mavis followed the woman up unswept stairs to the first floor, where the landlady fumbled with a key in the lock of a door.

"S'pose you know Foxy?" she queried.

"No. Who is he?"

"'E goes about the West End and brings me lady lodgers."

"I'm from the country," remarked Mavis.

"You a dear little bird from far away? You've fallen on a pretty perch, my dear, an' you can thank Gawd you ain't got with some as I could mention."

By this time, they had got into the room, where the landlady lighted one jet of a dirty chandelier.

"There now!" cried the landlady triumphantly.

Mavis looked about her at the gilt-framed glass over the mantelpiece, the table, the five chairs (including one arm), the sofa and the chiffonnier, which was pretty well all the furniture that the room contained. The remains of a fire untidied the grate; the flimsiest curtains were hung before the windows. The landlady was quick to notice the look of disappointment on the girl's face.

"See the bedroom, my dear, before you settle."

This proved to be even less inviting than the sitting-room: hardly any of the furniture was perfect; a dirty piece of stuff was pinned across the window; dust lay heavy on toilet glass and mantel. Happily contrasted with this squalor was the big bed, which was invitingly comfortable and clean.

Mavis was very tired; she looked longingly at the bed, with its luxurious, lace-fringed pillows. The landlady marked her indecision.

"It's very cheap, miss."

"What do you call cheap?"

"Two guineas a week; light an' coals extry."

"Two guineas a week!"

"You've perfec' liberty to bring in who you like."

Mavis stared at her in astonishment.

"An' no questions asked, my dear."

Mavis wondered if the woman were in her right senses.

"I thought you'd jump at it," she went on. "I could see it when you saw the bed. The gentlemen like a nice clean bed."

Mavis understood; clutching her bag, she walked to the door.

"Not goin' to 'ave 'em?" screeched the landlady.

Mavis hurried on.

"Guinea a week and what extries you like. There!"

Mavis ran down the stairs.

"Won't they give you more than five shillings?" shouted the woman over the banisters as Mavis reached the door.

"I s'pose your beat is the Park," the woman shrieked, as Mavis ran down the steps.

Mavis ran a few yards, to stop short. She trembled from head to foot; tears scalded her eyes, which, with a great effort, she kept back. She was crushed with humiliation and shame. At once she thought of the loved one, and how deeply he would resent the horrible insult to which his tenderly loved little Mavis had been subjected. But there was no time for vain imaginings. With the landlady's foul insinuations ringing in her ears, she set about looking for a house where she might get what she wanted. The rain, that had been threatening all day, began to fall, but her umbrella was at Paddington. She was not very far from the Tottenham Court Road. Fearful of catching cold in her present condition, she hurried to this thoroughfare, where she thought she might get shelter. When she got there, she found that places of vantage were already occupied to their utmost capacity by umbrellaless folk like herself. She hurried along till she came to what, from the pseudoclassic appearance of the structure, seemed a place of dissenting worship. She ran up the steps to the lobby, where she found the shelter she required. A door leading to the chapel was open, which enabled her to overhear the conclusion of the sermon. As the preacher's words fell on her ears, she listened intently, and edged nearer to the door communicating with the chapel. His message seemed meant expressly for her. It told her that, despite anything anyone might presume to urge to the contrary, God was ever the loving Father of His children; that He rejoiced when they rejoiced, suffered when they sorrowed; however much the faint-hearted might be led to believe that the world was ruled by remorseless law, that much faith and a little patience would enable even the veriest sinner to see how the seemingly cruellest inflictions of Providence were for the sufferer's ultimate good, and, therefore, happiness.

Presently, when the rain stopped, Mavis came away feeling mentally refreshed. As is usual with those in trouble, she applied anything pertinent she read or heard about sorrow to herself. The fact of her intercourse with Perigal having been in the nature of deadly sin did not trouble her so much as might have been expected. She felt that God would understand, and believed that to know all was to forgive all. Also, try as she might, she could not see that her sin was of such a deadly nature as it is made out to be by the Church. It seemed that her surrender to her lover at Polperro had been the natural and inevitable consequence of her love for him, and that, if the one were condemned, so also should love be itself, inasmuch as it was plainly responsible for what had happened. Now, she was glad to learn, on the authority of the pulpit, that, however much she suffered from her present extremity, it would be for her ultimate happiness.

She started afresh to look for a lodging. She needed all the resolution she could muster. Repulsive-looking foreign women opened most of the doors at which she knocked, whilst surly-looking men hovered in the background.

Mavis wished she had started earlier for Hammersmith, to see what she could find there. At last she went into a chemist's shop which she saw open, to ask if she could be recommended to any rooms. A burly, blotchy-faced, bearded man stood behind the bottle-laden counter. Mavis stated her wants.

"Married?" asked the man.

"Y—yes—but I'm living by myself for the present."

"Of course. But your husband would visit you," remarked the man with a leer.

Mavis looked at him in surprise.

"Well, we'll call it your husband," suggested the chemist.

Mavis walked from the shop.

It seemed that everyone was in league to insult her. Her heart was heavy with grief. She could not help thinking how the presence of the loved one, a word of encouragement from him, would instantly dissipate her soreness of heart and growing physical exhaustion.

She gave up the idea of looking for rooms in this disreputable corner of London. Her only concern was to get lodging for the night, so that she could resume her quest on the morrow in a more likely part of the great city. She stopped a policeman and asked to be directed to a reasonable hotel. The man told her that she would find what she wanted in the Euston Road. She walked along this depressing and sordid thoroughfare, where what were once front gardens before comfortable houses were now waste spaces, given over to the display of dilapidated signboards of strange and unfamiliar trades. Here she dragged herself up the steps of the hotels that abound in this road, to learn at each one she applied at that they were full for the night. If she had not been so tired, she would have wondered if they were speaking the truth, or if they divined her condition and did not consider her to be a respectable applicant. At the last at which she called, she was asked to write her name in the hotel book. She commenced to write Mavis Keeves, but remembered that she had decided to call herself Mrs Kenrick while in London. She crossed out what she had written, to substitute the name she had elected to bear. Whether or not this correction made the hotel people suspicious, she was soon informed that she could not be accommodated. Mavis, heartsore and weary, went out into the night. A different class of person to the one that she had met earlier in the evening began to infest the streets. Bold-eyed women, dressed in cheap finery, appeared here and there, either singly or in pairs. The vague, yet familiar fear, which she had experienced when she began to look for rooms, again took possession of her with gradually increasing force. She was soon on such familiar terms with this obsession, that she remembered when and how it had first originated in her mind. It was after her adventure with Mrs Hamilton and her chance meeting with the never-to-be-forgotten Mrs Ewer, when a horrid fear of London had possessed her soul. Now she saw, even plainer than before, the deep pitfalls and foul morasses which ever menace the feet of unprotected girls in London who have to earn their daily bread. If it were an effort for her to snatch a living from the great industrial machine when she was last in London, now, in her condition, it was practically hopeless to look for work. Mind and body were paralysed by a great fear. To add to her discomfiture, the rain again began to fall. Scarcely knowing what she was doing, she walked up a pathway, running parallel with the road, which flanked a row of forlorn-looking houses. Here she felt so faint that she was compelled to cling to the railings to save herself from falling. Two children passed, one of whom carried a jug, who stopped to stare at her.

"Please!" called Mavis weakly, at which one of the children approached her.

"Can you tell me where I can get a room?"

"I'll ask fader," replied the child, who spoke with a German accent.

Mavis remembered little beyond waiting an eternity of suspense, and then of being assisted into a house, up a flight of stairs to a room where she sank on the nearest thing handy. She opened her frock to clutch, as if for protection, the ring Perigal had given her, and which she always wore suspended on her heart. Then she was overtaken by unconsciousness.

When she awoke, she rubbed her eyes again and again, whilst a horrible pungent smell affected her nostrils. She could scarcely believe that she had got to where she found herself. She saw by the morning light, which was feebly straggling into the room, that she was lying, fully dressed, on an untidy, dirty bed. The room looked so abjectly wretched that she sprang from her resting-place and attempted to draw the curtains, in order to take complete stock of her surroundings—attempted, because the dark, cheap cretonne, of which they were made, refused to move, their tops being nailed to the upper woodwork of the window by tintacks. She tried the second window (the room boasted two), with the same result, owing to a like cause. For her safety's sake, she was relieved to find that the room overlooked the Euston Road.

After turning back the chintz curtains, she looked about her. She had never been in such a truly awful-looking room before. She had never imagined that any four walls could enclose such hopeless, dejected desolation as she saw. A round table stood in the middle of the carpetless room. There were several other tables about this one. Upon one stood a basin, in which was water that had some time ago been used for the ablutionary purposes of someone sadly in need of a wash. Thick rims of dirt encrusted the sides of the basin where the water had not reached. The looking glass was pimpled with droppings from lighted candles. Upon a further table was a tumbler filthy to look upon. The bed was painted iron; it wanted a leg, and to supply the deficiency a grocer's box had been thrust underneath. The blankets of the bed (which contained two pillows) were as grubby as the sheets. The pillows beside the one on which she had slept bore the impress of somebody's head. Over everything, walls, furniture, ceiling, and floor, lay a thick deposit of dust and grime. Misspelt lewd words were fingered on the dirt of the window-panes. The horror of the room seemed to grip Mavis by the throat. She coughed, to sicken at a foul feeling in her mouth, which seemed to be gritty from the unclean air of the room. This atmosphere was not only as if the windows had not been opened for years; it was as if it had been inhaled over and over again by alcohol-breathing lungs; also, the horrid memories of sordid lusts, of unnumbered bestial acts, seemed to lie heavy on the polluted fuggy air. To get away from the all-pervading stench, Mavis hurried to the door. This, she could not help noticing, hung loosely on its hinges; also, that about the doorplate were innumerable lock marks and screw holes, as if the door had been furnished with fastenings, times out of number, till the rotten wood refused to support any more. Mavis pulled open the door and walked on to a carpetless landing and stairs. She stamped with her foot, but this not attracting any attention, she called aloud. Her voice echoed as if she were in a vault. After some time, she heard a door unbolted, and a rough, unkempt man came up the stairs.

"How much?" asked Mavis.

"Five shillin'."

"For that?"

"Five shillin'," repeated the man doggedly.

Mavis did not further argue the point, as, when she opened her mouth, the stench of the room she had quitted seemed to fasten on her throat.

She paid the money and was about to fly down the stairs. Then she remembered her precious bag. Again holding her nose, she hurried back into the room where she had unwittingly passed the night. The bag was nowhere to be seen, although its outline was to be easily traced in the dust on the table where she had put it.

"My bag! my bag!" she cried.

"Vot bag?"

"The one I had last night. Here's its mark upon the table."

"I know nodinks about it," replied the man, as he disappeared down the stairs.

CHAPTER TWENTY-FIVE
A NEW ACQUAINTANCE

Mavis' heart seemed to stop. She knew the bag contained her trinkets, her reserve capital of twenty-three pounds, Perigal's letters, her powder-puff, and other feminine odds and ends. What she could not remember was if she had posted her note to Perigal, which contained the money she was returning to him. As much as her consternation would permit, she rapidly passed over in her mind everything that had happened since she had left the restaurant in Oxford Street. For the life of her, she could not recall going into a postoffice to purchase the stamp of which she had been in need. Her next thought was the quickest way to get back her property, at which the word police immediately suggested itself. Once outside the house, she made careful note of its number; she then walked quickly till she came upon a policeman, to whom she told her trouble.

"Was you there alone?" asked the constable.

Mavis looked at him inquiringly.

"I mean was you with a gentleman?"

Mavis bit her lip, but saw it would not help her to be indignant. She told the man how she got there, a statement which made him civil and sympathetic.

"It's a bad place, and we've had many complaints about it. You'd better complain to the inspector at the station, miss."

He directed her to where she should go. Exhausted with hunger and the fear of losing all her possessions, she followed the policeman's instructions, till she presently found herself telling an inspector at the station of the theft; he advised her to either make a charge, or, if she disliked the publicity of the police court, to instruct a solicitor. Believing that making a charge would be more effectual, besides speedier, she told the inspector of her decision.

"Very well. Your name, please?"

"Mavis Kenrick."

"Mrs," he wrote, as he glanced at the wedding ring which she now wore on her finger.

"What address, please?" was his next question.

"I haven't one at present."

The man looked at her in surprise, at which Mavis explained how she had come from Melkbridge the day before.

"At least you can give us your husband's address."

"He's abroad," declared Mavis, with as much resolution as she could muster.

"Then you might give me the address of your friends in Melkbridge."

"To write to?" asked Mavis.

"In case it should be necessary."

Mavis was at once aware of the inconvenient consequences to which an application for references to anyone at Melkbridge would give rise, especially as her name and state were alike incorrectly given. She hesitated for a few moments before telling the inspector that, disliking the publicity of the police court, she would prefer to instruct a solicitor. As she left the station, she would have felt considerably crestfallen, had she not been faint from want of food. She dragged her way to a tea-shop, to feel the better for a cup of tea and some toast. The taste of the room in which she had passed the night still fouled her mouth; its stench clung to her clothes. She asked her way to the nearest public baths, where she thought a shilling well spent in buying the luxury of a hot bath. Her next concern was to seek out a solicitor who would assist her to recover her stolen property. She had a healthy distrust of the tribe, and was wondering if, after all, it would not have been better to have risked the inspector's writing to any address she may have given at Melkbridge, rather than trust any chance lawyer with the matter, when she remembered that her old acquaintance, Miss Meakin, was engaged to a solicitor's clerk. She resolved to seek out Miss Meakin, and ask her to get her betrothed's advice and assistance. As she did not know Miss Meakin's present address, she thought the quickest way to obtain it was to call on her old friend Miss Nippett at Blomfield Road, Shepherd's Bush, who kept the register of all those who attended "Poulter's."

She had never quite lost touch with the elderly accompanist; they had sent each other cards at Christmas and infrequently exchanged picture postcards, Miss Nippett's invariably being a front view of "Poulter's," with Mr Poulter on the steps in such a position as not to obscure "Turpsichor" in the background.

Mavis travelled by the Underground to Shepherd's Bush, from where it was only five minutes' walk to Miss Nippett's. The whole way down, she was so dazed by her loss that she could give no thought to anything else. The calamities that now threatened her were infinitely more menacing than before her precious bag had been stolen. It seemed as if man and circumstance had conspired for her undoing. Her suspense of mind was such that it seemed long hours before she knocked at the blistered door in the Blomfield Road where Miss Nippett lived.

Miss Nippett was in, she learned from the red-nosed, chilblain-fingered slut who opened the door.

"What nyme?"

"Mrs Kenrick, who was Miss Keeves," replied Mavis.

"Will you go up?" said the slut when, a few minutes later, she came downstairs.

Mavis went upstairs, past the cupboard containing Miss Nippett's collection of unclaimed "overs," to the door directly beyond.

"Come in" cried a well-remembered voice, as Mavis knocked.

She entered, to see Miss Nippett half rising from a chair before the fire. She was startled by the great change which had taken place in the accompanist's appearance since she had last seen her. She looked many years older; her figure was quite bent; the familiar shawl was too ample for the narrow, stooping shoulders.

"Aren't you well?" asked Mavis, as she kissed her friend's cheek.

"Quite. Reely I am but for a slight cold. Mr Poulter, 'e's well too. Fancy you married!"

"Yes," said Mavis sadly.

But Miss Nippett took no notice of her dejection.

"I've never 'ad time to get married, there's so much to do at 'Poulter's.' You know! Still, there's no knowing."

Mavis, distressed as she was, could hardly restrain a smile.

"I've news too," went on Miss Nippett.

"Have you?" asked Mavis, who was burning to get to the reason of her call.

"Ain't you heard of it?"

"I can't say I have."

By way of explanation, Miss Nippett handed Mavis one of a pile of prospectuses at her elbow; she at once recognised the familiar pamphlet that extolled Mr Poulter's wares.

"See! 'E's got my name on the 'pectus. 'All particulars from Poulter's or Miss Nippett, 19 Blomfield Road, W.' Isn't that something to talk about and think over?"

Mavis hastily assented; she was about to ask for Miss Meakin's address, but Miss Nippett was too quick for her.

"D'ye think he'll win?"

"Who?"

"Mr Poulter, of course. 'Aven't you 'eard?"

"Tell me."

"Oh, I say, you are ignorant! He's competing for the great cotillion prize competition. I thought everybody knew about it."

"I think I've heard something. But could you tell me Miss Meakin's address?"

"11 Baynham Street, North Kensington, near Uxbridge Road station," Miss Nippett informed Mavis, after referring to an exercise book, to add: "This is the dooplicate register of 'Poulter's.' I always keep it here in case the other should get lost. Mr. Poulter, like all them great men, is that careless."

"Come again soon," said Miss Nippett, as Mavis rose to go.

Mavis promised that she would.

"How long have you been married?"

"Not long. Three months."

"Any baby?"

"After three months!" blushed Mavis.

"Working so at 'Poulter's' makes one forget them things. No offence," apologised Miss Nippett.

"Good-bye. I'll look in again soon."

"If you 'ave any babies, see they're taught dancing at 'Poulter's.'"

Between Notting Hill and Wormwood Scrubbs lies a vast desert of human dwellings. Fringing Notting Hill they are inhabited by lower middle-class folk, but, by scarcely perceptible degrees, there is a declension of so-called respectability, till at last the frankly working-class district of Latimer Road is reached. Baynham Street was one of the ill-conditioned, down-at-heel little roads which tenaciously fought an uphill fight with encroaching working-class thoroughfares. Its inhabitants referred with pride to the fact that Baynham Street overlooked a railway, which view could be obtained by craning the neck out of window at risk of dislocation. A brawny man was standing before the open door of No. 11 as Mavis walked up the steps.

"Is Bill coming?" asked the man, as he furtively lifted his hat.

Mavis looked surprised.

"To chuck out this 'ere lodger for Mrs. Scatchard wo' won't pay up," he explained.

"I know nothing about it," said Mavis.

"Ain't you Mrs Dancer, Bill's new second wife?"

Mavis explained that she had come to see Miss Meakin, at which the man walked into the passage and knocked at the first door on the left, as he called out:

"Lady to see you!"

"Who?" asked Miss Meakin, as she displayed a fraction of a scantily attired person through the barely opened door.

"Have you forgotten me?" asked Mavis, as she entered the passage.

"Dear Miss Keeves! So good of you to call!" cried Miss Meakin, not a little affectedly, so Mavis thought, as she raised her hand high above her head to shake hands with her friend in a manner that was once considered fashionable in exclusive Bayswater circles.

She then opened the door wide enough for Mavis to edge her way in. Mavis found herself in an apartment that was normally a pretentiously furnished drawing-room. Just now, a lately vacated bed was made up on the sofa; a recently used washing basin stood on a chair; whilst Miss Meakin's unassumed garments strewed the floor.

"And what's happened to you all this long time?" asked Miss Meakin, as she sat on the edge of a chair in the manner of one receiving a formal call.

"To begin with, I'm married," said Mavis hurriedly, at which piece of information her friend's face fell.

"Any family?" she asked anxiously.

"N-no—not yet."

"I could have married Mr Napper a month ago—in fact he begged me on his knees to," bridled Miss Meakin.

"Why didn't you?"

"We're going to his aunt's at Littlehampton for the honeymoon, but I'm certainly not going till it's the season there."

Mavis smiled.

"Would you?" asked Miss Meakin.

"Not if that sort of thing appealed to me."

When Miss Meakin had explained that she had got up late because she had been to a ball the night before, Mavis told her the reason of her visit, at which Miss Meakin declared that Mr Napper was the very man to help her. Mavis asked for his address. While her friend was writing it down, a violent commotion was heard descending the stairs and advancing along the passage. Mavis rightly guessed this was caused by the forcible ejection of the lodger who had failed with his rent.

To Mavis' surprise, Miss Meakin did not make any reference to this disturbance, but went on talking as if she were living in a refined atmosphere which was wholly removed from possibility of violation.

"There's one thing I should tell you," said Miss Meakin, as Mavis rose to take her leave. "Mr Napper's employer, Mr Keating, besides being a solicitor, sells pianos. Mr N. is expecting a lady friend, who is thinking of buying one 'on the monthly,' so mind you explain what you want."

"I won't forget," said Mavis, making an effort to go. But as voices raised in angry altercation could be heard immediately outside the front door, Miss Meakin detained Mavis, asking, in the politest tone, advice on the subject of the most fashionable material to wear at a select dinner party.

"I've quite given up 'Browning,'" she told Mavis, "he's so old-fashioned to up-to-date people. Now I'm going to be Mrs Napper, when the Littlehampton season comes round, I'm going in exclusively for smartness and fashion."

Mavis making as if she would go, and the disturbance not being finally quelled, Miss Meakin begged Mavis to stay to lunch. She repeatedly insisted on the word lunch, as if it conveyed a social distinction in the speaker.

Mavis had got as far as the door, when it burst open and an elderly woman of considerable avoirdupois broke into the room, to sink helplessly upon a flimsy chair which creaked ominously with its burden.

Miss Meakin introduced this person to Mavis as her aunt, Mrs Scatchard, and reminded the latter how Mavis had rescued her niece from the clutches of the bogus hospital nurse in Victoria Street so many months back.

"That you should call today of all days!" moaned the perspiring Mrs Scatchard.

"Why not today?" asked her niece innocently.

"The day I'm disgraced to the neighbourhood by a 'visitor' being turned out of doors."

"I knew nothing of it," protested Miss Meakin.

"And Mr Scatchard being a government official, as you might say."

"Indeed!" remarked Mavis, who was itching to be off.

"Almost a pillar of the throne, as you might say," moaned the poor woman.

"True enough," murmured her niece.

"A man who, as you might say, has had the eyes of Europe upon him."

"Ah!" sighed Miss Meakin.

"And me, too, who am, as it were, an outpost of blood in this no-class neighbourhood," continued Mrs Scatchard.

Mavis wondered when she would be able to get away.

"My father was a tax-collector," Mrs Scatchard informed Mavis.

"Indeed!" said the latter.

"And in a most select London suburb. Do you believe in blood?"

"I think so."

"Then you must come here often. Blood is so scarce in North Kensington."

"Thank you."

"Why not stay and have a bit of dinner?"

"Lunch," corrected Miss Meakin with a frown.

"We've a lovely sheep's heart and turnips," said Mrs Scatchard, disregarding her niece's pained interruption.

Mavis thanked kindly Mrs Scatchard, but said she must be off. She was not permitted to go before she promised to let Miss Meakin know the result of her visit to Mr Napper.

Mavis spent three of her precious pennies in getting to the office of Mr Keating, which was situated in a tiny court running out of Holborn. Upon the first door she came to was inscribed "A.F. Keating, Solicitor, Commissioner for Oaths," whilst upon an adjacent door was painted "Breibner, Importer of Pianofortes." She tried the handle of the solicitor's door, to find that it was locked. She was wondering what she should do when a tall, thin, podgy-faced man came in from the court. Mavis instinctively guessed that he was Mr Napper.

"'Ave you been waiting long, madam?" he asked.

"I've just come. Are you Mr Napper?"

"It is. Everybody knows me."

"I've come from Miss Meakin."

"Today?" he asked, as his white face lit up.

"I've come straight from her."

"And after what I said at last night's 'light fantastic,' she has sent you to me!" he cried excitedly, as he opened the door on which was inscribed "Breibner."

"RE consultation, madam. If you will be good enough to step this way, I shall be 'appy to take your instructions."

Mavis, despite her distress of mind, was not a little amused at this alteration in Mr Napper's manner. She followed him into Mr Keating's office, where she saw a very small office-boy, who, directly he set his eyes on Mr Napper, made great pretence of being busy. She was shown into an inner room, where she was offered an armchair. Upon taking it, Mr Napper gravely seated himself at a desk and said:

"Mr Keating is un'appily absent. Any confidence made to me is the same as made to 'im."

Mavis recited her trouble, of which Mr Napper put down the details.

When he had got these, Mavis waited in suspense. Mr Napper looked at his watch.

"Do you think you can do anything?" Mavis asked.

"I'm going to do my best, quite as much for Miss Meakin's sake as for the dignity of my profession," replied Mr Napper. "Please read through this, and, if it is correct, kindly sign."

Here he handed Mavis a statement of all she had told him in respect of her loss. After seeing that it was rightly set down, she signed "Mavis Kenrick" at the foot of the document.

"Vincent!" cried Mr Napper, as Mavis handed it back.

"Yessur," answered the tiny office-boy smartly, as he made the most of his height in the doorway.

"I am going out on important business."

"Yessur."

"I shan't be back for the best part of an hour."

"Yessur."

"If this lady cares to, she will wait till my return."

"Yessur."

Mr Napper dismissed Vincent and then turned to Mavis.

"If I may say so, I can see by your face that you're fond of literature," he said.

"I like reading."

"Law and music is my 'obby, as you might say. The higher literature is my intellect."

"Indeed!"

"Let me lend you something to read while you're waiting."

"You're very kind. But I've had nothing to eat. Would you mind if I took it out with me?"

"Delighted! What do you say to Locke's Human Understanding?" he asked, as he produced a book.

"Thank you very much."

"Or here's Butler's Anatomy of Melancholy."

"But—"

"Or 'Obbes's Leviathan," he suggested, producing a third volume.

"Thank you, but Locke will do to begin upon."

"Ask me to explain anything you don't understand," he urged.

"I won't fail to," she replied, at which Mr Napper took his leave.

Mavis went to a neighbouring tea-shop, where she obtained the food of which she was in need. When she returned to Mr Keating's office, she was shown into the inner room by Vincent, who shut the door as he left her. She was still a prey to anxiety, and succeeded in convincing herself how comparatively happy she would be if only she could get back her stolen goods. To distract her thoughts from her present trouble, she tried to be interested in the opening chapter of the work that Mr Napper had lent her. But it proved too formidable in her present state of mind. She would read a passage, to find that it conveyed no meaning; she was more interested in the clock on the mantel-piece and wondering how long it would be before she got any news. One peculiarity of Mr Napper's book attracted her attention: she saw that, whereas the first few pages were dog's-eared and thumb-marked, the succeeding ones were as fresh as when they issued from the bookseller's hands.

While she was thus waiting in suspense, she heard strange sounds coming from the office where Vincent worked. She went to the door, to look through that part of it which was of glass. She saw Vincent, who, so far as she could gather, was talking as if to an audience, the while he held an inkpot in one hand and the office cat in the other. When he had finished talking, he caused these to vanish, at which he acknowledged the applause of an imaginary audience with repeated bows. After another speech, he reproduced the cat and the inkpot, proceedings which led Mavis to think that the boy had conjuring aspirations.

Her heart beat quickly when Mr Napper re-entered the office.

"It's all right!" he hastened to assure her. "You're to come off with me to the station to identify your property."

Mavis thanked him heartfully when she learned that the police, having received a further complaint of the house where she had spent the night, had obtained a warrant and promptly raided the place, with the result that her bag (with other missing property) had been recovered. As they walked in the direction of the station, Mr. Napper asked her how she had got on with Locke's Human Understanding. Upon her replying that it was rather too much for her just then, he said:

"Just you listen to me."

Here he launched into an amazing farrago of scientific terms, in which the names of great thinkers and scientists were mingled at random. There was nothing connected in his talk; he seemed to be repeating, parrot fashion, words and formulas that he had chanced upon in his dipping into the works that he had boasted of comprehending.

Mavis looked at him in astonishment. He mistook her surprise for admiration.

"I'm afraid you haven't understood much of what I've been saying," he remarked.

"Not very much."

"You've paid me a great compliment," he said, looking highly pleased with himself.

Then he spoke of Miss Meakin.

"You'll tell her what I've done for you?"

"Most certainly."

"Last night, at the 'light fantastic' I told you of, we had a bit of a tiff, when I spoke my mind. Would you believe it, she only danced twenty hops with me out of the twenty-three set down?"

"What bad taste!"

"I'm glad you think that. Her sending you to me shows she isn't offended at what I said. I did give it her hot. I threw in plenty of scientific terms and all that."

"Poor girl!" remarked Mavis.

"Yes, she was to be pitied. But here we are at the station."

Mavis went inside with Mr Napper, where she proved her title to her stolen property by minutely describing the contents of her bag, from which she was rejoiced to find nothing had been taken. Her unposted letter to Perigal was with her other possessions.

As they were leaving the station, Mr Napper remarked:

"The day before yesterday I had the greatest compliment of my life paid me."

"And what was that?" asked Mavis.

"A lady told me that she'd known me three years, and that all that time she never understood what my scientific conversation was about."

CHAPTER TWENTY-SIX
TRAVAIL

If Mavis had believed that the recovery of her property would give her peace of mind, she soon discovered how grievously she was mistaken.

Directly she left the police station with Mr Napper, all her old fears and forebodings for the future resumed sway over her thoughts. As before, she sought to allay them by undiminished faith in her lover. She accepted Mr Napper's hospitality in the form of tea and toast at a branch of the Aerated Bread Company, where she asked him how much she was in his debt for his services. To her surprise, he replied, "Nothing at all," and added that he was only too glad to assist her, not only for Miss Meakin's sake, but because he felt that Mavis dimly appreciated his intellectuality. Upon Mavis untruthfully replying that she did, Mr Napper gave a further effort to impress, not only her, but others seated about them; he talked his jargon of scientific and philosophical phrases at the top of his voice. She was relieved when she was rid of his company. She then took train to Shepherd's Bush, where she called on Miss Meakin as promised. Much to her surprise, Miss Meakin, who was now robed in a flimsy and not too clean teagown, had not the slightest interest in knowing if Mavis had recovered her property; indeed, she had forgotten that Mavis had lost anything. She was only concerned to know what Mavis thought of Mr Napper, and what this person had said about herself: on this last matter, Mavis was repeatedly cross-questioned. Mavis then spoke of a matter she had thought of on the way down: that of engaging a room at Mrs Scatchard's if she had one to let. Miss Meakin, however, protested that she had nothing to do with the business arrangements of the house, and declared that her aunt had better be consulted.

Upon Mavis interviewing Mrs Scatchard on the matter, the latter declared that her niece had suggested the subject to her directly after Mavis had left in the morning, a statement which Miss Meakin did not appear to overhear. Mrs Scatchard showed Mavis a clean, homely little room. The walls were decorated with several photographs of celebrations, which, so far as she could see, were concerned with the doings of royalty. When it came to the discussion of terms, Mrs Scatchard pointed out to Mavis the advantage of being in a house rented by a man like Mr Scatchard, who was "so mixed up with royalty," as she phrased it; but, partly in consideration of the timely service which Mavis had once rendered Miss Meakin, and largely on the score that Mavis boasted of blood (she had done nothing of the kind), Mrs Scatchard offered her the room, together with use of the bathroom, for four-and-sixpence a week. Upon Mavis learning that the landlady would not object to Jill's presence, she closed with the offer. At Mrs Scatchard's invitation, she spent the evening in the sitting-room downstairs, where she was introduced to Mr Scatchard. If, as had been alleged, Mr Scatchard was a pillar of the throne, that august institution was in a parlous condition. He was a red-headed, red-eyed, clean-shaven man, in appearance not unlike an elderly cock; his blotchy face, thick utterance, and the smell of his breath, all told Mavis that he was addicted to drink. Mavis wondered how this fuddled man, whose wife let lodgings in a shabby corner of Shepherd's Bush, could be remotely associated with Government, till it leaked out that he had been for many years, and still was, one of the King's State trumpeters.

Mavis was grateful to the Scatchards for their humble hospitality, if only because it prevented her mind from dwelling on her extremity. She was so tired with all she had gone through, that, directly she got to bed, she fell asleep, to awake about five with a mind possessed by fears for the future. Try as she could, faith in her lover refused to supply the relief necessary to allow her further sleep.

About seven, kindly Mrs Scatchard brought her up some tea, her excuse for this attention being that "blood" could not be expected to get up without a cup of this stimulant. Mrs Scatchard, like most stout women, was of a nervous, kindly, ingenuous disposition. It hurt Mavis considerably to tell her the story she had concocted, of a husband in straitened circumstances in America, who was struggling to prepare a home for her. Mrs Scatchard was herself a bereaved mother. Much moved by her recollections, she gave Mavis needed and pertinent advice with reference to her condition.

"There is kindness in the world," thought Mavis, when she was alone.

After breakfast, that was supplied at a previously arranged charge of fourpence, Mavis, fearing the company of her thoughts, betook herself to Miss Nippett in the Blomfield Road.

She found her elderly friend in bed, a queer, hapless figure in her pink flannel nightgown.

"I haven't heard anything," said Miss Nippett, as soon as she caught sight of Mavis.

"Of what?"

"What luck Mr Poulter's had at the dancing competition! Haven't you come about that?"

"I came to see how you were."

"Don't you worry about me. I shall be right again soon; reely I shall."

Mavis tried to discover if Miss Nippett were properly looked after, but without result, Miss Nippett's mind being wholly possessed by "Poulter's" and its chief.

"He promised to send me a postcard to say how he got on, but I suppose he was too busy to remember," sighed Miss Nippett.

"Surely not!"

"He's like all these great men: all their 'earts in their fame, with no thought for their humble assistants," she complained, to add after a few moments' pause, "A pity you're married."

"Why?"

"'Cause, since I've been laid up, he's been in want of a reliable accompanist."

Mavis explained that she would be glad of some work, at which her friend said:

"Then off you go at once to the academy. He's often spoken of you, and quite nicely, and he's asked for you in family prayers. If he's won the prize, it's as sure as 'knife' that he'll give you the job. And mind you come and tell me if he's won."

Mavis thanked her wheezing, kind-hearted friend, and promised that she would return directly she had any news. Then, with hope in her heart, she hurried to the well-remembered academy, where she had sought work so many eventful months ago. As before, she looked into the impassive face of "Turpsichor" while she waited for the door to be answered.

A slatternly servant of the charwoman species replied to her summons. Upon Mavis saying that she wanted to see Mr Poulter immediately, she was shown into the "Ladies' Waiting Room," from which Mavis gathered that Mr Poulter had returned.

After a while, Mr Poulter came into the room with a shy, self-conscious smile upon his lovable face.

"You've heard?" he asked, as she shook hands.

Mavis looked at him in surprise.

"Of course you have, and have come to congratulate me," he continued.

"I'm glad you've been successful," said Mavis, now divining the reason of his elation.

"Yes" (here he sighed happily), "I've won the great cotillion prize competition. Just think of it!" Here he took a deep breath before saying, "All the dancing-masters in the United Kingdom competed, even including Gellybrand" (here his voice and face perceptibly hardened), "but I won."

"I congratulate you," said Mavis.

Mr Poulter's features weakened into a broad smile eloquent of an immense satisfaction.

"You can tell people you've been one of the first to congratulate me," he remarked.

"I won't forget. I was sorry to see that Miss Nippett is so unwell."

"It's most unfortunate; it so interferes with the evening classes."

"But she may get well soon."

"I fear not."

"Really?" asked Mavis, genuinely concerned for her friend's health.

"It's a great pity. Accompanists like her are hard to find. Besides, she was well acquainted with all the many ramifications of the academy."

Mavis recalled that, in the old days of her association with "Poulter's," she had noticed that otherwise kindly Mr Poulter took Miss Nippett's body and soul loyalty to him quite as a matter of course. Time, apparently, had not caused him to think otherwise of the faithful accompanist than as a once capable but now failing machine.

Mr Poulter asked Mavis what had happened to her since he had last seen her. She told him the fiction of her marriage; it hurt her to see how glibly the lie now fell from her lips.

After Mr Poulter had congratulated her and her absent husband, he said:

"I fear you would not care to undertake any accompanying."

"But I should."

"As you did before?"

"Certainly!"

It was then arranged that Mavis should commence work at the academy on that day, for much the same terms she was paid before. This matter being settled, she asked for notepaper and envelope, on which she wrote to Mrs Farthing, asking her to be so good as to send Jill at once, and to be sure to let her know by what train she would arrive at Paddington.

Mavis was careful to head the notepaper with the address of the academy; she did not wish anyone at Melkbridge to know her actual address. After taking leave of Mr Poulter and posting her letter, she repaired to Miss Nippett's as arranged. The accompanist was now out of bed, in a chair before the fire. Directly she caught sight of Mavis, she said:

"'As he won?"

"Yes, he's won the great cotillion prize competition."

A look of intense joy illumined Miss Nippett's face.

"Isn't he proud?" she asked.

"Very!"

"An' me not there to see him in his triumph." A cloud overspread Miss Nippett's features.

"What's the matter?" asked Mavis.

"Did he—did he send and tell you to tell me as 'ow he'd won."

The wistful old eyes were so pleading, that Mavis fibbed.

"Of course he sent me."

"I thought he wouldn't forget his old friend," she remarked with a sigh of relief. "'E'd surely know I was anxious to know."

Mavis told Miss Nippett of her engagement to play at "Poulter's" during the latter's absence.

"Don't you count on it being for long," said Miss Nippett.

"I hope it won't be, for your sake."

"I'm counting the minute' till I shall be back again at the academy," declared Miss Nippett.

Mavis, as she looked at the eager, pinched face, could well believe that she was speaking the truth.

"I shall buy you a bottle of port wine," said Mavis.

"What say?"

Mavis repeated her words.

"Oh, I say! Fancy me 'avin' port wine! I once 'ad a glass; it did make me feel 'appy."

Two days later, in accordance with the contents of a letter she had received from Mrs Farthing, Mavis met the train at Paddington that was to bring her dear Jill from Melkbridge. She discovered her friend huddled in a corner of the guard's van; her grief was piteous to behold, her eyes being full of tears, which the kindly attentions of the guard had not dissipated. Directly she saw her mistress, Jill uttered a cry that was almost human in its gladness, and tried to jump into Mavis' arms.

When Jill was released, Mavis hugged her in her arms, careless of the attention her devotion attracted.

With her friend restored to her, that evening was the happiest she had spent for some time.

For many succeeding weeks, Mavis passed her mornings with Jill, or Miss Nippett, or both; and most of her afternoons and all of her evenings at the academy. The long hours, together with the monotonous nature of the work, greatly taxed her energies, lessened as these were by the physical stress through which she was passing.

She obtained infrequent distraction from the peculiarities of the pupils. One, in particular, who was a fat Jewess, named Miss Hyman, greatly amused her. This person was desperately anxious to learn waltzing, but was handicapped by bandy legs. As she spun round and round the room with Mr Poulter, or any other partner, she would close her eyes and continually repeat aloud, "One, two, three; one, two, three," the while her feet kept step with the music.

Otherwise, her days were mostly drab-coloured, the only thing that at all kept up her spirits being her untiring faith in Perigal—a faith which, in time, became a mechanical action of mind. Strive as she might to quell rebellious thoughts, now and again she would rage soul and body at the web that fate, or Providence, had spun about her life. At these times, it hurt her to the quick to think that, instead of being the wife she deserved to be, she was in her present unprotected condition, with all its infinite possibilities of disaster. Again and again the thought would recur to her that she might have been Windebank's wife at any time that she had cared to encourage his overtures, and if she were desirable as a wife in his eyes, why not in Charlie Perigal's! Gregarious instincts ran in her blood. For all her frequent love of solitude, there were days when her soul ached for the companionship of her own social kind. This not being forthcoming-indeed (despite her faith in Perigal) there being little prospect of it—she avoided as much as possible the sight of, or physical contact with, those prosperous ones whom she knew to be, in some cases, her equals; in most, her social inferiors.

It was at night when she was most a prey to unquiet thoughts. Tired with her many hours' work at the piano, she would fall into a deep sleep, with every prospect of its continuing till Mrs Scatchard would bring up her morning cup of tea, when Mavis would suddenly awaken, to remain for interminable hours in wide-eyed thought. She would go over and over again events in her past life, more particularly those that had brought her to her present pass. The immediate future scarcely bothered her at all, because, for the present, she was pretty sure of employment at the academy. On the very rare occasions on which she suffered her mind to dwell on what would happen after her child was born, should Perigal not fulfil his repeated promises, her vivid imagination called up such appalling possibilities that she refused to consider them; she had enough sense to apply to her own case the wisdom contained in the words, "sufficient for the day is the evil thereof."

In these silent watches of the night, so protracted and awesome was the quiet, that it would seem to the girl's preternatural sensibilities as if the life of the world had come to a dead stop, and that only she and the little one within her were alive. Then she would wonder how many other girls in London were in a like situation to hers; if they were constantly kept awake obsessed by the same fears; also, if, like her, they comforted themselves by clasping a ring which they wore suspended on their hearts—a ring given them by the loved one, even as was hers. Then she would fall to realising the truth of the saying, "How easily things go wrong." It seemed such a little time since she had been a happy girl at Melkbridge (if she had only realised how really happy she was!), with more than enough for her everyday needs, when her heart was untrammelled by love; when she was healthful, and, apart from the hours which she was compelled to spend at the office, free. Now—An alert movement within her was more eloquent than thought.

Sometimes she would believe that her present visitation of nature was a punishment for her infringement of God's moral law; whilst at others she would rejoice with a pagan exultation that, whatever the future held in store, she had most gloriously lived in these crowded golden moments which were responsible for her present plight.

Once or twice her distress of mind was such that she could no longer bear the darkness; she would light the candle, when the confinement of the walls, the sight of the orderly and familiar furniture of the room, would suggest an imprisoning environment from which there was no escape. As if to make a desperate effort to free herself, she would jump out of bed, and, throwing the window up, would look out on the night, as if to implore from nature the succour that she failed to get elsewhere. If the night were clear, she would gaze up at the heavens, as if to wrest from its countless eyes some solution of, or, failing that, some sympathy for her extremity of mind. But, for all the eagerness with which her terror-stricken eyes would search the stars, these looked down indifferently, unpityingly, impersonally, as if they were so inured to the sight of sorrow that they were now careless of any pain they witnessed. Then, with a pang at her heart, she would wonder if Perigal were also awake and were thinking of her. She convinced herself again and again that her agonised communing with the night would in some mysterious way affect his heart, to incline it irresistibly to hers, as in those never-to-be-forgotten nights and days at Polperro.

She heard from him fairly regularly, when he wrote letters urging her for his sake to be brave, and telling of the many shocks he had received from the persistent ill luck which he was seeking to overcome. If he had known how eagerly she awaited the familiar writing, how she read and re-read, times without number, every line he wrote, how she treasured the letters, sleeping with them under her pillow at night, he would have surely written with more persistency and at greater length than he did. Occasionally he would enclose money; this she always returned, saying that, as she was now in employment, she had more than enough for her simple needs. Once, after sending back a five-pound note he had sent her, she received a letter by return of post—a letter which gave a death blow to certain hopes she had cherished. She had long debated in her mind if she should apply the gold-mounted dressing case which Windebank had sent her for a wedding present to a purchase very near to her heart. She knew that, if he could know of the purpose to which she contemplated devoting it, and of her straightened circumstances, he would wish her to do as she desired. Having no other money available, she was tempted to sell or pawn the dressing case, to buy with the proceeds a handsome outfit for the expected little life, one that should not be unworthy of a gentlewoman's child. She felt that, as, owing to the unconventional circumstances of its birth, the little one might presently be deprived of many of life's advantages, it should at least be appropriately clad in the early days of its existence. She had already selected the intended purchase, and was rejoicing in its richness and variety, when the reply came to her letter to Perigal that returned the five-pound note. This told Mavis what straitened circumstances her lover was in. He asked what she had done with the gold-mounted dressing case, and, if it were still in her possession, if she could possibly let him have the loan of it in order to weather an impending financial storm. With a heart that strove valiantly to be cheerful, Mavis renounced further thought of the contemplated layette, and sent off the dressing case to her lover. It was a further (and this time a dutiful) sacrifice of self on the altar of the loved one. Most of her spare time was now devoted to the making of the garments, which, in the ordinary course of nature, would be wanted in about two months. Sometimes, while working, she would sing little songs that would either stop short soon after they were started, or else would continue almost to the finish, when they would end abruptly in a sigh. Often she would wonder if the child, when born, would resemble its father or its mother; if her recent experiences would affect its nature: all the thousand and one things that that most holy thing on earth, an expectant, loving mother, thinks of the life which love has called into being.

At all times she told herself that, if her wishes were consulted, she would prefer the child to be a boy, despite the fact that it was a more serious matter to launch a son on the world than a daughter. But she knew well that, if anything were to happen to her lover (this was now her euphemism for his failing to keep his promise), a boy, when he came to man's estate, might find it in his heart to forgive his mother for the untoward circumstances of his birth, whereas a daughter would only feel resentment at the possible handicap with which the absence of a father and a name would inflict her life. Thus Mavis worked with her needle, and sang, and thought, and travailed; and daily the little life within her became more insistent.

CHAPTER TWENTY-SEVEN
THE NURSING HOME

A day came when Mavis's courage failed. Acting on the advice of kindly Mrs Scatchard, she had bought, for the sum of one guinea, a confinement outfit from a manufacturer of such things. She unpacked her purchase fearfully. Her heart beat painfully at the thought of the approaching ordeal that the sight of the various articles awakened.

At the same time, she saw Perigal's conduct in the cold light of reason. She was surprised to find how bitter she was with herself for loving a man who could behave as selfishly as he had done. While the mood possessed her, she went to a post-office and sent a reply-paid telegram to Perigal, telling him to come to town at once, and asking him to wire the train by which he would arrive. After sending the telegram, she somewhat repented of her precipitancy, and waited in much suspense to see what the answer would be. When, some two hours later, she heard the double knock of a telegraph boy at the door, her heart was filled with nervous apprehension, in which reawakened love for Perigal bore no inconsiderable part. She opened his reply with trembling hands. "Why? Wire or write reason—love—Charles," it ran.

In reply, she sat down and wrote a long letter, in which she told him how she was situated, reminded him of his promises, which, if he still loved her, as he had professed times out of number in his letters, it was now more than ever incumbent on him to fulfil; she concluded by imploring him to decide either one way or the other and put an end to her suspense. Two days later, the first post brought a letter from Wales. By the time it arrived Mavis had, in some measure, schooled her fears and rebellious doubtings of her lover; therefore, she was not so disappointed at its contents as she would otherwise have been. The letter was written in much the same strain as his other communications. While expressing unalterable love for Mavis, together with pride at the privileges she had permitted him to enjoy, it told her how he was beset by countless perplexities, and that directly he saw his way clear he would do as she wished: in the meantime, she was to trust him as implicitly as before.

Mavis sighed as she finished the letter; she then became lost in troubled thought, during which she was uncertain whether to laugh for joy or sorrow. She laughed for joy, perhaps because her mind, as once before when similarly confronted, had chosen the easier way of self-preservation, an instinct specially insistent in one of Mavis's years. She laughed for very happiness and persuaded herself that she was indeed a lucky girl to be loved so devotedly.

Although the colour soon went out of the blue sky of her joy-world, and its trees and flowers lacked much of their one-time freshness, she was not a little grateful for her short experience of its delights. It helped her to bear the slights and disappointments of the following days, of which she had no inconsiderable share.

As the year grew older, it became increasingly necessary for Mavis to discover a place where she might stay during, and for a while after, her confinement. Mrs Scatchard had told her from the first, that however much she might be disposed to let Mavis remain in the house for this event, Mr Scatchard strongly objected, at his age, to the inconvenience of a baby under the same roof. Mavis filled many weary hours in dragging herself up and down front-door steps in the quest for accommodation; but she spent her strength in vain. Directly landladies learned of the uses to which Mavis would put the room she wished to engage, they became resentful, and sullenly told her that they could not accommodate her. Little as Mavis was disposed to find harbourage for herself and little one in the unhomely places she inspected, she was hurt by the refusals encountered. It seemed to her that the act of gravely imperilling life in order to confer life was a situation which demanded loving care and devoted attention, necessities she lacked: the refusal of blowsy landladies to entertain her application hurt her more than the other indignities that she had, so far, been compelled to endure. One Sunday afternoon Mrs Scatchard brought up the People, in the advertising columns of which was a list of nursing homes. Mavis eagerly scanned the many particulars set forth, till she decided that "Nurse G.," who lived at New Cross, made the most seductive offer. This person advertised a comfortable home to married ladies during and after confinement; skilled care and loving attention were furnished for strictly moderate terms.

Mavis decided to call on Nurse G. the following day.

The atmosphere of the Scatchards' had recently been highly charged, as if in preparation for an event of moment. Whenever Mr Scatchard took his walks abroad, he was always accompanied by either his wife or niece, who, when they finally piloted him home, would wear a look of self-conscious triumph. When Mavis came down to breakfast, before setting out for New Cross, there was a hum of infinite preparation. Mr Scatchard was greasing his hair; gorgeous raiment was being packed into a bag; the final polish was being given to a silver trumpet. Both Mrs Scatchard and her niece, besides being cloaked and bonneted, wore an expression of grim resolution. Mr Scatchard had the look of a hunted animal at bay. Little was said, but just before Mavis started, Miss Meakin came to her and whispered:

"Wish us luck, dear."

"Luck?" queried Mavis.

"Don't you know of uncle and to-day's great doings?"

Mavis shook her head.

"Uncle and the King Emperor," explained Miss Meakin. "There's a royal kick up to-day, and uncle and the King Emperor will be there."

"Have you and your aunt had an invitation too?" asked Mavis mischievously.

"Not into the palace, as you might say. But we're both going as far as the gates with uncle, to see he gets there safely and isn't tempted by the way."

Soon after, Mr Scatchard left with the two women, looking, for all the world, like a prisoner in charge of lynx-eyed warders. Then Mavis made the long and tiring journey to New Cross. Nurse G. had advertised her nursing home as being at No. 9 Durley Road. This latter she found to be a depressing little thoroughfare of two-storeyed houses, all exactly alike. She could discover nothing particularly inviting in the outside appearance of No. 9. Soiled, worn, cotton lace curtains hung behind not over-clean windows; behind these again were dusty, carefully closed Venetian blinds. Mavis passed and repassed the house, uncertain whether or not to call. Before deciding which to do, she made a mental calculation (she was always doing this now) of exactly how much she would have left after being paid by Mr Poulter and settling up with Mrs Scatchard. As before, she reckoned to have exactly seven pounds fifteen shillings. She had no intention of asking Perigal for help, as in his last letter he had made copious reference to his straitened circumstances. Any debasing shifts and mean discomforts to which her poverty might expose her she looked on as a yet further sacrifice upon the altar of the loved one, faith in whom had become the cardinal feature of her life. The terms "strictly moderate" advertised by Nurse G. decided her. She opened the iron gate and walked to the door. Directly she knocked, she heard two or three windows thrown up in neighbouring houses, from which the bodies of unkempt women projected, to cast interested glances in Mavis's direction. As she waited, she could hear the faint puling of a baby within the house. Next, she was conscious that a lath of a Venetian blind was pulled aside and that someone was spying upon her from the aperture. She waited further, the while two of the curious women who leaned from the windows were loudly deciding the date on which

Mavis's baby would be born. Then, the door of No. 9 was suspiciously opened about six inches. Mavis found herself eagerly scanned by a fraction of a woman's face. The next moment, the woman, who had caught sight of Mavis's appearance, which was now very indicative of her condition, threw the door wide open and called cheerily:

"Come in, my dear; come in."

"I want Nurse G.," said Mavis.

"That's me: G—Gowler. Come inside."

"But—" hesitated Mavis, as she glanced at the repulsive face of the woman.

"Do either one thing or the other: come right in or keep out. The neighbours do that talk."

Mavis walked into the passage, at which the woman sharply closed the door. The puling of the baby was distinctly louder.

"We'll 'ave to talk 'ere," continued the woman, with some weakening of her previous cordiality, "we're that full up: two in a room an' all expectin'. But then it never rains but it pours, as you might say."

Mavis resisted an impulse to fly from the house. The more she saw of Mrs Gowler (the woman wore a wedding ring), the less she liked her. To begin with, her appearance had given Mavis much of a shock. Her alert fancy had conjured up a vision of a kindly, motherly woman, with soft eyes and voice, whose mere presence would have spoken of the sympathy and tenderness for which the lonely heart of Mavis ached. Nurse Gowler was short, fat, and puffy, with her head sunk right into her shoulders. Her pasty face, with its tiny eyes, contained a mouth of which the upper lip was insufficient to cover her teeth when her jaws were closed; some of these teeth were missing, but whole ones and stumps alike were discoloured with decay. It was her eyes which chiefly repelled Mavis: pupil, iris, and the part surrounding this last, were all of the same colour, a hard, bilious-looking green. Her face suggested to Mavis a flayed pig's head, such as can be seen in pork butchers' shops. As if this were not enough to disgust Mavis, the woman's manner soon lost the geniality with which she had greeted her; she stood still and impassively by Mavis, who could not help believing that Mrs Gowler was attentively studying her from her hat to her shoe leather.

Mavis began her story, to be interrupted by a repressed cry of pain proceeding from the partly open door on the right. Mrs Gowler quickly closed it.

Mavis resumed her story. When she got to the part where her supposed husband was in America, Mrs Gowler impatiently interrupted her by saying:

"Where 'e's making a 'ome for you."

"How did you know?" asked the astonished Mavis.

"It's always the way; we've lots of 'em like that here, occasionals and regulars."

"Occasionals and regulars!"

"Lor' bless you, some of 'em comes as punctual as the baked potato man in October. When was you expectin'?"

"I'm not quite certain," replied Mavis, at which Mrs Gowler plied her with a number of questions, leading the former to remark presently:

"I guess you're due next Friday two weeks. To prevent accidents, you'd better come on the Wednesday night. If you like to book a bed, I'll see it's kep'."

"But what are your charges?"

"'Ow much can you afford?"

After discussion, it was arranged that, if Mavis decided to stay with Mrs Gowler for three weeks certain, she was to pay twenty-two shillings a week, this sum to include the woman's skilled attendance and nursing, together with bed and board. In the event of Mavis wanting medical advice, Mrs Gowler had an arrangement with a doctor by which he charged the moderate fee of a shilling a visit to any of her patients that required his services. The extreme reasonableness of the terms inclined Mavis to decide on going to Mrs Gowler's.

"There's only one thing," she said: "I've a dog; she's a great pet and quite clean. If you wouldn't object to her coming, I might—"

"Bring her: bring her. Is she having dear little puppies?"

"Oh dear, no."

"A pity. The more the merrier. I love work."

This decided Mavis. With considerable misgiving, but spurred by poverty, she told the woman that she was coming.

"An' what about binding our bargain?" asked Mrs Gowler.

"How much do you want?" asked Mavis, as she produced her purse. "Will five shillings do?"

"It'll do," admitted Mrs Gowler grudgingly, although the deposit she usually received was half a crown.

"I feel rather faint. Is there anywhere I can sit down for a minute?" asked Mavis.

"If you don't mind the kitchen. P'raps you'd like a cup of tea. I always keep it ready on the fire."

Mavis thanked her and followed Mrs Gowler to the room indicated. Although it was late in May, a roaring fire was burning in the kitchen, about which, on various sized towel-horses, numerous articles of babies' attire were airing.

"Too 'ot for yer?" asked Mrs Gowler.

"I don't mind where it is so long as I sit down."

"'Ow do you like your tea?" asked her hostess. "Noo or stooed?"

"I'd like fresh tea if it isn't any trouble," replied Mavis.

The tea was quickly made, there being a plentiful supply of boiling water. Whilst Mavis was gratefully sipping hers, a noise of something falling was heard in the scullery behind.

"It's that dratted cat," cried Mrs Gowler, as she caught up a broom and waddled from the kitchen. She returned, a moment later, with something remotely approaching a look of tenderness in her eyes.

"It's awright; it's my Oscar," she remarked.

Then what appeared to be a youth of eighteen years of age entered the kitchen. He was dark, with a receding forehead; his chin, much too large for his face, seemed as if it had been made for somebody else. His absence of expression, together with the feeling of discomfort that at once seized Mavis, told her that he was an idiot.

"Go an' shake hands with the lady, Oscar."

Mavis shuddered to feel his damp palm upon hers.

"You wouldn't believe it, but 'e's six fingers on each 'and, and 'e's twenty-eight: ain't yer, Oscar?" remarked his mother proudly.

Oscar turned to grin at his mother, whilst Mavis, with all her maternal instinct aroused, avoided looking at or thinking of the idiot as much as possible.

Mrs Gowler waxed eloquent on the subject of her Oscar, to whom she was apparently devoted. She was just telling Mavis how he liked to amuse himself by torturing the cat, when a sharp cry penetrated into the kitchen, as if coming from the neighbourhood of the front door.

"Bella's coming on," she said, as she caught up an apron before leaving the kitchen. "Be nice to the lady, Oscar, and see her out, like the gent you are," cried Mrs Gowler, before shutting the door.

Alone with the grinning idiot, Mavis shut her eyes, the while she finished her tea. She did not want her baby to be in any way affected by the acute mental discomfort occasioned to its mother by the presence of Mrs Gowler's son, a contingency she had understood could easily be a reality. When she looked about for her hat and umbrella, she discovered, to her great relief, that she was alone, Oscar having apparently slipped out after his mother, the kitchen door being ajar. Mavis drew on her gloves, stopped her ears with her fingers as she passed along the passage, opened the door and hurried away from the house.

Once outside, the beauty of the sweet spring day emphasised the horror of the house she had left.

She set her lips grimly, thought lovingly of Perigal, and resolved to dwell on her approaching ordeal as little as possible. Before returning to Mrs Scatchard's, she looked in to see Miss Nippett, who, with the coming of summer, seemed to lose strength daily. She now hardly ever got up, but remained in bed all day, where she would talk softly to herself. She always brightened up when Mavis came into the room, and was ever keenly interested in the latest news from the academy, particularly in Mr Poulter's physical and economic wellbeing. Seeing how make-believe inquiries of Mr Poulter after his accompanist's health cheered the lonely old woman, Mavis had no compunction in employing these white lies to brighten Miss Nippett's monotonous days.

She raised herself in bed and nodded a welcome as Mavis entered the room. After assuring Mavis "that she was all right, reely she was," she asked:

"When are you going to 'ave your baby?"

"Very soon now," sighed Mavis.

"I don't think I shall ever 'ave one," remarked Miss Nippett.

"Indeed!"

"They're a great tie if one has a busy life," she said, to add wistfully, "Though it would be nice if one could get Mr Poulter for a godfather."

"Wouldn't it!" echoed Mavis.

"Give it a good start in the world, you know. It 'ud be something to talk about 'avin' 'im for a godfather."

Presently, when Mavis stooped to kiss the wan face before going, Miss Nippett said:

"If I was to die, d'ye know what 'ud make me die 'appy?"

"Don't talk such nonsense: at your age, too."

"If I could just be made a partner in 'Poulter's,'" continued Miss Nippett. "Not for the money, you understand, reely not for that; but for the honour, as you might say."

"I quite understand."

"But there, one mustn't be too ambitious. That's the worst of me. And it's the way to be un'appy," she sighed.

Mavis walked with heavy heart to her lodging; for all her own griefs, Miss Nippett's touching faith in "Poulter's" moved her deeply.

When Mavis got back, she found Mrs Scatchard and her niece in high feather. They insisted upon Mavis joining them at what they called a knife and fork tea, to which Mr Napper and two friends of the family had been invited. Mr Scatchard was not present, but no mention was made of his absence, it being looked upon as an inevitable relaxation after the work and fret of the day. The room was littered with evening papers.

"It all went off beautiful, my dear," Mrs Scatchard remarked to Mavis.

"I'm glad," said Mavis.

"We left him safe at the palace, and as there's nothing in the papers about anything going wrong, it must be all right."

"Of course," Mavis assented.

"We know Mr Scatchard has his weaknesses; but then, if he hadn't, he wouldn't be the musical artiste he is," declared his wife, at which Mavis, who was just then drinking tea, nearly swallowed it the wrong way.

Mr Napper soon dropped in, to be closely followed by a Mr Webb and a Miss Jennings, who had never met the solicitor's clerk before. Mr Webb and Miss Jennings were engaged to be married. As if to proclaim their unalterable affection to the world, they sat side by side with their arms about each other.

The presence of strangers moved Mr Napper to talk his farrago of philosophical nonsense. It did not take long for Mavis to see that Miss Jennings was much impressed by the flow of many-syllabled words which issued, without ceasing, from the lawyer's clerk's lips. The admiration expressed in the girl's eyes incited Mr Napper to further efforts.

He presently remarked to Miss Jennings:

"I can tell your character in two ticks."

Miss Jennings, who had been wholly resigned to the fact of her insignificance, began to take herself with becoming seriousness.

"How?" she asked, her eyes gleaming with interest.

"By your face or by your 'ead."

"Do tell me," she pleaded.

"'Ead or face?"

"Try the head," she said, as she sought to free herself from her lover's entangling embrace. But Mr Webb would not let her go; he grasped her firmly by the waist, and, despite her entreaties, would not relax his hold. Mr Napper made as if he would approach Miss Jennings, but was restrained by Miss Meakin, who stamped angrily on his corns, and, when he danced with pain, stared menacingly at him. When he recovered, Miss Jennings begged him to tell her character by her face.

Mr Napper, looking out of the corner of one eye at Miss Meakin, stared attentively at Miss Jennings, who was now fully conscious of the attention she was attracting. Mr Webb waited in suspense, with his eye on Mr Napper's face.

"You're very fond of draughts," said the latter presently.

"Right!" cried Miss Jennings, as she smiled triumphantly at her lover.

"But I shouldn't say you was much good at 'huffing,'" he continued.

"Right again!" smiled the delighted Miss Jennings.

"I should say your 'eart governed your 'ead," came next.

"Quite right!" cried Miss Jennings, who was now quite perked up.

"You're very fond of admiration," exclaimed Mr Napper, after a further pause.

"She isn't; she isn't," cried Mr Webb, as his hold tightened on the loved one's form.

More was said by Mr Napper in the same strain, which greatly increased not only Miss Jennings's sense of self-importance, but her interest in Mr Napper.

As Mavis perceived how his ridiculous talk captivated Miss Jennings, it occurred to her that the vanity of women was such, that this instance of one of their number being impressed by a foolish man's silly conversation was only typical of the manner in which the rest of the sex were fascinated.

CHAPTER TWENTY-EIGHT
MISS 'PETT'S APOTHEOSIS

Mavis was seriously alarmed for Miss Nippett. Her friend was so ill that she insisted upon a doctor being called in. After examining the patient, he told her that Miss Nippett was suffering from acute influenza; also, that complications were threatening. He warned Mavis of the risk of catching the disease, which, in her present condition, might have serious consequences; but she had not the heart to leave her friend to the intermittent care of the landlady. With the money that Miss Nippett instructed her to find in queer hiding-places, Mavis purchased bovril, eggs, and brandy, with which she did her best to patch up the enfeebled frame of the sick woman. Nothing that she or the doctor could do had any permanent effect; every evening, Miss Nippett's temperature would rise with alarming persistence.

"I wonder if she's anything on her mind that might account for it," the doctor said to Mavis, when leaving one evening.

"I don't see what she could have, unless—"

"Unless?"

"I believe she worries about a matter connected with her old occupation. I'll try and find out," said Mavis.

"'Ow did 'e say I was?" asked Miss Nippett, as Mavis rejoined her.

"Much better."

"I ain't."

"Nonsense!"

"Reely I ain't. If 'e says I'm better, 'e'd better stay away. That's the worst of these fash'nable 'Bush' doctors; they make fortunes out of flattering people they're better when they're not."

Mavis had more than a suspicion that Miss Nippett's retarded convalescence was due to not having attained that position in the academy to which she believed her years of faithful service entitled her. Mavis made reference to the matter; the nature of Miss Nippett's replies converted suspicion into certainty.

The next morning, Mavis called on Mr Poulter, whom she had not seen for two weeks, the increasing physical disabilities of her condition compelling her to give up work at the academy. She found him engaged in the invention of a new country dance for a forthcoming competition. Mavis explained her errand, but had some difficulty in convincing even kindly Mr Poulter of Miss Nippett's ambitious leanings: in the course of years, he had come to look on his devoted accompanist very much as he regarded "Turpsichor" who stood by the front door. Mavis's request surprised him almost as much as if he had been told that "Turpsichor" herself ached to waltz with him in the publicity of a long night.

"I don't believe she's very long to live," said Mavis. "If you could make her a partner, merely in an honorary sense, it would make her last days radiantly happy."

"It might be done, my dear," mused Mr Poulter.

"But, whatever you do, don't let her think I suggested it to you."

"'Poulter's' can be the soul of tact and discretion," he informed her.

After more conversation on the subject, Mavis was about to take her leave when the postman brought a parcel addressed to her at the academy, from her old Pennington friend, Mrs Trivett. It contained eggs, butter, and cream, together with a letter. This last told Mavis that things were in a bad way at the farm; in consequence, her husband was thinking of sub-letting his house, in order to migrate to Melkbridge, where he might earn a living by teaching music. It closed with repeated wishes for Mavis's welfare.

"These people will send things in my maiden name," said Mavis, as she wondered if Mr Poulter's suspicions had been aroused by similar packages having occasionally arrived for her addressed in the same way.

"It was only to be expected. From your professional association with the academy, they would think it only proper to address you by 'Miss' and your maiden name," remarked guileless Mr Poulter.

Upon Mavis's third visit to Miss Nippett after her interview with Mr Poulter, she noticed a change in the sick woman's appearance; she was sitting up in bed with a face wreathed in smiles.

"'Ave you 'eard?" she cried excitedly, when she saw Mavis.

"Heard what?" asked Mavis innocently.

"'Bout me an' 'Poulter's.' You don't mean to say you 'aven't 'eard!"

"I hope it's good news."

"Good! Good! It's wonderful! Jest you throw your eye over that."

Mavis read a formally worded letter from Mr Poulter, in which he informed Miss Nippett "that, in consideration of her many years' faithful service, he could think of no more fitting way to reward her than by taking her into partnership: in accordance with this resolve, what was formerly known as 'Poulter's' would in future be described for all time as 'Poulter and Nippett's.'"

"What d'ye think of that?" asked Miss Nippett.

"It's only what you deserved."

"There's no going back on it now it's in black and white."

"He wouldn't wish to."

"It's proof, ain't it, legal an' all that?"

"Absolute. I congratulate you," said Mavis, as she took the wan white hand in hers.

"Even now I can't b'lieve it's true," sighed the accompanist, as she sank exhausted on her pillows.

"You're overdoing it," said Mavis, as she mixed some brandy and milk.

"I 'ate the muck," declared Miss Nippett, when Mavis besought her to drink it.

"But if you don't do what you're told, you'll never get well."

"Reely!"

"Of course not. Take this at once," Mavis commanded.

"Here, I say, who are you talking to? Have you for gotten I'm a partner in—" Here the little woman broke off, to exclaim as she burst into tears: "It's true: it's true: it's reely, reely true."

Before Mavis went home, she soothed Miss Nippett's tears; she left her in a condition of radiant, enviable happiness. She had never seen anyone so possessed by calm abiding joy as the accompanist at her unlooked-for good fortune.

On her way back, Mavis marvelled at what she believed to be the all-wise arrangements of Providence, by which happiness was parcelled out to the humblest of human beings. With the exception of Windebank, she had not been friendly with a rich person since she had been a child, so could not, at present, have any opinion of how much happiness the wealthy enjoyed; but she could not help remarking how much joy and contentment she had encountered in the person seemingly most unlikely to be thus blessed. At this period of her life, it did not occur to her that the natural and proper egoism of the human mind finds expression in a vanity, that, if happily unchastened by knowledge or experience, is a source of undiluted joy to the possessor.

If time be measured by the amount of suffering endured, it was a little later that Mavis realised that to be ignorant is to be often happy, enlightenment begetting desires that there is no prospect of staying, and, therefore, discontentment ensues.

When Mavis next visited Miss Nippett, she rummaged, at her friend's request, in the cupboard containing the unclaimed "overs" for finery with which the accompanist wished to decorate her exalted state. If Miss Nippett had had her way and had appeared in the street wearing the gaudy, fluffy things she picked out, she would have been put down as a disreputable old lady. But, for all Miss Nippett's resolves, it was written in the book of fate that she was to take but one more journey out of doors, and that in the simplest of raiment. For all her prodigious elation at her public association with Mr Poulter, her health far from improved; her strength declined daily; she wasted away before Mavis' dismayed eyes. She did not suffer, but dozed away the hours with increasingly rare intervals in which she was stark awake. On these latter occasions, for all the latent happiness which had come into her life, she would fret because Mr Poulter rarely called to inquire after her health. Such was her distress at this remissness on the part of the dancing master, that more often than not, when Miss Nippett, after waking from sleep, asked with evident concern if Mr Poulter had been, Mavis would reply:

"Yes. But he didn't like to come upstairs and disturb you."

For five or six occasions Miss Nippett accepted this explanation, but, at last, she became skeptical of Mavis' statements.

"Funny 'e always comes when I'm asleep!" she would say. "S'pose he was too busy to send up 'is name an' chance waking me. Tell those stories to them as swallers them."

But a time came when Miss Nippett was too ill even to fret. For three days she lay in the dim borderland of death, during which the doctor, when he visited her, became more and more grave. A time came when he could do no more; he told Mavis that the accompanist would soon be beyond further need of mortal aid.

The news seemed to strike a chill to Mavis' heart. Owing to their frequent meetings, Miss Nippett had become endeared to her: she could hardly speak for emotion.

"How long will it be?" she asked.

"She'll probably drag through the night. But if I were you, I should go home in the morning."

"And leave her to die alone?"

"You have your own trouble to face. Hasn't she any friends?"

"None that I know of."

"No one she'd care to see?"

"There's one man, her old employer. But he's always so busy."

"Where does he live?"

Mavis told him.

"I'll find time to see him and ask him to come."

"It's very kind of you."

But the kindly doctor did not seem to hear what she said; he was sadly regarding Miss Nippett, who, just now, was dozing uneasily on her pillows. Then, without saying a word, he left the room.

Thus it came about that Mavis kept the long, sad night vigil beside the woman whom death was to claim so soon. As Miss Nippett's numbered moments remorselessly passed, the girl's heart went out to the pitiful, shrivelled figure in the bed. It seemed that an unfair contest was being fought between the might and majesty of death on the one hand, and an insignificant, work-worn woman on the other, in which the ailing body had not the ghost of a chance. Mavis found herself reflecting on the futility of life, if all it led to were such a pitifully unequal struggle as that going on before her eyes. Then she remembered how she had been taught that this world was but a preparation for the joyous life in the next; also, that directly Miss Nippett ceased to breathe it would mean that she was entering upon her existence in realms of bliss. Somehow, Mavis could not help smiling at the mental picture of her friend which had suddenly occurred to her. In this, she had imagined Miss Nippett with a crown on her head and a harp in her hand, singing celestial melodies at the top of her voice. The next moment, she reproached herself for this untimely thought; her heart ached at the extremity of the little old woman huddled up in the bed. Mavis had always lived her life among more or less healthy people, who were ceaselessly struggling in order to live; consequently, she had always disregarded the existence of death. The great destroyer seemed to find small employment amongst those who flocked to their work in the morning and left it at night; but here, in the meagre room, where human clay was, as it were, stripped of all adornments, in order not to lose the smallest chance in the fell tussle with disease, it was brought home to Mavis what frail opposition the bodies of men and women alike offer to the assaults of the many missioners of death. Things that she had not thought of before were laid bare before her eyes. The inevitable ending of life bestowed on all flesh an infinite pathos which she had never before remarked. The impotence of mankind to escape its destiny made life appear to her but as a tragic procession, in which all its distractions and vanities were only so much make-believe, in order to hide its destination from eyes that feared to see. The helplessness, the pitifulness of the passing away of the lonely old woman gave a dignity, a grandeur to her declining moments, which infected the common furniture of the room. The cheap, painted chest of drawers, the worn trunk at the foot of the bed, the dingy wall-paper, the shaded white glass lamp on the rickety table, all seemed invested with a nobility alien to their everyday common appearance, inasmuch as they assisted at the turning of a living thing, who had rejoiced, and toiled, and suffered, into unresponsive clay. Even the American clock on the mantelpiece acquired a fine distinction by reason of its measuring the last moments of a human being, with all its miserable sensibility to pain and joy—a distinction that was not a little increased, in Mavis' eyes, owing to the worldly insignificance of the doomed woman.

After Mavis had got ready to hand things that might be wanted in the night, she settled herself in a chair by the head of the bed in order to snatch what sleep she might. Before she dozed, she wondered if that day week, which she would be spending at Mrs Gowler's, would find her as prostrated by illness as was her friend. Two or three times in the dread silent watches of the night, she was awakened by Miss Nippett's continually talking to herself. Mavis would interrupt her by asking if she would take any nourishment; but Miss Nippett, vouchsafing no answer, would go on speaking as before, her talk being entirely concerned with matters connected with the academy. And all the time, the American clock on the mantelpiece remorselessly ticked off the accompanist's remaining moments.

Mavis, heartsick and weary, got little sleep. She watched the night grow paler and paler outside the window, till, presently, the shaded lamp at the bedside seemed absurdly wan. Birds greeted with their songs the coming of the day. The sun rose in another such a blue sky as that on which she and Charlie Perigal had enjoyed their never-to-be-forgotten visit to Llansallas Bay. Mavis was not a little jarred by the insensibility of the June day to Miss Nippett's approaching dissolution. She reflected in what a sad case would be humanity, if there were no loving Father to welcome the bruised and weary traveller, arrived at the end of life's pilgrimage, with loving words or healing sympathy. In her heart of hearts, she envied Miss

Nippett the heavenly solace and divine compassion which would soon be hers. Then her heart leapt to the glory of the young June day; she devoutly hoped that she would be spared to witness many, many such days as she now looked upon.

"Mrs Kenrick!" said a voice from the bed.

"Are you awake?" asked Mavis.

"Do draw that there blind. I can't stand that there sun."

"Does it worry you?"

"Give me the 'lectric, same as they have at the Athenaeum on long nights."

Mavis did as she was bid: the light of the lamp at once became an illumination of some importance.

"Now I want me shawl on again; the old one." "Don't you want any nourishment?" asked Mavis, as she fastened the familiar shawl about Miss Nippett's shoulders.

"What's the use?"

"To get better, of course."

"No getting better for me. I know: reely I do."

"Nonsense!"

Miss Nippett shook her head as resolutely as her bodily weakness permitted.

"What's the time?" she asked presently.

Mavis told her.

"Whatever 'appens, I shall go down to posterity as a partner in 'Poulter's'!"

"You've no business to think of such things," faltered Mavis.

"It's no use codding me. I know; reely I do."

"Then, if you don't believe me, wouldn't you like to see a clergyman?"

"There's someone else I'd much sooner see."

"Mr Poulter?"

"You've guessed right this time. Is there—is there any chance of his coming?" asked Miss Nippett wistfully.

"There's every chance. The doctor was going to tell him how ill you were."

"But you don't understand; these great, big, famous men ain't like me and you. They—they forget and—" Tears gathered in the red rims of Miss Nippett's eyes. Mavis wiped them gently away and softly kissed the puckered brow.

"There's somethin' I'd like to tell you," said Miss Nippett, some minutes later.

"Try and get some sleep," urged Mavis.

"But I want to tell someone. It isn't as if you was a larruping girl who'd laugh, but you're a wife, an' ever so big at that, with what you're expectin' next week."

"What is it?" asked Mavis.

"Bend over: you never know oo's listening."

Mavis did as she was asked.

"It's Mr Poulter—can't you guess?" faltered Miss Nippett.

"Tell me, dear."

"I b'lieve I love him: reely I do. Don't laugh."

"Why should I?"

"There was nothing in it—don't run away thinking there was—but how could there be, 'im so great and noble and famous, and me—"

Increasing weakness would not suffer Miss Nippett to finish the sentence.

Mavis forced her to take some nourishment, after which, Miss Nippett lay back on her pillow, with her eyes fixed on the clock. Mavis sat in the chair by the bedside. Now and again, her eyes would seek the timepiece. Whenever she heard a sound downstairs (for some time the people of the house could be heard moving about), Miss Nippett would listen intently and then look wistfully at Mavis.

The girl divined how heartfully the dying woman hungered for Mr Poulter's coming.

Thrice Mavis offered to seek him out, but on each occasion Miss Nippett's terrified pleadings not to be left alone constrained her to stay.

It wanted a few minutes to eight when Miss Nippett fell into a peaceful doze. Mavis took this opportunity of making herself a much-needed cup of tea. Whilst she was gratefully sipping it, Miss Nippett suddenly awoke to say:

"There! There's something I always meant to do."

"Never mind now," said Mavis soothingly.

"But I do. It is something to mind about—I never stood 'Turpsichor' a noo coat of paint."

"Don't worry about it."

"I always promised I would, but kep' putting it off an' off, an' now she'll never get it from me. Poor old 'Turpsichor'!"

Miss Nippett soon forgot her neglect of "Turpsichor" and fell into a further doze.

When she next awoke, she asked:

"Would you mind drawing them curtains?"

"Like that?"

"You are good to me: reely you are."

"Nonsense!"

"But then you ought to be: you've got a good man to love you an' give you babies."

"What is it you want?" asked Mavis sadly.

"Can you see the 'Scrubbs'?"

"The prison?"

"Yes, the 'Scrubbs.' Can you see 'em?"

"Yes."

"Quite distinct?"

"Quite."

"That's awright."

Miss Nippett sighed with some content.

"If 'e don't come soon, 'e'll be too late," murmured Miss Nippett after an interval of seeming exhaustion.

Mavis waited with ears straining for the sound of the knocker on the front door. Miss Nippett lay so that her weakening eyes could watch the door of the bedroom. Now and again, Mavis addressed one or two remarks to her, but the old woman merely shook her head, as if to convey that she had neither the wish nor the strength for further speech. Mavis, with a great fear, noted the failing light in her friend's eyes, but was convinced that, for all the weakening of the woman's physical processes, she desired as ardently as ever a sight of Mr Poulter before she died. A few minutes later, a greyness crept into Miss Nippett's face. Mavis repressed an inclination to fly from the room. Then, although she feared to believe the evidence of her ears, a knock was heard at the door. After what seemed an interval of centuries, she heard footsteps ascending the stairs. Mavis glanced at Miss Nippett. She was horrified to see that her friend was heedless of Mr Poulter's possible approach. She moved quickly to the door. To her unspeakable relief, Mr Poulter stood outside. She beckoned him quickly into the room. He hastened to the bedside, where, after gazing sadly at the all but unconscious Miss Nippett, he knelt to take the woman's wan, worn hand in his. To Mavis's surprise, Miss Nippett's fingers at once closed on those of Mr Poulter. As the realisation of his presence reached the dying woman's understanding, a smile of infinite gladness spread over her face: a rare, happy smile, which, as if by magic, effaced the puckered forehead, the wasted cheeks, the long upper lip, to substitute in their stead a great contentment, such as might be possessed by one who has found a deep joy, not only after much travail, but as if, till the last moment, the longed-for bliss had all but been denied. The wan fingers grasped tighter and tighter; the smile faded a little before becoming fixed.

Another moment, and "Poulter's" had lost the most devoted servant which it had ever possessed.

CHAPTER TWENTY-NINE
THE ORDEAL

Mavis and Jill stood outside Mrs Gowler's, in the late evening of the Wednesday after the day on which Miss Nippett had commenced her long, long rest. Mavis had left the trunk she was bringing at the station (a porter was trundling it on), but before opening the gate of No. 9 Durley Road, she instinctively paused to take what she thought might prove a last look at the world.

The contented serenity of the summer night enhanced the meanness of the little street; but Mavis's imagination soared over the roofs, not only of the road in which she stood, but of countless other roofs, till it winged its way to Melkbridge. Instead of the depressing road, with its infrequent down-at-heel passers-by, Mavis saw only the Avon as she had known it a year ago. The river flowed lazily beneath the pollard willows, as if complaisant enough to let these see their reflection in the water. Forget-me-nots jewelled the banks; ragged robin looked roguishly from, clumps of bushes; the scent of hay seemed to fill the world. That was then.

Now—! Before she had set out for Durley Road, she had penned a little note to Perigal. In this she had told him of the circumstances in which she was writing it, and had said that if it proved to be the last letter she should send him, that she would never cease to love and trust him in any world to which it might please God to take her. This was all she had written; but the moving simplicity of her words might have touched even Perigal's heart. Besides writing to her lover, Mavis had given Mrs Scatchard the address to which she was going, and had besought her, in the event of anything untoward happening, either to take Jill for her own or to find her a good home. Mrs Scatchard's promise to keep and cherish Jill herself, should anything happen to her mistress, cheered Mavis much.

Mavis took a last long look of the June night, sighed and entered the gate of No. 9: her nerves were so disordered that it seemed as if it shut behind her with a menacing clang. She knocked at the door, but, upon no one coming, she knocked again and again. She knew there was someone in the house, for the wailing of babies could be heard within. For all anyone cared, her baby might have been born on the step. After knocking and waiting for quite a long time, the door was opened by a sad-faced girl, who, with the remains of a fresh complexion, looked as if she were countryborn and bred.

"Mrs Gowler?" asked Mavis wearily.

Without making any reply, the young woman left the door open and disappeared up the stairs. Mavis, followed by Jill, dragged herself into the passage. The puling and smell of unwashed babies assailed her ears and nostrils to such an extent, that, to escape from these, she walked into the kitchen and closed the door. This room was empty, but, as on her last visit, a fire roared in the kitchener, before which innumerable rows of little garments were airing. Overpowered by the stifling heat, Mavis sank on a chair, where a horde of flies buzzed about her head and tried to settle on her face. She was about to seek the passage in preference to the stuffy kitchen, when she heard a loud single knock at the front door. Believing this to be the porter with her luggage, she went to the door, to find that her surmise was correct.

"Which room shall I take it to, miss?"

"It will do if you put it in the hall," replied Mavis.

When she had paid the man and shut the door, she sat upon her box in the passage. Jill nestled beside her, whilst Mavis rested with her fingers pressed well against her ears, to deaden the continual crying of babies which came from various rooms in the house.

As Mavis thus waited, disconsolate and alone, her heart sank within her. Her present case seemed to foreshadow the treatment she would receive at Mrs Gowler's hands during her confinement, which might now occur at any moment. As she waited, she lost all count of time; her whole being was concerned with an alteration in her habits of thought, which had been imminent during the last few months, but which needed a powerful stimulus to be completely effected. This was now supplied. Hitherto, when it became a question whether she should consider others before herself, she had, owing to an instinct in her blood, chosen the way of self-abnegation. She often suspected that others took advantage of this unselfishness, but found it hard to do otherwise than she had always done. Whether it was owing to all she had lately endured, or because her maternal instinct urged her to think only of her as yet unborn little one, she became aware of a hardening of heart which convinced her of the expediency of fighting for her own hand in the future. Mrs Gowler's absence was the immediate cause of this manifestation. Had she not loved Perigal so devotedly and trusted him so completely, she would have left the miserable house in Durley Road and gone to an expensive nursing home, to insist later upon his meeting the bill. For all her awakened instinct of self, the fact of her still deciding to remain at Mrs Gowler's was a yet further sacrifice on the altar of the loved one. Perhaps this further self-effacement where her lover was concerned urgently moved her to stand no trifling in respect of others. Consequently, when about half-past ten Mrs Gowler opened the door, accompanied by her idiot son, Oscar, who looked more imbecile than ever in elaborate clothes, she was not a little surprised to be greeted by Mavis with the words:

"What does this mean?"

"What does what mean?" replied Mrs Gowler, bridling.

"Keeping me waiting like this."

"Wot do you expect for wot you're payin'—brass banns and banners?"

"I don't expect impertinence from you!" cried Mavis.

"Imperence! imperence! And oo's Mrs Kenrick to give 'erself such airs! And before my Oscar too!"

"Listen to me," said Mavis.

"I wonder you don't send for your 'usband to go for me."

"But—"

"Your lovin' 'usband wot's in Ameriky a-making a snug little 'ome for you."

Mavis was, for the moment, vanquished by the adroitness of Mrs Gowler's thrust.

"I'm not well enough to quarrel. Please to show me my room."

"That's better. An' I'll be pleased to show you what you call 'my room' when I've given my Oscar 'is supper," shouted Mrs Gowler, as she sailed into the kitchen, followed by her gibbering son, who twice turned to stare at Mavis.

Alone in the unlit, stuffy passage, Mavis whispered her troubles to Jill. Tears came to her eyes, which she held back by thinking persistently of the loved one. While she waited, she heard the clatter of plates and the clink of glasses in the kitchen. Mavis would have gone for a short walk, but she had a superstitious fear of going out of doors again till after her baby was born.

The sharp cry, as of one suddenly assailed by pain, came from the floor overhead. Then a door opened, and footsteps came to the top of the first flight of stairs.

"Mrs Gowler! Mrs Gowler!" cried a woman's voice frantically. But the woman had to call many times before her voice triumphed over the thickness of the kitchen door and the noise of the meal.

"Oo is it?" asked Mrs Gowler, when she presently came from the kitchen, with her mouth full of bread, cheese, stout, and spring onions.

"Liz—Mrs Summerville!" replied the woman.

"'Arf a mo', an' I'll be up," grumbled Mrs Gowler, as she returned to the kitchen, to emerge a few seconds later pinning on her apron.

"You finish yer supper, Oscar, but don't drink all the stout," she called to her son, as she went up the stairs. Before she had got to the landing, the cry was heard again and yet again. It sounded to Mavis like some wounded animal being tortured beyond endurance. The cries continued, to seem louder when a door was opened, and to be correspondingly deadened when this was closed. Mavis shuddered; anticipation of the torment she would have to endure chilled the blood in her veins; cold shivers coursed down her back. It was as if she were imprisoned in a house of pain, from which she could only escape by enduring the most poignant of all torture inflicted by nature on sensitive human bodies. The cries became continuous. Mavis placed her fingers in her ears to shut them out. For all this precaution, a scream of pain penetrated to her hearing. A few moments later, when she had to use her hands in order to prevent Jill from jumping on to her lap, she did not hear a sound. Some quarter of an hour later, Mrs Gowler descended the stairs.

"A quick job that," she remarked to Mavis, who did not make any reply. "Let's 'ope you'll be as sharp," added the woman, as she disappeared into the kitchen.

Mavis gathered from these remarks that a mother had been delivered of a child during Mrs Gowler's brief sojourn upstairs. The latter confirmed this surmise by saying a little later, when she issued from the kitchen drying her hands and bared arms on a towel:

"The worst of these here nursing 'omes is that yer never knows when you're going to be on the job. I didn't expect Liz till termorrer."

Mavis made no reply.

"Would you like a glass of stout?" asked Mrs Gowler.

"No, thank you."

"I'm going to open another bottle an' thought you'd join, jes' friendly like, as you might say. What with the work an' the 'eat of the kitchen, I tell yer, I can do with it."

"I'm tired of sitting in this horrible passage. I wish you would show me to my room."

"Wait till it's ready," retorted Mrs Gowler, angry at her hospitality being refused.

"It ought to be ready. What else did I arrange to come for?"

"You can go up if you like, but Mrs May is bathing her baby, an' there's no room to move."

"Does—does that mean that you haven't given me a room to myself?" cried Mavis.

"Wot more d'ye expect for wot you're payin'?"

Mavis made up her mind.

"If you don't give me a room to myself, I shall go," declared Mavis.

"And 'ave yer baby in the street?"

"That's my affair."

Mavis rose as if to make good her words.

Seeing that she was in earnest, Mrs Gowler said:

"Don't be a mug. I'll see what I can do."

Mavis was much relieved when Mrs Gowler waddled up the stairs, taking with her an evil-smelling oil lamp. The woman's presence was beginning to inspire her with a nameless dread, which was alien to the repulsion inspired by her appearance and coarse speech. Now and again, Mavis caught a glimpse of terrifying depths of resolution in the woman's nature; then she seemed as if she would stick at nothing in order to gain her ends.

"This way, please, Mrs 'Aughty," Mrs Gowler presently called from the landing above Mavis's head.

Mavis walked up the two flights of stairs, followed by Jill, where she found Mrs Gowler in the passage leading to the two top-back rooms of the house. One of these was small, being little larger than a box-room, but to Mavis's eyes it presented the supreme advantage of being untenanted by any other patient.

"We'd better 'ave most of the furniture out, 'ceptin' the bed and washstand," declared Mrs Gowler.

"But where am I to keep my things?" asked Mavis.

"Can't you 'ave your box jes' outside the door? If there ain't no space, you might pop off before I could hop round the bed."

"Is it often dangerous?" faltered Mavis.

"That depends. 'Ave you walked much?"

"A good deal. Why?"

"That's in yer favour. But I 'ope nothin' will 'appen, for my sake. I can't do with any more scandals here. I've my Oscar to think of."

"Scandals?" queried Mavis.

"What about gettin' your box upstairs?" asked Mrs Gowler, as if wishful to change the subject.

"Isn't there anyone who can carry it up?"

"Not to-night. Yer can't expect my Oscar to soil 'is 'ands with menial work. I'm bringing him up to be the gent he is."

"Then I'll go down and fetch what I want for the night."

"Let me git 'em for yer," volunteered Mrs Gowler, as her eyes twinkled greedily.

"I won't trouble you."

Mavis went down to the passage, taking with her the evil-smelling lamp: the spilled oil upon the outside of this greased Mavis's fingers.

To save her strength, she cut the cords with which her trunk was bound with a kitchen knife, borrowed from Mrs Gowler for this purpose. She took from this box such articles as she might need for the night. Amongst other things, she obtained the American clock which had belonged to her old friend Miss Nippett. Mr Poulter, to whom the accompanist had left her few possessions, had prevailed on Mavis to accept this as a memento of her old friend.

Mavis toiled up the stairs with an armful of belongings, preceded by Mrs Gowler carrying the lamp, the woman impressed at the cut and material of which her last arrival's garments were made.

When Mavis had wound up the clock and placed it on the mantelpiece, and, with a few deft touches, had made the room a trifle less repellent, she saw her landlady come into the room with three bottles and two glasses (one of these latter had recently held stout) tucked under her arms.

"I thought we'd 'ave a friendly little chat, my dear," remarked Mrs Gowler, as if to explain her hospitality.

Just then, Mavis's heart ached for the sympathy and support of some motherly person in whom she could confide. A tender word, a hint of appreciation of her present extremity, would have done much to give her stay for the approaching dread ordeal. Perhaps this was why, for the time being, she stifled her dislike of Mrs Gowler and submitted to the woman's presence. Mrs Gowler unscrewed a bottle of stout, poured herself out a glass, drank it at one draught, and then half filled a glass for Mavis.

"Drink it, my dear. It will do us both good," cried Mrs Gowler, who already showed signs of having drunk more than she could conveniently carry.

Mavis, not to seem ungracious, sipped the stout as she sat on the bed.

"'Ow is it you ain't in a proper nursing 'ome?" asked Mrs Gowler, after she had opened the second bottle.

"Aren't I?" asked Mavis quickly.

"I've 'eard of better," answered Mrs Gowler guardedly. "Though, after all, I may be a better friend to you than all o' them together, with their doctors an' all."

"Indeed!" remarked Mavis, wondering what she meant.

"But that's tellin's," continued Mrs Gowler, looking greedily at Mavis from the depths of her little eyes.

"Is it?"

"Babies is little cusses; noisy, squally little brats."

"Not one's own."

"That's what I say. I love the little dears. Gawd's messages I call them. All the same, they're there, as you might say. An' yer can't explain them away."

"True," smiled Mavis.

"An' their cost!" grumbled Mrs Gowler, as she drained the second bottle by putting it to her lips. "They simply eat good money, an' never 'ave enough."

"One must look after one's own," remarked Mavis.

"Little dears! 'Ow I love their pretty prattle. It makes me think of 'eavens an' Gawd's angels," said Mrs Gowler. Then, as Mavis did not make any remark, she added: "Six was born 'ere last week."

"So many!"

"But onny three's alive."

"The other three are dead!"

"It costs five bob a week an' extries to let a kid live, to say nothin' of the lies and trouble an' all. An' no thanks you get for it."

"A mother loves and looks after her own," declared Mavis.

"Little dears! Ain't they pretty when they prattles their little prayers?" asked Mrs Gowler, as her lips parted in a terrible smile. "Many's the time I've given 'em gin from me own bottle to give the little angels sleep."

She said more to the same effect, to pause before saying, with a return to her practical manner:

"An' the gentlemen! They're always 'appy when anything 'appens to baby."

Mavis looked at the woman with questioning eyes; she wondered what she meant. For a few moments Mrs Gowler attempted to lull Mavis's uneasiness by extravagant praise of infants' ways, which culminated in a hideous imitation of baby language. Suddenly she stopped; her little eyes glared fiercely at Mavis, while her face became rigid.

"What's the matter?" asked the girl.

Mrs Gowler rose unsteadily to her feet and said:

"Ten quid down will save you from forking out five bob a week till you're blue in the face from paying it."

Mavis stared at her in astonishment. Mrs Gowler backed to the door.

"Told yer you'd fallen on your feet. Next time you'll know better. No pretty pretties: one little nightdress is all you'll want. But it's spot cash."

Mavis was alone; it was, comparatively, a long time before she gathered what Mrs Gowler meant. When she realised that the woman had as good as offered to murder her child, when born, for the sum of ten pounds, her first impulse was to leave the house. But it was now late; she was worn out with the day's happenings; also, she reflected that, with the scanty means at her disposal, a further move to a like house to Mrs Gowler's might find her worse off than she already was. Her heart was heavy with pain when she knelt by her bedside to say her prayers, but, try as she might, she could find no words with which to thank her heavenly Father for the blessings of the day and to implore their continuance for the next, as was her invariable custom. When she got up from her knees, she hoped that the disabilities of her present situation would atone for any remissness of which she had been guilty. Although she was very tired, it was a long time before she slept. She lay awake, to think long and lovingly of Perigal. This, and Jill's presence, were the two things that sustained her during those hours of sleeplessness in a strange, fearsome house, troubled as she was with the promise of infinite pain.

That night she loved Perigal more than she had ever done before. It seemed to her that she was his, body and soul, for ever and ever; that nothing could ever alter it. When she fell asleep, she did not rest for long at a stretch. Every now and then, she would awaken with a start, when, for some minutes, she would listen to the ticking of the American clock on the mantelpiece. Her mind went back to the vigil she had spent during Miss Nippett's kit night of life. Then, it had seemed as if the clock were remorselessly eager to diminish the remaining moments of the accompanist's allotted span. Now, it appeared to Mavis as if the clock were equally desirous of cutting short the moments that must elapse before her child was born.

The next morning, she was awakened soon after eight by the noise of a tray being banged down just inside the door, when she gathered that someone had brought her breakfast. This consisted of coarsely cut bread, daubed with disquieting-looking butter, a boiled shop egg, and a cup of thin, stewed tea. As Mavis drank the latter, she recollected the monstrous suggestion which Mrs Gowler had insinuated the previous evening. The horror of it filled her mind to the exclusion of everything else. She had quite decided to leave the house as soon as she could pack her things, when a pang of dull pain troubled her body. She wondered if this heralded the birth of her baby, which she had not expected for quite two days, when the pain passed. She got out of bed and was setting about getting up, when the pain attacked her again, to leave her as it had done before. She waited in considerable suspense, as she strove to believe that the pains were of no significance, when she experienced a further pang, this more insistent than the last. She washed and dressed with all dispatch. While thus occupied, the pains again assailed her. When ready, she went downstairs to the kitchen, followed by Jill, to find the room deserted. She called "Mrs Gowler" several times without getting any response. Before going to her box to get some things she wanted, she gave Jill a run in the enclosed space behind the house. When Mavis presently went upstairs with an armful of belongings from her box, she heard a voice call from the further side of a door she was passing:

"Was you wanting Piggy?"

"I wanted Mrs Gowler."

"She's gone out and taken Oscar with her."

"When will she be back?"

"Gawd knows. Was you wanting her pertikler?"

"Not very," answered Mavis, at which she sought her room.

For four hours, Mavis sat terrified and alone in the poky room, during which her pains gradually increased. They were still bearable, and not the least comparable to the mental tortures which continually threatened her, owing to the dreariness of her surroundings and her isolation from all human tenderness. Now and again, she would play with Jill, or she would remake her bed. When the horror of her position was violently insistent, she would think long and lovingly of Perigal, and of how he would overwhelm her with caresses and protestations of livelong devotion, could he ever learn of all she had suffered from her surrender at Looe.

About one, the door was thrust open, and Mrs Gowler, hot and perspiring, and wearing her bonnet, came into the room, carrying a plate, fork, knife, and spoon in one hand and a steaming pot in the other.

"'Elp yerself!" cried Mrs Gowler, as she threw the plate and spoon upon the bed and thrust the pot beneath Mavis's nose.

"It's coming on," said Mavis.

"You needn't tell me that. I see it in yer face. 'Elp yerself."

"But—"

"I'll talk to you when I've got the dinners. 'Elp yerself."

"What is it?" asked Mavis.

"Lovely boiled mutting. Eat all you can swaller. You can do with it before you've done," admonished the woman.

Six o'clock found Mavis lying face downwards on the bed, her body racked with pain. Mrs Gowler sat impassively on the only chair in the room, while Jill watched her mistress with frightened eyes from a corner. Now and again, when a specially violent pain tormented her body, Mavis would grip the head rail of the bed with her hands, or bite Perigal's ring, which she wore suspended from her neck. Once, when Mrs Gowler was considerate enough to wipe away the beads of sweat, which had gathered on the suffering girl's forehead, Mavis gasped:

"Is it nearly over?"

"What! Over!" laughed Mrs Gowler mirthlessly. "I call that the preliminary canter."

"Will it be much worse?"

"You're bound to be worse before you're better."

"I can't—I can't bear it!"

"Bite yer wedding ring and trus' in Gawd," remarked Mrs Gowler, in the manner of one mechanically repeating a formula. "This is what some of the gay gentlemen could do with."

"It's—it's terrible," moaned Mavis.

"'Cause it's your first. When you've been here a few times, it's as easy as kiss me 'and."

Very soon, Mavis was more than ever in the grip of the fiend who seemed bent on torturing her without ruth. She had no idea till then of the immense ingenuity which pain can display in its sport with prey. During one long-drawn pang, it would seem to Mavis as if the bones in her body were being sawn with a blunt saw; the next, she believed that her flesh was being torn from her bones with red-hot pincers. Then would follow a hallowed, blissful, cool interval from searing pain, which made her think that all she had endured was well worth the suffering, so vastly did she appreciate relief. Then she would fall to shivering. Once or twice, it seemed that she was an instrument on which pain was extemporising the most ingenious symphonies, each more involved than the last. Occasionally, she would wonder if, after all, she were mistaken, and if she were not enjoying delicious sensations of pleasure. Then, so far as her pain-racked body would permit, she found herself wondering at the apparently endless varieties of torment to which the body could be subjected.

Once, she asked to look at herself in the glass. She did not recognise anything resembling herself in the swollen, distorted features, the distended eyes, and the dilated nostrils which she saw in the glass which Mrs Gowler held before her. She was soon lost to all sense of her surroundings. She feared that she was going mad. She reassured herself, however, because, by a great effort of will, she would conjure up some recollection of the loved one's appearance, which she saw as if from a great distance. Then, after eternities of torment, she was possessed by a culminating agony. Sweat ran from her pores. Every nerve in her being vibrated with suffering, as if the accumulated pain of the ages was being conducted through her body. More and even more pain. Then, a supreme torment held her, which made all others seem trifling by comparison. The next moment, a new life was born into the world—a new life, with all its heritage of certain sorrow and possible joy; with all its infinite sensibility to pleasure or pain, to hope and love and disillusion.

CHAPTER THIRTY
THE "PERMANENT"

When Mavis regained a semblance of consciousness, something soft and warm lay on her heart. Jill was watching her with anxious eyes. A queer little female figure stood beside the bed.

"Better, dear?" asked this person.

"Where's Mrs Gowler?" whispered Mavis.

"She got tired of waiting, so I came in. I've been here a hour" (she pronounced the aspirate).

"Who are you?" asked Mavis.

"I'm the 'permanent.'"

"The what?"

"The 'permanent': at least, that's what they call me here. But you mustn't talk. You've 'ad a bad time."

"Is it a boy or a girl?" asked Mavis.

"A boy. Don't say no more."

Mavis did not know if she were pleased or otherwise with the sex of her child; she could only thankfully realise that she was free from torment. She lay back, enjoying to the full her delicious comparative ease, before lifting the bed clothes to press her lips against her baby's head. She held it closer to her heart as she realised that its father was the man she loved. Although the woman who had introduced herself as the "permanent" had told Mavis not to talk, she did not set the example of silence. While she busied herself about and in and out of the room, she talked incessantly, chiefly about herself. For a long time, Mavis was too occupied with her own thoughts to pay any attention to what she was saying. Before she listened to the woman's gossip, she was more intent on taking in the details of her appearance. Mavis could not make up her mind whether she was young, old, or middle-aged; she might so easily have been one of these. Her face was not unpleasant, although her largish dark eyes were quite close to her snub nose, over which the eyebrows met. Her expression was that of good-natured simplicity, while her movements and manner of speaking betrayed great self-consciousness, the result of an immense personal vanity. She was soon to be a mother.

"It's my eighth, and all by different fathers," she told Mavis, who wondered at the evident pride with which the admission was made, till the woman added: "When you have had eight, and all by different fathers, it proves how the gentlemen love you."

Mavis, for all her exhaustion, could not help smiling at the ingenuousness of the "permanent's" point of view. Seeing Mavis smile, the woman laughed also, but her hilarity was inspired by self-conscious pride.

"P'raps you wonder what's become of the little dears. Three's dead, two's 'dopted, an' two is paid for at five bob a week by the gentlemen," she informed Mavis. She then asked: "I'spose this is your first?"

Mavis nodded.

"My! You're a baby at it. I 'spect I'll have a dozen to your six."

Presently, she spoke of Mrs Gowler.

"I've had every kid here, all seven of 'em, before the one I'm 'spectin' on Sunday. That's why Piggy calls me the 'permanent.' Do you like Piggy?"

Mavis moved her head in a way that could either be interpreted as a nod or a negative shake.

"I don't care for her very much, though I must say that so long as you locks up yer things, and don't take notice of what she says or does when she's drunk, she's always quite the lady."

Mavis, for all her growing weariness, smiled.

"Do you know why I reely come here?" asked the "permanent." "'Cause I love Piggy's son, Oscar. Oh, he is that comic! He do make me laugh so, I never can see enough of him. Don't you love looking at Oscar?"

Mavis shook her head.

"Don't you think him comic?"

"No," whispered Mavis.

"Go h'on! But there, I nearly forgot!"

The "permanent" left the room, at which Mavis closed her eyes, thankful for a few moments' peace.

"Take this cornflour," said a voice at her elbow: the "permanent" had brought her a basinful of this food. "I made it meself, 'cause Piggy always burns it, an' Oscar puts his fingers in it."

"You're very kind," murmured Mavis.

"Hold yer jaw," remarked the "permanent" with mock roughness.

Mavis gratefully swallowed the stuff, to feel the better for it. When she had finished the last drop, she lay back to watch the "permanent," who arranged the room for the night. Candle, matches, and milk were put handy for Mavis to reach; an old skirt was put down for Jill; bed and pillows were made comfortable.

"If you want me, I'm in the left top front with Mrs Rabbidge."

"Not alone?" asked Mavis.

"Not me. Give me company when I 'ave kids. I'll bring yer tea in the morning."

Whatever misfortunes the fates had reserved for Mavis, they had endowed her with a magnificent constitution; consequently, despite the indifferent nursing, the incompetent advice, the ill-cooked food, she quickly recovered strength. Hourly she felt better, although the nursing of her baby was a continuous tax upon her vitality. Following the "permanent's" advice, who was an old hand in such matters, Mavis kept quite still and did not exert herself more than she could possibly help. But although her body was still, her mind was active. She fretted because she had received no reply to her last little letter to Perigal. Morning and evening, which was the time when she had been accustomed to get letters from Wales, she would wait in a fever of anxiety till the post arrived; when it brought no letter for her, she suffered acute distress of mind.

Upon the fifth evening after her baby was born, Mrs Gowler thrust an envelope beneath her door shortly after the postman had knocked. It was a yellow envelope, on which was printed "On His Majesty's Service." Mavis tore it open, to find her own letter to Perigal enclosed, which was marked "Gone, no address." A glance told her that it had been correctly addressed.

When, an hour later, Mrs Gowler came up to see if she wanted anything, she saw that Mavis was far from well. She took her hand and found it hot and dry.

"Does yer 'ead ache?" she asked of Mavis, whose eyes were wide open and staring.

"It's awful."

"If you're no better in the morning, you'd better 'ave a shillingsworth of Baldock."

If anything, Mavis was worse on the morrow. She had passed a restless night, which had been troubled with unpleasantly vivid dreams; moreover, the first post had brought no letter for her.

"Got a shillin'?" asked Mrs Gowler after she had made some pretence of examining her.

"What for?" asked Mavis.

"Doctor's fee. You'll be bad if you don't see 'im."

"Is he clever?" asked the patient.

"Clever! 'E be that clever, it drops orf 'im."

When, with the patient's consent, Mrs Gowler set out to fetch the doctor, she, also at the girl's request, sent a telegram to Mrs Scatchard, asking her to send on at once any letters that may have come for Mavis. She was sustained by a hope that Perigal may have written to her former address.

"Got yer shillin' ready?" asked Mrs Gowler, an hour or so later. "'E'll be up in a minute."

Two minutes later, Mrs Gowler threw the door wide open to admit Dr Baldock. Mavis saw a short, gross-looking, middle-aged man, who was dressed in a rusty frock-coat; he carried an old bowler hat and two odd left-hand gloves. Mrs Gowler detailed Mavis's symptoms, the while Dr Baldock stood stockstill with his eyes closed, as if intently listening to the nurse's words. When she had finished, the doctor caught hold of Mavis's wrist; at the same time, he fumbled for his watch in his waistcoat pocket; not finding it, he dropped her arm and asked her to put out her tongue. After examining this, and asking her a few questions, he told her to keep quiet; also, that he would look in again during the evening to see how she was getting on.

"Doctor's fee," said Mrs Gowler, as she thrust herself between the doctor and the bed.

Mavis put the shilling in her hand, at which the landlady left the room, to be quickly followed by the doctor, who seemed equally eager to go. Mavis, with aching head, wondered if the evening post would bring her the letter she hungered for from North Kensington.

An hour later, a note was thrust beneath her door. She got out of bed to fetch it, to read the following, scrawled with a pencil upon a soiled half sheet of paper:—

"Don't you go and be a fool and have no more of Piggy's doctors. He isn't a doctor at all, and is nothing more than a coal merchant's tally-man, who got the sack for taking home coals in the bag he carried his dinner in. My baby is all right, but he squints. Does yours?—I remain yours truly, the permannente, MILLY BURT."

Anger possessed Mavis at the trick Mrs Gowler had played in order to secure a further shilling from her already attenuated store, an emotion which increased her distress of mind. When Mrs Gowler brought in the midday meal, which to-day consisted of fried fish and potatoes from the neighbouring fried fish shop, Mavis said:

"If that man comes here again, I'll order him out."

"The doctor!" gasped Mrs Gowler.

"He's an impostor. He's no doctor."

"'E's as good as one any day, an' much cheaper."

"How dare he come into my room! I shall stop the shilling out of my bill."

"You will, will yer! You try it on," cried Mrs Gowler defiantly.

"I believe he could be prosecuted, if I told the police about it," remarked Mavis.

At the mention of "police," Mrs Gowler's face became rigid. She recovered herself and picked out for Mavis the least burned portion of fish; she also gave her a further helping of potatoes, as she said:

"We won't quarrel over that there shillin', an' a cup o' tea is yours whenever you want it."

Mavis smiled faintly. She was beginning to discover how it paid to stick up for herself.

As the comparative cool of the evening succeeded to the heat of the day, Mavis's agitation of mind was such that she could scarcely remain in bed. The fact of her physical helplessness served to increase the tension in her mind, consequently her temperature. She feared what would happen to her already over-taxed brain should she not receive the letter she desired. When she presently heard the postman's knock at the door, her heart beat painfully; she lay in an immense suspense, with her hands pressed against her throbbing head. After what seemed a great interval of time (it was really three minutes), Mrs Gowler waddled into the room, bringing a letter, which Mavis snatched from her hands. To her unspeakable relief, it was in

Perigal's handwriting, and bore the Melkbridge postmark. She tore it open, to read the following:—

"MY DEAREST GIRL,—Why no letter? Are you well? Have you any news in the way of a happy issue from all your afflictions? I have left Wales for good. Love as always, C. D. P."

These hastily scribbled words brought a healing joy to Mavis's heart. She read and re-read them, pressing her baby to her heart as she did so. As a special mark of favour, Jill was permitted to kiss the letter. If Mavis had thought that a communication, however scrappy, from her lover would bring her unalloyed gladness, she was mistaken. No sooner was her mind relieved of one load than it was weighted with another; the substitution of one care for another had long become a familiar process. The intimate association of mind and body being what it is, and Mavis's offspring being dependent on the latter for its well-being, it was no matter for surprise that her baby developed disquieting symptoms. Hence, Mavis's new cause for concern.

Contrary to the case of unwedded mothers, as usually described in the pages of fiction, Mavis's love for her baby had, so far, not been particularly active, this primal instinct having as yet been more slumbering than awake. As soon after his birth as she was capable of coherent thought, she had been much concerned at the undeniable existence of the new factor which had come into her life. There was no contradicting Mrs Gowler, who had said that "babies take a lot of explaining away." She reflected that, if the fight for daily bread had been severe when she had merely to fight for herself, it would be much harder to live now that there was another mouth to fill, to say nothing of the disabilities attending her unmarried state. The fact of her letter to Perigal having been returned through the medium of the dead-letter office had almost distracted her with worry, and it is a commonplace that this variety of care is inimical to the existence of any form of love.

Her baby's illness quickly called to life all the immense maternal instinct which she possessed, but, at the same time, her recent awakening to her own claims to consideration made her realise, with a heartfelt sigh, that, in loving her boy as she now did, she was only giving a further precious hostage to happiness.

For three days the mother was kept in a suspense that served to protract the boy's illness, but, at the end of this time, largely owing to Mrs Gowler's advice, he began to improve. The day that his disquieting symptoms disappeared, which was also the day on which he recovered his appetite, was signalised by the arrival of Perigal's reply to Mavis's letter from Durley Road, announcing the birth of their son. In this, he congratulated her on her fortitude, and assured her that her happiness and well-being would always be his first consideration. It also told her that she was the best and most charming girl he had ever met; meeting with other women only the more strengthened this conviction.

Mavis's heart leapt with a great joy. So long as she was easily first in her lover's eyes, nothing else mattered. She had been foolish ever to have done other than implicitly trust him. His love decorated the one-time sparrow that she was with feathers of gorgeous hue.

Days succeeded each other within the four walls of Mrs Gowler's nursing home much as anywhere else, although in each twenty-four hours there usually occurred what were to Mavis's sensitive eyes and ears unedifying sights, agonised cries of women in torment. All day and night, with scarcely any intermission, could be heard the wailing of one or more babies in different rooms in the house. Mrs Gowler's nursing home attracted numberless girls from all parts of the great city, whose condition necessitated their temporary retirement from employment, whatever it might be. Mavis gathered that they were mostly the mean sort of general servant, who had succumbed to the blandishments of the men who make it a practice to prey on this class of woman. So far as Mavis could see, they were mostly plain and uninteresting-looking; also, that the majority of them stayed only a few days, lack of means preventing them being at Mrs Gowler's long enough to recover their health. They would depart, hugging their baby and carrying their poor little parcel of luggage, to be swallowed up and lost in London's ravening and cavernous maw. As they sadly left the house, Mavis could not help thinking that these deserted women were indeed human sparrows, who needed no small share of their heavenly Father's loving kindness to prevent them from falling and being utterly lost in the mire of London. Once or twice during Mavis's stay, the house was so full that three would sleep in one room, each of whom would go downstairs to the parlour, which was the front room on the ground floor, for the dreaded ordeal, to be taken upstairs as soon as possible after the baby was born. Mavis, who had always looked on the birth of a child as something sacred and demanding the utmost privacy, was inexpressibly shocked at the wholesale fashion in which children were brought into the world at Mrs Gowler's.

There was much that was casual, and, therefore, callous about the circumstances attending the ceaseless succession of births; they might as well have been kittens, their mothers cats, so Mavis thought, owing to the mean indignities attaching to the initial stages of their motherhood. It did not occur to her how house-room, furniture, doctors, nurses, and servants supply dignity to a commonplace process of nature. It seemed to Mavis that Mrs Gowler lived in an atmosphere of horror and pain. At the same time, the girl had the sense to realise that Mrs Gowler had her use in life, inasmuch as she provided a refuge for the women, which salved their pride (no small matter) by enabling them to forego entering the workhouse infirmary, which otherwise could not have been avoided.

Oscar inspired Mavis with an inexpressible loathing. For the life of her, she could not understand why such terrible caricatures of humanity were permitted to live, and were not put out of existence at birth. The common trouble of Mrs Gowler's lodgers seemed to establish a feeling of fellowship amongst them during the time that they were there. Mavis was not a little surprised to receive one day a request from a woman, to the effect that she should give this person's baby a "feed," the mother not being so happily endowed in this respect as Mavis. The latter's indignant refusal gave rise to much comment in the place.

The "permanent" was soon on her feet, an advantage which she declared was owing to her previous fecundity. Mavis could see how the "permanent" despised her because she was merely nursing her first-born.

"'As Piggy 'ad a go at your box yet?" she one day asked Mavis, who replied:

"I'm too careful. I always keep it locked."

"Locks ain't nothin' to her. If you've any letters from a gentleman, as would compromise him, burn them."

"Why?"

"If she gets hold of 'em, she'll make money on 'em."

"Nonsense! She wouldn't dare."

"Wouldn't she! Piggy 'ud do anythink for gin or that there dear comic Oscar."

In further talks with the "permanent," Mavis discovered that, for all her acquaintance's good nature, she was much of a liar, although her frequent deviations from the truth were caused by the woman's boundless vanity. Time after time she would give Mavis varying accounts of the incidents attending her many lapses from virtue, in all of which drugging by officers of His Majesty's army played a conspicuous part.

Mavis, except at meal times, saw little of Mrs Gowler, who was usually in the downstair parlour or in other rooms of the house. Whenever she saw Mavis, however, she persistently urged her to board out her baby with one of the several desirable motherly females she was in a position to recommend. Mrs Gowler pointed out the many advantages of thus disposing of Mavis's boy till such time as would be more convenient for mother and son to live together. But Mavis now knew enough of Mrs Gowler and her ways; she refused to dance to the woman's assiduous piping. But Mrs Gowler was not to be denied. One day, when Mavis was sitting up in bed, Mrs Gowler burst into the room to announce proudly that Mrs Bale had come to see Mavis about taking her baby to nurse.

"Who is Mrs Bale?" asked Mavis, much annoyed at the intrusion.

"Wait till you see her," cried Mrs Gowler, as if her coming were a matter of rare good fortune.

Mavis had not long to wait. In a few moments a tall, spare, masculine-looking woman strode into the room. Mrs Bale's red face seemed to be framed in spacious black bonnet strings. Mavis thought that she had never seen such a long upper lip as this woman had. This was surmounted by a broken, turned-up nose, on either side of which were boiled, staring eyes, which did not hold expression of any kind. If Mavis had frequented music halls, she would have recognised the woman as the original of a type frequently seen on the boards of those resorts, played by male impersonators. Directly she saw Mavis, Mrs Bale hurried to the bedside and seized the baby, to dandle it in her arms, the while she made a clucking noise not unlike the cackling of a hen.

Mavis noticed that Mrs Bale's breath reeked of gin.

"Put my baby down," said Mavis.

"I'll leave you two ladies to settle it between yer," remarked Mrs Gowler, as she left the room.

"I'm not going to put my baby out to nurse. Good morning."

"Not for five shillings a week?" asked Mrs Bale.

"Good morning."

"Say I made it four and six?"

Mavis made no reply, at which Mrs Bale sat down and began to weep.

"What about the trouble and expense of coming all the way here?" asked Mrs Bale.

"I never asked you to come."

"Well, I shan't leave this room till you give me six-pence for refreshment to get me to the station."

"I won't give it to you; I'll give it to Mrs Gowler."

"An' a lot of it I'd see."

Mrs Gowler, who had been listening at the door, came into the room and demanded to know what Mrs Bale meant.

Then followed a stream of recriminations, in which each accused the other of a Newgate calendar of crime. Mavis at last got rid of them by giving them threepence each.

Three nights before Mavis left Durley Road, she was awakened by the noise of Jill's subdued growling. Thinking she heard someone outside her room, she went stealthily to the door; she opened it quickly, to find Mrs Gowler on hands and knees before her box, which she was trying to open with a bunch of keys.

"What are you doing?" asked Mavis.

The woman entered into a confused explanation, which Mavis cut short by saying:

"I've heard about your tricks. If I have any more bother from you, I shall go straight from here to the police station."

"Gawd's truth! Why did I ever take you in?" grumbled Mrs Gowler as she waddled downstairs. "I might 'ave known you was a cat by the colour of your 'air."

The time came when Mavis was able to leave Durley Road. Whither she was going she knew not. She paid her bill, refusing to discuss the many extras which Mrs Gowler tried to charge, had her box taken by a porter to the cloak room at the station, dressed her darling baby, said good-bye to Piggy and went downstairs, to shudder as she walked along the passage to the front door. She had not walked far, when an ordinary-looking man came up, who barely lifted his hat.

"Can I speak to you, m'am?"

"What is it?"

"You have just left 9 Durley Road?"

"Y-yes."

"I'm a detective officer. I'm engaged in watching the house. Have you any complaint to make?"

"I don't wish to, thank you."

"We know all sorts of things go on, but it's difficult to get evidence."

"I don't care to give you any because—because—"

"I understand, ma'm," said the man kindly. "I know what trouble is."

Mavis was feeling so physically and mentally low with all she had gone through, that the man's kindly words made the tears course down her cheeks.

She wiped them away, resettled the baby in her arms, and walked sorrowfully up the road, followed by the sympathetic glance of the plain-clothes detective.

CHAPTER THIRTY-ONE
PIMLICO

Mavis found a resting-place for her tired body in the unattractive district of Pimlico, which is the last halting-place of so many of London's young women before the road to perdition is irretrievably taken. Mavis had purposed going to Hammersmith, but the fates which decide these matters had other views. On the tedious underground journey from New Cross, she felt so unwell that she got out at Victoria to seek refuge in the ladies' cloak room. The woman in charge, who was old, wizened, and despondent, gave Mavis some water and held her baby the while she lamented her misfortunes: these were embodied in the fact that "yesterday there had only been three 'washies' and one torn dress"; also, that "in the whole of the last month there had been but three 'faints' and six ladies the worse for drink." Acting on the cloak-room attendant's advice, Mavis sought harbourage in one of the seemingly countless houses which, in Pimlico, are devoted to the letting of rooms. But Mavis was burdened with a baby; moreover, she could pay so little that no one wished to accommodate her. Directly she stated her simple wants, together with the sum that she could afford to pay, she was, in most cases, bundled into the street with scant consideration for her feelings. After two hours' fruitless search, she found refuge in a tiny milk-shop in a turning off the Vauxhall Bridge Road, where she bought herself a scone and a glass of milk; she also took advantage of the shop's seclusion to give her baby much-needed nourishment. Ultimately, she got a room in a straight street, flanked by stucco-faced high houses, which ran out of Lupus Street. Halverton Street has an atmosphere of its own; it suggests shabby vice, unclean living, as if its inhabitants' lives were mysterious, furtive deviations from the normal. Mavis, for all her weariness, was not insensible to the suggestions that Halverton Street offered; but it was a hot July day; she had not properly recovered from her confinement; she felt that if she did not soon sit down she would drop in the street. She got a room for four shillings a week at the fifth house at which she applied in this street. The door had been opened by a tall, thin, flat-chested girl, whose pasty face was plentifully peppered with pimples. The only room to let was on the ground floor at the back of the house; it was meagre, poorly furnished, but clean. Mavis paid a week's rent in advance and was left to her own devices. For all the presence of her baby and Jill, Mavis felt woefully alone. She bought, and made a meal of bloater paste, bread, butter, and a bottle of stout, to feel the better for it. She then telephoned to the station master at New Cross, to whom she gave the address to which he could forward her trunk. On her return from the shop where she had telephoned, she went into a grocer's, where, for twopence, she purchased a small packing case. With this she contrived to make a cradle for her baby, by knocking out the projecting nails with a hammer borrowed from the pimply-faced woman at her lodging. If the extemporised cradle lacked adornment, it was adorable by reason of the love and devotion with which she surrounded her little one. Her box arrived in the course of the evening, when Mavis set about making the room look as homelike as possible. This done, she made further inroads on her midday purchases of bread and bloater paste, washed, fed her baby, and said her prayers before undressing for the night. At ten o'clock, mother and child were asleep.

Mavis had occupied her room for some days before she learned anything of the house in which she lodged. It was kept by a Mr, Mrs, and Miss Gussle, who lived in the basement. It was Miss Gussle who had opened the door to Mavis on the day she came. Mrs Gussle was never seen. Mavis heard from one source that she was always drunk; from another, that she was a teetotaller and spent her time at devotions; from a third, that she neither drank nor prayed, but passed the day in reading novelettes. But it was Mr Gussle who appealed the most to Mavis's sense of character. He was a wisp of a bald-headed, elderly man, who was invariably dressed in a rusty black frockcoat suit, a not too clean dicky, and a made-up black bow tie, the ends of which were tucked beneath the flaps of a turned down paper collar. He had no business or trade, but did the menial work of the house. He made the beds, brought up the meals and water, laid the tables and emptied the slops; but, while thus engaged, he never made any remark, and when spoken to replied in monosyllables. The ground floor front was let to a third-rate Hebraic music-hall artiste, who perfunctorily attended his place of business. The second and third floors, and most of the top rooms, were let to good-looking young women, who were presumed to belong to the theatrical profession. If they were correctly described, there was no gainsaying their devotion to their calling. They would leave home well before the theatre doors were open to the public, with their faces made up all ready to go on the stage; also, they were apparently so reluctant to leave the scene of their labours that they would commonly not return till the small hours. The top front room was rented by an author, who made a precarious living by writing improving stories for weekly and monthly journals and magazines. Whenever the postman's knock was heard at the door, it was invariably followed by the appearance of the author in the passage, often in the scantiest of raiment, to discover whether the post had brought him any luck. Although his stories were the delight of the more staid among his readers, the writer was on the best of terms with the "theatrical" young women, he spending most of his time in their company. The lodgers at Mrs Gussle's were typical of the inhabitants of Halverton Street. And if a house influences the natures of those who dwell within its walls, how much more does the character of tenants find expression in the appearance of the place they inhabit? Hence the shabbiness and decay which Halverton Street suggested.

Mavis heard from Perigal at infrequent intervals, when he would write scrappy notes inquiring after her health, and particularly after his child. Once, he sent a sovereign, asking Mavis to have the boy photographed and to send him a copy. Mavis did as she was asked. The photographs cost eight shillings. Although she badly wanted a few shillings to get her boots soled and heeled, she returned the money which was over after paying for the photographs, to Perigal. She was resolved that no sordid question of money should soil their relationship, however attenuated this might become.

Much of Mavis's time was taken up with her baby. She washed, dressed, undressed, and took out her little one, duties which took up a considerable part of each day. From lack of means she was compelled to wash her own and the baby's body-linen, which she dried by suspending from cords stretched across the room. All these labours were an aspect of maternity which she had never encountered in books. Much of the work was debasing and menial; its performance left her weak and irritable; she believed that it was gradually breaking the little spirit she had brought from Mrs Gowler's nursing home. When she recalled the glowing periods she had chanced upon in her reading, which eulogised the supreme joys of motherhood, she supposed that they had been penned by writers with a sufficient staff of servants and with means that made a formidable laundry bill of no account. She wondered how working-class women with big families managed, who, in addition to attending to the wants of their children, had all the work of the house upon their hands. Mavis's spare time was filled by the answering of advertisements in the hope of getting sorely needed work; the sending of these to their destination cost money for postage stamps, which made sad inroads on her rapidly dwindling funds. But time and money were expended in vain. The address from which she wrote was a poor recommendation to possible employers. She could not make personal application, as she dared not leave her baby for long at a stretch. Sometimes, her lover's letters would not bring her the joy that they once occasioned; they affected her adversely, leaving her moody and depressed. Conversely, when she did not hear from Melkbridge for some days, she would be cheerful and light-hearted, when she would spend glad half-hours in reading the advertisements of houses to let and deciding which would suit her when she was married to Perigal. Sometimes, when burdened with care, she would catch sight of her reflection in the glass, to be not a little surprised at the strange, latent beauty which had come into her face. Maternity had invested her features with a surpassing dignity and sweetness, which added to the large share of distinction with which she had originally been endowed. At the same time, she noticed with a sigh that sorrow had sadly chastened the joyous light-heartedness which formerly found constant expression in her eyes.

Mavis had been at Mrs Gussle's about three weeks when she made the acquaintance of one of the "theatrical" young women upstairs. They had often met in the passage, when the girl had smiled sympathetically at Mavis. One afternoon, when the latter was feeling unusually depressed, a knock was heard at her door. She cried "Come in," when the girl opened the door a few inches to say:

"May I?"

"I didn't know it was you," remarked Mavis, distressed at her poverty being discovered.

"I came to ask if I could do anything for you," said the girl.

"That's very nice of you. Do come in."

The girl came in and stayed till it was time for her to commence the elaborate dressing demanded by her occupation. Mavis made her some tea, and the girl (who was called "Lil") prevailed upon her hostess to accept cigarettes. If the girl had been typical of her class, Mavis would have had nothing to do with her; but although Lil made a brave show of cynicism and gay worldliness, Mavis's keen wits perceived that these were assumed in order to conceal the girl's secret resentment against her habit of life. Mavis, also, saw that the girl's natural kindliness of heart and refined instincts entitled her to a better fate than the one which now gripped her. Lil was particularly interested in Mavis's baby. She asked continually about him; she sought him with her eyes when talking to Mavis, conduct that inclined the latter in her favour.

When Lil was going she asked:

"May I come again?"

"Why not?" asked Mavis.

"I didn't know I—I—So long," cried Lil, as she glanced in the direction of the baby.

On the occasion of her next visit, which took place two afternoons later, Lil asked:

"May I nurse your baby?" to add, as Mavis hesitated, "I promise I won't kiss him."

Mavis consented, greatly to Lil's delight, who played with the baby for the rest of the afternoon.

"You're fond of children?" commented Mavis.

The girl nodded, the while she bit her lip.

"I can see you've had baby brothers or sisters," remarked Mavis.

"How do you know?"

"By the way you hold him."

"What do you think of Gertie?" asked Lil quickly.

"Who's Gertie?"

"Mr Gussle. Upstairs we always call him Gertie."

"I can't make him out," said Mavis, at which she learned from Lil that Mr Gussle loathed his present means of earning a livelihood; also, that he hungered for respectability, and that, to satisfy his longing, he frequented, in his spare time, a tin tabernacle of evangelical leanings. Mavis also learned that the girls upstairs, knowing of Mr Gussle's proclivities, tempted him with cigarettes, spirits, and stimulating fleshly allurements.

One day, when Mavis had left her sleeping baby to go out for a few minutes, she returned to find Lil nursing her boy, the while tears fell from her eyes. Mavis pretended not to notice the girl's grief. She busied herself about the room, till Lil recovered herself. Later, when Mavis was getting seriously pressed for money, she came across odd half sovereigns in various parts of the room, which she rightly suspected had been put there by her friend. For all Lil's entreaties, Mavis insisted on returning the money. Lil constantly wore a frock to which Mavis took exception because it was garish. One day she spoke to Lil about it.

"Why do you so often wear that dress?" she asked.

"Don't you like it?"

"Not a bit. It's much too loud for you."

"I don't like it myself."

"Then why wear it?"

"It's my 'lucky dress.'"

"Your what?"

"'Lucky' dress. Don't you know all we girls have their 'lucky' dresses?"

This was news to Mavis.

"You mean a dress that—"

"Brings us luck with the gentlemen," interrupted Lil.

The subject thus opened, Lil became eloquent upon many aspects of her occupation. Presently she said:

"It isn't always the worst girls who are 'on the game.'"

"Indeed!"

"So many are there through no fault of their own."

"How is that?" asked Mavis.

"They get starved into it. It's all these big shops and places. They pay sweating wages, and to get food the girls pick up men. That's the beginning."

Mavis nodded assent. She remembered all she had heard and seen on this matter when at "Dawes'."

"And the small employers are getting just as bad. And of them the women are the worst. They don't care how much they grind poor girls down. If anything, I b'lieve they enjoy it. And if once a girl goes wrong, they're the ones to see she don't get back. Why is it they hate us so?"

"Give it up," replied Mavis, who added, "I should think it wanted an awful lot of courage."

"Courage! courage! You simply mustn't think. And that's where drink comes in."

Mavis sighed.

"Don't you ever take to the life," admonished Lil.

"I'm not likely to," shuddered Mavis.

"'Cause you ain't the least built that way. And thank God you ain't."

"I do; I do," said Mavis fervently.

"It's easy enough to blame, I know; but if you've a little one and no one in the wide world to turn to for help, and the little one's crying for food, what can a poor girl do?" asked Lil, as she became thoughtful and sad-looking.

A time came when Mavis was sorely pressed for money to buy the bare necessaries of life. She could not even afford soap with which to wash her own and her baby's clothes. Of late, she had made frequent visits to Mrs Scatchard's, where she had left many of her belongings. All of these that were saleable she had brought away and had disposed of either at pawnshops or at second-hand dealers in clothes. She had at last been constrained to part with her most prized trinkets, even including those which belonged to her father and the ring that Perigal had given her, and which she had worn suspended from her neck.

She now had but one and sixpence in the world. The manifold worries and perplexities consequent upon her poverty had affected her health. She was no longer able to supply her baby with its natural food. She was compelled to buy milk from the neighbouring dairy and to sterilise it to the best of her ability. To add to her distress, her boy's health suffered from the change of diet. Times without number, she had been on the point of writing to Perigal to tell him of all she had suffered and to ask for help, but pride had held her back. Now, the declension in her boy's health urged her to throw this pride to the winds, to do what common sense had been suggesting for so long. She had prayed eloquently, earnestly, often, for Divine assistance: so far, no reply had been vouchsafed. When evening came, she could bear no longer the restraint imposed by the four walls of her room. She had had nothing to eat that day; all she had had the day before was a crust of bread, which she had gleefully lighted upon at the back of her cupboard. This she would have shared with Jill, had not her friend despised such plain fare. Jill had lately developed a habit of running upstairs at meal times, when, after an interval, she would come down to lick her chops luxuriously before falling asleep.

Mavis was faint for lack of nourishment; hunger pains tore at her stomach. She felt that, if she did not get some air, she would die of the heat and exhaustion. Her baby was happily sleeping soundly, so she had no compunction in setting out. She crossed Lupus Street, where her nostrils were offended by the smell of vegetable refuse from the costermonger stalls, to walk in the direction of Victoria. The air was vapid and stale, but this did not prevent the dwellers in Pimlico from sitting at open windows or standing on doorsteps in order to escape the stuffiness of their houses. They were mostly vulgar lodging-house people, who were enjoying their ease following upon the burden of the day; but Mavis found herself envying them, if only for the fact that their bodies were well supplied with food. Hunger unloosed a savage rage within her, not only against everyone she encountered, but also against the conditions of her life. "What was the use of being of gentle birth?" she asked herself, if this were all it had done for her. She deeply regretted that she had not been born an ordinary London girl, in which case she would have been spared the possession of all those finer susceptibilities with which she now believed herself to be cursed, and which had prevented her from getting assistance from Perigal. She lingered by the cook shop in Denbigh Street, where she thought that she had never smelt anything so delicious as the greasy savours which came from the eating-house. It was only with a great effort of will that she stopped herself from spending her last one and sixpence (which she was keeping for emergency) in food. When she reached the Wilton Road, she walked of a set purpose on the station side of that thoroughfare. She feared that the restaurants opposite might prevail against her already weakened resolution. By the time she reached the Victoria Underground Station, her hunger was no longer under control. Her eyes searched the gutters greedily for anything that was fit to eat. She glared wolfishly at a ragged boy who picked up an over-ripe banana, which had been thrown on the pavement. The thought of the little one at home decided her. She turned in the direction of the post-office, having at last resolved to wire to her lover for help.

"Well, I'm blowed!" said a familiar voice at her side. Mavis turned, to see the ill-dressed figure of flat-chested, dumpy Miss Toombs.

"Miss Toombs!" she faltered.

"Didn't you see me staring at you?"

"Of course not. What are you doing in London?"

"I'm up here on a holiday. I am glad to see you."

"So am I. Good night."

"Eh!"

"I must go home. I said good night."

"You are a pig. I thought you'd come and have something to eat."

"I'm not—I'm not hungry."

"Well, sit down by me while I feed. I feel I want a jolly good blow out."

They had reached the doors of the restaurant opposite the main entrance to the underground railway. The issuing odours smote Mavis's hesitation hip and thigh.

"I—I really must be off," faltered Mavis, as she stood stockstill on the pavement.

By way of reply, Miss Toombs shoved the unresisting Mavis through the swing doors of the eating house; then, taking the lead, she piloted her to a secluded corner on the first floor, which was not nearly so crowded as the downstair rooms.

"It's nice to see good old Keeves again," remarked Miss Toombs, as she thrust a list of appetising foods under Mavis's nose.

"I'm really not a bit hungry," declared Mavis, who avoided looking at the toothsome-looking bread-rolls as far as her ravening hunger would permit. She grasped the tablecloth to stop herself from attacking these.

"Got any real turtle soup?" asked Miss Toombs of the polyglot waiter who now stood beside the table.

"Mock turtle," said the man, as he put his finger on this item in the menu card.

"Two oxtail soups," Miss Toombs demanded.

"Apres?"

"Two stewed scallops, and after that some lamb cutlets, new potatoes, and asparagus."

"Bon! Next, meiss," said the waiter, who began to think that the diner's prodigality warranted an unusually handsome tip.

Miss Toombs ordered roast ducklings and peas, together with other things, which included a big bottle of Burgundy, the while Mavis stared at her wide-eyed, open-mouthed; the starving girl could scarcely believe her ears.

"Is it—is it all true?" she murmured.

"Is what true?"

"Oh, meeting with you."

"Why? Have I altered much?"

It seemed a long time to Mavis till the soup was placed before her. Even when its savoury appeal made her faint with longing, she said:

"I'm—I'm really not a bit—"

She got no further. She had taken a mouthful of the soup, to hold it for a few moments in her mouth. She had no idea till then that it was possible to enjoy such delicious sensations. Once her fast was broken, the floodgates of appetite were open. She no longer made pretence of concealing her hunger; she would not have been able to if she had wished. She swallowed great mouthfuls of food greedily, silently, ravenously; she ate so fast that once or twice she was in danger of choking. If anyone had taken her food away, she would have fought to get it back. Thus Mavis devoured course after course, unaware, careless that Miss Toombs herself was eating next to nothing, and was watching her with quiet satisfaction from the corners of her eyes.

At last, Mavis was satisfied. She lay back silent and helpless on her plush seat, enjoying to the full the sensation of the rich, fat food nourishing her body. She closed her eyes and was falling into a deep sleep.

"Have some coffee and brandy," said Miss Toombs.

Mavis pulled herself together and drank the coffee.

"I'd give my soul for a cigarette," murmured Mavis, as she began to feel more awake.

"Blow you!" complained Miss Toombs, as she signalled to the waiter.

Mavis looked at her surprised, when her hostess said:

"You're prettier than ever. When I first saw you, I was delighted to think you were 'going off.'"

Mavis, regardless what others might think of her, lit the cigarette. Although she took deep, grateful puffs, which she wholly enjoyed, she soon let it go out; neither did she trouble to relight it, nor did she pay any attention to Miss Toombs's remarks. Mavis's physical content was by no means reflected in her mind. Her conscience was deeply troubled by the fact of her having, as it were, sailed with her benefactress under false colours.

Her cogitations were interrupted by Miss Toombs putting a box of expensive cigarettes (which she had got from the waiter) in her hand.

"Why are you so good to me?" asked Mavis.

"I've always really liked you."

"You wouldn't if you knew."

"Knew what?"

"Come. I'll show you."

After Miss Toombs had settled with the waiter, they left the restaurant. Miss Toombs accompanied Mavis along the Wilton Road and Denbigh Street. Halverton Street was presently reached. Mavis opened the door of Mrs Gussle's; with set face, she walked the passage to her room, followed by plain Miss Toombs. She unlocked the door of this and made way for her friend to enter. Clothes hung to dry from ropes stretched across the room: the baby slept in his rough, soap-box cradle.

Miss Toombs seemed to disregard the appearance of the room; her eyes sought the baby sleeping in the box.

"There!" cried Mavis. "Now you know."

"A baby!" gasped Miss Toombs.

"You've been kind to me. I had to let you know."

"Oh, you damn beast!" cried Miss Toombs.

Mavis looked at her defiantly.

"Oh, you damn beast!" cried Miss Toombs again. "You were always lucky!"

"Lucky!" echoed Mavis.

"To go and have a little baby and not me. Oh, it's too bad: too bad!"

Mavis looked inquiringly at her friend to see if she were sincere. The next moment, the two foolish women were weeping happy tears in each other's arms over the unconscious, sleeping form of Mavis's baby.

CHAPTER THIRTY-TWO
MISS TOOMBS REVEALS HERSELF

"Fancy you being like this," said Mavis, when she had dried her eyes.

"Like what?"

"Not minding my having a baby without being married."

"I'm not such a fool as to believe in that 'tosh,'" declared Miss Toombs.

"What 'tosh,' as you call it?"

"About thinking it a disgrace to have a child by the man you love."

"Isn't it?"

"How can it be if it's natural and inevitable?"

Mavis looked at Miss Toombs wide-eyed.

"Does the fact of people agreeing to think it wrong make it really wrong?" asked Miss Toombs, to add, "especially when the thinking what you call 'doing wrong' is actuated by selfish motives."

"How can morality possibly be selfish?" inquired Mavis.

"It's never anything else. If it weren't selfish it wouldn't be of use; if it weren't of use it couldn't go on existing."

"I'm afraid I don't follow you," declared Mavis, as she lit a cigarette.

"Wait. What would nearly all women do if you were mad enough to tell them what you've done?"

"Drop on me."

"Why?"

"Because I've done wrong."

"Are women 'down' on men for 'getting round' girls, or forgery, or anything else you like?"

Mavis was compelled to acknowledge her sex's lack of enthusiasm in the condemnation of such malpractices.

"Then why would they hunt you down?" cried Miss Toombs triumphantly. "Because, in doing as you've done, you've been a traitress to the economic interests of our sex. Women have mutually agreed to make marriage the price of their surrender to men. Girls who don't insist on this price choke men off marrying, and that's why they're never forgiven by other women."

"Is it you talking?"

"No, my dear Keeves; women, in this world, who look for marriage, have to play up to men and persuade them they're worth the price of a man losing his liberty."

"But fancy you talking like that!"

"If they're pretty, and play their cards properly, they're kept for life. If they're like you, and don't get married, it's a bad look-out. If they're pretty rotten, and have business instincts, they must make hay while the sun shines to keep them when it doesn't."

"And you don't really think the worse of me?"

"I think the more. It's always the good girls who go wrong."

"That means that you will."

"I haven't the chance. When girls are plain, like me, men don't notice them, and if they've no money of their own they have to earn a pittance in Melkbridge boot factories."

"I can't believe it's you, even now."

"I don't mind giving myself away, since you've done the same to me. And it's a relief to let off steam sometimes."

"And you really don't think the worse of me for having—having this?"

"I'd do the same myself to-morrow if I'd the chance and could afford to keep it, and knew it wouldn't curse me when it grew up."

Mavis winced to recover herself and say:

"But I may be married any day now."

"Whoever the father is, he seems a bit of a fool," remarked Miss Toombs, as she took the baby on her knee.

"To love me?"

"In not marrying you and getting you for life. From a man's point of view, you're a find, pretty Mavis."

"Nonsense!"

"I don't call it nonsense. Just look at your figure and your hips and the colour of your hair, your lovely white skin and all, to say nothing of the passion in your eyes."

"Is it staid Miss Toombs talking?"

"If I'm staid, it's because I have to be. No man 'ud ever want me. As for you, if I were a man, I'd go to hell, if there were such a place, if I could get you for all my very own."

"Don't you believe in hell?"

"Do you?"

"I don't know. Don't you?"

"The only hell I know is the jealous anger in a plain woman's heart. Of course there are others. You've only to dip into history to read of the hells that kings and priests, mostly priests, have made of this earth."

"What about Providence?" asked Mavis.

"Don't talk that 'tosh' to me," cried Miss Toombs vehemently.

"But is it 'tosh'?"

"If I were to give you a list of even the few things I've read about, the awful, cruel, blood-thirsty, wicked doings, it would make your blood boil at the injustice, the wantonness of it all. Read how the Spaniards treated the Netherlanders once upon a time, the internal history of Russia, the story of Red Rubber, loads of things, and over and over again you'd ask, 'What was God doing to allow such unnecessary torture?'"

Miss Toombs paused for breath. Seeing Mavis looking at her with open-mouthed astonishment, she said:

"Have I astonished you?"

"You have."

"Haven't you heard anyone else talk like that?"

"What I was thinking of was, that you, of all people, should preach revolt against accepted ideas. I always thought you so straitlaced."

"Never mind about me."

"But I do. If you believe all you say, why do you go to church and all that?"

"What does it matter to anyone what an ugly person like me thinks or does?"

"Anyway, you're quite interesting to me."

"Really: really interesting?" asked Miss Toombs, with an inflection of genuine surprise in her voice.

"Why should I say so if I didn't think so?"

A flush of pleasure overspread the plain woman's face as she said:

"I believe you're speaking the truth. If ever I play the hypocrite, it's because I'm a hopeless coward."

"Really!" laughed Mavis, who was beginning to recover her spirits.

"Although I believe my cowardice is justified," declared Miss Toombs. "I haven't a friend or relation in the world. If I were to get ill, or lose my job to-morrow, I've no one to turn to. I've a bad circulation and get indigestion whenever I eat meat. I've only one pleasure in life, and I do all I know to keep my job so that I can indulge in it."

"What's that?"

"You'll laugh when I tell you."

"Nothing that gives a human being innocent pleasure can be ridiculous," remarked Mavis.

"My happiness comes in winter," declared Miss Toombs. "I love nothing better than to go home and have tea and hot buttered toast before the blazing fire in my bed-sitting room. Then, about seven, I make up the fire and go to bed with my book and hot-water bottles. It's stuffy, but it's my idea of heaven."

Mavis did not offer any comment.

"Now laugh at me," said Miss Toombs.

Instead of doing any such thing, Mavis bent over to kiss Miss Toombs's cheek.

"No one's ever wanted to kiss me before," complained Miss Toombs.

"Because you've never let anyone know you as you really are," rejoined Mavis.

"Now we've talked quite enough about me. Let's hear a little more about yourself."

"My history is written in this room."

"Don't talk rot. I suppose it all happened when you went away for your holidays last year?"

"You didn't think—"

"No. I didn't think you had the pluck."

"It doesn't require much of that."

"Doesn't it? There are loads of girls, nice girls too, who'd do as you've done to-morrow if they only dared," declared Miss Toombs. "And why not?" she added defiantly.

"You take my breath away," laughed Mavis.

"Don't laugh, dear. It's much too serious to laugh at," remonstrated Miss Toombs. "We're here for such a short time, and so much of that is taken up with youth and age and illness and work that it's our duty to get as much happiness as we can. And if two people love each other—"

"The woman can be brought down to this."

"And wasn't it worth it?" cried Miss Toombs hotly.

"Worth it!" echoed Mavis.

"Didn't you have a lovely time when you were away?"

"Heavenly!"

"Didn't he kiss your hands and feet and hair and tell you you were the most beautiful woman in the whole world, as they do in books?"

Mavis nodded.

"And didn't he hold you to his heart all the night through, and didn't you think you were in heaven? No—no, don't tell me. It would make me miserable and jealous for weeks."

"Why should it?"

"Who's ever wanted to love and kiss my feet and hands? But there it is—you're a pretty girl, and all that, but you can't have everything in this world. You've had to pay one of the chief penalties for your attractiveness."

Just then Mavis's baby began to cry.

"It's my hard knee," remarked Miss Toombs ruefully. "They always cry when I nurse them."

"I think he's hungry," remarked Mavis.

"Then give the boy his supper. Don't mind me."

Mavis busied herself with the preparations for sterilising the milk, but the boy cried so lustily that, to quiet him, Mavis blushingly undid her bodice to put the nipple of her firm, white breast in his mouth.

"It's the only thing to quiet him," explained Mavis.

"No wonder. He's got taste, has that boy. Don't turn away. It's all so beautiful, and there's nothing wrong in nature."

"What are you thinking of?" asked Miss Toombs presently, after Mavis had been silent for a while. "Don't you feel at home with me?"

"Don't be silly! You know you profess not to believe in Providence."

"What of it?"

"I've been in a bad way lately and I've prayed for help. Surely meeting with you in a huge place like London is an answer to my prayer."

"Meeting you, when you were hard up, was like something out of a book, eh?"

"Something out of a very good book," replied Mavis.

"Well, it wasn't chance at all. These sort of things never happen when they're wanted to. I've been up in town looking for you."

"What!"

"And thereby hangs a very romantic tale."

"You've been looking for me?"

"What's the time?"

"You're not thinking of going yet? Why were you looking for me?"

"It's nearly ten," declared Miss Toombs, as she looked at her watch. "Unless I stay the night here, I must be off."

"Where are you staying?"

"Notting Hill. I beg its pardon—North Kensington. They're quiet people. If I'm not back soon, my character will be lost and I shall be locked out for the night."

"I'd love you to stay. But there's scarcely room for you in this poky little hole."

"Can't I engage another room?"

"But the expense?"

"Blow that! See if they can put me up."

Mavis talked to Miss Gussle on the subject. Very soon, Mr Gussle could be heard panting up the stairs with an iron chair bedstead, which was set up, with other conveniences, in the music-hall agent's office.

"Nice if he comes back and came into my room in the night," remarked Miss Toombs.

"What on earth would you do?" asked Mavis.

"Lock the door to keep him in," replied Miss Toombs quickly, at which the two friends laughed immoderately.

As Miss Toombs was leaving the room to wire to her landlady to tell her that she was staying with friends for the night, she kissed her hand to Mavis's baby.

"What are you going to call him?" she asked.

"Charlie, of course," promptly replied Mavis.

The next moment, she could have bitten off her tongue for having given Miss Toombs a possible clue to her lover's identity: she had resolved never to betray him to a living soul.

But Mavis comforted herself on the score that her friend received her information without betraying interest or surprise. Twenty minutes later, Miss Toombs came back, staggering beneath the weight of an accumulation of parcels, which contained a variety of things that Mavis might want.

"How could you spend your money on me?" asked Mavis, as the different purchases were unpacked.

"If one can't have a romance oneself, the next best thing is to be mixed up in someone else's," replied Miss Toombs.

Mavis and her friend sat down to a supper of strawberries and cream, whilst they drank claret and soda water. Jill was not forgotten; Miss Toombs had bought her a pound of meat scraps from the butcher's, which the dog critically consumed in a corner.

"Let me hear about your romance and all the Melkbridge news," said Mavis, as she stopped her friend from pouring more cream upon her plate of strawberries.

"Blow Melkbridge!" exclaimed Miss Toombs, her face hardening.

"But I love it. I'm always thinking about it, and I'd give anything to go back there."

"Eh!"

"I said I'd give anything to be back there."

"Rot!"

"Why rot?"

"You mustn't dream of going back," cried Miss Toombs anxiously.

"Why on earth not?"

"Eh! Oh, because I say so."

"Does anyone down there know?"

"Not that I'm aware of."

"Then why shouldn't I go back?"

"There's no reason, only—"

"Only what?"

"Let me tell you of my romance."

"Very well, only—"

"When I tell you I'm in love, I don't think you ought to interrupt," remarked Miss Toombs.

"I only wanted to know why I mustn't dream of going back to Melkbridge," said Mavis anxiously.

"Because I can get you a better job elsewhere. There now!"

"Let's hear of your love affair," said Mavis, partly satisfied by Miss Toombs's reason for not wishing her to return to the place where her lover was.

"Five weeks ago, a man strode into our office at the factory; tall, big, upright, sunburned."

"Who was he?" asked Mavis.

"He wasn't a man at all; he was a god. And his clothes! Oh, my dear, my heart came up in my mouth. And when he gave me his card—"

"Who was he?" interrupted Mavis.

"Can't you guess?"

"Give it up."

"Captain Sir Archibald Windebank."

"Really!"

"I wish it hadn't been. I've never forgotten him since."

"What did he want?"

"You!"

"Me?"

"You, you lucky girl! Has he ever kissed you?"

"Once."

"Damn you! No, I don't mean that. You were made for love. But why didn't you hold him in your arms and never let him go? I should have."

"That's not a proper suggestion," laughed Mavis. "What did he want me for?"

"He wanted to find out what had become of you."

"What did you tell him?"

"I didn't get much chance. Directly he saw Miss Hunter was nice-looking, he addressed all his remarks to her."

"Not really?"

"A fact. Then I got sulky and got on with my work."

"What did she say?"

"What could she say? But, my goodness, wouldn't she have told some lies if I hadn't been there, and she had had him all to herself!"

"Lies about me?"

"She hated the sight of you. She never could forgive you because you were better born than she. And, would you believe it, she started to set her cap at him."

"Little cat!"

"He said he would come again to see if we heard any more of you, and, when he went, she actually made eyes at him. And, if that weren't enough, she wore her best dress and all her nick-knacks every day till he came again."

"He did come again?"

"This time he spoke to me. He went soon after I told him we hadn't heard of you."

"Did he send you to town to look for me?"

"I did that on my own. I traced you to a dancing academy, then to North Kensington, and then to New Cross."

"Where at New Cross?" asked Mavis, fearful that her friend had inquired for her at Mrs Gowler's.

"I'd been given an address, but I lost it on the way. I described you to the station master and asked if he could help me. He remembered a lady answering your description having a box sent to an address in Pimlico. When I told him you were a missing relative, he turned it up."

"Why didn't you call?"

"I didn't know if you were Mrs Kenrick, and, if you were, how you would take my 'nosing' into your affairs."

"Why did you bother?"

"I always liked you, and when I feared you'd got into a scrape for love of a man, my heart went out to you and I wanted to help you."

Mavis bent over to kiss her friend before saying: "I only hope I live to do you a good turn."

"You've done it already by making friends with me. But isn't Hunter a pig?"

"I hate her," said Mavis emphatically.

"She tried to get my time for her holidays, but it's now arranged that she goes away when I get back."

"Where is she going?" asked Mavis absently.

"Cornwall."

"Cornwall? Which part?"

"South, I believe. Why?"

"Curiosity," replied Mavis.

Then Miss Toombs told Mavis the rest of the Melkbridge news. She learned how Mr and Mrs Trivett had given up Pennington Farm and were now living in Melkbridge, where Miss Toombs had heard that they had a hard struggle to get along. Miss Toombs mentioned several other names well known to Mavis; but she did not speak of Charlie Perigal.

It was a long time before Mavis slept that night. She had long and earnestly thanked her Heavenly Father for having sent kindly Miss Toombs to help her in her distress. She then lay awake for quite a long while, wondering why Miss Toombs had been against her going to Melkbridge.

Vague, intangible fears hovered about her, which were associated with her lover and his many promises to marry her. He also was at Melkbridge. Mavis tried to persuade herself that Miss Toombs's objection to her going to the same place could have nothing in common with the fact of her lover's presence there.

The next morning, while the two friends were breakfasting, Mavis again spoke of the matter.

"I can't make out why you were so against my going to Melkbridge," she said.

"Have you been worrying about it?" asked Miss Toombs.

"Yes. Is there any reason why I shouldn't go back?"

"You great big silly! The reason why I didn't want you to go there is because I might get you a better job in town."

"But you told me last night you were friendless. Friendless girls can't get others work in town. So don't try and get over me by saying that."

Miss Toombs explained how the manager of a London house, which had extensive dealings with Devitt's boot factory, was indebted to her for certain crooked business ways that she had made straight. She told Mavis that she had gone to see this man on Mr Devitt's behalf since she had been in town, and that he was anxious to keep in her good books. She thought that a word from her would get Mavis employment.

Mavis thanked her friend; she made no further mention of the matter which occasionally disturbed her peace of mind.

For all her friend's kindly offer, she longed to tread the familiar ways of the country town which was so intimately associated with the chief event of her life.

During the five unexpired days of Miss Toombs's holiday, the two women were rarely apart. Of a morning they would take the baby to the grounds of Chelsea Hospital, which, save for the presence of the few who were familiar with its quietude, they had to themselves. Once or twice, they took a 'bus to the further side of the river, when they would sit in a remote corner of Battersea Park. They also went to Kew Gardens and Richmond Park. Mavis had not, for many long weeks, known such happiness as that furnished by Miss Toombs's society. Her broad views of life diminished Mavis's concern at the fact of her being a mother without being a wife.

The time came when Mavis set out for Paddington (she left the baby behind in charge of Jill), in order to see her friend go by the afternoon train to Melkbridge. Mavis was silent. She wished that she were journeying over the hundred miles which lay between where she stood and her lover. Miss Toombs was strangely cheerful: to such an extent, that Mavis wondered if her friend guessed the secret of her lover's identity, and, divining her heart's longings, was endeavouring to distract her thoughts from their probable preoccupation. Mavis thanked her friend again and again for all she had done for her. Miss Toombs had that morning received a letter from her London boot acquaintance in reply to one she had written concerning Mavis. This letter had told Miss Toombs that her friend should fill the first vacancy that might occur. Upon the strength of this promise, Miss Toombs had prevailed on Mavis to accept five pounds from her; but Mavis had only taken it upon the understanding that the money was a loan.

While they were talking outside Miss Toombs's third class compartment, Mavis saw Montague Devitt pass on his way to a first, followed by two porters, who were staggering beneath the weight of a variety of parcels. Mavis hoped that he would not see her; but the fates willed otherwise. One of the porters dropped a package, which fell with a resounding thwack at Mavis's feet. Devitt turned, to see Mavis.

"Miss Keeves!" he said, raising his hat.

Mavis bowed.

"May I speak to you a moment?" he asked, after glancing at Miss Toombs, and furtively lifting his hat to this person.

Mavis joined him.

"What has become of you all this time?"

"I've been working in London."

"I've often thought of you. What are you doing now?"

"I'm looking for something to do."

"I suppose you'd never care to come back and work for me in Melkbridge?"

"Nothing I should like better," remarked Mavis, as her heart leapt.

They talked for two or three minutes longer, when, the train being on the point of starting, Devitt said:

"Send me your address and I'll see you have your old work again."

Mavis thanked him.

"Just met Miss Toombs?" he asked.

"She's been staying with me. Thank you so much."

Mavis hurried from the man's carriage to that containing her friend, who was standing anxiously by the window.

"It's all right!" cried Mavis excitedly.

"What's all right, dear?" cried Miss Toombs as the train began to move.

"I'm coming to work at Melkbridge. It's au revoir, dear!"

Mavis was astonished, and not a little disquieted, to see the expression of concern which came over her friend's disappearing face at this announcement.

CHAPTER THIRTY-THREE
AN OLD FRIEND

Four days later, Mavis spent the late afternoon with her baby and Jill in the grounds of Chelsea Hospital. She then took a 'bus to Ebury Bridge (Jill running behind), to get out here and walk to her lodging. As she went up Halverton Street, she noticed, in the failing light, a tall, soldierly looking man standing on the other side of the road. But the presence of men of military bearing, even in Halverton Street, was not sufficiently infrequent to call for remark. Mavis opened her door with the key and went to her room. Here, she fed her baby and ate something herself. When her boy fell asleep, Mavis left him in charge of Jill and went out to do some shopping. She had not gone far when she heard footsteps behind her, as if seeking to overtake her. Mavis, who was well used to being accosted by night prowlers, quickened her steps, but to no purpose: a moment or two later, someone touched her arm. She turned angrily, to see Windebank beside her. Her expression relaxed, to become very hard.

"Don't you know me?" he asked huskily.

She stopped, but did not reply. She recalled the man she had seen standing on the other side of the road, and whom she now believed to have been Windebank. If it were he, and he had been waiting to see her, he had undoubtedly seen her baby. Rage, self-pity at the realisation of her helplessness, defiance, desire to protect the good name of the loved one, filled her being. She walked for some moments in silence, he following.

"Are you very angry?" he asked.

"Yes."

"I'm sorry."

The deep note of sincerity in his voice might have arrested her wrath. If anything, his emotion stimulated her anger.

"Why do, you take pleasure in spying on me?" she cried. "I always knew you were a beast."

"Eh! Oh, rot!" he replied.

"Why can't you leave me alone? You would if you knew how I hated you."

"Do you mean that?" he asked quietly.

"You shouldn't have spied on me."

"Don't be angry: at least not very. You wouldn't if you knew how I've longed to see you again, to find out what's become of you."

"You know now!" she exclaimed defiantly.

"And since I know, what is the use of your getting angry?"

"I hate meanness," cried Mavis.

"Eh!"

"Spying's meanness. It's hateful: hateful."

"So are fools," he cried, with a vehemence approaching hers.

She looked at him, surprised. He went on:

"I hate fools, and much, much as I think of you and much as you will always be to me, I can't help telling you what a fool you've been."

"Not so loud," urged Mavis. They had now reached the corner of much-frequented Lupus Street, where the man's emphatic voice would attract attention.

"I'll say what I please. And if I choose to tell you I think you a precious fool, nothing on earth shall stop me."

"That's right: insult me," remarked Mavis, who was secretly pleased at his unrestrained anger.

"'Insult' be hanged! You're an arrant, downright fool! You'd only to say the word to have been my wife."

"What an honour!" laughed Mavis, saying the first words which came into her head. The next moment she would have given much to have been able to recall them.

"For me," said Windebank gravely. "And I know I'd have made you happy."

"I believe you would," admitted Mavis, wishing to atone for her thoughtless remark.

As if moved by a common impulse, they crossed Lupus Street and sought the first quiet thoroughfare which presented itself. This happened to be Cambridge Street, along the shabby pretentiousness of which they walked for some minutes in silence, each occupied with their thoughts.

"How did you find out where I was?" she asked.

"Miss Toombs."

"You've seen her?"

"She sent me 'Halverton Street' written on a piece of paper. I guessed what it meant."

"You spoke to her before about me?"

"Yes. I was anxious to know what had become of you."

"You needn't have bothered."

"I couldn't help myself."

"You really, really cared?"

"A bit. And now I see what a fool you've been——"

"It won't make any difference," she interrupted.

"What do you mean?" he asked quickly.

"It won't make any difference to me. I'm to be married any day now."

"What's that?" he asked quickly.

Mavis repeated her statement.

"To whom?"

"The man I love; whom else?"

"Are you counting on that?"

"Of course," she answered, surprised at the question.

She wondered what he could mean, but she could get no enlightenment from his face, which preserved a sphinx-like impenetrability.

"What are you thinking of?" she asked.

"How best to help you."

"I'm not in need of help: besides, I can take care of myself."

"H'm! Where were you going when I met you?"

"Shopping."

"May I come too?"

"It wouldn't interest you."

"How long can you spare?"

"Not long. Why?"

They had now reached the Wilton Road. By way of reply to her question, he elbowed her into one of the pretentious restaurants which lined the side of the thoroughfare on which they walked.

"I'm not hungry," she protested.

"Do as you're told," he replied, urging her to a table.

He called the waiter and ordered an elaborate meal to be brought with all dispatch. He then took off the light overcoat covering his evening clothes before joining Mavis, who was surprised to see how much older he was looking.

"What are you staring at?" he asked.

"You. Have you had trouble?"

"Yes," he replied, looking her hard in the eyes.

"I'm sorry," she remarked, dropping hers.

As if to leaven her previous ungraciousness, Mavis ate as much of the food as she could. She noticed, however, that, beyond sipping his wine, Windebank merely made pretence of eating: but for all his remissness with regard to his own needs, he was full of tender concern for her comfort.

"You're eating nothing," she presently remarked.

"Like our other meal in Regent Street."

She nodded reminiscently.

"You hadn't forgotten?"

"It was the night I left you in the fog."

"Like the little fool you were!"

She did not make any reply. He seemed preoccupied for the remainder of the meal, an absent-mindedness which was now and again interrupted by sparks of forced gaiety.

She wondered if he had anything on his mind. She had previously resolved to wish him good-bye when they left the restaurant; but, somehow, when they went out together, she made no objection to his accompanying her in the direction of Halverton Street, the reason being that she felt wholly at home with him; he seemed so potent to protect her; he was so concerned for her happiness and well-being. She revelled in the unaccustomed security which his presence inspired.

"What are you going to buy?" he asked, as they again approached Lupus Street.

"Odds and ends."

"You must let me carry them."

She smiled a little sadly, but otherwise made no reply to Windebank's suggestion. She was bent on enjoying to the full her new-found sensation of security. When they reached Lupus Street, she went into the mean shops to order or get (in either case to pay for) the simple things she needed. These comprised bovril, tea, bacon, sugar, methylated spirit, bread, milk, a chop, a cauliflower, six bottles of stout, and three pounds of potatoes. Whatever shop she entered, Windebank insisted on accompanying her, and, in most cases, quadrupled her order; in others, bought all kinds of things which he thought she might want. In any other locality, the sight of a man in evening dress, with prosperity written all over him, accompanying a shabbily-dressed girl, as Mavis then was, in her shopping, would have excited comment; but in Pimlico, anything of this nature was not considered at all out of the way.

Windebank, loaded with parcels, accompanied Mavis to the door of her lodging. Here, she opened the door, and in three or four journeys to her room relieved Windebank of his burdens. She was loth to let him go. Seeing that her baby was sleeping peacefully, she said to Windebank, when she joined him outside:

"I'll walk a little way with you."

"It's very good of you."

As they walked towards Victoria, neither of them seemed eager for speech. They were both oppressed by the realisation of the inevitable roads to which life's travellers are bound, despite the personal predilections of the wayfarers.

"Little Mavis! little Mavis! what is going to happen?" he presently asked.

"I'm going to be married and live happily ever after," she answered.

"I've had shocking luck. I mean with regard to you," he continued.

Mavis making no reply to this remark, he went on:

"But what I can't understand is, why you ran away that night when I got you out of Mrs Hamilton's."

"I escaped in the fog."

"But why? Why? Little Mavis! little Mavis! these things are much too sacred to play the fool with."

"I ran away out of consideration for you."

"Eh?"

"Why else should I? I didn't want you to burden your life with a nobody like me."

"Are you serious?"

She laughed bitterly.

"Well, I'm hanged!" he cried.

"It's no use worrying now."

"One can't altogether help it. Why hadn't you a better sense of your value? I'd have married you; I'd have lived for you, and I swear I'd have made you happy."

"I know you would," she assented.

"And now I find you like this."

"I'll be going back now."

"I'll turn with you if I may."

"You'll be late."

"I'll chance that," he laughed. "Months before I met you at Mrs Hamilton's, I heard about you from Devitt."

"What did he say?"

"It was just before you were going down to see him, from some school you were at, about taking a governess's billet. He told me of this, and I sent you a message."

"I never had it."

"Not really?"

"A fact. What was it?"

"I said that my people and myself were no end of keen on seeing you again and that we wanted you to come down and stay."

"You told him that?"

"One day in the market-place at Melkbridge. Afterwards, I often asked about you, if he knew your address and all that; but I never got anything out of him."

"But he knew all the time where I was. I don't understand."

"Little Mavis is very young."

"That's right: insult me," she laughed.

"Those sort of people with a marriageable daughter aren't going to handicap their chances by having sweet Mavis about the house."

"People aren't really like that!"

"Not a bit; they're as artless as you. My dear little Mavis, one 'ud think you'd never left the nursery."

"But I have."

"Curse it, you have! Why did you? Oh! why did you?"

"Do as I've done?"

"Yes. Why did you?"

"I loved him."

"Eh?"

"The only possible reason—I loved him."

"And if you'd loved me, you'd have done the same for me?"

"If you'd asked me."

"For me? For me?"

"If I loved you, and if you asked me."

"But that's just it. If a chap truly loves a girl, he'd rather die than injure a hair of her head. And if you loved me, my one idea would be to protect my darling little Mavis from all harm. Why——"

He stopped. Mavis's face was drawn as if she were in great pain.

"What's the matter?" he asked.

"How dare you? Oh, how dare you?"

"Dare I what?" he asked, much perplexed at her sudden anger.

"Insult the man I love. If what you say is true, it would mean he didn't truly love me. You lie! I tell you he does! You lie—you lie!"

"You're right," assented Windebank sadly, after a moment's thought. "You're quite right. I made a mistake. I ask everyone's pardon. How could any man fail to appreciate you?"

Much to his surprise, her anger soon abated. A not too convincing light-heartedness took the place of this stormy ebullition. If Windebank had been more skilled in the mechanism of a woman's heart, he would have promptly divined the girl's gaiety had been wilfully assumed, in order to conceal from herself the anxiety that Windebank's words, with reference to the proper conduct of a true lover, had inspired. By the time they had reached her door, she had expended her fund of forced gaiety; she was again the subdued Mavis whom trouble had fashioned. She thanked Windebank many times for his kindness; although she was tired, she was in no mood to leave him. She liked the restfulness that she discovered in his company; also, she dreaded to-night the society of her own thoughts.

They were now standing in the street immediately outside the door of her lodging. They had been silent for some moments. Mavis regretfully realised that he must soon leave her.

"Will you do me a favour?" he asked suddenly.

She looked up inquiringly.

"May I see——?" he continued softly. "May I see——?"

"My boy?" she asked, divining his wish.

She thought for a moment before slipping into the house. A little later, she came out carrying the sleeping baby in her arms. Mavis's heart inclined to Windebank for his request; at the same time, she knew well that, were she a man, and in his present situation, she would not be the least interested in the loved woman's child, whose father was a successful rival.

Windebank uncovered the little one's face. He looked at it intently for a while. He then bent down to kiss the baby's forehead.

"God bless you, little boy!" he murmured. "God bless you and your beautiful mother!"

He then covered the baby's face, and walked quickly away in the direction of Victoria.

That night, Mavis saw dawn touch the eastern sky with light before she slept. She lay awake, wondering at and trying to resolve into coherence the many things which had gone to the shaping of her life. What impressed her most was that so many events of moment had been brought about by trivial incidents to which she had attached no importance at the time of their happening. Strive as she might, she could not hide from herself how much happier would have been her lot if she had loved and married Windebank. It also seemed to her as if fate had done much to bring them together. She recalled, in this connection, how she again met this friend of her early youth at Mrs Hamilton's, of all places, where he had not only told her of the nature of the house into which she had been decoyed, but had set her free of the place. Then had followed the revelation of her hitherto concealed identity, a confession which had called into being all his old-time, boyish infatuation for her. To prevent possible developments of this passion for a portionless girl from interfering with his career, she had left him, to lose herself in the fog. If her present situation were a misfortune, it had arisen from her abnormal, and, as it had turned out, mischievous consideration for his welfare. But scruples of the nature which she had displayed were assuredly numbered amongst the virtues, and to arrive at the conclusion that evil had arisen from the practice of virtue was unthinkable. Such a sorry sequence could not be; God would not permit it.

Mavis's head ached. Life to her seemed an inexplicable tangle, from which one fact stood out with insistent prominence. This, that although Windebank's thoughtless words about the safety of a woman with the man who truly loved her had awakened considerable apprehension in her heart, she realised how necessary it was to trust Perigal even more (if that were possible) than she had ever done before. He was her life, her love, her all. She trusted and believed in him implicitly. She was sure that she would love him till the last moment of her life. With this thought in her heart, with his name on her lips, the while she clutched Perigal's ring, which Miss Toombs's generosity had enabled her to get out of pawn, she fell asleep.

The first post brought two letters. One was from Miss Toombs's business acquaintance, offering her a berth at twenty-eight shillings a week; the other was from Montague Devitt, confirming the offer he had made Mavis at Paddington. Devitt's letter told her that she could resume work on the following Monday fortnight. It did not take Mavis the fraction of a second to decide which of the two offers she would accept. She sat down and wrote to Mr Devitt to thank him for his letter; she said that the would be pleased to commence her duties at the time suggested. The question of where and how she was to lodge her baby at Melkbridge, and, at the same time, avoid all possible risk of its identity being discovered, she left for future consideration. She was coming back from posting the letter, when she was overtaken by Windebank, who was driving a superb motor car. He pulled up by the kerb of the pavement on which she was walking.

"Good morning," he cried cheerily. "I was coming to take you out."

"Shopping?" she asked.

"To have a day in the country. Jump in and we'll drive back for the youngster."

"It's very kind of you, but——"

"There are no 'buts.' I insist."

"I really mustn't go," said Mavis, thinking longingly of the peace of the country.

"But you must. Remember you've someone else to think of besides yourself."

"You?"

"The youngster. A change to country air would do him no end of good."

"Do you really think it would?" asked Mavis, hesitating before accepting his offer.

"Think! I know. If you don't want to come, it's your duty to sacrifice yourself for the boy's health."

This decided Mavis. Less than an hour later, they were driving in the cool of Surrey lanes, where the sweet air and the novelty of the motion brought colour to Mavis's cheeks.

They lunched at a wayside inn, to sit, when the simple meal was over, in the garden where the air was musical with bees.

"This is peace," exclaimed Mavis, who was entranced with the change from dirty, mean Pimlico.

"As your life should always be, little Mavis."

"It is going to be."

"But what are you going to do till this marriage comes off?"

Mavis told him how it was arranged that she was soon to commence work at Melkbridge. Much to her surprise and considerably to her mind's disquiet, Windebank hotly attempted to dissuade her from this course. He urged a variety of reasons, the chief of which was the risk she ran of the fact of her motherhood being discovered. But he might as well have talked to Jill, who accompanied the party. Mavis's mind was made up. The obstacles he sought to put in her way, if anything, strengthened her determination. One concession, however, he wrung from her—this, that if ever she were in trouble she would not hesitate to seek his aid. On the return home in the cool of the evening, Windebank asked if he could secure her better accommodation than where she now lived until she left for Wiltshire. Mavis would not hear of it, till Windebank pointed out that her child's health might be permanently injured by further residence in unwholesome Halverton Street. Before Mavis fell in with his request, she stipulated that she was not to pay more than a pound a week for any rooms she might engage. When she got back, she was overwhelmed with inquiries from Lil, the girl upstairs, with reference to "the mug" whom she (Mavis) had captured. But Mavis scarcely listened to the girl's questions; she was wondering why, first of all, Miss Toombs and then Windebank should be against her going to Melkbridge. Her renewed faith in Perigal prevented her from believing that any act of his was responsible for their anxiety in the matter. She could only conclude that they believed that in journeying to Melkbridge, as she purposed, she ran a great risk of her motherhood being discovered.

The next morning, Mavis set about looking for the new rooms which she had promised Windebank to get. Now she could afford to pay a reasonable price for accommodation, she was enabled to insist upon good value for the money. The neat appearance of a house in Cambridge Street, which announced that lodgings were to let, attracted her. A clean, white-capped servant showed her two comfortably furnished rooms, which were to let at the price Mavis was prepared to pay. She learned that the landlady was a Mrs Taylor. Upon asking to see her, a woman, whose face still displayed considerable beauty, glided into the room.

Mrs Taylor spoke in a low, sweet voice; she would like to accommodate Mavis, but she had to be very, very particular: one had to be so careful nowadays. Could Mavis furnish references; failing that, would Mavis tell her what place of worship she attended? Mavis referred Mrs Taylor to Miss Toombs at Melkbridge and Mrs Scatchard at North Kensington, which satisfied the landlady. When, twenty-four hours later, Mavis moved in, she found that Windebank had already sent in a profusion of wines, meats, fruit and flowers for her use. She was wishing she could send them back, when Mrs Taylor came into her sitting-room with her hands to her head.

Upon Mavis asking what was amiss, she learned that Mrs Taylor had a violent headache and the only thing that did her any good was champagne, which she could not possibly afford. Mavis hastened to offer Mrs Taylor a bottle of the two dozen of champagne which were among the things that Windebank had sent in.

Under the influence of champagne, Mrs Taylor became expansive. She had already noted the abundance with which Mavis was surrounded.

"Have you a gentleman friend, dear?" she presently asked in her soft, caressing voice.

"I have one very dear friend," remarked Mavis, thinking of Windebank.

"I hope you're very careful," remarked Mrs Taylor.

"What do you mean?"

"Excuse my mentioning it, but gentlemen will be gentlemen where a pretty girl is concerned."

"Thank you, but I am quite, quite safe," replied Mavis hotly. "And do you know why?"

Mrs Taylor shook her auburn head.

"I'll tell you. It's because he loves me more than anything else in the world. And, therefore, I'm safe," she declared proudly.

CHAPTER THIRTY-FOUR
MAVIS GOES TO MELKBRIDGE

On the following Sunday fortnight, Mavis left the train at Dippenham quite late in the evening. She purposed driving with her baby and Jill in a fly the seven miles necessary to take her to Melkbridge. She choose this means of locomotion in order to secure the privacy which might not be hers if she took the train to her destination.

During the last few days, her boy had not enjoyed his usual health; he had lost appetite and could not sleep for any length of time. Mavis believed the stuffy atmosphere of Pimlico to be responsible for her baby's ailing; she had great hopes of the Melkbridge air effecting an improvement in his health.

She had travelled down in a reserved first-class compartment, which Windebank, who had seen her off at Paddington, had secured. He had only been a few minutes on the platform, as he had to catch the boat train at Charing Cross, he being due at Breslau the following day, to witness the German army manoeuvres on a special commission from the War Office.

Mavis had seen much of him during her stay at Mrs Taylor's. At all times, he had urged upon Mavis the inadvisability of going to Melkbridge. He was so against this contemplated proceeding that he had vainly offered to settle money on her if only it would induce her to forego her intention. Miss Toombs had by letter joined her entreaties to Windebank's. She pointed out that if Mavis brought her child to Melkbridge, as she purposed doing, it was pretty certain that its identity would be discovered. But Windebank pleaded and Miss Toombs wrote to no purpose. Before Windebank had said good-bye at Paddington, he again made Mavis promise that she would not hesitate to communicate at once with him should she meet with further trouble.

The gravity with which he made this request awakened disquiet in her mind, which diminished as her proximity to Melkbridge increased. Impatient to lessen the distance that separated her from her destination, she quickly selected a fly. A porter helped the driver with her luggage; she settled herself with her baby and Jill, and very soon they were lumbering down the ill-paved street. Her mind was so intent on the fact of her increasing nearness to the loved one, that she gave but a passing remembrance to the occasion of her last visit to Dippenham, when she had met Perigal after letting him know that she was about to become a mother. Her eyes strained eagerly from the window of the fly in the direction of

Melkbridge. She was blind, deaf, indifferent to anything, other than her approaching meeting with her lover, which she was sure could not long be delayed now she had come to live so near his home. She was to lodge with her old friend Mrs Trivett, who had moved into a cottage on the Broughton Road.

Mavis had written to tell Mrs Trivett the old story of her fictitious marriage; she had, also, stated that for the present she wished this fact, together with the parentage of her child, to be kept a strict secret. Mavis little recked the risk she ran of discovery. She was obsessed by the desire to breathe the Melkbridge air. She believed that her presence there would in some way or other make straight the tangle into which she had got her life. The fly had left Dippenham well behind, and was ambling up and down the inclines of the road. Mavis looked out at the stone walls which, in these parts, take the place of hedgerows: she recognised with delight this reminder that she was again in Wiltshire. Four miles further, she would pass a lodge gate and the grounds of Major Perigal's place. She might even catch a glimpse of the house amongst the trees as she passed. As the miles were wearily surmounted and the dwelling of the loved one came ever nearer, Mavis's heart beat fast with excitement. She continually craned her neck from the window to see if the spot she longed to feast her eyes upon were in sight. When it ultimately crept into view, she could scarcely contain herself for joy. She caught up her baby from the seat to hold him as high as it was possible in order that he might catch a glimpse of his darling daddy's home.

The baby arms were hot and dry to the touch, but Mavis was too intent on looking eagerly across the expanse of park to notice this just now. Many lights flashed in her eyes, to be hidden immediately behind trees. Her lover's home was unusually illuminated to-night—unusually, because, at other times, when she had passed it, only one or two lights had been visible, Major Perigal living the life of a recluse who disliked intercourse with his species. Half an hour later, Mavis was putting her baby to bed at Mrs Trivett's. His face was flushed, his eyes staring and wide awake; but Mavis put down these manifestations to the trying journey from town. She went downstairs to eat a few mouthfuls with Mr and Mrs Trivett before returning to his side. She found them much altered; they had aged considerably and were weighted with care. Music teaching in Melkbridge was a sorry crutch on which to lean for support. During the short meal, neither husband nor wife said much. Mavis wondered if this taciturnity were due to any suspicions they might entertain of Mavis's unwedded state. But when Mrs Trivett came upstairs with her, she sat on the bed and burst into tears.

Upon Mavis asking what was amiss, Mrs Trivett told her that they were overwhelmed with debt and consequent difficulties to such an extent, that they did not know from one day to another if they would continue to have a roof over their heads. She also told Mavis that her coming as a lodger had been in the nature of a godsend, and that she had returned to Melkbridge upon the anniversary of the day on which her husband had commenced his disastrous tenancy of Pennington Farm.

Mavis slept little that night. Her baby was restless and wailed fitfully throughout the long hours, during which the anxious mother did her best to comfort him. Mavis made up her mind to call in a doctor if he were not better in the morning. When she was dressing, the baby seemed calmer and more inclined to sleep, therefore she had small compunction in leaving him in Mrs Trivett's motherly arms when, some two hours later, she left the Broughton Road for the boot factory. Miss Toombs was already at the office when she got there. Mavis scarcely recognised her friend, so altered was she in appearance. Dark rings encircled her eyes; her skin was even more pasty than was its wont. Mavis noticed that when her friend kissed her, she was trembling.

"What's the matter, dear?" asked Mavis.

"Indigestion. It's nothing at all."

The two friends talked quickly and quietly till Miss Hunter joined them. Beyond giving Mavis the curtest of nods, this young person took no notice of her.

Mavis was more grateful than otherwise for Miss Hunter's indifference; she had feared a series of searching questions with regard to all that had happened since she had been away from Melkbridge.

Miss Toombs's appearance and conduct at meeting with Mavis was not the only strange behaviour which she displayed. When anyone came into the office, she seemed in a fever of apprehension; also, when anyone spoke to Mavis, her friend would at once approach and speak in such a manner as to send them about their business as soon as possible. Mavis wondered what it could mean.

Her boy did not seem quite so well when she got back to Mrs Trivett's for the midday meal. During the afternoon's work, her anxiety was such that she could scarcely concentrate her attention on what she was doing. When she hurried home in the evening, the boy was decidedly worse; there was no gainsaying the seriousness of his symptoms. Every time Mavis tried to make him take nourishment, he would cry out as if it hurt him to swallow.

Mrs Trivett, who had had much experience with the ailments of a sister's big family, feared that the baby was sickening for something. Mavis would have sent for a doctor at once, but Mrs Trivett pointed out that doctors could do next to nothing for sick babies beyond ordering them to be kept warm and to have nourishment in the shape of two drops of brandy in water every two hours; also, that if it were necessary to have skilled advice, the doctor had better be sent for when Mavis was at the boot factory; otherwise, he might ask questions bearing on matters which, just now, Mavis would prefer not to make public. Mrs Trivett had much trouble in making the distraught mother appreciate the wisdom of this advice. She only fell in with the woman's views when she reflected, quite without cause, that the doctor's inevitable questioning might, in some remote way, compromise her lover. Late in the evening, when it was dark, Miss Toombs came round to see how matters were going.

"It's all your fault, foolish Mavis, for coming to Melkbridge," she remarked, when Mavis had told her of her perplexities.

"But how was I to know?"

"The only way to have guarded against complications was to keep away altogether. I suppose you wouldn't go even now?"

"He's much too ill to move. Besides——"

"Will you go when he's better, if I tell you something?"

"What?" asked Mavis, seriously alarmed by the deadly earnestness of her friend's manner.

"Miss Hunter!"

"What of her?"

"First tell me, where was it you went for your—your honeymoon?"

"Polperro. Why?"

"That's one of the places she's been to."

"And you think——?"

"Her manner's so funny. And you wondered why I was so jolly keen on your not coming to Melkbridge!"

"I thought—I hoped my troubles were at an end," murmured Mavis.

"Whatever happens, you can rely on me till the death—when it's after dark."

"What do you mean?" asked Mavis.

"Why, that much, much as I love you, I'm not going to risk the loss of my winter fire, hot-water bottles, and books, for getting mixed up in any scrape pretty Mavis gets herself into."

The next morning Mavis went to business in a state bordering on distraction. The baby was not one whit better, and even hopeful Mrs Trivett had shaken her head sadly. But she had pointed out that Mavis could not help matters by remaining at home; she also promised to send for a doctor should the baby's health not improve in the course of the morning. Mavis was so distraught that she stared wildly at the one or two people she chanced to meet, who, knowing her, seemed disposed to stop and speak. She wondered if she should let her lover know the disquieting state of his son's health. So far, she had not told him of her coming to Melkbridge, wishing the inevitable meeting to come as a delightful surprise. When she got to the office, she found a long letter from Windebank, which she scarcely read, so greatly was her mind disturbed. She only noted the request on which he was always insisting, namely, that she was at once to communicate with him should she find herself in trouble.

When she got back at midday, she found that, the baby being no better, Mrs Trivett had sent her husband for a doctor who had recently come to Melkbridge; also, that he had promised to call directly after lunch. With this information, Mavis had to possess herself in patience till she learned the doctor's report. That afternoon, the moments were weighted with leaden feet. Three o'clock came; Mavis was beginning to congratulate herself that, if the doctor had pronounced anything seriously amiss with her child, Mrs Trivett would not have failed to communicate with her, when a boy came into the office to ask for Miss Keeves.

She jumped up excitedly, and the boy put a note into her hand. A faintness overwhelmed her so that she could hardly find strength with which to tear open the missive. When she finally did so, she read: "Come at once, much trouble," scrawled in Mrs Trivett's writing.

Mavis, scarcely knowing what she was doing, reached for her hat, the while Miss Toombs watched her with sympathetic eyes. At the same time, one of the factory foremen came into the office and put an envelope into Mavis's hand. She paid no attention to this last beyond stuffing it into a pocket of her frock. Her one concern was to reach the Broughton Road with as little delay as possible. Once outside the factory, she closely questioned the boy as he ran beside her, but he could tell her nothing beyond that Mrs Trivett had given him a penny to bring Mavis the note. When Mavis, breathless and faint, arrived at Mrs Trivett's gate, she saw two or three people staring curiously at the cottage. She all but fell against the door, and was at once admitted by Mrs Trivett.

"The worst! Let me know the worst!" gasped the terror-stricken girl.

Mavis was told that her baby was ill with diphtheria; also, that a broker's man was in possession at Mrs Trivett's.

"Will he get over it?" was Mavis's next question.

"It's for a lot of money. It's just on thirty pounds."

"I mean my boy."

"The doctor has hopes. He's coming in again presently."

Mavis hurried to the stairs leading to her bedroom. As she went up these, she brushed against a surly-looking man who was coming down. She rightly judged him to be the man in possession. She found the little sufferer stretched upon his bed of pain with wildly dilating eyes; it wrung Mavis's heart to see what difficulty he had with his breathing. If she could only have done something to ease her baby's sufferings, she would have been better able to bear the intolerable suspense. She realised that she could do nothing till the doctor paid his next visit. But she had forgotten; one thing she could do: she could pray for divine assistance to the Heavenly Father who was able to heal all earthly ills. This she did. Mavis prayed long and earnestly, with words that came from her heart. She told Him how she had endured pain, sorrow, countless debasing indignities without murmuring; if only in consideration of these, she begged that the life of her little one might be spared.

Whilst thus engaged, Mavis heard a tap at the door. She got up impatiently as she called to whomsoever it might be to enter.

Mrs Trivett came in with many apologies for disturbing Mavis. She then told her lodger that the broker's man was aware of the illness from which Mavis's baby was suffering; also that, as he was a family man, he objected to being in a house where there was a contagious disease, and that, if the child were not removed to the local fever hospital by the evening, he would inform the authorities. Mrs Trivett's information spelt further trouble for Mavis. Apart from her natural disinclination to confide her dearly loved child to the care of strangers, she saw a direct menace to herself should the man carry out his threat of insisting on the removal of the child. Montague Devitt was much bound up with the town's municipal authorities. In this capacity, it was conceivable that he might discover the identity of the child's mother; failing this, her visits to the hospital to learn the child's progress would probably excite comment, which, in a small town like Melkbridge, could easily be translated into gossip that must reach the ears of the Devitt family. The cloud of trouble hung heavily over Mavis.

"Can't—can't anything be done?" she asked desperately.

"It's either the hospital or paying the broker."

"How much is it?"

"Twenty-nine pounds sixteen."

"That's easily got," remarked Mavis. "At once?" asked Mrs Trivett, as her worn face brightened.

"I don't suppose I could get it till the morrow. It would be then too late?"

"But if you're sure of getting it, something might be arranged."

"Would the man take my word?"

"No. But he might know someone who would lend the money in a way that would be convenient."

"See him at once. Find out if anything can be done," urged the distracted mother.

Five minutes later, whilst Mavis was waiting in suspense, Mrs Trivett came up to say that the doctor had come again. Mavis had no time to ask her landlady what she had done with the broker's man, as the doctor came into the room directly after he had been announced. He was quite a young doctor, on whom the manners of an elderly man sat incongruously. He glanced keenly at Mavis as he bowed to her; then, without saying a word, he fell to examining the child's throat.

"Well?" asked Mavis breathlessly, when he had satisfied himself of its condition.

"I must ask you a few questions," replied the doctor.

"What do you wish to know?" she asked with anxious heart.

He asked her much about the baby's place of birth, subsequent health and diet.

When Mavis told him of the Pimlico supplied milk, which she had sterilised herself, he shook his head.

"That accounts for the whole trouble," he remarked. "You should have fed him yourself."

"It didn't agree with him, and then it went away," Mavis told him.

"Ah, you had worry?"

"A bit. Do you think he'll pull through?"

"I'll tell you more to-night," he informed her.

Mavis attracted men. The doctor, not being blind to her fascinations, was not indisposed to linger for a moment's conversation, after he had treated the baby's throat, during which Mavis thought it necessary to tell him the old story of the husband in America who was preparing a home for her.

"Some chap's been low enough to land that charming girl with that baby," thought the doctor as he walked home. "She's as innocent as they make 'em, otherwise she wouldn't have told me that silly husband yarn. If she were an old hand, she'd have kept her mouth shut."

Meanwhile, Mavis had been summoned downstairs to a conference, in which the broker's man (his name was Gunner), Mrs Trivett, and a man named Hutton, whom Mr Trivett had fetched, took part.

Mavis was informed that Mr Hutton would lend her the money needed to get rid of Mr Gunner's embarrassing presence, for which she was to pay two pounds interest, if repaid in a month, and eight pounds interest a year during which the capital sum was being repaid by monthly instalments.

"I will telegraph to Germany," said Mavis. "You shall have the money next week at latest."

Mr Hutton wanted guarantees; failing these, was Mavis in any kind of employment?

Mavis told him how she was employed by Mr Devitt.

The man opened his eyes. Had the lady proof of this statement?

Mavis thrust her hand into her pocket, believing she might find the letter which Montague Devitt had written to Pimlico. She brought out, instead, the letter the foreman had put into her hand when she was leaving in reply to Mrs Trivett's summons. The envelope of this was addressed in Mr Devitt's hand.

"Here's a letter from him here," declared Mavis, as she tore it open to glance at its contents before passing it on to Hutton.

But the glance hardened into a look of deadly seriousness as her eyes fell on what was written. She re-read the letter two or three times before she grasped its import.

> "Dear Miss Keeves," it ran, "it is with the very deepest regret that I write to say that certain facts have come to my knowledge with regard

to the way in which you spent your holiday last year at Polperro. I, also, gather that your sudden departure from Melkbridge was in connection with this visit. As a strict moral rectitude is a sine qua non amongst those I employ, I must ask you to be good enough to resign your appointment. I enclose cheque for present and next week's salary.—Truly yours,

"MONTAGUE S.T. DEVITT."

The faces about her faded from her view; the room seemed as if it were going round.

"What's the matter, ma'am?" asked Mrs Trivett anxiously.

"I can't give the guarantee," gasped Mavis.

Mr Hutton rose and buttoned his coat.

"What about Germany?" put in Mrs Trivett.

"I'd forgotten that," said Mavis. "I'll write a telegram at once."

Mr Hutton unbuttoned his coat.

"Here's ink and paper, ma'am."

Mavis took up the pen, at which Mr Hutton sat down. But she could not remember the address. With swimming head, she dived her hand into the pockets of her frock, but could not find Windebank's letter.

"I must have left it at the office," she murmured.

"What is it you want?" asked Mrs Trivett.

"His letter for the address."

Mr Hutton got up.

"What time is it?" asked Mavis.

"Just six o'clock."

"The factory would be locked for the night. Won't they take my word?" she asked. "I don't want to be parted from my child while I go to the factory."

Mr Hutton buttoned his coat.

Mavis made an impassioned appeal to the man in possession and his friend. She might as well have talked to the stone walls which lined the Dippenham Road for any impression she produced.

"This address will find me up to ten o'clock to-night, mum," said Mr Hutton, as he threw a soiled envelope on the table. "An' if I'm woke up arter, I charge it on the interest."

When Mr Hutton had taken his leave, Mavis fought an attack of hysterics. Realising that Gunner, the broker's man, would prove as good as his word in the matter of having her sick child removed, if the money were not forthcoming, Mavis saw that there was no time to be lost. She quickly wrote two notes, one of which was to Miss Toombs, the other to Charlie Perigal. In these she briefly recounted the circumstances of her necessity. Trivett was dispatched to Miss Toombs, whilst his wife undertook to deliver Perigal's note at his father's house.

Mavis waited by her beloved boy's side while the messengers sped upon their respective errands. Her child was doubly dear to her now that their separation was threatened. As his troubled eyes looked helplessly (sometimes it seemed appealingly) into hers, she vowed again and again that he should never be taken away to be nursed by strangers. Something would happen, something must happen to prevent such a mutilation of her holiest feelings as would be occasioned by her enforced separation from her sick boy. Of course, why had she not thought of it before? Her lover, the boy's father, would return with the messenger, to be reconciled to her over the nursing of the ailing little life back to health and strength. She had read much the same sort of thing in books, which were always informed with life.

The minutes of the American clock, which had belonged to Miss Nippett, laboriously totalled into an hour. Mavis could hear Gunner uneasily shuffling in the room below. The late August evening was drawing in. Mavis quite succeeded in persuading herself that this would prove the last night of her misfortunes.

Mr Trivett was the first to return. He brought six pounds from Miss Toombs, with a note saying that it was all she could lay hands upon. This, with the four which Mavis possessed, made ten. Gunner smiled amiably and set about collecting his clay pipes, which he had left in odd corners of the cottage. Then, after half an hour of weary waiting, Mrs Trivett came to the door, which Mavis opened with trembling hands. She was alone. Her face proclaimed the fruitlessness of her errand.

"Mr Charles Perigal was out for the evening and would not be back till quite late," she had been told.

This decided Mavis to act upon a resolve that, had been formulating in her mind while waiting for Mrs Trivett's return.

"Give me half an hour," she said to the sullen Gunner. "I'll make it well worth your while." She then went upstairs to kiss her baby before setting out.

"Where are you going, ma'am?" asked tearful Mrs Trivett, who had followed her upstairs.

"To Mr Devitt. He's kind at heart. I know, if I can see him, he'll give me what I want."

"But will he see you?"

"I'll see to that. Promise you won't leave baby while I'm gone."

Mavis took a last look of her darling as she went out of the door. She then let herself out and sped in the direction of the Bathminster Road. She scarcely knew, she did not care, what she should say when she came face to face with Devitt. She had almost forgotten that he had been informed of her secret. All she knew was that she was in peril of losing her sick child, and that she was fighting for its possession with the weapons that came handiest. Nothing else in the world was of the smallest account. She also dimly realised that she was fighting for her lover's approval, to whom she would soon have to render an account of her stewardship to his son. This gave edge to her determination. She knocked at the door of the brightly lit, pretentious-looking house in the Bathminster Road.

"I want to see Mr Devitt privately," she told the fat butler who opened the door.

He would have shown her into a room, but she preferred to wait in the hall, which, just now, was littered with trunks.

"I think he's with Mr Harold," said the man, as he walked to a door at the further end of the hall.

The trunk labels were written in a firm, bold hand, which caught Mavis's eye. "Harold Devitt, Esq., Homeleigh, Swanage, Dorset," was the apparent destination of the luggage.

"Mr Devitt must be in the drawing-room," said Hayter, as he reappeared to walk up the stairs.

Mavis, scarcely knowing what she was doing, followed the man up the heavily carpeted stairs, which did not betray her footfalls.

The man opened the door of the drawing-room.

As she followed close on his heels, she heard a terrific peal at the front door bell. Recollection of what she saw in the drawing-room is burned into Mavis's memory and will remain there till her last moment of consciousness.

Montague Devitt, in evening dress, was lolling before the fireplace. His wife and her sister were busily engaged in unpacking showy articles from boxes, which Mavis divined to be wedding gifts. Victoria Devitt, sumptuously dressed, was seated on a low chair. Bending over her shoulder in an attitude of unconcealed devotion was Charlie Perigal.

Mavis took in the significance of all that she saw at a glance. Her blood went ice cold. Something snapped in her head. She opened her lips to speak, but no words issued. Instead, one arm was uplifted to accuse. Then she became rigid; only her eyes were eloquent.

Perigal was struck dumb by the apparently miraculous appearance of Mavis in the room. Then, as her still body continued to menace him with a gesture of seemingly eternal accusation, he became shamefaced. A hum of voices sounded in Mavis's ears, but she was indifferent to what they were saying.

Next, as if from a great distance, she heard her name called by a familiar voice. She was impelled to turn in the direction from which it came, to see Mrs Trivett, tearful, distraught, standing in the doorway. Mavis's eyes expressed a fearful inquiry.

"Don't come back! don't come back," wailed the woman.

Thus, almost in the same breath, Mavis learned how she had lost both lover and child.

CHAPTER THIRTY-FIVE
THE VALLEY OF THE SHADOW

Mavis never left the still, white body of her little one. She was convinced that they were all mistaken, and that he must soon awaken from the sleep into which he had fallen. She watched, with never-wearying eyes, for the first signs of consciousness, which she firmly believed could not long be delayed. Now and again she would hold its cold form for an hour at a stretch to her heart, in the hope that the warmth of her breasts would be communicated to her child. Once, during her long watch, she fancied that she saw his lips twitch. She excitedly called to Mrs Trivett, to whom, when she came upstairs, she told the glad news. To humour the bereaved mother, Mrs Trivett waited for further signs of animation, the absence of which by no means diminished Mavis's confidence in their ultimate appearance. Her faith in her baby's returning vitality, that never waned, that nothing could disturb, was so unwaveringly steadfast, that, at last, Mrs Trivett feared to approach her. Letters arrived from Miss Toombs, Perigal, Windebank, and Montague Devitt, Mavis did not open them; they accumulated on the table on which lay her untasted food. The funeral had been fixed for some days later (Mavis was indifferent as to who gave the orders), but, owing to the hot weather, it was necessary that this dread event should take place two days earlier than had originally been arranged. The night came when Mavis was compelled to take a last farewell of her loved one.

She looked at his still form with greedy, dry eyes, which never flinched. By and by, Mrs Trivett gently touched her arm, at which Mavis went downstairs without saying a word. The change from the room upstairs to the homely little parlour had the effect of making her, in some measure, realise her loss: she looked about her with wide, fearful eyes.

"My head! my head!" she suddenly cried.

"What is it, dear?" asked Mrs Trivett.

"Hold it! Hold it, someone! It's going to burst."

Mrs Trivett held the girl's burning head firmly in her hands.

"Tighter! tighter!" cried Mavis.

"Oh, deary, deary! Why isn't your husband here to comfort you?" sobbed Mrs Trivett.

Mavis's face hardened. She repressed an inclination to laugh. Then she became immersed in a stupor of despair. She knew that it would have done her a world of good if she had been able to shed tears; but the founts of emotion were dry within her. She felt as if her heart had withered. Then, it seemed as if the walls and ceiling of the room were closing in upon her; she had difficulty in breathing; she believed that if she did not get some air she would choke. She got up without saying a word, opened the door, and went out. Trivett, at a sign from his wife, rose and followed.

The night was warm and still. Mavis soon began to feel relief from the stifling sensations which had threatened her. But this relief only increased her pain, her sensibilities being now only the more capable of suffering. As Mavis walked up the deserted Broughton Road, her eyes sought the sky, which to-night was bountifully spread with stars. It occurred to her how it was just another such a night when she had walked home from Llansallas Bay; then, she had fearfully and, at the same time, tenderly held her lover's hand. The recollection neither increased nor diminished her pain; she thought of that night with such a supreme detachment of self that it seemed as if her heart were utterly dead. She turned by the dye factory and stood on the stone bridge which here crosses the Avon. The blurred reflection of the stars in the slowly moving water caused her eyes again to seek the skies.

Thought Mavis: "Beyond those myriad lights was heaven, where now was her beloved little one. At least, he was happy and free from pain, so what cause had she, who loved him, to grieve, when it was written that some day they would be reunited for ever and ever?"

Mavis looked questioningly at the stars. It would have helped her much if they had been able to betray the slightest consciousness of her longings. But they made no sign; they twinkled with aloof indifference to the grief that wrung her being. Distraught with agonised despair, and shadowed by Trivett, she walked up the principal street of the town, now bereft of any sign of life. Unwittingly, her steps strayed in the direction of the river. She walked the road lying between the churchyard and the cemetery, opened the wicket gate by the church school, and struck across the well-remembered meadows. When she came to the river, she stood awhile on the bank and watched the endless procession of water which flowed beneath her. The movement of the stream seemed, in some measure, to assuage her grief, perhaps because her mind, seeking any means of preservation, seized upon the moving water, this providing the readiest distraction that offered.

Mavis walked along the bank (shadowed by the faithful Trivett) in the direction of her nook. Still with the same detachment of mind which had affected her when she had looked at the stars in the Broughton Road, she paused at the spot where she had first seen Perigal parting the rushes upon the river bank. Unknown to him, she had marked the spot with three large stones, which, after much search, she had discovered in the adjacent meadow. As of old, the stones were where she had placed them. Something impelled her to kick them in the river, but she forbore as she remembered that this glimpse of Perigal which they commemorated was, in effect, the first breath which her boy had drawn within her. And now——! Mavis was racked with pain. As if to escape from its clutch, she ran across the meadows in the direction of Melkbridge, closely followed by Trivett. Memories of the dead child's father crowded upon her as she ran. It seemed that she was for ever alone, separated from everything that made life tolerable by an impassable barrier of pain. When she came to the road between the churchyard and the cemetery, she felt as if she could go no further. She was bowed with anguish; to such an extent did she suffer, that she leaned on the low parapet of the cemetery for support. The ever-increasing colony of the dead was spread before her eyes. She examined its characteristics with an immense but dread curiosity. It seemed to Mavis that, even in death, the hateful distinctions between rich and poor found expression. The well-to-do had pretentious monuments which bordered the most considerable avenue; their graves were trim, well-kept, filled with expensive blooms, whilst all that testified to remembrance on the part of the living on the resting-places of the poor were a few wild flowers stuck in a gallipot. Away in a corner was the solid monument of the deceased members of a county family. They appeared, even in death, to shun companionship with those of their species they had avoided in life. It, also, seemed as if most of the dead were as gregarious as the living; well-to-do and poor appeared to want company; hence, the graves were all huddled together. There were exceptions. Now and again, one little outpost of death had invaded a level spread of turf, much in the manner of human beings who dislike, and live remote from, their kind.

But it was the personal application of all she saw before her which tugged at her heartstrings. It made her rage to think that the little life to which her agony of body had given birth should be torn from the warmth of her arms to sleep for ever in this unnatural solitude. It could not be. She despairingly rebelled against the merciless fate which had overridden her. In her agony, she beat the stones of the parapet with her hands. Perhaps she believed that in so doing she would awaken to find her sorrows to have been a horrid dream. The fact that she did not start from sleep brought home the grim reality of her griefs. There was no delusion: her baby lay dead at home; her lover, to whom she had confided her very soul, was to be married to someone else. There was no escape; biting sorrow held her in its grip. She was borne down by an overwhelming torrent of suffering; she flung herself upon the parapet and cried helplessly aloud. Someone touched her arm. She turned, to see Trivett's homely form.

"I can't bear it: I can't, I can't!" she cried.

Trivett looked pitifully distressed for a few moments before saying:

"Would you like me to play?"

Mavis nodded.

"I don't know if the church is open; but, if it is, they've been decorating it for—for—Would you very much mind?"

"Play to me: play to me!" cried Mavis.

The musician, whose whole appearance was eloquent of the soil, clumped across the gravelled path of the churchyard, followed by Mavis. He tried many doors, all of which were locked, till he came to a small door in the tower; this was unfastened.

He admitted Mavis, and then struck a wax match to enable her to see. The cold smell of the church at once took her mind back to when she had entered it as a happy, careless child. With heart filled with dumb despair, she sat in the first seat she came to. As she waited, the gloom was slowly dissipated, to reveal the familiar outlines of the church. At the same time, her nostrils were assailed by the pervading and exotic smell of hot-house blooms.

The noise made by the opening of the organ shutters cracked above her head and reverberated through the building. While she waited, none of the sacred associations of the church spoke to her heart; her soul was bruised with pain, rendering her incapable of being moved by the ordinary suggestions of the place. Then Trivett played. Mavis's highly-strung, distraught mind ever, when sick as now, seeking the way of health, listened intently, devoutly, to the message of the music. Sorrow was the musician's theme: not individual grief, but the travail of an aged world. There had been, there was, such an immense accumulation of anguish that, by comparison with the sum of this, her own griefs now seemed infinitesimal. Then the organ became eloquent of the majesty of sorrow. It was of no dumb, almost grateful, resignation to the will of a Heavenly Father, who imposed suffering upon His erring children for their ultimate good, of which it spoke. Rather was the instrument eloquent of the power wielded by a pagan god of pain, before whose throne was a vast aggregation of torment, to which every human thing, and particularly loving women, were, by the conditions consequent on their nature, condemned to contribute. In return for this inevitable sacrifice, the god of pain bestowed a dignity of mind and bearing upon his votaries, which set them apart, as though they were remote from the thoughtless ruck.

While Trivett played, Mavis was eased of some of her pain, her mind being ever receptive to any message that music might offer. When the organ stopped, the cold outlines of the church chilled her to the marrow. The snap occasioned by the shutting up of the instrument seemed a signal on the part of some invisible inquisitor that her torments were to recommence. Before Trivett joined her, the sound of the church clock striking the hour smote her ear with its vibrant, insistent notes. This reminder of the measuring of time recalled to Mavis the swift flight, not only of the hours, but of the days and years. It enabled her dimly to realise the infinitesimal speck upon the chart of recorded time which even the most prolonged span of individual life occupied. So fleeting was this stay, that it almost seemed as if it were a matter of no moment if life should happen to be abbreviated by untimely death. Whilst the girl's mind thus struggled to alleviate its pain and to mend the gaps made by the slings and arrows of poignant grief in its defences, Trivett stumbled downstairs and blundered against the pews as he approached. Then the two walked home, where Mavis resumed her lonely vigil beside the ark which contained all that was mortal of her baby. No matter what further anguish this watch inflicted, she could not suffer her boy to be alone during the last night of his brief stay on earth.

The next afternoon, about two, when all Melkbridge was agog with excitement at the wedding of Major Perigal's son to Victoria Devitt, two funeral carriages might have been seen drawing up at a cottage in the Broughton Road. Under the driver's seat of the first was quickly placed a small coffin, which was smothered with wreaths, while a tall, comely, fair young woman, clad in deep mourning, stepped into the coach, the blinds of which were closely drawn. A homely, elderly man, accompanied by his wife, got into the next, and the two carriages drove off at a smart trot in the direction of the town. Soon after the little procession had started, a black spaniel might have been seen escaping into the road, where it followed the carriages with its nose to the ground, much in the same way as it had been used to follow the Pimlico 'buses in which its mistress travelled when she had carried her baby.

Mavis, white and drawn, lay back in the carriage that was proceeding on its relentless way. She did not know, she did not care, who had made the arrangements for this dismal ride. All she knew was that all she had left of life seemed confined in the glass case beneath the driver's seat.

During the morning, Mrs Trivett had brought in wreaths of flowers from Windebank, Miss Toombs, herself, and her husband. A last one had arrived, which bore upon the attached card, "From C.P., with all imaginable sympathy." Mavis, after glancing at the well-remembered writing, had trodden the flowers underfoot and then had passionately kicked the ruined wreath from the room.

He, at least, should have no part in her sorrowful lot. As she drove into the town, she was now and again met by gay carriages which were returning from setting down wedding guests at the church door. The drivers of these wore wedding favours pinned to their coats, while their whips were decorated with white satin ribbons. As each carriage passed, Mavis felt a sharp tugging at her heart. She guessed that she was not being driven to Melkbridge; she wondered with an almost impersonal curiosity whither they were bound. She had been told, but she had not listened. She had reached such depths of suffering—indeed, she had quite touched bottom—that it now needed an event of considerable moment to make the least impression on her mutilated sensibilities. When they reached the market-place and bore to the right, she gathered that they were going to Pennington.

The day was perfect—a day that in happier circumstances Mavis would have loved. The sun reigned in a cloudless sky, the blue of which was mellowed with a touch of autumn dignity. The grasses waved gladly by the road-side, and along the ditches; patches of sunlight played delightful games of hide-and-seek on hedge-rows and among the trees. Most of the bushes were gay with song, while the birds seemed to laugh in very defiance of winter when the sun was so warm. The unrestrained joy and vivacity of the day emphasised the gloom that rilled the first of the two funeral carriages. Mavis stared with dull surprise at the rollicking gaiety of the afternoon: its callousness to her anguish irked her. It made her think how unnecessary and altogether bootless was the loss she had sustained. She tried to realise that God had singled her out for suffering as a mark of His favour. But at the bottom of her heart she nourished something in the nature of resentment against the Most High. She knew that, if only life could be restored to the child, she would be base enough to forfeit her chances of eternal life in exchange for the boon. As she passed a by-lane, a smart cart, containing a youngish man and a gaily-clad, handsome, happy-looking girl, pulled up sharply in coming from this in order to avoid a collision. Mavis saw the gladness fade from the faces of the occupants of the cart as they realised the nature of the procession they had encountered. The man took off his cap; the girl looked away with frightened eyes.

Five minutes later, the two carriages entered the gates of Pennington Churchyard. The wind was blowing from Melkbridge, therefore she had not heard before the measured tolling of the bell, which now seemed, every time it struck, to stab her soul to the quick. The carriage pulled up at the door of the tiny church. After waiting a few moments, Mavis got out.

Scarcely knowing what she was doing, she walked up the church, to sit in a pew near the top. Although she never took her eyes from the flower-covered coffin, she was aware that Windebank was sitting at the back, whilst, a few moments later, Miss Toombs strolled into the church with the manner of one who had got there by the merest chance.

"Man that is born of woman hath but a short time to live."

Mavis stood up directly those words were spoken; otherwise, she paid no attention to the exquisite periods of the burial service: her heart was with her boy. The present was as much as she could endure; she was nerving herself for the time when she should leave the church. Till now, she felt that her baby was part of this life and herself; then, without further ado, he would be torn from her cognisance to be put out of sight in the ground.

The inexorable minutes passed. Mavis stood before the open grave. Miss Toombs, ashamed of her earlier timidity, stood beside her. Windebank, erect and bare-headed, was a little behind. As the box containing her baby disappeared, Mavis felt as if the life were being mercilessly drawn from her. It was as if she stood there for untold ages. Then it seemed as if her heart were torn out by the roots. Blinded with pain, she found herself being led by Miss Toombs towards the carriage in which she had been driven from Melkbridge. But Mavis would not get into this. Followed by her friend, she struck into a by-path which led into a lane. Here she walked dry-eyed, numbed with pain, in a world that was hatefully strange. Then Miss Toombs made brave efforts to talk commonplaces, while tears streamed from her eyes. The top of Mavis's head seemed both hot and cold at the same time; she wondered if it would burst. Then, with a sharp bark of delight, Jill sprang from the hedge to jump delightedly about her mistress. Mavis knelt down and pressed her lips to her faithful friend's nose. At the same moment, the wind carried certain sounds to her ears from the direction of Melkbridge. Mavis looked up. The expression of fear which Miss Toombs's face wore confirmed her suspicions. Suddenly, Miss Toombs flung herself upon Mavis, and clapped her hands against the suffering woman's ears.

"Don't listen! don't listen!" screamed Miss Toombs.

But Mavis thrust aside the other woman's arms, to hear the sound of wedding bells, which were borne to her by the wind.

Mavis listened intently for some moments, the while Miss Toombs fearfully watched her. Then, Mavis placed her hands to her head, and laughed and laughed and laughed, till Miss Toombs thought that she was never going to stop.

CHAPTER THIRTY-SIX
A VISIT

Mavis's ride to Pennington was her last appearance out of doors for many a long day. For weeks she lay at Mrs Trivett's on the borderland of death. For nights on end, it was the merest chance whether or not she would live to see another dawn; but, in the end, youth, aided by skilful doctoring and careful nursing, prevailed against the dread illness which had fastened on her brain. As she slowly got better, the blurred shadows which had previously hovered about her took shape into doctor, nurses, and Mrs Trivett. When they told her how ill she had been, and how much better she was, despair filled her heart. She had no wish to live; her one desire was to join her little one beyond the grave.

A time came when the improvement which had set in was not maintained; she failed to get better, yet did not become worse, although Mavis rejoiced in the belief that her health was daily declining. Often, she would wake in the night to listen with glad ears to the incessant ticking of the American clock on the mantelpiece. If alone she would say:

"Go on, go on, little clock, and shorten the time till I again see my dearest."

As if in obedience to her behest, the clock seemed to tick with renewed energy.

Sometimes she would try and picture the unspeakable bliss which would be hers when the desire of her heart was gratified. She often thanked God that she would soon be with Him and her little one. She believed that He found His happiness in witnessing the joy of mothers at again meeting with their children from whom they had been parted for so long.

She had no idea who paid the expenses of her illness; she was assured by Mrs Trivett, whom she often questioned on the subject, that there was no cause for uneasiness on the matter. Her health still refusing to improve, a further medical adviser was called in. He suggested foreign travel as the most beneficial course for Mavis to pursue. But the patient flatly refused to go abroad; for a reason she could not divine, the name of Swanage constantly recurred to her mind. She did not at once remember that she had seen the name on the labels of the luggage which had cumbered the hall on the night when she had called at the Devitts. She often spoke of this watering-place, till at last it was decided that, as she had this resort so constantly in her mind, it might do her good to go there. Even then, it was many more weeks before she was well enough to be moved. She remained in a condition of torpor which the visits of Windebank or Miss Toombs failed to dissipate. At last, when a mild February came, it was deemed possible for her to make the journey. The day before it was arranged that she should start, she was told that a gentleman, who would give no name, and who had come in a carriage of which the blinds were drawn, wished to see her. When she went down to the parlour, she saw a spare old man, with a face much lined and wrinkled, who was clad in ill-fitting, old-fashioned clothes, fidgeting about the room.

"You wish to see me?" asked Mavis, as she wondered who he could be.

"Yes. My name's Perigal: Major Perigal."

Mavis did not speak.

The man seemed surprised at her silence.

"I—I knew your father," he remarked.

"I knew your son," said Mavis icily.

"More's the pity!"

Mavis looked up, mildly surprised. The man continued:

"He's mean: mean right through. I've nothing good to say of him. I know him too well."

Mavis kept silent. Major Perigal went on:

"A nice mess you've made of it."

The girl's eyes held the ghost of a smile. He continued:

"I did my best for you, but you thought yourself too clever."

Mavis looked up inquiringly.

"When I heard who it was he was going to marry, I wanted to do you a good turn for your father's sake, as I knew Charles could never make you happy. I forbade the marriage, knowing he wouldn't face poverty for you. He's hateful: hateful right through."

"And if we'd married?"

"I'd have come round, especially after seeing you. You're a daughter-in-law any man would be proud of. And now he's married that Devitt girl for her money."

"For her money?" queried Mavis.

"What little she has. Never mind her: I want to speak of you. For all your fine looks, you were too clever by half."

"What do you mean?" she asked, with dull, even voice.

"What I say. That for all your grand appearance you were much too knowing. Since you couldn't get him one way, you thought you'd have him another."

"You mean——"

"By doing as you did."

"You insult me!" cried Mavis, now roused from her lethargy.

"Eh?"

"Insult me. And that is why you came. But since you're here, you may as well know I made a mess of it, as you call it, because I loved your son. If I'd the time over again, I suppose I'd be just such another fool. I can't help it. I loved him. I wish you good morning."

Major Pengal had never been so taken aback in his life. Mavis's words and manner carried conviction to his heart.

"I didn't know—I beg your pardon—I take hack my words," he said confusedly.

Mavis relapsed into her previous torpor.

"I didn't know there was such a woman in the world," he continued. "What you must have been through!"

Mavis did not speak.

"May I have the honour of calling on you again?" he asked with old-fashioned courtesy.

"It would be useless. I go away to-morrow."

"For good?"

"For some weeks."

"If you return, perhaps you would honour me by calling on me. I never see anyone. But, if you would permit me to say so, your friendship would be an honour."

"Thank you, but I don't know what I shall be doing," said Mavis wearily.

A few moments later, Major Perigal took his leave, but without recovering from his unaffected surprise at Mavis's honesty. He looked at her many times, to say, as he went out of the door of the parlour:

"I always believed Charles to have brains: now I know him to be a cursed fool."

The following day, Mavis, accompanied by Mrs Trivett and Jill, set out for Swanage. They took train to Dorchester, where they changed into the South-Western system, which carried them to Swanage, after making a further change at ancient Wareham. Arrived at Swanage station, they took a fly to the house of a Mrs Budd, where lodgings, at the doctor's recommendation, had been secured. On their way to Mrs Budd's, Mavis noticed a young man in a hand-propelled tricycle, which the fly overtook. The nature of the machine told Mavis that its occupant was a cripple.

If she had encountered him eighteen months ago, her heart would have filled with pity at seeing the comely young man's extremity: now, she looked at him very much as she might have noticed a cat crossing the road.

Mrs Budd was waiting on the doorstep in anxious expectation of her lodgers. To see her white hair, all but toothless mouth, and wrinkled face, she looked seventy, which was about her age; but to watch her alert, brisk movements, it would seem as if she enjoyed the energy of twenty. She ushered Mavis into her apartments, talking volubly the while; but the latter could not help seeing that, whereas she was treated with the greatest deference by the landlady, this person quite ignored the existence of Mrs Trivett.

It was with a feeling of relief that Mavis sat down to a meal after the door had been closed on Mrs Budd's chatter. The change had already done her good. Her eyes rested approvingly on the spotless table appointments.

"Poor dear!" exclaimed Mrs Trivett in pitying tones, who waited to see if Mavis had everything she wanted before eating with Mrs Budd in the kitchen.

"What's the matter?" asked Mavis.

"I knew something dreadful would happen. It's the anniversary of the day on which I had my first lot of new teeth, which gave me such dreadful pain."

"What's wrong?"

"That Mrs Budd. I took a dislike to her directly I saw her."

Mavis stared at Mrs Trivett in surprise.

"I do hope you'll be comfortable," continued Mrs Trivett. "But I fear you won't be. She looks the sort of person who would give anyone damp sheets and steal the sugar."

Mrs Trivett said more to the same effect. Mavis, remembering Mrs Budd's behaviour to her, could scarcely keep back a smile; it was the first time since her illness that anything had appeared at all amusing.

But this was not the sum of Mrs Trivett's resentment against Mrs Budd. After the meal was over, she rejoined Mavis with perspiration dropping from her forehead.

"The kitchen's like an oven, and I've nearly been roasted," complained Mrs Trivett. "And her horrid old husband is there, who can't do anything for himself."

"Why didn't you leave before you got so hot?" asked Mavis.

"It's that there Mrs Budd's fault. She's only one tooth, and it takes her all her time to eat."

"I meant, why didn't you leave so that you could finish eating in here?"

"I didn't like to, ma'am, but if you wouldn't very much mind in future——"

"By all means, eat with me if you wish it."

"Thank you kindly. I'm sure that woman and me would come to blows before many days was over."

Mavis rested for the remainder of the day and only saw Mrs Budd during the few minutes in which the table was being either laid or cleared away; but these few minutes were enough for the landlady to tell Mavis pretty well everything of moment in her life. Mavis learned how Mrs Budd's husband had been head gardener to a neighbouring baronet, until increasing infirmities had compelled him to give up work; also, that as he had spent most of his life in hot-houses, the kitchen had always to have a big fire blazing in order that the old man might have the heat necessary for his comfort. It appeared that Mrs Budd's third daughter had died from curvature of the spine. The mother related with great pride how that, just before death, the girl's spine had formed the figure of a perfect "hess." Mavis was also informed that Mrs Budd could not think of knowing her next-door neighbour, because this person paid a penny a pound less for her suet than she herself did.

When Mavis was going upstairs to bed, she came upon Mrs Budd laboriously dragging her husband, a big, heavy man, up to bed by means of a cord slung about her shoulders and fastened to his waist. Mavis subsequently learned that Mrs Budd had performed this feat every night for the last four years, her husband having lost the use of his limbs.

After Mavis had been a few days at Mrs Budd's, she was sufficiently recovered to walk about Swanage. One day she was even strong enough to get as far as the Tilly Whim caves, where she was both surprised and disgusted to find that some surpassing mediocrity had had the fatuousness to deface the sheer glory of the cliffs with improving texts, such as represent the sum of the world's wisdom to the mind of a successful grocer, who has a hankering after the natural science which is retailed in ninepenny popular handbooks. Often in these walks, Mavis encountered the man whom she had seen upon the day of her arrival; as before, he was pulling himself along on his tricycle. The first two or three times they met, the cripple looked very hard at Jill, who always accompanied her mistress. Afterwards, he took no notice of the dog; he had eyes only for Mavis, in whom he appeared to take a lively interest. Mavis, who was well used to being stared at by men, paid no heed to the man's frequent glances in her direction.

The sea air and the change did much for Mavis's health; she was gradually roused from the lethargy from which she had suffered for so long. But with the improvement in her condition came a firmer realisation of the hard lot which was hers. Her love for Charlie Perigal had resulted in the birth of a child. Although her lover had broken his vows, she could, in some measure, have consoled herself for his loss by devoting her life to the upbringing of her boy. Now her little one had been taken from her, leaving a vast emptiness in her life which nothing could fill. God, fate, chance, whatever power it was that ruled her life, had indeed dealt hardly with her. She felt an old woman, although still a girl in years. She had no interest in life: she had nothing, no one to live for.

One bright March day, Mavis held two letters in her hand as she sat by the window of her sitting-room at Mrs Budd's. She read and re-read them, after which her eyes would glance with much perplexity in the direction of the daffodils now opening in the garden in front of the house. She pondered the contents of the letters; then, as if to distract her thoughts from an unpalatable conclusion, which the subject matter of one of the letters brought home to her, she fell to thinking of the daffodils as though they were the unselfish nurses of the other flowers, insomuch as they risked their frail lives in order to see if the world were yet warm enough for the other blossoms now abed snugly under the earth. The least important of the two letters was from Major Perigal; it had been forwarded on from Melkbridge. In his cramped, odd hand, he expressed further admiration for Mavis's conduct; he begged her to let him know directly she returned to

Melkbridge, so that he might have the honour of calling on her again. The other letter was from Windebank, in which he briefly asked Mavis if she would honour him by becoming his wife. Mavis was much distressed. However brutally her heart had been bruised by the events of the last few months, she sometimes believed (this when the sun was shining) that some day it would be possible for her to conjure up some semblance of affection for Windebank, especially if she saw much of him. His mere presence radiated an atmosphere of protection. It offered a welcome harbourage after the many bufferings she had suffered upon storm-tossed seas. If she could have gone to him as she had to Perigal, she would not have hesitated a moment. Now, so far as she was concerned, there was all the difference in the world. Although she knew that her soul was not defiled by her experience with Perigal, she had dim perceptions of the way in which men, particularly manly males, looked upon such happenings. It was not in the nature of things, after all that had occurred, for Windebank to want her in a way in which she would wish to be desired by the man of her choice. Here was, apparently, no overmastering passion, but pity excited by her misfortunes. Mavis had got out of Mrs Trivett (who had long since left for Melkbridge) that it was Windebank who had insisted on paying the expenses of her illness and stay at Swanage, in spite of Major Perigal's and his son's desire to meet all costs that had been incurred. Mavis also learned that Windebank and Charles Perigal had had words on the subject—words which had culminated in blows when Windebank had told Perigal in unmeasured terms what he thought of his conduct to Mavis.

As Mavis recalled Windebank's generosity with regard to her illness, it seemed to her that this proposal of marriage was all of a piece with his other behaviour since her baby had died. Consideration for her, not love, moved his heart. If she were indeed so much to him, why did he not come down and beg her with passionate words to join her life to his?

Mavis made no allowance for the man's natural delicacy for her feelings, which he considered must have been cruelly harrowed by all she had lately suffered. Just now, there was no room in her world for the more delicate susceptibilities of emotion. She wholly misjudged him, and the more she thought of it, the more she believed that his letter was dictated by pity rather than love. This pity irked her pride and made her disinclined to accept his offer.

Then Mavis thought of Major Perigal's letter. It flattered her to think how her personality appealed to those of her own social kind. She began to realise what a desirable wife she would have made if it had not been for her meeting and subsequent attachment to Charlie Perigal. Any man, Windebank, but for this experience, would have been proud to have made her his wife. She believed that her whole-hearted devotion to a worthless man had for ever cut her off from love, wifehood, motherhood—things for which her being starved. Then she tried to fathom the why and wherefore of it all. She had always tried to do right: in situations where events were foreign to her control, she had trusted to her Heavenly Father for protection. "Why was it," she asked herself, "that her lot had not been definitely thrown in with Windebank before she had met with Charles Perigal? Why?" Such was her resentment at the ordering of events, that she set her teeth and banged her clenched fist upon the arm of her chair.

At that moment the crippled man wheeled himself past the house on his self-propelled tricycle. He looked intently at the window of the room that Mavis occupied. At the same moment Mrs Budd came into the room to ask what Mavis would like for luncheon.

"Who is that passing?" asked Mavis.

The old woman ran lightly to the window.

"The gentleman on that machine?"

"Yes. I've often seen him about."

"It's Mr Harold Devitt, miss."

"Harold Devitt! Where does he come from?" asked Mavis of Mrs Budd, who had a genius for gleaning the gossip of the place.

"Melkbridge. He's the eldest son of Mr Montague Devitt, a very rich gentleman. Mr Harold lives at Mrs Buck's with a male nurse to look after him, poor fellow."

Mrs Budd went on talking, but Mavis did not hear what she was saying. Mention of the name of Devitt was the spark that set alight a raging conflagration in her being. She had lost a happy married life with Windebank, to be as she now was, entirely owing to the Devitts. Now it was all plain enough—so plain that she wondered how she had not seen it before. It was the selfish action of the Devitts, who wished to secure Windebank for their daughter, which had prevented Montague from giving Mavis the message that Windebank had given to him. It was the Devitts who had not taken her into their house, because they feared how she might meet Windebank in Melkbridge. It was the Devitts who had given her work in a boot factory, which resulted in her meeting with Perigal. It was the Devitts, in the person of Victoria, who had prevented Perigal from keeping his many times repeated promises to marry Mavis. The Devitts had blighted her life. Black hate filled her heart, overflowed and poisoned her being. She hungered to be revenged on these Devitts, to repay them with heavy interest for the irreparable injury to her life for which she believed them responsible. Then, she remembered how tenderly Montague Devitt had always spoken of his invalid boy Harold; a soft light had come into his eyes on the few occasions on which Mavis had asked after him. A sudden resolution possessed her, to be immediately weakened by re-collections of Montague's affection for his son. Then a procession of the events in her life, which were for ever seared into her memory, passed before her mind's eye—the terror that possessed her when she learned that she was to be a mother; her interview with Perigal at Dippenham; her first night in London, when she had awakened in the room in the Euston Road; Mrs Gowler's; her days of starvation in Halverton Street; the death and burial, not only of her boy, but of her love for and faith in Perigal—all were remembered. Mavis's mind was made up. She went to her bedroom, where, with infinite deliberation, she dressed for going out.

"Mr Harold Devitt!" she said, when she came upon him waiting on his tricycle by the foolish little monument raised to the memory of one of Alfred the Great's victories over invading Danes.

The man raised his hat, while he looked intently at Mavis.

"I have to thank you for almost the dearest treasure I've ever possessed. Do you remember Jill?"

"Of course: I wondered if it might prove to be she when I first saw her. But is your name, by any chance, Miss Keeves?"

Mavis nodded.

"I've often wondered if I were ever going to meet you. And when I saw you about——"

"You noticed me?"

"Who could help it? I'm in luck."

"What do you mean?" she asked lightly.

"Meeting with you down here."

Thus they talked for quite a long while. Long before they separated for the day, Mavis's eyes had been smiling into his.

CHAPTER THIRTY-SEVEN
MAVIS AND HAROLD

"You're late!"

"I always am. I've been trying to make myself charming."

"That wouldn't be difficult."

"You think so?"

"I'm sure of it."

Mavis spoke lightly, but Harold's voice was eloquent of conviction.

"I'm sure of it," he repeated, as if to himself.

"Am I so perfect?" she asked, as her eyes sought the ground.

"In my eyes. But, then, I'm different from other men."

"You are."

"You needn't remind me of it."

"Isn't it nice to be different from others?"

"And wheel myself about because I can't walk?"

"Is that what you meant? Believe me, I didn't mean that. I was thinking how different you were to talk to, to other men I've met."

"You flatter me."

"It's the truth."

"Then, since I'm so exceptional, will you do something for me?"

"Perhaps."

"Never be later than you can help. I worry, fearing something's happened to you."

"Not really?"

"You are scarcely a subject I should fib about."

This was the beginning of a conversation that took place a fortnight after Mavis's first meeting with Harold by the sea. During this time, they had seen each other for the best part of every day when the weather was fine enough for Harold to be out of doors; as it was an exceptionally fine spring, they met constantly. Mavis was still moved by an immense hatred of the Devitt family, whom, more than ever before, she believed to be responsible for the wrongs and sufferings she had endured. In her determination to injure this family by making Harold infatuated with her, she was not a little surprised at the powers of dissimulation which she had never before suspected that she possessed. She was both ashamed and proud of this latent manifestation of her individuality—proud because she was inclined to rejoice in the power that it conferred. But, at times, this elation was diluted with self-reproaches, chiefly when she was with Harold, but not looking at him; then his deep, rich voice would awaken strange tremors in her being.

However much Mavis was occasionally moved to pity his physical misfortune, the recollection of her griefs was more than enough to harden her heart.

"Very, very strange that I should have run against you here," he went on.

"Why?"

"I was at home when your old schoolmistress's letter came about you. I remember she dragged in Ruskin."

"Poor Miss Mee!"

"I was always interested in you, and when I was in the South of France, I was always asking my people to do their best for you."

Mavis's eyes grew hard as she asked:

"You've kept your promise to me?"

"That I shouldn't tell my people I'd met you?"

"I made it because—"

"Never mind why. You made it: that is enough for me."

Mavis's eyes softened. Then she and Harold fell to talking of Melkbridge and Montague Devitt; presently of Victoria.

"I hope she was kind to you at Melkbridge," said Harold.

"Very," declared Mavis, saying what was untrue.

"Dear Vic is a little disappointing. I'm always reproaching myself I don't love her more than I do. Have you ever met the man she married?"

"Mr. Perigal? I've met him," replied Mavis.

"Do you like him?"

"I scarcely remember."

"I don't overmuch. I'm sorry Vic married him, although my people were, of course, delighted."

"Why?"

"We're quite new people, while the Perigals are a county family. But, somehow, I don't think he'll make Vic happy."

"What makes you say that?"

"He's not happy himself. Everything he takes up he wearies of; he gets pleasure out of nothing. And the pity of it is, he's no fool; if anything, he's too many brains."

"How can anyone have too many?"

"Take Perigal's case. He's too analytical; he sees too clearly into things. It's a sort of Rontgen ray intelligence, which I wouldn't have for worlds. Isn't it old Solomon who says, 'In much wisdom there is much sorrow'?"

"Solomon says a good many things," said Mavis gravely, as she remembered how the recollection of certain passion-charged verses from the "Song" had caused her to linger by the canal at Melkbridge on a certain memorable evening of her life, with, as it proved, disastrous consequences to herself.

"Have you ever read the 'Song'?" asked Harold.

"Yes."

"I love it, but I daren't read it now."

"Why?"

"More than most things, it brings home to me my—my helplessness."

The poison, begotten of hatred, made Mavis thankful that the Devitt family had not had it all their own way in life.

When she next looked at Harold, he was intently regarding her. Mavis's glance dropped.

"But now there's something more than reading the 'Song' that makes me curse my luck," he remarked.

"And that?"

"Can't you guess?" he asked earnestly.

Mavis did not try; she was already aware of the fascination she possessed for the invalid.

For the rest of the time they were together, Mavis could get nothing out of Harold; he was depressed and absent-minded when spoken to. Mavis, of set purpose, did her utmost to take Harold out of himself.

"Thank you," he said, as she was going.

"What for?"

"Wasting your time on me and helping me to forget."

"Forget what?"

"Never mind," he said, as he wheeled himself away.

When Mavis got back to Mrs Budd's, she found a bustle of preparation afoot. Mrs Budd was running up and downstairs, carrying clean linen with all her wonted energy; whilst Hannah, her sour-faced assistant, perspired about the house with dustpan and brushes.

"Expecting a new lodger?" asked Mavis.

"It's my daughter, Mrs Perkins; she's telegraphed to say she's coming down from Kensington for a few days."

"She'll be a help."

Mrs Budd's face fell as she said:

"Well, miss, she comes from Kensington, and she has a baby."

"Is she bringing that too?"

"And her nurse," declared Mrs Budd, not without a touch of pride.

When Mrs Perkins arrived, she was wearing a picture hat, decorated with white ostrich feathers, a soiled fawn dust-coat, and high-heeled patent leather shoes. She brought with her innumerable flimsy parcels (causing, by comparison, a collapsible Japanese basket to look substantially built), and a gaily-dressed baby carried by a London slut, whose face had been polished with soap and water for the occasion.

After the dust-cloak had settled with the driver, it advanced self-consciously to the steps leading to the front door, the while it called to the London slut:

"Come along, nurse, and be careful of baby."

Mavis, who saw and heard this from the window of her sitting-room, noticed that Mrs Perkins greeted her mother, who was waiting at the door, with some condescension. When the last flimsy parcel had been taken within, Mrs Budd brought in Mrs Perkins and the baby to introduce them to Mavis. Mrs Perkins sat down and assumed a manner of superfine gentility, while she talked with a Cockney accent. Her mother remained standing. The dust-cloak lived in Kensington, it informed Mavis, "which was so convenient for the West End: it was only an hour's 'bus ride from town."

"Less than that," said Mavis to the dust-cloak.

"I have known it to take fifty-five minutes when it hasn't been stopped by funerals," declared Mrs Perkins.

Mavis looked at the dust-cloak in surprise.

"I always thought it took a quarter of an hour at the outside," remarked Mavis.

"For my part, when I go to London, I'm afraid of the 'buses," said Mrs Budd. "I always take the train to Willesden Junction. Florrie's house is only five minutes from there."

Mrs Perkins frowned, coughed, and then violently changed the subject. Mavis gave no heed to what she was saying. Her eyes were fixed on the baby, which Mrs Budd had put in her arms.

Passionate regrets filled her mind, while a dull pain assailed her heart. She held the baby with a tense grip as Mrs Perkins talked at her, the while the mother kept one eye self-consciously upon her offspring.

Baby that and baby this, she was saying, as Mavis continued to stare with dry-eyed grief at the baby's pasty face. Then blind rage possessed her.

"Why should this common brat, which, even at this early age, carried his origin in his features, live, while my sweet boy is beneath the ground in Pennington Churchyard?" she asked herself.

It was cruel, unjust. Mavis's rage was such that she was within measurable distance of dashing the baby to the ground. Perhaps the dust-cloak's maternal sensibilities scented danger, for, rather abruptly, it got up to go, giving as an excuse that it must rest in order to fulfil social engagements in Swanage. When Mrs Budd, her daughter and grandson, had gone, Mavis still sat in her chair. Her hands grasped its arms; her eyes stared before her. If, at any time, Harold's personality had caused her hatred of his family to wane, the sight of Mrs Perkins's baby was sufficient to restore its vigour.

Then it occurred to Mavis how her love for Perigal, which she had thought to be as stable as the universe, had unconsciously withered within her. It was as if there had been an immense reaction from her one-time implicit faith in her lover, making her despise, where once she had had unbounded confidence. This awakening to the declension that had taken place in her love gave her many anxious hours.

For some days Mavis saw nothing of Harold. She walked on the sweep of sea front and in the streets of the little town in the hope of meeting him, but in vain. She wondered if he had gone home, but persuaded herself that he would not have left Swanage without letting her know.

Mavis was not a little irked at Harold's indifference to her friendship; it hurt her self-esteem, which had been enhanced by the influence she had so palpably wielded over him. It also angered her to think that, after all, she would not be able to drink the draught of revenge which she had promised herself at the Devitts' expense.

All this time she had given no further thought to Windebank's letter; it remained unanswered. As the days passed, and she saw nothing of Harold, she began to think considerably of the man who had written to offer her marriage. These thoughts were largely coloured with resentment at the fact of Windebank's not having followed up his unanswered letter by either another communication or a personal appeal. Soon she was torn by two emotions: hatred of the Devitts and awakened interest in Windebank; she did not know which influenced her the more. She all but made up her mind to write some sort of a reply to Windebank, when she met Harold pulling himself along the road towards the sea.

He had changed in the fortnight that had elapsed since she had last seen him; his face had lost flesh; he looked worn and anxious.

When he saw her, he pulled up. She gave him a formal bow, and was about to pass him, when the hurt expression on the invalid's face caused her to stop irresolutely by his side.

"At last!" he said.

Mavis looked at him inquiringly.

"I could bear it no longer," he went on.

"Bear what?"

He did not reply; indeed, he did not appear to listen to her words, but said:

"I feared you'd gone for good."

"I've seen nothing of you either."

"Then you missed me? Tell me that you did."

"I don't know."

"I have missed YOU."

"Indeed!"

"I daren't say how much. Where are you going now?"

"Nowhere."

"May I come too?" he asked pleadingly. "I'll go a little way," she remarked.

"Meet me by the sea in ten minutes."

"Why not go there together?"

"I'd far rather meet you."

"Don't you like being seen with me?"

"Yes and no. Yes, because I am very proud at being seen with you."

"And 'no'?"

"It's why I wanted you to meet me by the sea."

"Why?"

"Can't you guess?"

"If I could I wouldn't ask."

"I'll tell you. When you walk with me, I'm afraid you notice my infirmity the more."

"I'll only go on one condition," declared Mavis.

"That——?"

"That we go straight there from here."

"I'm helpless where you're concerned," he sighed, as he started his tricycle.

They went to the road bordering the sea, which just now they had to themselves. On the way they said little; each was occupied with their thoughts.

Mavis was touched by Harold's devotion; also, by his anxiety not to obtrude his infirmity upon her notice. She looked at him, to see in his eyes unfathomable depths of sadness. She repressed an inclination to shed tears. She had never been so near foregoing her resolve to make him the instrument of her hatred of his family. But the forces that decide these matters had other views. Mavis was staring out to sea, in order to hide her emotion from Harold's distress, when the sight of the haze where sea and sky met arrested her attention. Something in her memory struggled for expression, to be assisted by the smell of seaweed which assailed her nostrils.

In the twinkling of an eye, Mavis, in imagination, was at Llansallas Bay, with passionate love and boundless trust in her heart for the lover at her side, to whom she had surrendered so much. The merest recollection of how her love had been betrayed was enough to dissipate the consideration that she was beginning to feel for Harold. Her heart turned to stone; determination possessed her.

"Still silent!" she exclaimed.

"I have to be."

"Who said so?"

"The little sense that's left me."

"Sense is often nonsense."

"It's a bitter truth to me."

"Particularly now?"

"Now and always."

"May I know?"

"Why did you come into my life?" he asked, as if he had not heard her request.

"Why shouldn't I?"

"Why have you? Why have you?"

"You're not the only one who can ask that question," she murmured.

He looked at her for some moments in amazement before saying:

"Say that again."

"I shan't."

"If I were other than I am, I should compel you."

"How could you?"

"With my lips. As it is——"

"Yes—tell me."

"My infirmity stops me from saying and doing what I would."

"Why let it?" asked Mavis in a low voice, while her eyes sought the ground.

"You—you mean that?" he asked, in the manner of one who scarcely believed the evidence of his ears.

"I mean it."

He did not speak for such a long time that Mavis began to wonder if he regretted his words. When she stole a look at him, she saw that his eyes were staring straight before him, as if his mind were all but overwhelmed by the subject matter of its concern.

Mavis touched his arm. He shivered slightly and glanced at her as if surprised, before he realised that she was beside him.

"Listen!" he said. "You asked—you shall know; whether you like or hate me for it. I love you. Women have never come into my life; they've always looked on me with pitying eyes. I would rather it were so. But you— you—you are beautiful, with a heart like your face, both rare and wonderful. Perhaps I love you so much because you are young and healthy. It hurts me."

His eyes held such a piteously fearful look that Mavis was moved in spite of herself. He went on:

"If my disposition were like my twisted body, it wouldn't matter. But I love life, movement, struggling. Were I as I used to be, I should love to have a beautiful, responsive woman for my own. I should love to have you."

Before Mavis knew what she had done, she had put her hand on his. Then he said, as if speaking to himself:

"What have I to offer besides a helpless, envious love? My wife would be a nurse, not a mistress, as she should be."

"Stop! stop!" she pleaded.

"No, I will not stop," he cried, as he bent over to hold her head so that her eyes looked into his. "You shall listen and then decide. I love you. If it's good enough, I'm yours. You know what I have to offer, and I ask you to be my wife because I can't help myself. Because—"

Mavis had closed her eyes for fear that he should read her heart. He passionately kissed the closed lids before sinking back exhausted in his chair.

"Listen to me," said Mavis after a while. "It's I who am to blame. Let me go away so that you can forget me."

"Forget you! forget you!" he cried. "No, you shall not go away; not till you've said 'yes' or 'no' to what I ask."

"When shall I answer?"

"Give yourself time—only—"

"Only?"

"Don't keep me waiting longer than you can help."

For three days, Mavis drifted upon uncertain tides. She was borne rapidly in one direction only to float as certainly in another. She lacked sufficient strength of purpose to cast anchor and abide by the consequences. She deplored her irresolution, but, try as she might, she found it a matter of great difficulty to give her mind to the consideration of Harold's offer. Otherwise, the most trivial happenings imprinted themselves on her brain: the aspect of the food she ate, the lines on her landlady's face, the flittings in and out of the front door of the "dust-cloak" on its way to trumpery social engagements, the while its mother minded the baby, all acquired in her eyes a prominence foreign to their importance. Also, thoughts of Windebank now and again flooded her mind. Then she remembered all he had done for her, at which gratitude welled from her soul. At such times she would be moved by a morbid consideration for his feelings; she longed to pay back the money he had spent on her illness, and felt that her mind would never be at ease on the matter till she had.

If only he would come down, and, despite anything she could say or do, insist on marrying her and determine to win her heart; failing that, if he would only write words of passionate longing which might awaken some echo in her being! She read and re-read the letter in which he offered her marriage; she tried to see in his formal phrases some approximation to a consuming love, but in vain.

She had never answered this letter; she reproached herself for not having done so. Mavis sat down to write a few words, which would reach Windebank by the first post in the morning, when she found that the ink had dried in the pot. She rang the bell. While waiting, a vision of the piteous look on Harold's face when he had told her of his love came into her mind. Accompanying this was the recollection of the cause of which her friendship with Harold was an effect. Hatred of the Devitts possessed her. She remembered, and rejoiced, that it was now in her power to be revenged for all she believed she had suffered at their hands. So black was the quality of this hate that she wondered why she had delayed so long.

When the ink was brought, it was to Harold that she was about to write; Windebank was forgotten.

As Mavis wrote the day of the month at the head of the page, she seemed to hear echoes of Harold's resonant voice vibrating with love for her. She sighed and put down her pen. If only she were less infirm of purpose. Her hesitations were interrupted by Mrs Budd bringing in a letter for Mavis that the postman had just left. It was from Mrs Trivett. It described with a wealth of detail a visit that the writer had paid to Pennington Churchyard, where she had taken flowers to lay on the little grave. Certain nerves in the bereaved mother's face quivered as she read. Memories of the long-drawn agony which had followed upon her boy's death crowded into her mind. Mavis hardened her heart.

CHAPTER THIRTY-EIGHT
MAVIS'S REVENGE

Upon a day on which the trees and hedges were again frocked in spring finery in honour of approaching summer, Mrs Devitt was sitting with her sister in the drawing-room of Melkbridge House. Mrs Devitt was trying to fix her mind on an article in one of the monthly reviews dealing with the voluntary limitation of families on the part of married folk. Mrs Devitt could not give her usual stolid attention to her reading, because, now and again, her thoughts wandered to an interview between her husband and Lowther which was taking place in the library downstairs. This private talk between father and son on the subject of certain snares which beset the feet of moneyed youth when in London, and in which the unhappy Lowther had been caught. Mrs Devitt was sufficiently vexed at the prospect of her husband having to fork out some hundreds of pounds, without the further promise of revelations in which light-hearted, lighter living young women were concerned. Debts were forgivable, perhaps excusable, in a young gentleman of Lowther's standing, but immorality, in Mrs Devitt's eyes, was a horse of quite another colour; anything of this nature acted upon Mrs Devitt's susceptibilities much in the same way as seeing red afreets an angry bull.

Miss Spraggs, whom the last eighteen months had aged in appearance, looked up from the rough draft of a letter she was composing.

"Did you hear anything?" she asked, as she listened intently.

"Hear what?"

"The door open downstairs. Lowther's been in such a time with Montague."

"I suppose Lowther is confessing everything," sighed Mrs Devitt.

"Nothing of the sort," remarked Miss Spraggs.

"What do you mean?"

"No one ever does confess everything: something is always kept back."

"Don't you think, Eva, you look at things from a very material point of view?"

Eva shrugged her narrow shoulders. Mrs Devitt continued:

"Now and again, you seem to ignore the good which is implanted in us all."

"Perhaps because it's buried so deep down that it's difficult to see."

Half an hour afterwards, it occurred to Mrs Devitt that she might have retorted, "What one saw depended on the power of one's perceptions," but just now, all she could think of to say was:

"Quite so; but there's so much good in the world, I wonder you don't see more of it."

"What are you reading?" asked Miss Spraggs, as she revised the draft of her letter.

The scribbling virgin often made a point of talking while writing, in order to show how little mental concentration was required for her literary efforts.

"An article on voluntary limitations of family. It's by the Bishop of Westmoreland. He censures such practices: I agree with him."

Mrs Devitt spoke from her heart. The daughter of a commercial house, which owed its prosperity to an abundant supply of cheap labour, she realised (although she never acknowledged it to herself) that the practices the worthy bishop condemned, if widely exercised, must, in course of time, reduce the number of hands eager to work for a pittance, and, therefore, the fat profits of their employers.

"So do I," declared Miss Spraggs, who only wished she had the ghost of a chance of contributing (legitimately) to the sum of the population.

"There's an admirable article about Carlyle in the same number of the National Review," said Miss Spraggs presently.

"I never read anything about Carlyle," declared Mrs Devitt.

Miss Spraggs raised her straight eyebrows.

"He didn't get on with his wife," said Mrs Devitt, in a manner suggesting that this fact effectually disposed in advance of any arguments Miss Spraggs might offer.

Soon after, Montague Devitt came into the room, to be received with inquiring glances by the two women. He walked to the fireplace, where he stood in moody silence.

"Well?" said his wife presently.

"Well!" replied Devitt.

"What has Lowther confessed?"

"The usual."

"Money?"

"And other things."

"Ah! What were the other things?"

"We'll talk it over presently," replied Montague, as he glanced at Miss Spraggs.

"Am I so very young and innocent that I shouldn't learn what has happened?" asked Miss Spraggs, who, in her heart of hearts, enjoyed revelations of masculine profligacy.

"I'd rather speak later," urged Montague gloomily, to add, "It never rains but it pours."

"Why do you say that?" asked his wife quickly.

"I'd a letter from Charlie Perigal this mornin'."

"Where from?"

"The same Earl's Court private hotel. He wants somethin' to do."

"Something to do!" cried the two sisters together.

"His father hasn't done for him what he led me to believe he would," explained Devitt gloomily.

"You can find him something?" suggested Miss Spraggs.

"And, till you do, I'd better ask them to stay down here," said his wife.

"That part of it's all right," remarked Devitt. "But somehow I don't think Charlie——"

"What?" interrupted Mrs Devitt.

"Is much of a hand at work," replied her husband.

No one said anything for a few minutes.

Mrs Devitt spoke next.

"I'm scarcely surprised at Major Perigal's refusal to do anything for Charles," she remarked.

"Why?" asked her husband.

"Can you ask?"

"You mean all that business with poor Mavis Keeves?"

"I mean all that business, as you call it, with that abandoned creature whom we were so misguided as to assist."

Devitt said nothing; he was well used to his wife's emphatic views on the subject—views which were endorsed by her sister.

"The whole thing was too distressing for words," she continued. "I'd have broken off the marriage, even at the last moment, for Charles's share in it, but for the terrible scandal which would have been caused."

"Well, well; it's all over and done with now," sighed Devitt.

"I'm not so sure; one never knows what an abandoned girl, as Miss Keeves has proved herself to be, is capable of!"

"True!" remarked Miss Spraggs.

"Come! come!" said Devitt. "The poor girl was at the point of death for weeks after her baby died."

"What of that?" asked his wife.

"Girls who suffer like that aren't so very bad."

"You take her part, as you've always done. She's hopelessly bad, and I'm as convinced as I'm sitting here that it was she who led poor Charlie astray."

"It's all very unfortunate," said Devitt moodily.

"And we all but had her in the house," urged Mrs Devitt, much irritated at her husband's tacit support of the girl.

"Anyway, she's far away from us now," said Devitt.

"Where has she gone?" asked Miss Spraggs.

"Somewhere in Dorsetshire," Devitt informed her.

"If she hadn't gone, I should have made it my duty to urge her to leave Melkbridge," remarked Mrs Devitt.

"She's not so bad as all that," declared Devitt.

"I can't understand why men stand up for loose women," said his wife.

"She's not a loose woman: far from it. If she were, Windebank would not be so interested in her."

Devitt could not have said anything more calculated to anger the two women.

Miss Spraggs threw down her pen, whilst Mrs Devitt became white.

"She must be bad to have fascinated Sir Archibald as she has done," she declared.

"Windebank is no fool," urged her husband.

"I suppose the next thing we shall hear is that she's living under his protection," cried Mrs Devitt.

"In St John's Wood," added Miss Spraggs, whose information on such matters was thirty years behind the times.

"More likely he'll marry her," remarked Devitt.

"What!" cried the two women.

"I believe he'd give his eyes to get her," the man continued.

"He's only to ask," snapped Miss Spraggs.

"Anyway, we shall see," said Devitt.

"Should that happen, I trust you will never wish me to invite her to the house," said Mrs Devitt, rising to her full height.

"It's all very sad," remarked Devitt gloomily.

"It is: that you should take her part in the way you do, Montague," retorted his wife.

"I'm sorry if you're upset," her husband replied. "But I knew Miss Keeves as a little girl, when she was always laughin' and happy. It's all very, very sad."

Mrs Devitt moved to a window, where she stood staring out at the foliage which, just now, was looking self-conscious in its new finery.

"Who heard from Harold last?" asked Devitt presently.

"I did," replied Miss Spraggs. "It was on Tuesday he wrote."

"How did he write?"

"Quite light-heartedly. He has now for some weeks: such a change for him."

"H'm!"

"Why do you ask?" said Mrs Devitt.

"I saw Pritchett when I was in town yesterday."

"Harold's doctor?" queried Miss Spraggs.

"He told me he'd seen Harold last week."

"At Swanage?"

"Harold had wired for him. I wondered if anythin' was up."

"What should be 'up,' as you call it, beyond his being either better or worse?"

"That's what I want to know."

"What do you mean?"

"Why, that it was more from Pritchett's manner than from anything else that I gathered somethin' had happened."

"So long as he's well, there's nothing to worry about," said Mrs Devitt reassuringly.

The late afternoon post brought a letter for Montague from his son Harold. This told his father that a supreme happiness had come in his life; that, by great good fortune, he had met and quietly married Mavis Keeves; that, by her wish, the marriage had been kept a secret for three weeks; it ended by saying how he hoped to bring his wife to his father's house early in the following week. Montague Devitt stared stupidly at the paper on which this information was conveyed; then he leaned against the mantelpiece for support. He looked as if he had been struck brutally and unexpectedly between the eyes. "Montague! Montague!" cried his wife, as she noticed his distress.

The letter fell from his hands.

"Read!" he said faintly.

"Harold's writing!" exclaimed Mrs Devitt, as she caught up the letter.

Devitt watched her as she read; he saw her face grow hard; then her jaw dropped; her eyes stared fixedly before her. When Miss Spraggs read the letter, as she very soon did, she went into hysterics; she had a great affection for Harold. The hand of fate had struck the Devitts remorselessly; they were stunned by the blow for quite a long while. For her part, Mrs Devitt could not believe that Providence would allow her to suffer such a terrible affliction as was provided by the fact of her stepson's marriage to Mavis; again and again she looked at the letter, as if she found it impossible to believe the evidence of her eyes.

"What's—what's to be done?" gasped Mrs Devitt, when she was presently able to speak.

"Don't ask me!" replied her husband.

"Can't you do anything?" asked Miss Spraggs, during a pause in her hysterical weeping.

"Do what?"

"Something: anything. You're a man."

"I haven't grasped it yet. I must think it out," he said, as he began to walk up and down the room so far as the crowded furniture would permit.

"We must try and think it's God's will," said his wife, making an effort to get her thoughts under control.

"What!" cried Devitt, stopping short in his walk to look at his wife with absent eyes.

"God has singled us out for this bitter punishment," snuffled Mrs Devitt, as her eyes glanced at the heavily gilded chandelier.

With a gesture of impatience, Devitt resumed his walk, while Miss Spraggs quickly went to windows and door, which she threw open to their utmost capacity for admitting air.

"One thing must be done," declared Devitt.

"Yes?" asked his wife eagerly.

"That Hunter girl who split on Mavis Keeves havin' been at Polperro with Perigal."

"She knows everything; we shall be disgraced," wailed Mrs Devitt.

"Not at all. I'll see to that," replied her husband grimly.

"What will you do?"

"Give her a good job in some place as far from here as possible, and tell her that, if her tongue wags on a certain subject, she'll get the sack."

"What!" asked his wife, surprised at her husband's decision and the way in which he expressed himself.

"Suggest somethin' better."

"I was wondering if it were right."

"Right be blowed! We're fightin' for our own hand."

With this view of the matter, Mrs Devitt was fain to be content.

It was a dismal and forlorn family party which sat down to dinner that evening under the eye of the fat butler. Husband, wife, and Miss Spraggs looked grey and old in the light of the table lamps. By this time Lowther had been told of the trouble which had descended so suddenly upon the family. His comment on hearing of it was characteristic.

"Good God! But she hasn't a penny!" he said. He realised that the prospects of his father assisting him out of his many scrapes had declined since news had arrived of Harold's unlooked-for marriage. When the scarcely tasted meal was over, Montague sent Lowther upstairs "to give the ladies company," while he smoked an admirable cigar and drank the best part of a bottle of old port wine. The tobacco and the wine brought a philosophical calm to his unquiet mind; he was enabled to look on the marriage from its least unfavourable aspects. He had always liked Mavis and would have done much more for her than he had already accomplished, if his womenfolk had permitted him to follow the leanings of his heart; he knew her well enough to know that she was not the girl to bestow herself lightly upon Charlie Perigal. He had not liked Perigal's share in the matter at all, and the whole business was still much of a mystery. Although grieved beyond measure that the girl had married his dearly loved boy, he realised that with Harold's ignorance of women he might have done infinitely worse.

"What are you going to do?" asked Mrs Devitt of her husband in the seclusion of their bedroom.

"Try and make the best of it. After all, she's a lady."

"What! You're not going to try and have the marriage annulled?"

It was her husband's turn to express astonishment.

"Surely you'll do something?" she urged.

"What can I do?"

"As you know, it can't be a marriage in—in the worldly sense; when it's like that something can surely be done," said Mrs Devitt, annoyed at having to make distant allusions to a subject hateful to her heart.

"What about Harold's feelin's?"

"But—"

"He probably loves her dearly. What of his feelin's if he knew—all that we know?"

"I did not think of that. Oh dear! oh dear! it gets more and more complicated. What can be done?"

- 416 -

"Wait."

"What for?"

"Till we see them. Then we can learn the why and the wherefore of it all and judge accordin'ly."

With this advice Mrs Devitt had to be content, but for all the comfort it may have contained it was a long time before husband or wife fell asleep that night.

But even the short period of twenty-four hours is enough to accustom people to trouble sufficiently to make it tolerable. When this time had passed, Mrs Devitt's mind was well used to the news which yesterday afternoon's post had brought. Her mind harked back to Christian martyrs; she wondered if the fortitude with which they met their sufferings was at all comparable to the resolution she displayed in the face of affliction. The morning's post had brought a letter from Victoria, to whom her brother had written to much the same effect as he had communicated with his father. In this she expressed herself as admirably as was her wont; she also treated the matter with a sympathetic tact which, under the circumstances, did her credit. She trusted that anything that had happened would not influence the love and duty she owed her husband. Harold's marriage to Miss Keeves was in the nature of a great surprise, but if it brought her brother happiness she would be the last to regret it; she hoped that, despite past events, she would be able to welcome her brother's wife as a sister; she would not fail to come in time to greet her sister-in-law, but she would leave her husband in town, as he had important business to transact.

Some half hour before the time by which Harold and his wife could arrive at Melkbridge House, the Devitt family were assembled in the library; in this room, because it was on the ground floor, and, therefore, more convenient for Harold's use, he having to be carried up and down stairs if going to other floors of the house.

Devitt was frankly ill at ease. His wife did her best to bear herself in the manner of the noblest traditions (as she conceived them) of British matronhood. Miss Spraggs talked in whispers to her sister of "that scheming adventuress," as she called Mavis. Victoria chastened agitated expectation with resignation; while Lowther sat with his hands thrust deep into his trouser pockets. At last a ring was heard at the front door bell, at which Devitt and Lowther went out to welcome bride and bridegroom. Those left in the room waited while Harold was lifted out of the motor and put into the hand-propelled carriage which he used in the house. The Devitt women nerved themselves to meet with becoming resolution the adventuress's triumph.

Through the open door they could hear that Mavis had been received in all but silence; only Harold's voice sounded cheerily. The men made way for Mavis to enter the library. It was by no means the triumphant, richly garbed Mavis whom the women had expected who came into the room. It was a subdued, carelessly frocked Mavis, who, after accepting their chastened greetings, kept her eyes on her husband. When the door was closed, Harold was the first to speak.

"Mother, if I may call you that! father! all of you! I want you to hear what I have to say," he began, in his deep, soothing voice. "You know what my accident has made me; you know how I can never be other than I am. For all that, this winsome, wonderful girl, out of the pity and goodness of her loving heart, has been moved to throw in her lot with mine—even now I can hardly realise my immense good fortune" (here Mavis dropped her eyes), "but there it is, and if I did what was right, I should thank God for her every moment of my life. Now you know what she is to me; how with her youth and glorious looks she has blessed my life, I hope that you, all of you, will take her to your hearts."

A silence that could almost be heard succeeded his words; but Harold did not notice this; he had eyes only for his wife.

Tea was brought in, when, to relieve the tension, Victoria went over to Mavis and sat by her side; but to her remarks Harold's wife replied in monosyllables; she had only eyes for her husband. The Devitts could make nothing of her; her behaviour was so utterly alien to the scarcely suppressed triumph which they had expected. But just now they did not give very much attention to her; they were chiefly concerned for Harold, whose manner betrayed an extra-ordinary elation quite foreign to the depression which had troubled him before his departure for Swanage. Now a joyous gladness possessed him; from the frequent tender glances he cast in his wife's direction, there was little doubt of its cause. Harold's love for his wife commenced by much impressing his family, but ended by frightening them; they feared the effect on his mind when he discovered, as he undoubtedly must, when his wife had thrown off the mask, that he had wedded a heartless adventuress, who had married him for his money. At the same time, the Devitts were forced to admit that Mavis's conduct was unlike that of the scheming woman of their fancies; they wondered at the reason of her humility, but did not learn the cause till the family, other than Harold, were assembled upstairs in the drawing-room waiting for dinner to be announced. When Mavis had come into the room, the others had been struck by the contrast between the blackness of her frock and the milky whiteness of her skin; they were little prepared for what was to follow.

"Now we are alone, I have something to say to you," she began. The frigid silence which met her words made her task the harder; the atmosphere of the room was eloquent of antagonism. With an effort she continued: "I don't know what you all think of me—I haven't tried to think—but I'm worse—oh! ever so much worse than you believe."

The others wondered what revelations were toward. Devitt's mind went back to the night when Mavis had last stood in the drawing-room. Mavis went on:

"When I was away my heart was filled with hate: I hated you all and longed to be revenged."

Mavis's audience were uncomfortable; it was an axiom of their existence to shy at any expression of emotion.

The Devitts longed for the appearance of the fat butler, who would announce that dinner was served. But to-night his coming was delayed till Mavis had spoken.

"Chance threw Harold in my way," she went on. "He loved me at once, and I took advantage of his love, thinking to be revenged on you for all I believed—yes, I must tell you everything—for all I believed you had done against me."

Here Mrs Devitt lifted up her hands, as if filled with righteous anger at this statement.

Mavis took no notice, but continued:

"That is why I married him. That was then. Now I am punished, as the wicked always are, punished over and over again. Why did I do it? Why? Why?"

Here a look of terror came into her eyes; these looked helplessly about the room, as if nothing could save her from the torment that pursued her.

"He is ill; very ill. His doctor told me. How long do you think he will live?"

"Pritchett?" asked Devitt.

"Yes, when he came down to Swanage. What he told me only makes it worse."

"Makes what worse?" asked Devitt, who was eager to end this painful scene.

"My punishment. He thinks me good—everything I ought to be. I love him! I love him! I love him! He's all goodness and love. He believes in me as he believes in God. I love him! How long do you think he'll live? I love him! I love him! I love him!"

CHAPTER THIRTY-NINE
A SURPRISE

Mavis spoke truly. She loved her husband, although with a different love from that which she had known for Perigal. She had adored the father of her child with her soul and with her body, but in her affection for her husband there was no trace of physical passion, of which she had no small share. This new-born love was, in truth, an immense maternal devotion which seemed to satisfy an insistent longing of her being.

Upon the day of their wedding, Mavis was already wondering if she were beginning to love Harold; but for all this uncertainty, she believed that if the marriage were to be a physical as well as a civil union, she would have confessed before the ceremony took place her previous intimacy with Perigal. After the marriage, the holy fervour with which Harold had regarded Mavis bewildered her. The more his nature was revealed to her, the better she was enabled to realise the cold-blooded brutality with which the supreme Power (Mavis's thoughts did not run so easily in the direction of a Heavenly Father as was once their wont) had permanently mutilated Harold's life, which had been of the rarest promise. Still ignorant of her real sentiments for her husband, she had persuaded him, for no apparent reason, to delay acquainting his family with the news of their marriage. Truth soon illumined Mavis's mind. Directly she realised how devotedly she loved her husband (the maternal aspect of her love did not occur to her), her punishment for her previous duplicity began. She was constantly overwhelmed with bitter reproaches because of her having set out to marry her husband from motives of revenge against his family.

Mavis's confession to the Devitts temporarily eased her mind, but, as her husband's solicitude for her happiness redoubled, her torments recommenced with all their old-time persistency. Harold's declining health gave her innumerable anguished hours; she realised that, so long as he lived, she would suffer for the deception she had practised. She believed that, if she survived him, her remaining days would be filled with grief.

Whichever way she looked, trouble confronted her with hard, unbending features.

She was enmeshed in a net of sorrow from which there was no escape.

In order to stifle any hints or rumours which might have got about Melkbridge of Mavis having been a mother without being a wife, she was pressed by the Devitts to make a stay of some length at Melkbridge House. Guessing the reason of this invitation, she accepted, although she, as well as her husband, were eager to get into a quaint, weather-beaten farmhouse which Harold had bought in the neighbourhood.

To make her stay as tolerable as possible, Mavis set herself to win the hearts of the Devitt family, the feminine members of which, she was convinced, were bitterly hostile to her. The men of the household, to the scarcely concealed dismay of the women, quickly came over to her side. Lowther she appreciated at his worth; her studied indifference to him went a long way towards securing that youth's approval, which was not unmingled with admiration for her person. Montague she was beginning to like. For his part, he was quickly sensible of the feminine distinction which Mavis's presence bestowed upon his home. The fine figure she cut in evening dress at dinner parties, when the Devitts feasted their world; her conversation in the drawing-room afterwards; the emotion she put into her playing and singing (it was the only expression Mavis could give to the abiding griefs gnawing at her heart), were social assets of no small value, which Devitt was the first to appreciate. Mrs Harold Devitt's appearance and parts gave to his assemblies a piquancy which was sadly lacking when his friends repaid his hospitality. Mavis, also, pointed out to Devitt the advisability of rescuing from the lumber rooms several fine old pieces of furniture which were hidden away in disgrace, largely because they had belonged to Montague's humble grandfather. The handiwork of Chippendale and Hepplewhite was furbished up and put about the house, replacing Tottenham Court Road monstrosities. When the old furniture epidemic presently seized upon Melkbridge, the Devitts could flatter themselves that they had done much to influence local fashion in the matter.

Montague came to take pleasure in Mavis's society, when he would drop his blustering manner to become his kindly self. They had many long talks together, which enabled Mavis to realise the loneliness of the man's life. The more Montague saw of her the more he disliked his son-in-law's share in the paternity of Mavis's dead child.

Now and again he would discuss business worries with her, which established a community of interest between them. His friendship gave Mavis confidence in her endeavours to placate the female Devitts. This latter was uphill work: Mrs Devitt and her sister entrenched themselves in a civil reserve which resisted Mavis's most strenuous assaults. With Victoria, Mavis believed, at first, that she had better luck, Mrs Charlie Perigal's sentiments and manner of expressing them being all that the most exigent fancy might desire; but as time wore on, Mavis got no further with her sister-in-law; she could never feel that she and Victoria had a single heart beat in common.

As with so many others, Mavis began by liking but ended by being repelled by Victoria's inhuman flawlessness.

Thus Mavis lived for the weeks she stayed at Melkbridge House. But at all times, no matter what she might be doing, she was liable to be attacked by bitter, heart-rending grief at the loss of her child. Mavis had already suffered so much that she was now able to distinguish the pains peculiar to the different varieties of sorrow. This particular grief took the shape of a piteous, persistent heart hunger which nothing could stay. Joined to this was a ceaseless longing for the lost one, which cast drear shadows upon the bright hues of life. The way in which she was compelled to isolate her pain from all human sympathy did not diminish its violence.

One night, when the Devitts were entertaining their kind, the conversation at dinner touched upon a local petty sessions case, in which the nursemaid of one of those present had been punished for concealing the birth of an illegitimate child, who had since died.

"It was a great worry to me," complained the nurse's mistress. "She was such a perfect nurse."

"I hope you'll do something for her when she comes out," urged Harold.

The woman stared at Harold in astonishment.

"Think how the poor girl's suffered," he continued.

"Do you really think so?" asked the woman.

"She's lost her child."

"But I always understood that those who lose children out of wedlock cannot possible grieve like married women who have the same loss."

In a moment Mavis's thoughts flew to Pennington Churchyard, where her heart seemed buried deep below the grass; certain of her facial nerves twitched, while tears filled her eyes. Devitt's voice recalled her to her surroundings; she looked up, to catch his eyes looking kindly into hers. Although she made an effort to join in the talk, she was mentally bowing her head, the while her being ached with anguish. She did not recover her spirits for the rest of the evening.

There came a day when one of the big guns of the financial world was expected to dinner. Mavis had many times met at Melkbridge House some of the lesser artillery of successful business men, when she had been surprised to discover what dull, uninteresting folk they were; apart from their devotion to the cult of money-getting, they did not seem to have another interest in life, the ceaseless quest for gold absorbing all their vitality. This big gun was a Sir Frederick Buntz, whose interest Devitt, as he told Mavis, was anxious to secure in one of his company-promoting schemes. In order to do Devitt a good turn, Mavis laid herself out to please the elderly Sir Frederick, who happened to have an eye for an attractive woman. Sir Frederick scarcely spoke to anyone else but Mavis throughout dinner; at the end of the evening, he asked her if she advised him to join Devitt's venture.

Mavis's behaviour formed the subject of a complaint made by Mrs Devitt when alone with Montague in their bedroom.

"Didn't you notice the shameless way she behaved?" asked Mrs Devitt.

"Nonsense!" replied her well-pleased lord.

"Everyone noticed it. She's rapidly going from bad to worse."

"Anyway, it's as good as put five thousand in my pocket, if not more."

"What do you mean?"

Montague's explanation modified his wife's ill opinion of Mavis. The next morning, when Devitt thanked his daughter-in-law for influencing Sir Frederick in the way she had done, Mavis said:

"I want something in return."

"Some shares for yourself?"

"A rise of a pound a week for Miss Toombs."

"That plain, unhealthy little woman at the boot factory!"

"She's a heart of gold. I know you'll do it for me," said Mavis, who was now conscious of her power over Devitt.

Having won her way, Mavis set out to intercept Miss Toombs, who about this time would be on her way to business. They had not met since Mavis's marriage to Harold, Miss Toombs refusing to answer Mavis's many letters and always being out when her old friend called.

Mavis ran against Miss Toombs by the market-place; her friend looked in worse health than when she had last seen her.

"Good morning," said Mavis.

"Don't talk to me," cried Miss Toombs. "I hate the sight of you."

"No, you don't. And I've done you a good turn."

"I'm sorry to hear it. I wish you good morning."

"What have I done to upset you?" asked Mavis.

"Don't pretend you don't know."

"But I don't."

"What! Then I'll tell you. You've married young Devitt, when there's a man worth all the women who ever lived eating his heart out for you."

Mavis stopped, amazed at the other woman's vehemence.

"A man who you've treated like the beast you are," continued Miss Toombs hotly. "After all that's happened, he longed to marry you, and that's more than most men would have done."

"You don't know—you can't understand," faltered Mavis.

"Yes, I do. You're not really bad; you're only a precious big fool and don't know when you've got a good thing."

"I—I love my husband."

"Rot! You may think you do, but you don't. You're much too hot-blooded to stick that kind of marriage long. I know I wouldn't. And it serves you right if you ever make a mess of it."

"I thought Sir Archibald only pitied me," said Mavis, in extenuation of her marriage.

"Pity! pity! He's a man, not a bloodless nincompoop," said Miss Toombs. "And it's you I have to thank for seeing him so often," she added, as her anger again flamed up.

"Sir Archibald?" asked Mavis.

"He sees me to talk about you," said Miss Toombs sorrowfully. "And he never looks twice at me. He doesn't even like me enough to ask me to go away for a week-end with him. I'm simply nothing to him, and that's the truth."

"I think you a dear, anyway. And I've got you a rise of a pound a week."

"What?"

Mavis repeated her information.

"That'll buy me some summer muslins I've long had my eye on, and one or two bits of jewellery. Then, perhaps, he'll look at me," declared Miss Toombs.

The next moment she caught sight of her reflection in Perrott's (the grocer's) window, at which she cried:

"Just look at me! What on earth could ever make that attractive?"

"Your kind nature," replied Mavis. "You're much too fond of under-valuing your appearance."

"It's all damned unfair!" cried Miss Toombs passionately. "What use are your looks to you? What fun do you get out of life? Why—oh why haven't I your face and figure?"

"What would you do with it?" asked Mavis.

"Get him, get him somehow. If he wouldn't marry me I'd manage to 'live.' And he's not a cad like Charlie Perigal," cried Miss Toombs, as she hurried off to work.

When Mavis got back, she learned that the morning post had brought an invitation for the Devitts and herself for a dinner that Major Perigal was giving in two weeks' time. Major Perigal, also, wrote privately to Mavis, urging her to give him the honour of her company; he assured her that his son would not be present.

Little else but the approaching dinner was discussed by the Devitts for the rest of the day. As if to palliate their interest in the matter, they explained to Mavis how the proffered hospitality was alien to the ways of the giver of the feast. At heart they were greatly pleased with the invitation; it promised a meeting with county folk on equal terms, together with a termination to the aloofness with which Major Perigal had treated the Devitts since his son's marriage to Victoria. They accepted with alacrity. Mavis, alone, hesitated.

Her husband urged her to go, although his physical disability would prevent him from accompanying her.

"I want my dearest to go," he said. "It will give me so much pleasure to know how wonderful you looked, and how everyone admired you."

Mavis decided to accept the invitation, largely because it was her husband's wish; a little, because she had the curiosity to meet those who would have been acquaintances and friends had her father been alive. Her lot had been thrown so much among those who worked for daily bread, that she was not a little eager to mix, if it were only for a few hours, with her own social kind.

Mavis, again at Harold's wish, reluctantly ordered an expensive frock for the dinner. It was of grey taffetas embroidered upon bodice and skirt with black velvet butterflies. The night of the dinner, when Mavis was ready to go, she showed herself to her husband before setting out. He looked at her long and intently before saying:

"I shall always remember you like this."

"What do you mean?" she asked, a little afraid.

"It isn't what I expect. It's what I deserve for marrying a glorious young creature like you."

"Am I discontented?" she asked proudly.

"God bless you. You're as good as you're beautiful," he replied.

As she stooped to kiss him, the prayer of her heart was:

"May he never know why I married him."

His eyes, alight with love, followed her as she left the room.

Major Perigal received his guests in the drawing-room. The first person whom Mavis encountered after she had greeted her host was Windebank. She recalled that she had not seen him since her illness at Mrs Trivett's, He had written to congratulate her on her marriage when she had come to stay with the Devitts; since then, she had not heard from him.

Although Mavis knew that she might see him to-night, she was so taken aback at meeting him that she could think of nothing to say. He relieved her embarrassment by talking commonplace.

"Here's someone who much wishes to meet you," he said presently. "It's Sir William Ludlow; he served with your father in India."

Mavis knew the name of Sir William Ludlow as that of a general with a long record of distinguished service.

When he was introduced by Windebank, Mavis saw that he had soldier written all over his wiry, spare person; she congratulated herself upon meeting a man who might talk of the stirring events in which he had taken so prominent a part. He had only time to tell Mavis how she more resembled her mother than her father when a move was made for the dining-room. Mavis was taken down by Windebank.

"Thank you," she said in an undertone, when they had reached the landing.

"What for?"

"All you've done."

He turned on her such a look of pain that she did not say any more.

Windebank sat on her right; General Sir William Ludlow on her left. Directly opposite was a little pasty-faced woman with small, bright eyes. Victoria, by virtue of her relationship to Major Perigal, faced her father-in-law at the bottom of the table; upon her right sat the most distinguished-looking man Mavis had ever seen. Tall, finely proportioned, with noble, regular features, surmounted by grey hair, he suggested to Mavis a fighting bishop of the middle ages: she wondered who he was. The soldier on her left talked incessantly, but, to Mavis's surprise, he made no mention of his campaigns; he spoke of nothing else but rose culture, his persistent ill-luck at flower shows, the unfairness of the judging. The meal was long and, even to Mavis, to whom a dinner party was in the nature of an experience, tedious.

Infrequent relief was supplied by the pasty-faced woman opposite, who was the General's wife; she did her best to shock the susceptibilities of those present by being in perpetual opposition to their stolid views.

An elderly woman, whose face showed the ravages of time upon what must have been considerable beauty (somehow she looked rather disreputable), had referred to visits she had paid, when in London for the season, to a sister who lived in Eccleston Square.

"Such a dreadful neighbourhood!" she complained. "It made me quite ill to go there."

"I love it," declared Lady Ludlow.

"That part of London!" exclaimed the faded beauty.

"Why not? Whatever life may be there, it is honest in its unconcealment. And to be genuine is to be noble."

"You're joking, Kate," protested the faded beauty.

"I'm doing nothing of the kind. Give me Pimlico," declared Lady Ludlow emphatically.

At mention of Pimlico, Mavis and Windebank involuntarily glanced into each other's eyes; the name of this district recalled many memories to their minds.

When dinner was over, Mavis had hardly reached the drawing-room with the women-folk, when Lady Ludlow pounced upon her.

"I've been so anxious to meet you," she declared. "You're one of the lucky ones."

"Since when am I lucky?" asked Mavis.

"Since your father died and you had to earn your living till you were married. Old Jimmy Perigal told me all about it. You're to be envied."

"I fail to see why."

"You've mixed with the world and have escaped living with all these stuffy bores."

"They don't know how lucky they are," remarked Mavis with conviction.

"Nonsense! Give me life and the lower orders. What did my husband talk about during dinner?"

"Roses."

"Of course. When he was at his wars, I had some peace. Now I'm bored to death with flowers."

"Who was that distinguished-looking man who sat on Mrs Charles Perigal's right?" asked Mavis.

"That's Lord Robert Keevil, whose brother is the great tin-god 'Seend.'"

"The Marquis of Seend?" queried Mavis.

"That's it: he was foreign minister in the last Government. But Bobbie Keevil is adorable till he's foolish enough to open his mouth. Then he gives the game away."

"What do you mean?"

"He's the complete fool. If he would only hold his tongue, he might be a success. His wife is over there. Her eyes are always weeping for the loss of her beauty. Your father wanted to marry her in his youth. But give me people who don't bother about such tiresome conventionalities as marriage."

Mavis looked curiously at the woman whom her father had loved. Doubtless, she was comely in her youth, but now Mavis saw pouched eyes, thin hair, a care-lined face not altogether innocent of paint and powder. And it was those cracked lips her father had longed to kiss; those dim eyes, the thought of which had, perhaps, shortened his hours of rest! The sight of the faded beauty brought home to Mavis the vanity of earthly love, till she reflected that, had the one-time desire of her father's heart been gratified, the sorrow they would have shared in common would ever endear her to his heart, and keep her the fairest woman the earth possessed, for all the defacement time might make in her appearance.

When the men came up from the dining-room, there was intermittent music in which Mavis took part. The sincerity of her voice, together with its message of tears, awoke genuine approval in her audience.

"An artiste, my dear," declared Lady Ludlow. "Artistes have always a touch of vulgarity in their natures, or they wouldn't make their appeal. We must be great friends. I'm sick to death of correct people."

For the rest of the evening, Mavis noticed how she herself was constantly watched by Windebank and Major Perigal, the former of whom dropped his eyes when he saw that Mavis perceived the direction of his glance. As the evening wore on, Mavis was faintly bored and not a little troubled. She reflected that it was in these very rooms that Charlie Perigal had read her piteous little letters from London, and from where he probably penned his lying replies. Mavis would have liked to have been alone so that she could try to appreciate the whys and wherefores of the most significant events in her life. The conditions of her last stay in London and those of her present life were as the poles apart so far as material well-being was concerned; her mind ached to fasten upon some explanation that would reconcile the tragic events in her life with her one-time implicit faith in the certain protection extended by a Heavenly Father to His trusting children. Perhaps it was as well that Mavis was again asked to sing; the effort of remembering her words put all such thoughts from her mind.

Whatever clouds may have gathered about Mavis's appreciation of the evening, there was no doubt of the enjoyment of those Devitts who were present. The dinner was, to them, an event of social moment in their lives. Although they looked as if they had got into the dignified atmosphere of Major Perigal's drawing-room by mistake, they were greatly delighted with their evening; afterwards, they did not fail to make copious references to those they had met at dinner to their Melkbridge friends.

A month after the dinner, Major Perigal died suddenly in his chair. Two days after he was buried, Mavis received an intimation from his solicitors, which requested her presence at the reading of his will. Wondering what was toward, Mavis made an appointment. To her boundless astonishment, she learned that Major Perigal, "on account of the esteem in which he held the daughter of his old friend, Colonel Keeves," had left Mavis all his worldly goods, with the exception of bequests to servants and five hundred pounds to his son Charles.

CHAPTER FORTY
A MIDNIGHT WALK

Thus it would seem as if fate wished to make amends for the sorry tricks it had played Mavis. Her first impressions after hearing the news were of such a contradictory nature that she was quite bewildered. Those present at the reading of the will, together with Montague Devitt, who had accompanied her, hastened to offer their congratulations (those of Devitt being chastened by the reflection of how much his daughter Victoria suffered from Mavis's good fortune), but, even while these were talking and shaking her hand, two salient emotions were already emerging from the welter in Mavis's mind. One of these was an immeasurable, passionate regret for her child's untimely death. If he had lived, she would now have been able to devote her sudden enrichment to providing him, not only with the comforts that wealth can secure, but also with a career when he should come to man's estate. The other emotion possessing her was the inevitable effect of unexpected good fortune on a great and persistent remorse: more than ever, she suffered tortures of self-reproach for having set out to marry her husband from motives of revenge against his family. Whilst thus occupied with her thoughts, she became conscious that someone was watching her; she turned in the direction from which she believed she was being regarded, to see Charlie Perigal with his eyes fixed on her. She looked him full in the eyes, the while she was relieved to find that his presence did not affect the beating of her heart. Seeing that she did not avoid his glance, he came over to her.

"I congratulate you," he said.

"Thank you," she replied indifferently.

"I have also to congratulate you on your marriage—that is, if you are happy."

"I am very happy," she declared with conviction.

"That's more than I am."

"Indeed!" she remarked carelessly.

"Although, in some respects, I deserve all I've got—I'm bad and mean right through."

"Indeed!" said Mavis, as before.

"But there's something to be said for me. To begin with, no one can help being what they are. There's no more merit in your being good than there is demerit in my being what I am."

"Did I ever lay claim to goodness?"

"Because you didn't, it goes nearer to making you good and admirable than anything else you could do. Directly virtue becomes self-conscious, it is vulgar."

Mavis began to wonder if it would ease the pain at her heart if she were to confess her duplicity to her husband.

Perigal continued:

"An act is judged by its results; it is considered either virtuous or vicious according as its results are harmful or helpful to the person affected."

"Indeed!" said Mavis absently.

"Once upon a time, there was no right and no wrong, till one man in the human tribe got more than his fair share of arrow-heads—then, his wish to keep them without fighting for them led to the begetting of vice and virtue as we know it."

"How was that?" asked Mavis, striving to escape from her distracting emotions by following what Perigal was saying.

"The man with the arrow-heads hired a chap with a gift of the gab to tell the others how wrong it was to want things someone else had collared. That was the first lesson in morality, and the preacher, seeing there was money in the game, started the first priesthood. Yes, morality owes its existence to the fact of the well-to-do requiring to be confirmed in their possessions without having to defend them by force."

Mavis was now paying no attention to Perigal's talk: mind and heart were in Pennington Churchyard. Perigal, thinking he was interesting Mavis, went on:

"You mayn't think it, but a bad egg like me does no end of a lot of good in the world, although downright criminals do more. If it weren't for people who interfered with others' belongings, the race would get slack and deteriorate. It's having to look after one's property which keeps people alert and up to the mark, and, therefore, those who're the cause of this fitness have their uses. No, my dear Mavis, evil is a necessary ingredient of the body politic, and if it were abolished to-morrow the race would go to 'pot.'"

Perigal said more to the same effect. Mavis was, presently, moved to remark:

"You take the loss of the money you expected very calmly."

"No wonder!"

"No wonder?" she queried, without expressing any surprise in her voice.

"To begin with, you have it. Then I've seen you."

Mavis thought for a moment before saying:

"I suppose, as I'm another man's wife, I ought to be angry at that remark."

"Aren't you?" he asked eagerly.

She did not reply directly; perhaps some recognition of the coldness with which she regarded him penetrated his understanding, for he added pleadingly:

"Don't say you don't mind because you're absolutely indifferent to me!"

"Why not?"

"Anything but that," he said, while a distressed look crept into his eyes. "But then, if you speak the truth, you couldn't say that after all that has—

"I'm going to speak the truth," she interrupted. "It doesn't interest me to say anything else."

"Well?" he exclaimed anxiously.

"I don't in the least mind what you said. And I'm not in the least offended, because, whatever you might ever say or do, it would never interest me."

He stared at her helplessly for a few moments before saying:

"Serve me jolly well right."

Mavis did not say any more, at which Perigal got up to leave her.

"I've been a precious fool," he muttered, after glancing at Mavis's face before moving away.

Devitt scarcely spoke whilst driving Mavis home; consequently, her thoughts had free play. It would certainly ease her mind, she reflected, if she made full confession to her husband of the reasons that impelled her to make his acquaintance and accept his offer of marriage; but it then occurred to her that this tranquillity of soul would be bought at the price, not only of his implicit faith in her, but of his happiness. Therefore, whatever pangs of remorse it was destined for her to suffer, he must never know; she being the offender, it was not meet that she should shift the burden of pain from her shoulders to his. Her sufferings were her punishment for her wrongdoing.

Mrs Devitt and Miss Spraggs were silent when they learned of Mavis's good fortune; they were torn between enhanced respect for Harold's wife and concern for Victoria, who had married a penniless man. Mavis could not gauge the effect of the news on Victoria, as she had gone back to London after Major Perigal's funeral, her husband remaining at Melkbridge for the reading of the will. Harold, alone among the Devitts, exhibited frank dismay at his wife's good fortune.

"Aren't you glad, dearest?" asked Mavis.

"For your sake."

"Why not for yours?"

"It's the thing most likely to separate us."

"Separate us!" she cried in amazement.

"Why not? This money will put you in the place in life you are entitled to fill."

Mavis stared at him in astonishment.

"With your appearance and talents you should be a great social success with the people who matter," he continued.

"Nonsense!"

"You undervalue your wonderful self. I should never have been so selfish as to marry you."

"You don't regret it?"

"For the great happiness it has brought me—no. But when I think how you might have made a great marriage and had a real home—"

"Aren't we going to have a real home?" she interrupted.

"Are we?"

"If it's love that makes the home, we have one whatever our condition," declared Mavis.

"Thank you for saying that. But what I meant was that children are wanted to make the perfect home."

Mavis's face fell.

"You, with your rare nature, must want to have a child," he continued. "I don't know which must be worse: for a childless woman to long for a child or to have one and lose it."

Mavis grasped the arm of the chair for support.

"What's the matter?" he asked, alarmed.

"What you said. Don't, don't say I'm dissatisfied any more."

Thus Mavis and those nearest to her learned of the alteration in her fortunes.

Mavis was not long in discovering that the command of money provided her with a means of escape from the prepossessions afflicting her mind. The first thing she did was to summon the most renowned nerve specialists to Melkbridge, where they held a lengthy consultation in respect of Harold's physical condition. Mavis was anxious to know if anything could be done to strengthen the slender thread of his life; she was much distressed to learn that the specialists' united skill could do nothing to stay the pitiless course of his disease. This verdict provided a further sorrow for Mavis, which she had to keep resolutely to herself, inasmuch as she told Harold that the doctors had spoken most favourably of the chances of his obtaining considerable alleviation of his physical distresses.

"And then you regret my coming into all this money, when it can do so much for you," she said, with a fine assumption of cheerfulness.

To get some distraction from her many troubles, Mavis next set about seeking out all the people who had ever been kind to her in order that they should benefit from her good fortune.

It did not take her long to discover that Miss Annie Mee was dead; but for all she and her solicitors were able to do, they could find no trace of 'Melia. Mavis paid Mr Poulter's debts, gave him a present of a hundred pounds (endowing the academy he called it), and, in memory of Miss Nippett, she gave "Turpsichor" two fine new coats of paint. Mavis also discovered where Miss Nippett was buried, and, finding that the grave had no headstone, she ordered one. To Mrs Scatchard and her niece she made handsome presents, and gave Mr Napper a finely bound edition of the hundred best books; whilst Mr and Mrs Trivett were made comfortable for life. Mavis was unable to find two people she was anxious to help. These were the "Permanent" and the "Lil" of Halverton Street days. One day, clad in shabby garments, she went to Mrs Gowler's address at New Cross to get news of the former. But the house of evil remembrance was to let; a woman at the next door house told Mavis that Mrs Gowler had been arrested and had got ten years for the misdeeds which the police had at last been able to prove. Mavis went on a similar errand to Halverton Street, to find that Lil had long since left and that there was no one in the house who knew of her whereabouts. She had been lost in one of the many foul undercurrents of London life. The one remaining person Mavis wished to benefit was Miss Toombs. For a long time, this independent-minded young woman resisted the offers that Mavis made her. One day, however, when Miss Toombs was laid up with acute indigestion, Mavis prevailed on her to accept a handsome cheque which would enable her to do what she pleased for the rest of her life, without endangering the happiness she derived from tea, buttered toast, and hot-water bottles in winter.

"It was unkind of you not to take it before," said Mavis.

Miss Toombs looked stupidly at her benefactor.

"Now I know you want to thank me. Good night," said Mavis, as she put out her hand.

Miss Toombs took it, gripped it, and then turned round with her face to the wall. The next morning, Mavis received a letter from her in pencil. In this, she told Mavis that the desire of her life had been for independence; but that she had held out against taking the money because she had latterly become jealous of Mavis, owing to Windebank's lifelong infatuation for her.

In addition to these benefactions, Mavis insisted on repaying Windebank for all the expense he had been put to for her illness, her child's funeral, and for her long stay at Swanage.

Thus, Mavis's first concern was to benefit those who had shown her kindness; whether or not she added to the sum of their individual happiness is another matter. Mr Poulter, doubtless, thought that dear Mrs Harold Devitt, while she was about it, might just as well have gilded "Turpsichor's" head and face. Mrs Scatchard, and particularly Miss Meakin, were probably resentful that Mavis did not ask them to mix with her swell friends; whilst Miss Toombs had plenty of time on her hands in which to indulge in vain regrets because she was not as attractive and finely formed as Mavis.

Beyond these gifts, it was a long time before Mavis could get into the habit of spending her substance freely, and without thought of whether she could really afford to part with money; the reason being that, for so many years in her life, she had had to consider so carefully every penny she spent, that she found it difficult to break away from these habits of economy. Late in the year, she moved up from her Melkbridge place (which she had long since gone into) to the house in town which Major Perigal had been in the habit of letting, or, if a tenant were not forthcoming, shutting up.

When she got there with Harold and Jill, she welcomed the distractions that London life offered, and in which her husband joined so far as his physical disability would permit. Windebank, to whom Harold took a great liking, and Lady Ludlow introduced Mavis to their many acquaintances. In a very short time, Mavis had more dear, devoted friends than she knew what to do with. The women, who praised her and her devotion "to a perfect dear of a husband" to her face, would, after enjoying her hospitality, go away to discuss openly how soon she would elope with Windebank, or any other man they fancied was paying her attention.

Mavis was not a little surprised by the almost uniform behaviour of the men who frequented her house. Old or young, rich or impecunious, directly they perceived how comely Mavis was, and that her husband was an invalid, did not hesitate to consider her fair game to be bagged as soon as may be. Looks, manners, veiled words, betrayed their thoughts; but, somehow, even the hardiest veteran amongst them did not get so far as a declaration of love. Something in Mavis's demeanour suggested a dispassionate summing up of their desires and limitations, in which the latter made the former appear a trifle ridiculous, and restrained the words that were ever on their tongues. This propensity on the part of men who, Mavis thought, ought to know better, occasioned her much disquiet. She confided these tribulations to Lady Ludlow's ear.

"Men are all alike all the world over," remarked the latter, on hearing Mavis's complaint. "You can't trust 'em further than you can see 'em."

"Not all, surely," replied Mavis, thinking of the innocuous young men, indigenous to Shepherd's Bush, whom she had so often danced with at "Poulter's."

"Anyhow, men in our class of life are all at one on that point. Directly they see a pretty woman, their one idea is to get hold of her."

"I wouldn't believe it, unless I'd seen for myself the truth of it."

"It's a great pity all of our sex didn't realise it; but then it would make the untempted more morally righteous than ever," declared Lady Ludlow.

"But if a man really and truly loves a woman—"

"That's another story altogether. A woman is always safe with the man who loves her."

"Because his love is her best protection?"

"Assuredly."

The sudden reflection that Perigal had never really loved her produced, strangely enough, in Mavis a sharp but short-lived revulsion of feeling in his favour. On the whole, Mavis's, heart inclined to social gaiety. To begin with, the constant change afforded by a succession of events which, although all of a piece, were to her unseasoned senses ever varying, provided some relief from the remorse and suffering that were always more or less in possession of her heart. Also, having for all her life been cut off from the gaieties natural to her age and kind, her present innocent dissipations were a satisfaction of this long repressed social instinct.

But, at all times, Windebank's conduct was a puzzle. Although he had the run of the house, although scarcely a day passed without Mavis seeing a good deal of him, he never betrayed by word or look the love which Miss Toombs declared burned within him for Mavis. He had left the service in order to devote more time to his Wiltshire property, but his duties seemed to consist chiefly in making himself useful to Mavis or her husband. Womanlike, Mavis would sometimes try to discover her power over him, but although no trouble was too great for him to take in order to oblige her, Mavis's most provoking moods neither weakened his allegiance nor made him other than his calm, collected self.

"No! Miss Toombs is mistaken," thought Mavis. "He doesn't love me; he but understands and pities me."

A week before Christmas, Mavis and her husband returned to Melkbridge. Christmas Day that year fell on a Sunday. Upon the preceding Saturday, she bade her many Melkbridge acquaintances to the feast. When this was over, she wished her guests good night and a happy Christmas. After seeing her husband safely abed and asleep, she set about making preparations for a project that she had long had in her mind. Going to her room, she put on the plainest and most inconspicuous hat she could find; she also donned a long cloak and concealed face and hair in a thick veil. Unlocking a box, she got out a cross made of holly, which she concealed under her cloak. Then, after listening to see if the house were quiet, she went downstairs in her stockings, and carrying the thick boots she purposed wearing. Arrived at the front door, the bolts and bars of which she had secretly oiled, she opened this after putting on her boots, and let herself out into the night. Vigorous clouds now and again obscured the stars: the world seemed full of a great peace. Mavis waited to satisfy herself that she had not awakened anyone in the house; she then struck out in the direction of Pennington. It was only on the rarest occasions that Mavis could visit her boy's grave, when she had to employ the greatest circumspection to avoid being seen. Although since her translation from insignificance to affluence and local importance, she was remarkably well known in and about Melkbridge, and although her lightest acts were subjects of common gossip, she could not let Christmas go by without taking the risk that a visit to the churchyard at Pennington would entail. Her greatest fear of detection was in going through the town, but she kept well under the shadows of the town hall side of the market-place, so that the policeman, who was there on duty, walking-stick in hand, would not see her. Once in the comparative security of the Pennington road, she hurried past dark inanimate cottages and farmsteads, whilst overhead familiar constellations sprawled in a now clear sky. Several times on her progress, she fancied that she heard footsteps striking the hard, firm road behind her, but, whenever she stopped to listen, she could not hear a sound. Just as she reached the brewery at Pennington, clouds obscured the stars; she had some difficulty in picking her way in the darkness. When she got to the churchyard gate, happily unlocked, it was still so dark that she had to light matches in order to avoid stumbling on the graves. Even with the help of matches, it was as much as she could do to find her way to the plain white stone on which only the initials of her boy and the dates of his birth and death were recorded. When she got to the grave, the wind had blown out so many of her matches that she had only four left. One of these she lit in order to place the holly cross on the grave; she had just time to put it where she wanted it to lie, when the match went out. She knelt on the ground, while her heart went out to what was lying so many feet beneath.

"Oh, my dear! my dear!" she cried, but the sound of her own voice startled her into silence. The cry of her heart was:

"What is all that I have worth without you! How gladly would I give up my all, if only I could hold you warm and breathing in my arms!"

Then she fell to thinking what a joyous time would be hers at this season of the year, were her boy alive and if they were going to spend Christmas together. Pain possessed her; its operation seemed to isolate her from the world that she had lately known. She breathed an atmosphere of anguish; the mourning that the presence of those in the churchyard had caused their loved ones seemed to find expression in her heart, till, happily, tears eased her pain.

Then she became conscious of the physical discomfort occasioned by kneeling on the ground in the cold night air.

She got up. In order to take a last look at the grave, she lit another match. This burned steadily, enabling her to glance about her to see what companionship her boy possessed on this drear December night. The feeble match flame intensified the gloom and emphasised the deep, black quietude of the place. This hamlet of the dead was amazingly remote from all suggestions of life. It appeared to hug itself for its complete detachment from human interests. It seemed desolate, alone, forgotten by the world. As Mavis left its stillness, she thought:

"At least he's found a great peace."

Before Mavis left the churchyard, the stars enabled her to discern her path. She hastened in the direction of Melkbridge, wondering if her absence had been discovered. As before, she believed that she was followed, but strove to think that the footsteps she was all but certain she heard were the echo of her own. As she hurried through the town, this impression became a conviction. She was alarmed, and resolved to find out who it was who had elected to spy upon her actions. When she came to the place where the road branched off to her house, she concealed herself in the shadow of the wall. She had not long to wait. Very soon, the tall upright figure of a man swung into the road in which she was standing. One glance was enough to tell her that it was Windebank. As he was about to pass her, he paused as if to listen.

"Who are you looking for?" asked Mavis, who was anxious to discover what he was doing out of doors.

"Let me see you home," he said coldly.

"If anyone sees us, they will think—" she began.

"We shan't meet anyone. It's not safe for you to be out."

They walked in silence. As he did not express the least surprise at finding her out alone in the small hours of the morning, Mavis believed that he had divined her intention of going to Pennington and had hung about the house till she had come out, when he had followed, all the way to and from her destination, in order to protect her from harm.

"Good night," he said, as he stopped just before they reached the nearest lodge gates of her grounds.

"Good night and thank you," replied Mavis.

"I won't wish you a very happy Christmas."

"May I wish you one?"

"Good night," he answered curtly.

CHAPTER FORTY-ONE
TRIBULATION

Although, as time went on, Mavis became used to her griefs, and although she got pleasure from the opulent, cultured atmosphere with which she was surrounded, she was neither physically nor spiritually happy. It was not that the mutual love existing between herself and Harold abated one jot; neither was it that she had lost overmuch of her old joyousness in nature and life. But there were two voids in her being (one of which she knew could never be filled) which were the cause of her distress. A woman of strong domestic instincts, she would have loved nothing better than to have had one or two children. Owing to her changed circumstances, maternity would not be associated with the acute discomforts which she had once experienced. Whenever she heard of a woman of her acquaintance having a baby, her face would change, her heart would be charged with a consuming envy. Illustrations of children's garments in the advertisement columns of women's journals caused her to turn the page quickly. Whenever little ones visited her, she would often, particularly if the guest were a boy, furtively hug him to her heart. Once or twice, on these occasions, she caught Windebank's eye, when she wondered if he understood her longing.

Her other hunger was for things of the spirit. She was as one adrift upon a sea of doubt; many havens noticed her signals of distress, but, despite the arrant display of their attractions, she could not find one that promised anchorage to which she could completely trust. Her old-time implicit faith in the existence of a Heavenly Father, who cared for the sparrows of life, had waned. Whenever the simple belief recurred to her, as it sometimes did, she would think of Mrs Gowler's, to shudder and put the thought of beneficent interference with the things of the world from her mind.

At the same time she could not forget that when there had seemed every prospect of her being lost in the mire of London, or in the slough of anguish following upon her boy's death, she had, as if by a miracle, escaped.

Now and again, she would find herself wondering if, after all, the barque of her life had been steered by a guiding Hand, which, although it had taken her over storm-tossed seas and stranded her on lone beaches, had brought her safely, if troubled by the wrack of the waters she had passed, into harbour.

Incapable of clear thought, she could arrive at no conclusion that satisfied her.

At last, she went to Windebank to see if he could help.

"What is one to do if one isn't altogether happy?" she asked.

"Who isn't happy?"

"I'm not altogether."

"You! But you've everything to make you."

"I know. But I'll try and explain."

"You needn't."

"Why? You don't know what troubles me."

"That's nothing to do with it. All troubles are alike in this respect, that the only thing to be done is to mend what's wrong. If you can't, you must make the best of it," he declared grimly.

After this rough-and-ready advice, Mavis felt that it would be futile to attempt a further explanation of her disquiet.

"Thanks; but it isn't so easy as it sounds," she said.

"Really!" he remarked, not without a suggestion of sarcasm in his exclamation.

About this time, Mavis saw a good deal of Perigal. He rented from her husband the farm that Harold had purchased soon after his marriage, and in which he had purposed living. Perigal had long since spent the ten thousand pounds he had inherited from his mother; he was now living on the four hundred a year his wife possessed. If anything, Mavis encouraged his frequent visits; his illuminating comments on men and things took her out of herself; also, if the truth be told, Mavis's heart held resentment against the man who had played so considerable a part in her life. Whenever Mavis was in London, the sight of a fallen woman always fed this dislike; she reflected that, but for the timely help she had enjoyed, she might have been driven to a like means of getting money if her child had been in want. Another thing that urged her against Perigal was that she constantly noticed how negligently many of the married women of her acquaintance interpreted their wifely duties, and, in most cases, to husbands who had dowered their mates with affection and worldly goods. She reflected that, by all the laws of justice, Perigal should have appreciated to the full the treasure of love and passion which she had poured out so lavishly at his feet.

Perigal, all unconscious of the way in which Mavis regarded him, went out of his way to pay her attention.

One summer afternoon, while Harold rested indoors, Mavis gave Perigal tea beneath the shade of a witch-elm on the lawn. She was looking particularly alluring; if she were at all doubtful of this fact, the admiration expressed in Perigal's eyes would have reassured her. They had been talking lightly, brightly, each in secret pursuing the bent of their own feelings for the other, when the spectre of Mavis's spiritual troublings blotted out the sunlight and the brilliant gladness of the summer afternoon. She was silent for awhile, presently to be aware that Perigal's eyes were fixed on her face. She looked towards him, at which he sighed deeply.

"Aren't you happy?" she asked.

"How can I be?"

"You've everything you want in life."

"Have I? Since when?"

"The day you married."

"Rot!"

"What do you mean?"

"I can tell you after all that" (here he caught Mavis's eye)—"after we've been such friends—as far as I'm concerned, my marriage has been a ghastly failure."

"You mustn't tell me that," declared Mavis, to whom the news brought a secret joy.

"I can surely tell you after—after we've been such dear friends. But we don't hit it off at all. I can't stick Vic at any price."

"Nonsense! She's pretty and charming. Everyone who knows her says the same."

"When they first know her; then they think no end of a lot of her; but after a time everyone's 'off' her, although they haven't spotted the reason."

"Have you?"

"Unfortunately, that's been my privilege. Vic has enough imagination to tell her to do the right thing and all that; but otherwise, she's utterly, constitutionally cold."

"Nonsense! She must have sympathy to 'do the right thing,' as you call it."

"Not necessarily. Hers comes from the imagination, as I told you; but her graceful tact chills one in no time. I might as well have married an icicle."

"I'm sorry," remarked Mavis, saying what was untrue.

"And then Vic has a conventional mind: it annoys me awfully. Conventions are the cosmetics of morality."

"Where did you read that?"

"And these conventions, that are the rudiments of what were once full-blooded necessities, are most practised by those who have the least call for their protection. Pity me."

"I do."

Perigal's eyes brightened.

"I'm unhappy too," said Mavis, after a pause.

"Not really?"

"I wondered if you would help me."

"Try me."

Perigal's eyes glittered, a manifestation which Mavis noticed.

"You know how you used to laugh at my belief in Providence."

"Is that how you want me to help?"

"If you will."

Perigal's face fell.

"Fire away," he said, as he lit a cigarette.

Mavis told him something of her perplexities.

"I want to see things clearly. I want to find out exactly where I am. Everything's so confusing and contradictory. I shan't be really happy till I know what I really and truly believe."

"How can I help you? You have to believe what you do believe."

"But why do I believe what I do believe?"

"Because you can't help yourself. Your present condition of mind is the result of all you have experienced in your existence acting upon the peculiar kind of intelligence with which your parents started you in life. Take my advice, don't worry about these things. If you look them squarely in the face, you only come to brutal conclusions. Life's a beastly struggle to live, and then, when subsistence is secured, to be happy. It's nature's doing; it sees to it that we're always sharpening our weapons."

Mavis did not speak for a few moments; when she did, it was to say:

"I can't understand how I escaped."

"From utter disaster?" he asked.

"Scarcely that."

"I hope not, indeed. But you were a fool not to write to me and let me have it for my selfishness. But I take it that at the worst you'd have written, when, of course, I should have done all I could."

"All?"

"Well—all I reasonably could."

"I wasn't thinking so much of that," said Mavis. "What I can't understand is why I've dropped into all this good fortune, even if it's at your expense."

"You owe it to the fact of your being your father's daughter and that he was friendly with the pater. Next, you must thank your personality; but the chief thing was that you are your father's daughter."

"And I often and often wished I'd been born a London shop-girl, so that I should never long for things that were then out of my reach. So there was really something in my birth after all."

"I should jolly well think there was. It's no end of an asset. But to go back to what we were talking about."

"About nature's designs to make us all fight for our own?"

"Yes. Look at yourself. You're now ever so much harder than you were."

"Are you surprised?" she asked vehemently, as she all but betrayed her hatred.

"It's really a good thing from your point of view. It's made you more fitted to take your own part in the struggle."

"Then, those who injured me were the strong preying on the weak?" she asked.

"It's the unalterable law of life. It's a disagreeable one, but it's true. It's the only way the predominance of the species is assured."

"I think I'll have a cigarette," said Mavis.

"One of mine?"

"One of my own, thanks."

"You're very unkind to me," said Perigal.

"In not taking your cigarette?"

"You ignore everything that's been between us. You look on me as heartless, callous; you don't make allowances."

"For what?"

"My cursed temperament. No one knows better than I what a snob I am at heart. When you were poor, I did not value you. Now—"

"Now?"

"Can you ask?"

A joy possessed Mavis's heart; she felt that her moment of triumph was near.

Perigal went on:

"Still, I deserve all I get, and that's so rare in life that it's something in the nature of an experience."

Mavis did not speak. She was hoping no one would come to interrupt them.

"There's one thing you might have told me about," he went on.

"What?"

Perigal dropped his eyes as he said:

"Someone who died."

Mavis's heart was pitiless.

"Why should I?"

"He was mine as much as yours. There are several things I want to know. And if it were the last word I utter, all that happened over that has 'hipped' me more than anything."

"I shall tell you nothing," declared Mavis.

"I've a right to know."

"No."

"Why not?"

"I tell you, no. You left me to fight alone; it was all so terrible, I daren't think of it more than I can help."

"But—"

"There are no 'buts,' no anything. I bore the sorrow alone, and I shall keep to myself all the tenderness that remains: nothing can ever alter it."

"You say that as if you hated me. Don't do that, little Mavis. I love you more than I do my mean selfish self."

"You love me!"

"I do now. I wanted you to know. Once or twice, I hoped—never mind what. But from the way you said what you said just now, I see it's utterly 'off.'"

"You never said anything truer. And do you know why?" she asked with flaming eye.

"Because I left you in the lurch?"

"Not altogether that, but because you were a coward, and, above all, a fool, in the first place. I know what I was. I see what other women are, and it makes me realise my value. I realise my value as, if you'd married me, I'd have faced death, anything with you. Pretty women with a few brains who'll stick to a man are rather scarce nowadays. But it wasn't good enough for you: you wouldn't take the risk. You've no—no stuffing. That is why, if you and I were left alone in the world together for the rest of our lives, I should never do anything but despise you."

Perigal's face went white. He bit his thin lips. Then he smiled as he said:

"Retributive justice."

"I'm sorry to be so candid. But it's what I've been thinking for months. I've only waited for an opportunity to say it."

"We've both scored," he said. "You can't take away what you've given, and that's a lot to be thankful for—but—but—"

"Well?"

"I'm dependent for my bread and butter on a woman who bores me to death, and have to look to a family for any odd jobs I may get—a family that, whatever they may do for me, I should always despise. That, and because I see what a fool I've been to lose you, is where you've scored."

As he strolled away, wondering how Mavis could be so indifferent to him after all that had happened, she did not trouble to glance after his retreating form.

Henceforth, Mavis was left much to herself. Perigal avoided her; whilst Windebank, about this time, to her annoyance, discontinued his frequent visits. Having so much time on her hands, Mavis returned to her old prepossessions about the why and wherefore of the varied happenings in her life.

Looking back, she found that her loving trust, her faith in her lover, her girlish innocence of the ways of sensual men had been chiefly responsible for her griefs; that it was indeed, as Perigal said, that she in her weakness had been preyed upon by the strong. Thus, it followed that girlish confidence in the loved one's word, the primal instinct of abnegation of self to the adored one, whole-hearted faith—all these characteristics (which were above price) of a loving heart were in the nature of a handicap in the struggle for happiness. It also followed that a girl thus equipped would be at a great disadvantage in rivalry with one who was cold, selfish, calculating. Mavis shuddered as she reached this conclusion.

Her introspections were interrupted by an event that, for the time, put all such thoughts from her mind.

One morning, upon going into Harold's room, she found that he did not recognise her. The local doctor, who usually attended him, was called in; he immediately asked for another opinion. This being obtained from London, the remedies the specialist prescribed proved so far beneficial that the patient dimly recovered the use of his senses, with the faint promise of further improvement if the medical instructions were obeyed to the letter. Then followed for Mavis long, scarcely endurable night watches, which were so protracted that often it seemed as if the hand of time had stopped, as if darkness for ever enshrouded the world. When, at last, day came, she would make an effort to snatch a few hours' sleep in order to fit her for the next night's attendance on the loved one. The shock of her husband's illness immediately increased her faith in Divine Providence. It was as if her powerlessness in the face of this new disaster were such that she relied on something more than human aid to give her help. Always, before she tried to sleep, she prayed long and fervently to the Most High that He would restore her beloved husband to comparative health; that He would interfere to arrest the fell disease with which he was afflicted. She prayed as a mother for a child, sick unto death. At the back of her mind she had formed a resolution that, if her prayer were answered, she would believe in God for the rest of her life with all her old-time fervour. She dared not voice this resolve to herself; she believed that, if she did so, it would be in the nature of a threat to the Almighty; also, she feared that, if her husband got worse, it would be consequently incumbent on her to lose the much needed faith in things not of this world. Thus, when Mavis knelt she poured out her heart in supplication. She was not only praying for her husband but for herself.

But Mavis's prayer was unheard. Her husband steadily got worse. One night, when the blackness of the sky seemed as a pall thrown over the corpse of her hopes, she took up a chance magazine, in which some verses, written to God by an author, for whose wide humanity Mavis had a great regard, attracted her.

The substance of these lines was a complaint of His pitiless disregard of the world's sorrow. One phrase particularly attracted her: it was "His unweeting way."

"That is it," thought Mavis. "That expresses exactly what I feel. There is, there must be, a God, but His ways are truly unweeting. He has seen so much pain that He has got used to it and grown callous."

CHAPTER FORTY-TWO
THE WELL-BELOVED

One morning, when Mavis was leaving Harold, she was recalled by one of the nurses. He had signalled that he wished to see her again. Upon Mavis hastening to his side, he tried to speak, but could not. His eyes seemed to smile a last farewell till unconsciousness possessed him.

As before, Mavis called in the most expensive medical advice, which told her that nothing could be done. It appeared that Harold's spine had commenced to curve in such a manner that his lungs were seriously affected. It was only a question of months before the slight thread, by which his life hung, would be snapped. Mavis knew of many cases in which enfeebled lungs had been bolstered up for quite a long time by a change to suitable climates; she was eager to know if the same held good in her husband's case.

"Oh yes," said the great specialist. "There were parts of South Africa where the veld air was so rarefied that a patient with scarcely any lung at all might live for several years. But—"

"But what?" asked Mavis.

"If I may say so, he will never be other than what he now is. Would it be advisable to prolong—?"

The expression on Mavis's face stopped him short in the middle of his question.

"Of course, if you've decided to send him, it's quite another matter," he went on. "In that case, you cannot be too careful in seeing he has the most reliable attendants procurable."

Mavis hesitated the fraction of a second before replying:

"I should go with him."

It needed only that brief moment for Mavis to make up her mind. She would do her utmost to prolong her husband's life; she would accompany him wherever he went to obtain this end.

In making this last resolve, Mavis knew well the trials and discomforts to which she would expose herself. Her well-ordered days, her present existence, which seemed to run on oiled wheels, the friends and refinements with which she had surrounded herself, the more particularly appealed to her when contrasted with the lean years of her earlier life. Her days of want, joined to her natural inclinations, had created a hunger for the good things of the earth, which her present opulence had not yet stayed. She still held out her hands to grasp the beautiful, satisfying things which money, guided by a mind of some force and a natural refinement, can buy. Therefore, it was a considerable sacrifice for Mavis to give up the advantage she not only possessed, but keenly appreciated, to tend a man who was a physical and mental wreck, in a part of the world remote from civilising influences. But, together with her grief for the loss of her boy, there lived in her heart an immense and ineradicable remorse for having married her husband from motives of revenge against his family.

Harold's living faith in her goodness kept these regrets green; otherwise, the kindly hand of time would have rooted them from her heart.

"Do you believe?" Mavis had once asked of her husband on a day when she had been troubled by things of the spirit.

"In you," he had replied, which was all she could get from him on the subject.

His reply was typical of the whole-hearted reverence with which he regarded her.

Mavis believed that to tend her husband in the land where existence might prolong his life would be some atonement for the deception she had practised. When she got a further eminent medical opinion, which confirmed the previous doctor's diagnosis, she set about making preparations for the melancholy journey. These took her several times to London; they proved to be of a greater magnitude than she had believed to be possible.

When driving to a surgical appliance manufacturer on one of these visits, she saw an acquaintance of her old days playing outside a public house. It was Mr Baffy, the bass viol player, who was fiddling his instrument as helplessly as ever, while he stared before him with vacant eyes. Mavis stopped her cab, went up to his bent form and put a sovereign into his hand as she said:

"Do you remember me?"

The vacant manner in which his eyes stared into hers told Mavis that he had forgotten her.

When Mavis's friends learned of her resolution, they were unanimous in urging her to reconsider what they called her Quixotic fancy. Lady Ludlow was greatly concerned at losing her friend for an indefinite period; she pointed out the uselessness of the proceeding; she endeavoured to overwhelm Mavis's obstinacy in the matter with a torrent of argument. She may as well have talked to the Jersey cows which grazed about Mavis's house, for any impression she produced. After a while, Mavis's friends, seeing, that she was determined, went their several ways, leaving her to make her seemingly endless preparations in peace.

Alone among her friends, Windebank had not contributed to the appeals to Mavis with reference to her leaving England with her husband: for all this forbearing to express an opinion, he made himself useful to Mavis in the many preparations she was making for her departure and stay in South Africa. So ungrudgingly did he give his time and assistance, that Mavis undervalued his aid, taking it as a matter of course.

Three days before it was arranged that Mavis should leave Southampton with Harold, her resolution faltered. The prospect of leaving her home, which she had grown to love, increased its attractions a thousand-fold. The familiar objects about her, some of which she had purchased, had enabled her to sustain her manifold griefs. Cattle in the stables (many of which were her dear friends), with the passage of time had become part and parcel of her lot. A maimed wild duck, which she had saved from death, waited for her outside the front door, and followed her with delighted quacks when she walked in the gardens. All of these seemed to make their several appeals, as if beseeching her not to leave them to the care of alien hands. Her dearly loved Jill she was taking with her. Another deprivation that she would keenly feel would be the music her soul loved. Whenever she was assailed by her remorseless troubles in London, she would hasten, if it were possible, to either the handiest and best orchestral concert, or a pianoforte recital where Chopin was to be played. The loneliness, sorrowings, and longings of which the master makers of music (and particularly the consumptive Pole) were eloquent, found kinship with her own unquiet thoughts, and companionship is a notorious assuager of griefs.

Physical, and particularly mental illness, was hateful to her. If the truth be told, it was as much as she could do to overcome the repugnance with which her husband's presence often inspired her, despite the maternal instinct of which her love for Harold was, for the most part, composed. In going with him abroad, she was, in truth, atoning for any wrong she may have done him.

Two days later, Mavis occupied many hours in saying a last farewell to her home. It was one of the October days which she loved, when milk-white clouds sailed lazily across the hazy blue peculiar to the robust ripe age of the year. This time of year appealed to Mavis, because it seemed as if its mellow wisdom, born of experience, corresponded to a like period in the life of her worldly knowledge. The prize-bred Jersey cows grazed peacefully in the park grounds. Now and again, she would encounter an assiduous bee, which was taking advantage of the fineness of the day to pick up any odds and ends of honey which had been overlooked by his less painstaking brethren. Mavis, with heavy heart, visited stables, dairies, poultry-runs. These last were well at the back of the house; beyond them, the fields were tipped up at all angles; they sprawled over a hill as if each were anxious to see what was going on in the meadow beneath it. Followed by Jill and Sally, her lame duck, Mavis went to the first of the hill-fields, where geese, scarcely out of their adolescence, clamoured about her hands with their soothing, self-contented piping. Even the fierce old gander, which was the terror of stray children and timid maid-servants, deigned to notice her with a tolerant eye. Mavis sighed and went indoors.

Just before tea, she was standing at a window sorrowfully watching the sun's early retirement. The angle of the house prevented her from seeing her favourite cows, but she could hear the tearing sound their teeth made as they seized the grass.

She had seen nothing of her friends (even including Windebank) for the last few days. They had realised that she was not to be stopped from going on what they considered to be her mad enterprise, and had given her up as a bad job. No one seemed to care what became of her; it was as if she were deserted by the world. A sullen anger raged within her; she would not acknowledge to herself that much of it was due to Windebank's latent defection. She longed to get away and have done with it; the suspense of waiting till the morrow was becoming intolerable. As the servants were bringing in tea, Mavis could no longer bear the confinement of the house; she hurried past the two men to go out of the front door.

She walked at random, going anywhere so long as she obeyed the passion for movement which possessed her. Some way from the house, she chanced upon Windebank, who was standing under a tree.

"Why are you here?" she asked, as she stood before him.

"I was making up my mind."

"What about?"

"If I should see you again."

"You needn't. Do you hear? You needn't," she said passionately. He looked at her surprised. She went on:

"Everyone's forgotten me and doesn't care one bit what becomes of me. You're the worst of all."

"I?"

"You. They're honest and stay away. You, in your heart, don't wish to trouble to say good-bye, but you haven't the pluck to act up to your wishes. I hate you!"

"But, Mavis—"

"Don't call me that. You haven't the courage of your convictions. I hate you! I hate you! I hate you! I wish I'd never seen you. Be honest and go away and leave me."

"No!" cried Windebank, as he seized her arm.

"That's right! Strike me!" cried Mavis, reckless of what she said.

"I'm going to be honest at last and tell you something," he declared.

"More insults!"

"It is an insult this time, but all the same you'll hear it."

Mavis was a little awed by the resolution in his face and manner. He went on now a trifle hoarsely:

"Little Mavis, I love you more than I ever believed it possible for man to love woman. I've tried to forget you, but I want you more and more."

"How—how dare you!" she cried.

"Because I love you. And because I do, I've fought against seeing you; but as you've come to me and you're going away to-morrow, I must tell you."

Mavis was less resentful of his words; she resisted an inclination to tremble violently.

"Don't go," urged Windebank.

"Where?"

"Abroad. Don't go and leave me. I love you."

"How can you! Harold was your friend."

"My enemy. He took you from me when I was sure of you; my enemy, I tell you. Oh, little Mavis, let me make you happy. You can do no good going with him, so why not stay? I'd give my life to hold you in my arms, and I know I'd make you happy."

"You mustn't; you mustn't," murmured Mavis, as she strove to believe that his words and the grasp of his hand on her arm did not minister to the repressed, but, none the less ardent longings of her being.

"I must. I tell you I haven't been near a woman since I struck you again in Pimlico, and all for love of you. I've waited. Now, I'll get you."

Windebank placed his arms about her and kissed her lips, eyes, and hair many, many times. Then he held her at arm's length, while his eyes looked fixedly into hers.

A delicious inertia stole over Mavis's senses. He had only to kiss her again for her to fall helplessly into his arms.

Although she realised the enormity of his offence, something within her seemed to impel her to wind her arm about his neck and draw his lips to hers. Instead, she summoned all her resolution; striking him full in the face, she freed herself to run quickly from him. As she ran, she strove to hide from herself that, in her inmost heart, she was longing for him to overtake her, seize her about the body, and carry her off, as might some primeval man, to some lair of his own, where he would defend her with his life against any who might seek to disturb her peace.

But Windebank did not follow her. That night she sobbed herself to sleep. The next morning, Mavis left with Harold for Southampton.

Many months later, Mavis, clad in black, stood, with Jill at her side, on the deck of a ship that was rapidly steaming up Southampton water. Her eyes were fixed on the place where they told her she would land. The faint blurs on the landing pier gradually assumed human shape; one on which she fixed her eyes became suspiciously like Windebank. When she could no longer doubt that he was waiting to greet her, she went downstairs to her cabin, to pin a bright ribbon on her frock. When he joined her on the steamer, neither of them spoke for a few moments.

"I got your letter from—" he began.

"Don't say anything about it," she interrupted. "I know you're sorry, but I'd rather not talk of it."

Windebank turned his attentions to Jill, to say presently to Mavis:

"Are you staying here or going on?"

"I don't know. I think I'll stay a little. And you?"

"I'll stay too, if you've no objection."

"I should like it."

Windebank saw to the luggage and drove Mavis to the barrack-like South-Western Hotel; then, after seeing she had all she wanted, he went to his own hotel to dress for his solitary dinner. He had scarcely finished this meal when he was told that a lady wished to speak to him on the telephone. She proved to be Mavis, who said:

"If you've nothing better to do, come and take me out for some air."

The next few days, they were continually together, when they would mostly ramble by the old-world fortifications of the town. During all this time, neither of them made any mention of events in the past in which they were both concerned.

One evening, an unexpected shower of rain disappointed Windebank's expectation of seeing Mavis after dinner. He telephoned to her, saying that, after coming from a hot climate, she must not trust herself out in the wet.

He was cursing the weather and wondering how he would get through the evening without her, when a servant announced that a lady wished to see him. The next moment, Mavis entered his sitting-room. He noticed that she had changed her black frock for one of brighter hue.

"Why have you come?" he asked, when the servant had gone.

"To see you. Don't you want me?"

"Yes, but—"

"Then sit down and talk; or rather don't. I want to think."

"You could have done that better alone."

"I want to think," she repeated.

They sat for some time in silence, during which Windebank longed to take her in his arms and shower kisses on her lips.

Presently, when she got up to leave, she found so much to say that she continually put off going. At last, when they were standing near the door, Mavis put her face provokingly near his. He bent, meaning to kiss her hair, but instead his lips fell on hers.

To his surprise, Mavis covered his mouth with kisses. Windebank's eyes expressed astonishment, while his arm gripped her form.

"Forgive me; forgive me," she murmured.

"What for?" he gasped.

"I've been a brute, a beast, and you've never once complained."

"Dearest!"

"It's true enough; too true. All your life you've given me love, and all I've given you are doubts and misunderstandings. But I'll atone, I'll atone now. I'm yours to do what you will with, whenever you please, now, here, if you wish it. You needn't marry me; I won't bind you down; I only ask you to be kind to me for a little, I've suffered so much."

"You mean—you mean—"

"That you've loved me so long and so much that I can only reward you by giving you myself."

She opened her arms. He looked at her steadily for a while, till, with a great effort, he tore himself from her presence and left the room.

The next morning, Mavis received a letter from Windebank.

"My own dearest love," it ran, "don't think me a mug for leaving you last night as I did, but I love you so dearly that I want to get you for life and don't wish to run any risk of losing what I treasure most on earth. I am making arrangements so that we can get married at the very earliest date, which I believe is three days from now. And then—"

Mavis did not read any more just then.

"When and where you please," she scribbled on the first piece of paper she could find. Lady Ludlow's words occurred to her as she sent off her note by special messenger: "A woman is always safe with the man who loves her."

Three days later, Windebank and Mavis were made man and wife. For all Windebank's outward impassivity, Mavis noticed that, when he put the ring on her finger, his hand trembled so violently that he all but dropped it. Directly the wedding was over, Windebank and Mavis got into the former's motor, which was waiting outside the church.

"At last!" said Windebank, as he sat beside his wife.

"Where next?" asked Mavis.

"To get Jill and your things and then we'll get away."

"Where to? I hope it's right away, somewhere peaceful in the country."

"We'll go on till you come to a place you like."

They went west. They had lunched in high spirits at a wayside inn, which took Mavis's fancy, to continue travelling till the late afternoon, when the machine came to a dead stop.

"We'll have to camp in a ditch," said Mavis.

"How you'd curse me if we had to!" said her husband.

"It would be heaven with you," she declared.

Windebank reverently kissed her.

He saw that the car wanted spirit, which he learned could be bought at a village a short way ahead. Mavis and Jill accompanied Windebank to the general shop where petrol was sold.

"I can't let you out of my sight," she said, as they set out.

"Why not?"

"You might run off."

He laughed. By the time they reached the shop, Mavis had quite emerged from the sobriety of her demeanour to become an approximation to her old light-hearted self.

"That's how I love to see you," remarked Windebank.

When they entered the shop, Mavis' face fell.

"What's the matter?" he asked, all concern for his wife.

"Don't you smell paraffin?"

"What of it?"

"It takes me back to Pimlico—that night when we went shopping together—you bought me a shilling's worth."

"I wish someone would come; then we'd get out of it," remarked Windebank.

But his wife did not appear to listen; she was lost in thought. Then she clung desperately to his arm.

"What is it?" he asked tenderly.

"It's love I want; love. Nothing else matters. Love me: love me: love me. A little love will help me to forget."

Milton Keynes UK
Ingram Content Group UK Ltd.
UKHW011123050624
443649UK00006B/503

9 789361 477768